The Collected Supernatural
& Weird Fiction of
Sir Arthur Conan Doyle: 1

The Collected Supernatural & Weird Fiction of Sir Arthur Conan Doyle: 1

Including the Novella 'The Maracot Deep,'
Two Novelettes and Sixteen Short Stories
of Terror and Unease

Sir Arthur Conan Doyle

LEONAUR

The Collected Supernatural & Weird Fiction of Sir Arthur Conan Doyle: 1
Including the Novella 'The Maracot Deep,' Two Novelettes and Sixteen
Short Stories of Terror and Unease
by Sir Arthur Conan Doyle

Leonaur is an imprint of Oakpast Ltd

Material original to this edition and
this editorial selection
copyright © 2009 Oakpast Ltd

ISBN: 978-1-84677-838-4 (hardcover)
ISBN: 978-1-84677-837-7 (softcover)

http://www.leonaur.com

Publisher's Notes

The views expressed in this book are not necessarily
those of the publisher.

Contents

The Maracot Deep

Chapter 1

Since these papers have been put into my hands to edit, I will begin by reminding the public of the sad loss of the steamship *Stratford*, which started a year ago upon a voyage for the purpose of oceanography and the study of deep-sea life. The expedition had been organized by Dr. Maracot, the famous author of *Pseudo-Coralline Formations* and *The Morphology of the Lamellibranchs*. Dr. Maracot had with him Mr. Cyrus Headley, formerly assistant at the Zoological Institute of Cambridge, Massachusetts, and at the time of the voyage Rhodes Scholar at Oxford. Captain Howie, an experienced navigator, was in charge of the vessel, and there was a crew of twenty-three men, including an American mechanic from the Merribank Works, Philadelphia.

This whole party has utterly disappeared, and the only word ever heard of the ill-fated steamer was from the report of a Norwegian barque which actually saw a ship, closely corresponding with her description, go down in the great gale of the autumn of 1926. A lifeboat marked *Stratford* was found later in the neighbourhood of the tragedy, together with some deck gratings, a lifebuoy, and a spar. This, coupled with the long silence, seemed to make it absolutely sure that the vessel and her crew would never be heard of more. Her fate is rendered more certain by the strange wireless message received at the time, which, though incomprehensible in parts, left little doubt as to the fate of the vessel. This I will quote later.

There were some remarkable points about the voyage of the *Stratford* which caused comment at the time. One was the curious secrecy observed by Professor Maracot. He was famous for his dislike and distrust of the Press, but it was pushed to an extreme upon this occasion, when he would neither give information to reporters nor would he permit the representative of any paper to set foot in the vessel during the weeks that it lay in the Albert Dock. There were rumours abroad of some curious and novel construction of the ship which would fit it for deep-sea work, and these rumours were confirmed from the yard of Hunter and Company of West Hartlepool, where the structural changes had actually been carried out. It was at one time said that the whole bottom of the vessel was detachable, a report which attracted the attention of the underwriters at Lloyd's, who were, with some difficulty, satisfied upon the point. The matter was soon forgotten, but it assumed an importance now when the fate of the expedition has been brought once more in so extraordinary manner to the notice of the public.

So much for the beginning of the voyage of the *Stratford*. There are now four documents which cover the facts so far as they are known. The first is the letter which was written by Mr. Cyrus Headley, from the capital of the Grand Canary, to his friend, Sir James Talbot, of Trinity College, Oxford, upon the only occasion, so far as is known, when the *Stratford* touched land after leaving the Thames. The second is the strange wireless call to which I have alluded. The third is that portion of the log of the *Arabella Knowles* which deals with the vitreous ball. The fourth and last is the amazing contents of that receptacle, which either represent a most cruel and complex mystification, or else open up a fresh chapter in human experience the importance of which cannot be exaggerated. With this preamble I will now give Mr. Headley's letter, which I owe to the courtesy of Sir James Talbot, and which has not previously been published. It is dated October 1st, 1926.

I am mailing this, my dear Talbot, from Porta de la Luz, where we have put in for a few days of rest. My principal companion in the voyage has been Bill Scanlan, the head mechanic, who, as a fellow-countryman and also as a very entertaining character, has become my natural associate. However, I am alone this morning as he has what he describes as 'a date with a skirt'. You see, he talks as Englishmen expect every real American to talk. He would be accepted as the true breed. The mere force of suggestion makes me 'guess' and 'reckon' when I am with my English friends. I feel that they would never really understand that I was a Yankee if I did not. However, I am not on those terms with you, so let me assure you right now that you will not find anything but pure Oxford in the epistle which I am now mailing to you.

You met Maracot at the Mitre, so you know the dry chip of a man that he is. I told you, I think, how he came to pitch upon me for the job. He inquired from old Somerville of the Zoological Institute, who sent him my prize essay on the pelagic crabs, and that did the trick. Of course, it is splendid to be on such a congenial errand, but I wish it wasn't with such an animated mummy as Maracot. He is inhuman in his isolation and his devotion to his work. 'The world's stiffest stiff,' says Bill Scanlan: And yet you can't but admire such complete devotion. Nothing exists outside his own science. I remember that you laughed when I asked him what I ought to read as a preparation, and he said that for serious study I should read the collected edition of his own works, but for relaxation Haeckel's *Plankton-Studien*.

I know him no better now than I did in that little parlour looking out on the Oxford High. He says nothing, and his gaunt, austere face—the face of a Savonarola, or rather, perhaps, of a Torquemada—never relapses into geniality. The long, thin, aggressive nose, the two small gleaming grey eyes set closely together under a thatch of eyebrows, the thin-lipped, compressed mouth, the cheeks worn into hollows by constant thought and ascetic life, are all uncompanionable. He lives on some mental mountaintop, out of reach of ordinary mortals. Sometimes I think he is a little mad. For example, this extraordinary instrument that he has made ... but I'll tell things in their due order and then you can judge for yourself.

I'll take our voyage from the start. The *Stratford* is a fine seaworthy little boat, specially fitted for her job. She is twelve hundred tons, with clear decks and a good broad beam, furnished with every possible appliance for sounding, trawling, dredging and tow-netting. She has, of course, powerful steam winches for hauling the trawls, and a number of other gadgets of various kinds, some of which are familiar enough, and some are strange. Below these are comfortable quarters with a well—fitted laboratory for our special studies.

We had the reputation of being a mystery ship before we started, and I soon found that it was not undeserved. Our first proceedings were commonplace enough. We took a turn up the North Sea and dropped our trawls for a scrape or two, but, as the average depth is not much over sixty feet and we were specially fitted for very deep-sea work, it seemed rather a waste of time. Anyhow, save for familiar table fish, dog-fish, squids, jelly-fish and some terrigenous bottom deposits of the usual alluvial clay-mud, we got nothing worth writing home about. Then we rounded Scotland, sighted the Faroes, and came down the Wyville-Thomson Ridge, where we had better luck. Thence we worked south to our proper cruising-ground, which was between the African coast and these islands. We nearly grounded on Fuert-Eventura one moonless night, but save for that our voyage was uneventful.

During these first weeks I tried to make friends with Maracot, but it was not easy work. First of all, he is the most absorbed and absent-minded man in the world. You will remember how you smiled when he gave the elevator boy a penny under the impression that he was in a street car. Half the time he is utterly lost in his thoughts, and seems hardly aware of where he is or what he is doing. Then in the second place he is secretive to the last degree. He is continually working at papers and charts, which he shuffles away when I happen to enter the cabin. It is my firm belief that the man has some secret project in his mind, but that so long as

12

we are due to touch at any port he will keep it to himself. That is the impression which I have received, and I find that Bill Scanlan is of the same opinion.

'Say, Mr. Headley,' said he one evening, when I was seated in the laboratory testing out the salinity of samples from our hydrographic soundings, 'what d'you figure out that this guy has in his mind? What d'you reckon that he means to do?'

'I suppose,' said I, 'that we shall do what the Challenger and a dozen other exploring ships have done before us, and add a few more species to the list of fish and a few more entries to the bathymetric chart.'

'Not on your life,' said he. 'If that's your opinion you've got to guess again. First of all, what am I here for, anyhow?'

'In case the machinery goes wrong,' I hazarded.

'Machinery nothing! The ship's machinery is in charge of MacLaren, the Scotch engineer. No, sir, it wasn't to run a donkey-engine that the Merribank folk sent out their star performer. If I pull down fifty bucks a week it's not for nix. Come here, and I'll make you wise to it..'

He took a key from his pocket and opened a door at the back of the laboratory which led us down a companion ladder to a section of the hold which was cleared right across save for four large glittering objects half-exposed amid the straw of their huge packing-cases. They were flat sheets of steel with elaborate bolts and rivets along the edges. Each sheet was about ten feet square and an inch and a half thick, with a circular gap of eighteen inches in the middle.

'What in thunder is it?' I asked.

Bill Scanlan's queer face—he looks half-way between a vaudeville comic and a prize-fighter—broke into a grin at my astonishment.

'That's my baby, sir,' he quoted. 'Yes, Mr. Headley, that's what I am here for. There is a steel bottom to the thing. It's in that big case yonder. Then there is a top, kind of arched, and a great ring for a chain or rope. Now, look here at the bottom of the ship.'

There was a square wooden platform there, with projecting screws at each corner which showed that it was detachable.

'There is a double bottom,' said Scanlan. 'It may be that this guy is clean loco, or it may be that he has more in his block than we know, but if I read him right he means to build up a kind of room—the windows are in storage here—and lower it through the bottom of the ship. He's got electric searchlights here, and I allow that he plans to shine 'em through the round portholes and see what's goin' on around.'

'He could have put a crystal sheet into the ship, like the Catalina Island boats, if that was all that was in his mind,' said I.

'You've said a mouthful,' said Bill Scanlan, scratching his head. 'I can't figger it out nohow. The only one sure thing is, that I've been sent to be under his orders and to help him with the darn fool thing all I can. He has said nothin' up to now, so I've said the same, but I'll just snoop around, and if I wait long enough I'll learn all there is to know.'

So that was how I first got on to the edge of our mystery. We ran into some dirty weather after that, and then we got to work doing some deep-sea trawling north-west of Cape Juba, just outside the Continental Slope, and taking temperature readings and salinity records. It's a sporting proposition, this deep-sea dragging with a Peterson otter trawl gaping twenty feet wide for everything that comes its way—sometimes down a quarter of a mile and bringing up one lot of fish, sometimes half a mile and quite a different lot, every stratum of ocean with its own inhabitants as separate as so many continents. Sometimes from the bottom we would just bring up half a ton of clear pink jelly, the raw material of life, or, maybe, it would be a scoop of *pteropod* ooze, breaking up under the microscope into millions of tiny round reticulated balls with amorphous mud between. I won't bore you with all the *brotulids* and *macrurids*, the *ascidians* and *holothurians* and *polyzoa* and *echinoderms*—anyhow, you can reckon that there is a great harvest in the sea, and that we have been diligent reapers. But always I had the same feeling that the heart of Maracot was not in the job, and that other plans were in that queer high, narrow Egyptian mummy of a head. It all seemed to me to be a try-out of men and things until the real business got going.

I had got as far as this in my letter when I went ashore to have a last stretch, for we sail in the early morning. It's as well, perhaps, that I did go, for there was no end of a barney going on upon the pier, with Maracot and Bill Scanlan right in the heart of it. Bill is a bit of a scrapper, and has what he calls a mean wallop in both mitts, but with half a dozen Dagoes with knives all round them things looked ugly, and it was time that I butted in. It seems that the Doctor had hired one of the things they call cabs, and had driven half over the island inspecting the geology, but had clean forgotten that he had no money on him. When it came to paying, he could not make these country hicks understand, and the cabman had grabbed his watch so as to make sure. That brought Bill Scanlan into action, and they would have both been on the floor with their backs like pin-cushions if I had not squared the matter up, with a dollar or two over for the driver and a five-dollar bonus for the chap with the mouse under his eye. So all ended well, and Maracot was more human than ever I saw him yet. When we got to the ship he called me into the little cabin which he reserves for himself and he thanked me.

'By the way, Mr. Headley,' he said, 'I understand that you are not a married man?'

'No,' said I, 'I am not.'

'No one depending upon you?'

'No.'

'Good!' said he. 'I have not spoken of the object of this voyage because I have, for my own reasons, desired it to be secret. One of those reasons was that I feared to be forestalled. When scientific plans get about one may be served as Scott was served by Amundsen. Had Scott kept his counsel as I have done, it would be he and not Amundsen who would have been the first at the South Pole. For my part, I have quite as important a destination as the South Pole, and so I have been silent. But now we are on the eve of our great adventure and no rival has time to steal my plans. Tomorrow we start for our real goal.'

'And what is that?' I asked.

He leaned forward, his ascetic face all lit up with the enthusiasm of the fanatic.

15

'Our goal,' said he, 'is the bottom of the Atlantic Ocean.'

And right here I ought to stop, for I expect it has taken away your breath as it did mine. If I were a story-writer, I guess I should leave it at that. But as I am just a chronicler of what occurred, I may tell you that I stayed another hour in the cabin of old man Maracot, and that I learned a lot, which there is still just time for me to tell you before the last shore boat leaves.

'Yes, young man,' said he, 'you may write freely now, for by the time your letter reaches England we shall have made the plunge.'

This started him sniggering, for he has a queer dry sense of humour of his own.

'Yes, sir, the plunge is the right word on this occasion, a plunge which will be historic in the annals of Science. Let me tell you, in the first place, that I am well convinced that the current doctrine as to the extreme pressure of the ocean at great depths is entirely misleading. It is perfectly clear that other factors exist which neutralize the effect, though I am not yet prepared to say what those factors may be. That is one of the problems which we may settle. Now, what pressure, may I ask, have you been led to expect under a mile of water?' He glowered at me through his big horn spectacles.

'Not less than a ton to the square inch,' I answered. 'Surely that has been clearly shown.'

'The task of the pioneer has always been to disprove the thing which has been clearly shown. Use your brains, young man. You have been for the last month fishing up some of the most delicate Bathic forms of life, creatures so delicate that you could hardly transfer them from the net to the tank without marring their sensitive shapes. Did you find that there was evidence upon them of this extreme pressure?'

'The pressure,' said I, 'equalized itself. It was the same within as without.'

'Words—mere words!' he cried, shaking his lean head impatiently. 'You have brought up round fish, such fish as *Gastrostomus globulus*. Would they not have been squeezed flat had the pressure been as you imagine? Or look at our otter-boards. They are not squeezed together at the mouth of the trawl.'

'But the experience of divers?'

'Certainly it holds good up to a point. They do find a sufficient increase of pressure to influence what is perhaps the most sensitive organ of the body, the interior of the ear. But as I plan it, we shall not be exposed to any pressure at all. We shall be lowered in a steel cage with crystal windows on each side for observation. If the pressure is not strong enough to break in an inch and a half of toughened double-nickelled steel, then it cannot hurt us. It is an extension of the experiment of the Williamson Brothers at Nassau, with which no doubt you are familiar. If my calculation is wrong—well, you say that no one is dependent upon you. We shall die in a great adventure. Of course, if you would rather stand clear, I can go alone.'

It seemed to me the maddest kind of scheme, and yet you know how difficult it is to refuse a dare. I played for time while I thought it over.

'How deep do you propose to go, sir?' I asked.

He had a chart pinned upon the table, and he placed the end of his compasses upon a point which lies to the south-west of the Canaries.

'Last year I did some sounding in this part,' said he.

'There is a pit of great depth. We got twenty-five thousand feet there. I was the first to report it. Indeed, I trust that you will find it on the charts of the future as the "Maracot Deep".'

'But, good God, sir!' I cried, 'you don't propose to descend into an abyss like that?'

'No, no,' he answered, smiling. 'Neither our lowering chain nor our air tubes reach beyond half a mile. But I was going to explain to you that round this deep crevasse, which has no doubt been formed by volcanic forces long ago, there is a varied ridge or narrow plateau, which is not more than three hundred fathoms under the surface.'

'Three hundred fathoms! A third of a mile!'

'Yes, roughly a third of a mile. It is my present intention that we shall be lowered in our little pressure-proof look-out station on to this submarine bank. There we shall make such observations as we can. A speaking-tube will connect us with the ship so that

17

we can give our directions. There should be no difficulty in the mater. When we wish to be hauled up we have only to say so.'

'And the air?'

'Will be pumped down to us.'

'But it will be pitch-dark.'

'That, I fear, is undoubtedly true. The experiments of Fol and Sarasin at the Lake of Geneva show that even the ultra-violet rays are absent at that depth. But does it matter? We shall be provided with the powerful electric illumination from the ship's engines, supplemented by six two-volt Hellesens dry cells connected together so as to give a current of twelve volts. That, with a Lucas army signalling lamp as a movable reflector, should serve our turn. Any other difficulties?'

'If our air lines tangle?'

'They won't tangle. And as a reserve we have compressed air in tubes which would last us twenty—four hours. Well, have I satisfied you? Will you come?'

It was not an easy decision. The brain works quickly and imagination is a mighty vivid thing. I seemed to realize that black box down in the primeval depths, to feel the foul twice-breathed air, and then to see the walls sagging, bulging inwards, rending at the joints with the water spouting in at every rivet-hole and crevice and crawling up from below. It was a slow, dreadful death to die. But I looked up, and there were the old man's fiery eyes fixed upon me with the exaltation of a martyr to Science. It's catching, that sort of enthusiasm, and if it be crazy, it is at least noble and unselfish. I caught fire from his great flame, and I sprang to my feet with my hand out.

'Doctor, I'm with you to the end,' said I.

'I knew it,' said he. 'It was not for your smattering of learning that I picked you, my young friend, nor,' he added, smiling, 'for your intimate acquaintance with the pelagic crabs. There are other qualities which may be more immediately useful, and they are loyalty and courage.'

So with that little bit of sugar I was dismissed, with my future pledged and my whole scheme of life in ruins. Well, the last shore boat is leaving. They are calling for the mail. You will either not hear from me again, my dear Talbot, or you will get a letter worth reading. If you don't hear you can have a floating headstone and drop it somewhere south of the Canaries with the inscription:

> HERE, OR HEREABOUTS, LIES ALL THAT THE FISHES
> HAVE LEFT OF MY FRIEND CYRUS J. HEADLEY

****

The second document in the case is the unintelligible wireless message which was intercepted by several vessels, including the Royal Mail steamer *Arroya*. It was received at 3 p.m. October 3rd, 1926, which shows that it was dispatched only two days after the *Stratford* left the Grand Canary, as shown in the previous letter, and it corresponds roughly with the time when the Norwegian barque saw a steamer founder in a cyclone two hundred miles to the south-west of Porta de la Luz. It ran thus:

Blown on our beam ends. Fear position hopeless. Have already lost Maracot, Headley, Scanlan. Situation incomprehensible. Headley handkerchief end of deep sea sounding wire. God help us!
S. S. *Stratford*.

****

This was the last, incoherent message which came from the ill-fated vessel, and part of it was so strange that it was put down to delirium on the part of the operator. It seemed, however, to leave no doubt as to the fate of the ship.

The explanation—if it can be accepted as an explanation—of the matter is to be found in the narrative concealed inside the vitreous ball, and first it would be as well to amplify the very brief account which has hitherto appeared in the Press of the finding of the ball. I take it verbatim from the log of the *Arabella Knowles*, master Amos Green, outward bound with coals from Cardiff to Buenos Aires:

Wednesday, Jan. 5th, 1927. Lat. 27.14, Long. 28 West. Calm weather. Blue sky with low banks of cirrus clouds. Sea like glass.

At two bells of the middle watch the first officer reported that he had seen a shining object bound high out of the sea, and then fall back into it. His first impression was that it was some strange fish, but on examination with his glasses he observed that it was a silvery globe, or ball, which was so light that it lay, rather than floated, on the surface of the water. I was called and saw it, as large as a football, gleaming brightly about half a mile off on our starboard beam. I stopped the engines and called away the quarter-boat under the second mate, who picked the thing up and brought it aboard.

On examination it proved to be a ball made of some sort of very tough glass, and filled with a substance so light that when it was tossed in the air it wavered about like a child's balloon. It was nearly transparent, and we could see what looked like a roll of paper inside it. The material was so tough, however, that we had the greatest possible difficulty in breaking the ball open and getting at the contents. A hammer would not crack it, and it was only when the chief engineer nipped it in the throw of the engine that we were able to smash it. Then I am sorry to say that it dissolved into sparkling dust, so that it was impossible to collect any good-sized piece for examination. We got the paper, however, and, having examined it and concluded that it was of great importance, we laid it aside with the intention of handing it over to the British Consul when we reached the Plate River. Man and boy, I have been at sea for five-and-thirty years, but this is the strangest thing that ever befell me, and so says every man aboard this ship. I leave the meaning of it all to wiser heads than mine.

****

So much for the genesis of the narrative of Cyrus J. Headley, which we will now give exactly as written:

Whom am I writing to? Well, I suppose I may say to the whole wide world, but as that is rather a vague address I'll aim at my friend Sir James Talbot, of Oxford University, for the reason that my last letter was to him and this may be regarded as a continuation. I expect the odds are a hundred to one that this ball, even if it should see the light of day and not be gulped by a shark in passing, will toss about on the waves and never catch the eye of the passing sailor, and yet it's worth trying, and Maracot is sending up another, so, between us, it may be that we shall get our wonderful story to the world. Whether the world will believe it is another matter, I guess, but when folk look at the ball with its vitrine cover and note its contents of levigen gas, they will surely see for themselves that there is something here that is out of the ordinary. You at any rate, Talbot, will not throw it aside unread.

If anyone wants to know how the thing began, and what we were trying to do, he can find it all in a letter I wrote you on October 1st last year, the night before we left Porta de la Luz. By George! If I had known what was in store for us, I think I should have sneaked into a shore boat that night. And yet—well, maybe, even with my eyes open I would have stood by the Doctor and seen it through. On second thoughts I have not a doubt that I would.

Well, starting from the day that we left Grand Canary I will carry on with my experiences.

The moment we were clear, of the port, old man Maracot fairly broke into flames. The time for action had come at last and all the damped-down energy of the man came flaring up. I tell you he took hold of that ship and of everyone and everything in it, and bent it all to his will. The dry, creaking, absent-minded scholar had suddenly vanished, and instead there emerged a human electrical machine, crackling with vitality and quivering from the great driving force within. His eyes gleamed behind his glasses like flames in a lantern. He seemed to be everywhere at once, working out distances on his chart, comparing reckonings with the skipper, driving Bill Scanlan along, setting me on to a hundred odd jobs, but it was all full of method and with a definite end. He developed an unexpected knowledge of electricity and of mechanics and spent much of his time working at the machinery which Scanlan, under his supervision, was now carefully piecing together.

'Say, Mr. Headley, it's just dandy,' said Bill, on the morning of the second day. 'Come in here and have a look. The Doc. is a regular fellow and a whale of a slick mechanic.'

I had a most unpleasant impression that it was my own coffin at which I was gazing, but, even so, I had to admit that it was a very adequate mausoleum. The floor had been clamped to the four steel walls, and the porthole windows screwed into the centre of each. A small trapdoor at the top gave admission, and there was a second one at the base. The steel cage was supported by a thin but very powerful steel hawser, which ran over a drum, and was paid out or rolled in by the strong engine which we used for our deep-sea trawls. The hawser, as I understood, was nearly half a mile in length, the slack of it coiled round bollards on the deck. The rubber breathing-tubes were of the same length, and the telephone wire was connected with them, and also the wire by which the electric lights within could be operated from the ship's batteries, though we had an independent instalment as well.

It was on the evening of that day that the engines were stopped. The glass was low, and a thick black cloud rising upon the horizon gave warning of coming trouble. The only ship in sight was a barque flying the Norwegian colours, and we observed that it was reefed down, as if expecting trouble. For the moment, however, all was propitious and the *Stratford* rolled gently upon a deep blue ocean, white-capped here and there from the breath of the trade wind. Bill Scanlan came to me in my laboratory with more show of excitement than his easy-going temperament had ever permitted him to show.

'Look it here, Mr. Headley,' said he, 'they've lowered that contraption into a well in the bottom of the ship. D'you figure that the Boss is going down in it?'

'Certain sure, Bill. And I am going with him.'

'Well, well, you are sure bughouse, the two of you, to think of such a thing. But I'd feel a cheap skate if I let you go alone.'

'It is no business of yours, Bill.!

'Well, I just feel that it is. Sure, I'd be as yellow as a Chink with the jaundice if I let you go alone. Merribanks sent me here to look after the machinery, and if the machinery is down at the bottom of the sea, then it's a sure thing that it's me for the bottom. Where those steel castings are—that's the address of Bill Scanlan—whether the folk round him are crazy or no.'

It was useless to argue with him, so one more was added to our little suicide club and we just waited for our orders.

All night they were hard at work upon the fittings, and it was after an early breakfast that we descended into the hold ready for our adventure. The steel cage had been half lowered into the false bottom, and we now descended one by one through the upper trap-door, which was closed and screwed down behind us, Captain Howie with a most lugubrious face having shaken hands with each of us as we passed him. We were then lowered a few more feet, the shutter drawn above our heads, and the water admitted to test how far we were really seaworthy. The cage stood the trial well, every joint fitted exactly, and there was no sign of any leakage. Then the lower flap in the hold was loosened and we hung suspended in the ocean beneath the level of the keel.

It was really a very snug little room, and I marvelled at the skill and foresight with which everything had been arranged. The electric illumination had not been turned on, but the semi—tropical sun shone brightly through the bottle-green water at either porthole. Some small fish were flickering here and there, streaks of silver against the green background. Inside there was a settee round the little room, with a bathymetric dial, a thermometer, and other instruments ranged above it. Beneath the settee was a row of pipes which represented our reserve supply of compressed air in case the tubes should fail us. Those tubes opened out above our heads, and the telephonic apparatus hung beside them. We could all hear the mournful voice of the captain outside.

'Are you really determined to go?' he asked.

'We are quite all right,' the Doctor answered, impatiently. 'You will lower slowly and have someone at the receiver all the time. I will report conditions. When we reach the bottom, remain as you are until I give instructions. It will not do to put too much strain upon the hawser, but a slow movement of a couple of knots an hour should be well within its strength. And now "Lower away!"'

He yelled out the two words with the scream of a lunatic. It was the supreme moment of his life, the fruition of all his brooding dreams. For an instant I was shaken by the thought that we were really in the power of a cunning, plausible monomaniac. Bill Scanlan had the same thought, for he looked across at me with a rueful grin and touched his forehead. But after that one wild outburst our leader was instantly his sober, self-contained self once more. Indeed, one had but to look at the order and forethought which showed itself in every detail around us to be reassured as to the power of his mind.

But now all our attention was diverted to the wonderful new experience which every instant was providing. Slowly the cage was sinking into the depths of the ocean. Light green water turned to dark olive. That again deepened into a wonderful blue, a rich deep blue gradually thickening to a dusky purple. Lower and lower we sank—a hundred feet, two hundred feet, three hundred. The valves were acting to perfection. Our breathing was as free and natural as upon the deck of the vessel. Slowly the bathymeter needle moved round the luminous dial. Four hundred, five hundred, six hundred. 'How are you?' roared an anxious voice from above us.

'Nothing could be better,' cried Maracot in reply. But the light was failing. There was now only a dim grey twilight which rapidly changed to utter darkness. 'Stop her!' shouted our leader. We ceased to move and hung suspended at seven hundred feet below the surface of the ocean. I heard the click of the switch, and the next instant we were flooded with glorious golden light which poured out through each of our side windows and sent long glimmering vistas into the waste of waters round us. With our faces against the thick glass, each at our own porthole, we gazed out into such a prospect as man had never seen.

Up to now we had known these strata by the sight of the few fish which had been too slow to avoid our clumsy trawl, or too stupid to escape a drag-net. Now we saw the wonderful world of water as it really was. If the object of creation was the production of man, it is strange that the ocean is so much more populous than the land. Broadway on a Saturday night, Lombard

Street on a week-day afternoon, are not more crowded than the great sea spaces which lay before us. We had passed those surface strata where fish are either colourless or of the true maritime tints of ultramarine above and silver below. Here there were creatures of every conceivable tint and form which pelagic life can show. Delicate *leptocephali* or eel larva shot like streaks of burnished silver across the tunnel of radiance. The slow snake-like form of *muroena*, the deep-sea lamprey, writhed and twisted by, or the black *ceratia*, all spikes and mouth, gaped foolishly back at our peering faces. Sometimes it was the squat cuttlefish which drifted across and glanced at us with human sinister eyes, some-times it was some crystal-clear pelagic form of life, *cystoma* or *glaucus*, which lent a flower—like charm to the scene. One huge *caranx*, or horse mackerel, butted savagely again and again against our window until the dark shadow of a seven-foot shark came across him, and he vanished into its gaping jaws. Dr. Maracot sat entranced, his notebook upon his knee, scribbling down his observations and keeping up a muttered monologue of scien-tific comment. 'What's that? What's that?' I would hear. 'Yes, yes, *chimoera mirabilis* as taken by the Michael Sars. Dear me, there is *lepidion*, but a new species as I should judge. Observe that *macru-nus*, Mr. Headley; its colouring is quite different to what we get in the net.' Once only was he taken quite aback. It was when a long oval object shot with great speed past his window from above, and left a vibrating tail behind it which extended as far as we could see above us and below. I admit that I was as puz-zled for the moment as the Doctor, and it was Bill Scanlan who solved the mystery.

'I guess that boob, John Sweeney, has heaved his lead along-side of us. Kind of a joke, maybe, to prevent us from feeling lonesome.'

'To be sure! To be sure!' said Maracot, sniggering. '*Plumbus long-icaudatus*—a new genus, Mr. Headley, with a piano-wire tail and lead in its nose. But, indeed, it is very necessary they should take soundings so as to keep above the bank, which is circumscribed in size. All well, Captain!' he shouted. 'You may drop us down.'

And down we went. Dr. Maracot turned off the electric light

and all was pitch-darkness once more save for the bathymeter's luminous face, which ticked off our steady fall. There was a gentle sway, but otherwise we were hardly conscious of any motion. Only that moving hand upon the dial told us of our terrific, our inconceivable, position. Now we were at the thousand-foot level, and the air had become distinctly foul. Scanlan oiled the valve of the discharge tube and things were better. At fifteen hundred feet we stopped and swung in mid-ocean with our lights blazing once more. Some great dark mass passed us here, but whether swordfish or deep-sea shark, or monster of unknown breed, was more than we could determine. The Doctor hurriedly turned off the lights. 'There lies our chief danger,' said he; 'there are creatures in the deep before whose charge this steel-plated room would have as much chance as a beehive before the rush of a rhinoceros.'

'Whales, maybe,' said Scanlan.

'Whales may sound to a great depth,' the savant answered. 'A Greenland whale has been known to take out nearly a mile of line in a perpendicular dive. But unless hurt or badly frightened no whale would descend so low. It may have been a giant squid: They are found at every level.'

'Well, I guess squids are too soft to hurt us. The laugh would be with the squid if he could claw a hole in Merribanks' nickel steel.'

'Their bodies may be soft,' the Professor answered, 'but the beak of a large squid would sheer through a bar of iron, and one peck of that beak might go through these inch-thick windows as if they were parchment.'

'Gee Whittaker!' cried Bill, as we resumed our downward journey.

And then at last, quite softly and gently, we came to rest. So delicate was the impact that we should hardly have known of it had it not been that the light when turned on showed great coils of the hawser all around us. The wire was a danger to our breathing tubes, for it might foul them, and at the urgent cry of Maracot it was pulled taut from above once more. The dial marked eighteen hundred feet. We lay motionless on a volcanic ridge at the bottom of the Atlantic.

Chapter 2

For a time I think that we all had the same feeling. We did not want to do anything or to see anything. We just wanted to sit quiet and try to realize the wonder of it—that we should be resting in the plumb centre of one of the great oceans of the world. But soon the strange scene round us, illuminated in all directions by our lights, drew us to the windows.

We had settled upon a bed of high algae ('*Cutleria multifida*,' said Maracot), the yellow fronds of which waved around us, moved by some deep-sea current, exactly as branches would move in a summer breeze. They were not long enough to obscure our view, though their great flat leaves, deep golden in the light, flowed occasionally across our vision. Beyond them lay slopes of some blackish slag-like material which were dotted with lovely coloured creatures, *holothurians*, *ascidians*, echini and *echinoderms*, as thickly as ever an English spring time bank was sprinkled with hyacinths and primroses. These living flowers of the sea, vivid scarlet, rich purple and delicate pink, were spread in profusion upon that coal-black background. Here and there great sponges bristled out from the crevices of the dark rocks, and a few fish of the middle depths, themselves showing up as flashes of colour, shot across our circle of vivid radiance. We were gazing enraptured at the fairy scene when an anxious voice came down the tube:

'Well, how do you like the bottom? Is all well with you? Don't be too long, for the glass is dropping and I don't like the look of it. Giving you air enough? Anything more we can do?'

'All right, Captain!' cried Maracot, cheerily. 'We won't be long. You are nursing us well. We are quite as comfortable as in our own cabin. Stand by presently to move us slowly forwards.'

We had come into the region of the luminous fishes, and it amused us to turn out our own lights, and in the absolute pitch-darkness—a darkness in which a sensitive plate can be suspended for an hour without a trace even of the ultra-violet ray—to look out at the phosphorescent activity of the ocean. As against a black velvet curtain one saw little points of brilliant light moving steadily along as a liner at night might shed light through its long line of portholes. One terrifying creature had luminous teeth which gnashed in Biblical fashion in the outer darkness. Another had long golden antennae, and yet another a plume of flame above its head. As far as our vision carried, brilliant points flashed in the darkness, each little being bent upon its own business, and lighting up its own course as surely as the nightly taxicab at the theatre-hour in the Strand. Soon we had our own lights up again and the Doctor was making his observations of the sea-bottom.

'Deep as we are, we are not deep enough to get any of the characteristic Bathic deposits,' said he. 'These are entirely beyond our possible range. Perhaps on another occasion with a longer hawser—'

'Cut it out!' growled Bill. 'Forget it!'

Maracot smiled. 'You will soon get acclimatized to the depths, Scanlan. This will not be our only descent.'

'The Hell you say!' muttered Bill.

'You will think no more of it than of going down into the hold of the *Stratford*. You will observe, Mr. Headley, that the groundwork here, so far as we can observe it through the dense growth of *hydrozoa* and *silicious* sponges, is pumice stone and the black slag of basalt, pointing to ancient plutonic activities. Indeed, I am inclined to think that it confirms my previous view that this ridge is part of a volcanic formation and that the Maracot Deep,' he rolled out the words as if he loved them, 'represents the outer slope of the mountain. It has struck me that it would be an interesting experiment to move our cage slowly

28

onwards until we come to the edge of the Deep, and see exactly what the formation may be at that point. I should expect to find a precipice of majestic dimensions extending downwards at a sharp angle into the extreme depths of the ocean.'

The experiment seemed to me to be a dangerous one, for who could say how far our thin hawser could bear the strain of lateral movement; but with Maracot danger, either to himself or to anyone else, simply did not exist when a scientific observation had to be made. I held my breath, and so I observed did Bill Scanlan, when a slow movement of our steel shell, brushing aside the waving fronds of seaweed, showed that the full strain was upon the line. It stood it nobly, however, and with a very gentle sweeping progression we began to glide over the bottom of the ocean, Maracot, with a compass in the hollow of his hand, shouting his direction as to the course to follow, and occasionally ordering the shell to be raised so as to avoid some obstacle in our path.

'This basaltic ridge can hardly be more than a mile across,' he explained. 'I had marked the abyss as being to the west of the point where we took our plunge. At this rate, we should certainly reach it in a very short time.'

We slid without any check over the volcanic plain, all feathered by the waving golden algae and made beautiful by the gorgeous jewels of Nature's cutting, flaming out from their setting of jet. Suddenly the Doctor dashed to the telephone.

'Stop her!' he cried. 'We are there!'

A monstrous gap had opened suddenly before us. It was a fearsome place, the vision of a nightmare. Black shining cliffs of basalt fell sheer down into the unknown. Their edges were fringed with dangling *laminaria* as ferns might overhang some earthly gorge, but beneath that tossing, vibrating rim there were only the black gleaming walls of the chasm. The rocky edge curved away from us, but the abyss might be of any breadth, for our lights failed to penetrate the gloom which lay before us. When a Lucas signalling lamp was turned downwards it shot out a long golden lane of parallel beams extending down, down, down until it was quenched in the gloom of the terrible chasm beneath us.

'It is indeed wonderful!' cried Maracot, gazing out with a

pleased proprietary expression upon his thin, eager face. 'For depth I need not say that it has often been exceeded. There is the Challenger Deep of twenty-six thousand feet near the Ladrone Islands, the Planet Deep of thirty-two thousand feet off the Philippines, and many others, but it is probable that the Maracot Deep stands alone in the declivity of its descent, and is remarkable also for its escape from the observation of so many hydrographic explorers who have charted the Atlantic. It can hardly be doubted—'

He had stopped in the middle of a sentence and a look of intense interest and surprise had frozen upon his face. Bill Scanlan and I, gazing over his shoulders, were petrified by that which met our startled eyes.

Some great creature was coming up the tunnel of light which we had projected into the abyss. Far down where it tailed off into the darkness of the pit we could dimly see the vague black lurchings and heavings of some monstrous body in slow upward progression. Paddling in clumsy fashion, it was rising with dim flickerings to the edge of the gulf. Now, as it came nearer, it was right in the beam, and we could see its dreadful form more clearly. It was a beast unknown to Science, and yet with an analogy to much with which we are familiar. Too long for a huge crab and too short for a giant lobster, it was moulded more upon the lines of the crayfish, with two monstrous nippers outstretched on either side, and a pair of sixteen-foot antennae which quivered in front of its black dull sullen eyes. The carapace, light yellow in colour, may have been ten feet across, and its total length, apart from the antennae, must have been not less than thirty.

'Wonderful!' cried Maracot, scribbling desperately in his notebook. 'Semi-pediculated eyes, elastic lamellae, family *crustacea*, species unknown. *Crustaceus Maracoti*—why not? Why not?'

'By gosh, I'll pass its name, but it seems to me it's coming our way!' cried Bill. 'Say, Doc, what about putting our light out?'

'Just one moment while I note the reticulations!' cried the naturalist. 'Yes, yes, that will do.' He clicked off the switch and we were back in our inky darkness, with only the darting lights outside like meteors on a moonless night.

'That beast is sure the world's worst,' said Bill, wiping his forehead. 'I felt like the morning after a bottle of Prohibition Hoosh.'

'It is certainly terrible to look at,' Maracot remarked, 'and perhaps terrible to deal with also if we were really exposed to those monstrous claws. But inside our steel case we can afford to examine him in safety and at our ease.'

He had hardly spoken when there came a rap as from a pick-axe upon our outer wall. Then there was a long drawn rasping and scratching, ending in another sharp rap.

'Say, he wants to come in!' cried Bill Scanlan in alarm. 'By gosh! we want "No Admission" painted on this shack.' His shaking voice showed how forced was his merriment, and I confess that my own knees were knocking together as I was aware of the stealthy monster closing up with an even blacker darkness each of our windows in succession, as he explored this strange shell which, could he but crack it, might contain his food.

'He can't hurt us,' said Maracot, but there was less assurance in his tone. 'Maybe it would be as well to shake the brute off.' He hailed the Captain up the tube.

'Pull us up twenty or thirty feet,' he cried.

A few seconds later we rose from the lava plain and swung gently in the still water. But the terrible beast was pertinacious. After a very short interval we heard once more the raspings of his feelers and the sharp tappings of his claws as he felt us round. It was terrible to sit silently in the dark and know that death was so near. If that mighty claw fell upon the window, would it stand the strain? That was the unspoken question in each of our minds.

But suddenly an unexpected and more urgent danger presented itself. The tappings had gone to the roof of our little dwelling, and now we began to sway with a rhythmic movement to and fro.

'Good God!' I cried. 'It has hold of the hawser. It will surely snap it.'

'Say, Doc, it's mine for the surface. I guess we've seen what we came to see, and it's home, sweet home for Bill Scanlan. Ring up the elevator and get her going.'

'But our work is not half done,' croaked Maracot. 'We have

only begun to explore the edges of the Deep. Let us at least see how broad it is. When we have reached the other side I shall be content to return.' Then up the tube: 'All well, Captain. Move on at two knots until I call for a stop.'

We moved slowly out over the edge of the abyss. Since darkness had not saved us from attack we now turned on our lights. One of the portholes was entirely obscured by what appeared to be the creature's lower stomach. Its head and its great nippers were at work above us, and we still swayed like a clanging bell. The strength of the beast must have been enormous. Were ever mortals placed in such a situation, with five miles of water beneath—and that deadly monster above? The oscillations became more and more violent. An excited shout came down the tube from the Captain as he became aware of the jerks upon the hawser, and Maracot sprang to his feet with his hands thrown upwards in despair. Even within the shell we were aware of the jar of the broken wires, and an instant later we were falling into the mighty gulf beneath us.

As I look back at that awful moment I can remember hearing a wild cry from Maracot.

'The hawser has parted! You can do nothing! We are all dead men!' he yelled, grabbing at the telephone tube, and then, 'Goodbye, Captain, goodbye to all.' They were our last words to the world of men.

We did not fall swiftly down, as you might have imagined. In spite of our weight our hollow shell gave us some sustaining buoyancy, and we sank slowly and gently into the abyss. I heard the long scrape as we slid through the claws of the horrible creature who had been our ruin, and then with a smooth gyration we went circling downwards into the abysmal depths. It may have been fully five minutes, and it seemed like an hour, before we reached the limit of our telephone wire and snapped it like a thread. Our air tube broke off at almost the same moment and the salt water came spouting through the vents. With quick, deft hands Bill Scanlan tied cords round each of the rubber tubes and so stopped the inrush, while the Doctor released the top of our compressed air which came hissing forth from the tubes. The lights had gone out when the wire snapped, but even in the dark the Doctor was able to connect up the Hellesens dry cells which lit a number of lamps in the roof.

'It should last us a week,' he said, with a wry smile. 'We shall at least have light to die in.' Then he shook his head sadly and a kindly smile came over his gaunt features. 'It is all right for me. I am an old man and have done my work in the world. My one regret is that I should have allowed you two young fellows to come with me. I should have taken the risk alone.'

I simply shook his hand in reassurance, for indeed there was nothing I could say. Bill Scanlan, too, was silent. Slowly we sank, marking our pace by the dark fish shadows which flitted past our windows. It seemed as if they were flying upwards rather than that we were sinking down. We still oscillated, and there was nothing so far as I could see to prevent us from falling on our side, or even turning upside down. Our weight, however, was, fortunately, very evenly balanced and we kept a level floor. Glancing up at the bathymeter I saw that we had already reached the depth of a mile.

'You see, it is as I said,' remarked Maracot, with some complacency. 'You may have seen my paper in the Proceedings of the Oceanographical Society upon the relation of pressure and depth. I wish I could get one word back to the world, if only to confute Bulow of Giessen, who ventured to contradict me.'

'My gosh! If I could get a word back to the world I wouldn't waste it on a square-head highbrow,' said the mechanic. 'There is a little wren in Philadelphia that will have tears in her pretty eyes when she hears that Bill Scanlan has passed out. Well, it sure does seem a darned queer way of doing it, anyhow.'

'You should never have come,' I said, putting my hand on his.

'What sort of tin-horn sport should I have been if I had quitted?' he answered. 'No, it's my job, and I am glad I stuck it.'

'How long have we?' I asked the Doctor, after a pause.

He shrugged his shoulders.

'We shall have time to see the real bottom of the ocean, anyhow,' said he. 'There is air enough in our tubes for the best part of a day. Our trouble is with the waste products. That is what is going to choke us. If we could get rid of our carbon dioxide—'

'That I can see is impossible.'

'There is one tube of pure oxygen. I put it in in case of accidents. A little of that from time to time will help to keep us alive. You will observe that we are now more than two miles deep.'

'Why should we try to keep ourselves alive? The sooner it is over the better,' said I.

'That's the dope,' cried Scanlan. 'Cut loose and have done with it.'

'And miss the most wonderful sight that man's eye has ever seen!' said Maracot. 'It would be treason to Science. Let us record facts to the end, even if they should be for ever buried with our bodies. Play the game out.'

'Some sport, the Doc!' cried Scanlan. 'I guess he has the best guts of the bunch. Let us see the spiel to an end.'

We sat patiently on the settee, the three of us, gripping the edges of it with strained fingers as it swayed and rocked, while the fishes still flashed swiftly upwards athwart the portholes.

'It is now three miles,' remarked Maracot. 'I will turn on the oxygen, Mr. Headley, for it is certainly very close. There is one thing,' he added, with his dry, cackling laugh, 'it will certainly be the Maracot Deep from this time onwards. When Captain Howie takes back the news my colleagues will see to it that my grave is also my monument. Even Bulow of Giessen—' He babbled on about some unintelligible scientific grievance.

We sat in silence again, watching the needle as it crawled on to its fourth mile. At one point we struck something heavy, which shook us so violently that I feared that we would turn upon our side. It may have been a huge fish, or conceivably we may have bumped upon some projection of the cliff over the edge of which we had been precipitated. That edge had seemed to us at the time to be such a wondrous depth, and now looking back at it from our dreadful abyss it might almost have been the surface. Still we swirled and circled lower and lower through the dark green waste of waters. Twenty-five thousand feet now was registered upon the dial.

'We are nearly at our journey's end,' said Maracot. 'My Scott's recorder gave me twenty-six thousand seven hundred last year at the deepest point. We shall know our fate within a few minutes. It may be that the shock will crush us. It may be—'

And at that moment we landed.

There was never a babe lowered by its mother on to a feather-bed who nestled down more gently than we on to the extreme bottom of the Atlantic Ocean. The soft thick elastic ooze upon which we lit was a perfect buffer, which saved us from the slightest jar. We hardly moved upon our seats, and it is as well that we did not, for we had perched upon some sort of a projecting hummock, clothed thickly with the viscous gelatinous mud, and there we were balanced rocking gently with nearly half our base projecting and unsupported. There was a danger that we would tip over on our side, but finally we steadied down and remained motionless. As we did so Dr. Maracot, staring out through his porthole, gave a cry of surprise and hurriedly turned out our electric light.

To our amazement we could still see clearly. There was a dim, misty light outside which streamed through our porthole, like the cold radiance of a winter morning. We looked out at the strange scene, and with no help from our own lights we could see clearly for some hundred yards in each direction. It was impossible, inconceivable, but none the less the evidence of our senses told us that it was a fact. The great ocean floor is luminous.

'Why not?' cried Maracot, when we had stood for a minute or two in silent wonder. 'Should I not have foreseen it? What is this *pteropod* or globigerina ooze? Is it not the product of decay, the mouldering bodies of a billion billion organic creatures? And is decay not associated with phosphorescent luminosity? Where, in all creation, would it be seen if it were not here? Ah! It is indeed hard that we should have such a demonstration and be unable to send our knowledge back to the world.'

'And yet,' I remarked, 'we have scooped half a ton of radiolarian jelly at a time and detected no such radiance.'

'It would lose it, doubtless, in its long journey to the surface. And what is half a ton compared to these far-stretching plains of slow putrescence? And see, see,' he cried in uncontrollable excitement, 'the deep-sea creatures graze upon this organic carpet even as our herds on land graze upon the meadows!'

As he spoke a flock of big black fish, heavy and squat, came slowly over the ocean bed towards us, nuzzling among the spongy growths and nibbling away as they advanced. Another huge red creature, like a foolish cow of the ocean, was chewing the cud in front of my porthole, and others were grazing here and there, raising their heads from, time to time to gaze at this strange object which had so suddenly appeared among them.

I could only marvel at Maracot, who in that foul atmosphere, seated under the very shadow of death, still obeyed the call of Science and scribbled his observations in his notebook. Without following his precise methods, I none the less made my own mental notes, which will remain for ever as a picture stamped upon my brain. The lowest plains of ocean consist of red clay, but here it was overlaid by the grey *bathybian* slime which formed an undulating plain as far as our eyes could reach. This plain was not smooth, but was broken by numerous strange rounded hillocks like that upon which we had perched, all glimmering in the spectral light. Between these little hills there darted great clouds of strange fish, many of them quite unknown to Science, exhibiting every shade of colour, but black and red predominating. Maracot watched them with suppressed excitement and chronicled them in his notes.

The air had become very foul, and again we were only able to save ourselves by a fresh emission of oxygen. Curiously enough, we were all hungry—I should rather say ravenous—and we fell upon the potted beef with bread and butter, washed down by whisky and water, which the foresight of Maracot had provided. With my perceptions stimulated by this refreshment, I was seated at my lookout portal and longing for a last cigarette, when my eyes caught something which sent a whirl of strange thoughts and anticipations through my mind.

I have said that the undulating grey plain on every side of us was studded with what seemed like hummocks. A particularly large one was in front of my porthole, and I looked out at it within a range of thirty feet. There was some peculiar mark upon the side of it, and as I glanced along I saw to my surprise that this mark was repeated again and again until it was lost round the curve. When one is so near death it takes much to give one a thrill about anything connected with this world, but my breath failed me for a moment and my heart stood still as I suddenly realized that it was a frieze at which I was looking and that, barnacled and worn as it was, the hand of man had surely at some time carved these faded figures. Maracot and Scanlan crowded to my porthole and gazed out in utter amazement at these signs of the omnipresent energies of man.

'It is carving, for sure!' cried Scanlan. 'I guess this dump has been the roof of a building. Then these other ones are buildings also. Say, boss, we've dropped plumb on to a regular burg.'

'It is, indeed, an ancient city,' said Maracot. 'Geology teaches that the seas have once been continents and the continents seas, but I have always distrusted the idea that in times so recent as the quaternary there could have been an Atlantic subsidence. Plato's report of Egyptian gossip had then a foundation of fact. These volcanic formations confirm the view that this subsidence was due to seismic activity.'

'There is regularity about these domes,' I remarked. 'I begin to think that they are not separate houses, but that they are cupolas and form the ornaments of the roof of some huge building.'

'I guess you are right,' said Scanlan. 'There are four big ones at the corners and the small ones in lines between. It's some building, if we could see the whole of it! You could put the whole Merribank plant inside it—and then some.'

'It has been buried up to the roof by the constant dropping from above,' said Maracot. 'On the other hand, it has not decayed. We have a constant temperature of a little over 32° Fahrenheit in the great depths, which would arrest destructive processes. Even the dissolution of the Bathic remains which pave the floor of the ocean and incidentally give us this luminosity must be a very slow one. But, dear me! this marking is not a frieze but an inscription.'

There was no doubt that he was right. The same symbol re-curred every here and there. These marks were unquestionably letters of some archaic alphabet.

'I have made a study of Phoenician antiquities, and there is certainly something suggestive and familiar in these characters,' said our leader. 'Well, we have seen a buried city of ancient days, my friends, and we carry a wonderful piece of knowledge with us to the grave. There is no more to be learned. Our book of knowledge is closed. I agree with you that the sooner the end comes the better.'

It could not now be long delayed. The air was stagnant and dreadful. So heavy was it with carbon products that the oxygen could hardly force its way out against the pressure. By standing on the settee one was able to get a gulp of purer air, but the mephitic reek was slowly rising. Dr. Maracot folded his arms with an air of resignation and sank his head upon his breast. Scanlan was now overpowered by the fumes and was already sprawling upon the floor. My own head was swimming, and I felt an intolerable weight at my chest. I closed my eyes and my senses were rapidly slipping away. Then I opened them for one last glimpse of that world which I was leaving, and as I did so I staggered to my feet with a hoarse scream of amazement.

A human face was looking in at us through the porthole!

Was it my delirium? I clutched at the shoulder of Maracot and shook him violently. He sat up and stared, wonder-struck and speechless at this apparition. If he saw it as well as I, it was no figment of the brain. The face was long and thin, dark in complexion, with a short, pointed beard, and two vivid eyes darting here and there in quick, questioning glances which took in every detail of our situation. The utmost amazement was visible upon the man's face. Our lights were now full on, and it must indeed have been a strange and vivid picture which presented itself to his gaze in that tiny chamber of death, where one man lay senseless and two others glared out at him with the twisted, contorted features of dying men, cyanosed by incipient asphyxiation. We both had our hands to our throats, and our heaving chests carried their message of despair. The man gave a wave of his hand and hurried away.

'He has deserted us!' cried Maracot.

'Or gone for help. Let us get Scanlan on the couch. It's death for him down there.'

We dragged the mechanic on to the settee and propped his head against the cushions. His face was grey and he murmured in delirium, but his pulse was still perceptible.

'There is hope for us yet,' I croaked.

'But it is madness!' cried Maracot. 'How can man live at the bottom of the ocean? How can he breathe? It is collective hallucination. My young friend, we are going mad.'

Looking out at the bleak, lonely grey landscape in the dreary spectral light, I felt that it might be as Maracot said. Then suddenly I was aware of movement. Shadows were flitting through the distant water. They hardened and thickened into moving figures. A crowd of people were hurrying across the ocean bed in our direction. An instant later they had assembled in front of the porthole and were pointing and gesticulating in animated debate. There were several women in the crowd, but the greater part were men, one of whom, a powerful figure with a very large head and a full black beard, was clearly a person of authority. He made a swift inspection of our steel shell, and, since the edge of our base projected over the place on which we rested, he was able to see that there was a hinged trap-door at the bottom. He now sent a messenger flying back, while he made energetic and commanding signs to us to open the door from within.

'Why not?' I asked. 'We may as well be drowned as be smothered. I can stand it no longer.'

'We may not be drowned,' said Maracot. 'The water entering from below cannot rise above the level of the compressed air. Give Scanlan some brandy. He must make an effort, if it is his last one.'

I forced a drink down the mechanic's throat. He gulped and looked round him with wondering eyes. Between us we got him erect on the settee and stood on either side of him. He was still half-dazed, but in a few words I explained the situation.

'There is a chance of chlorine poisoning if the water reaches the batteries,' said Maracot. 'Open every air tube, for the more pressure we can get the less water may enter. Now help me while I pull upon the lever.'

We bent our weight upon it and yanked up the circular plate

from the bottom of our little home, though I felt like a suicide as I did so. The green water, sparkling and gleaming under our light, came gurgling and surging in. It rose rapidly to our feet, to our knees, to our waists, and there it stopped. But the pressure of the air was intolerable. Our heads buzzed and the drums of our ears were bursting. We could not have lived in such an atmosphere for long. Only by clutching at the rack could we save ourselves from falling back into the waters beneath us.

From our higher position we could no longer see through the portholes, nor could we imagine what steps were being taken for our deliverance. Indeed, that any effective help could come to us seemed beyond the power of thought, and yet there was a commanding and purposeful air about these people, and especially about that squat bearded chieftain, which inspired vague hopes. Suddenly we were aware of his face looking up at us through the water beneath and an instant later he had passed through the circular opening and had clambered on to the settee, so that he was standing by our side—a short sturdy figure, not higher than my shoulder, but surveying us with large brown eyes, which were full of a half-amused confidence, as who should say, 'You poor devils; you think you are in a very bad way, but I can clearly see the road out.'

Only now was I aware of a very amazing thing. The man, if indeed he was of the same humanity as ourselves, had a transparent envelope all round him which enveloped his head and body, while his arms and legs were free. So translucent was it that no one could detect it in the water, but now that he was in the air beside us it glistened like silver, though it remained as clear as the finest glass. On either shoulder he had a curious rounded projection beneath the clear protective sheath. It looked like an oblong box pierced with many holes, and gave him an appearance as if he were wearing epaulettes.

When our new friend had joined us another face appeared in the aperture of the bottom and thrust through it what seemed like a great bubble of glass. Three of these in succession were passed in and floated upon the surface of the water. Then six small boxes were handed up and our new acquaintance tied one with the straps attached to them to each of our shoulders, whence they stood up like his own. Already I began to surmise that no infraction of natural law was involved in the life of these strange people, and that while one box in some new fashion was a producer of air the other was an absorber of waste products. He now passed the transparent suits over our heads, and we felt that they clasped us tightly in the upper arm and waist by elastic bands, so that no water could penetrate. Within we breathed with perfect ease, and it was a joy to me to see Maracot looking out at me with his eyes twinkling as of old behind his glasses, while Bill Scanlan's grin assured me that the life-giving oxygen had done its work, and that he was his cheerful self once more. Our rescuer looked from one to another of us with grave satisfaction, and then motioned to us to follow him through the trap-door and out on to the floor of the ocean. A dozen willing hands were outstretched to pull us through and to sustain our first faltering steps as we staggered with our feet deep in the slimy ooze.

Even now I cannot get past the marvel of it! There we were, the three of us, unhurt and at our ease at the bottom of a five-mile abyss of water. Where was that terrific pressure which had exercised the imagination of so many scientists? We were no more affected by it than were the dainty fish which swam around us. It is true that, so far as our bodies were concerned, we were protected by these delicate bells of vitrine, which were in truth tougher than the strongest steel, but even our limbs, which were exposed, felt no more than a firm constriction from the water which one learned in time to disregard. It was wonderful to stand together and to look back at the shell from which we had emerged. We had left the batteries at work, and it was a wondrous object with its streams of yellow light flooding out from each side, while clouds of fishes gathered at each window. As we watched it the leader took Maracot by the hand, and we followed them both across the watery morass, clumping heavily through the sticky surface.

And now a most surprising incident occurred, which was clearly as astonishing to these strange new companions of ours as to ourselves. Above our heads there appeared a small, dark object, descending from the darkness above us and swinging down until it reached the bed of the ocean within a very short distance from where we stood. It was, of course, the deep-sea lead from the *Stratford* above us, making a sounding of that watery gulf with which the name of the expedition was to be associated. We had seen it already upon its downward path, and we could well understand that the tragedy of our disappearance had suspended the operation, but that after a pause it had been concluded, with little thought that it would finish almost at our feet. They were unconscious, apparently, that they had touched bottom, for the lead lay motionless in the ooze. Above me stretched the taut piano wire which connected me through five miles of water with the deck of our vessel. Oh, that it were possible to write a note and to attach it! The idea was absurd, and yet could I not send some message which would show them that we were still conscious? My coat was covered by my glass bell and the pockets were unapproachable, but I was free below the waist and my handkerchief chanced to be in my trousers pocket. I pulled it out and tied it above the top of the lead. The weight at once disengaged itself by its automatic mechanism, and presently I saw my white wisp of linen flying upwards to that world which I may never see again. Our new acquaintances examined the seventy-five pounds of lead with great interest, and finally carried it off with us as we went upon our way.

We had only walked a couple of hundred yards, threading our way among the hummocks, when we halted before a small square-cut door with solid pillars on either side and an inscription across the lintel. It was open, and we passed through it into a large, bare chamber. There was a sliding partition worked by a crank from within, and this was drawn across behind us. We could, of course, hear nothing in our glass helmets, but after standing a few minutes we were aware that a powerful pump must be at work, for we saw the level of the water sinking rapidly above us. In less than a quarter of an hour we were standing upon a sloppy stone-flagged pavement, while our new friends were busy in undoing the fastenings of our transparent suits.

An instant later there we stood, breathing perfectly pure air in a warm, well-lighted atmosphere, while the dark people of the abyss, smiling and chattering, crowded round us with hand-shakings and friendly pattings. It was a strange, rasping tongue that they spoke, and no word of it was intelligible to us, but the smile on the face and the light of friendship in the eye are un-derstandable even in the waters under the earth. The glass suits were hung on numbered pegs upon the wall, and the kindly folk half led and half pushed us to an inner door which opened on to a long downward-sloping corridor. When it closed again behind us there was nothing to remind us of the stupendous fact that we were the involuntary guests of an unknown race at the bot-tom of the Atlantic ocean and cut off for ever from the world to which we belonged.

Now that the terrific strain had been so suddenly eased we were all exhausted. Even Bill Scanlan, who was a pocket Her-cules, dragged his feet along the floor, while Maracot and I were only too glad to lean heavily upon our guides. Yet, weary as I was, I took in every detail as we passed. That the air came from some air-making machine was very evident, for it issued in puffs from circular openings in the walls. The light was diffused and was clearly an extension of that fluor system which was already engaging the attention of our European engineers when the filament and lamp were dispensed with. It shone from long cyl-inders of clear glass which were suspended along the cornices of the passages. So much I had observed when our descent was checked and we were ushered into a large sitting-room, thickly carpeted and well furnished with gilded chairs and sloping sofas which brought back vague memories of Egyptian tombs. The crowd had been dismissed and only the bearded man with two attendants remained. 'Manda' he repeated several times, tapping himself upon the chest. Then he pointed to each of us in turn and repeated the words Maracot, Headley and Scanlan until he had them perfect. He then motioned us to be seated and said a word to one of the attendants, who left the room and returned presently, escorting a very ancient gentleman, white-haired and long-bearded, with a curious conical cap of black cloth upon his head. I should have said that all these folk were dressed in coloured tunics, which extended to their knees, with high boots of fish skin or *shagreen*. The venerable newcomer was clearly a physician, for he examined each of us in turn, placing his hand upon our brows and closing his own eyes as if receiving a mental impression as to our condition. Apparently he was by no means satisfied, for he shook his head and said a few grave words to Manda. The latter at once sent the attendant out once more, and he brought in a tray of eatables and a flask of wine, which were laid before us. We were too weary to ask ourselves what they were, but we felt the better for the meal. We were then led to another room, where three beds had been prepared, and on one of these I flung myself down. I have a dim recollection of Bill Scanlan coming across and sitting beside me.

'Say, Bo, that jolt of brandy saved my life,' said he. 'But where are we, anyhow?'

'I know no more than you do.'

'Well, I am ready to hit the hay,' he said, sleepily, as he turned to his bed. 'Say, that wine was fine. Thank God, Volstead never got down here.' They were the last words I heard as I sank into the most profound sleep that I can ever recall.

Chapter 3

When I came to myself I could not at first imagine where I was. The events of the previous day were like some blurred nightmare, and I could not believe that I had to accept them as facts. I looked round in bewilderment at the large, bare, windowless room with drab-coloured walls, at the lines of quivering purplish light which flowed along the cornices, at the scattered articles of furniture, and finally at the two other beds, from one of which came the high-pitched, strident snore which I had learned aboard the *Stratford*, to associate with Maracot. It was too grotesque to be true, and it was only when I fingered my bed cover and observed the curious woven material, the dried fibres of some sea plant, from which it was made, that I was able to realize this inconceivable adventure which had befallen us. I was still pondering it when there came a loud explosion of laughter, and Bill Scanlan sat up in bed.

'Mornin', Bo!' he cried, amid his chuckles, on seeing that I was awake.

'You seem in good spirits,' said I, rather testily. 'I can't see that we have much to laugh about.'

'Well, I had a grouch on me, the same as you, when first I woke up,' he answered. 'Then came a real cute idea, and it was that that made me laugh.'

'I could do with a laugh myself,' said I. 'What's the idea?'

'Well, Bo, I thought how durned funny it would have been if we had all tied ourselves on to that deep-sea line. I allow with those glass dinguses we could have kept breathing all right.

45

Then when old man Howie looked over the side there would have been the whole bunch of us comin' up at him through the water. He would have figured that he had hooked us, sure. Gee, what a spiel!'

Our united laughter woke the Doctor, who sat up in bed with the same amazed expression upon his face which had previously been upon my own. I forgot our troubles as I listened in amusement to his disjointed comments, which alternated between ecstatic joy at the prospect of such a field of study, and profound sorrow that he could never hope to convey his results to his scientific confreres of the earth. Finally he got back to the actual needs of the moment.

'It is nine o'clock,' he said, looking at his watch. We all registered the same hour, but there was nothing to show if it was night or morning.

'We must keep our own calendar,' said Maracot; 'we descended upon October 3rd. We reached this place on the evening of the same day. How long have we slept?'

'My gosh, it may have been a month,' said Scanlan, 'I've not been so deep since Mickey Scott got me on the point in the six round try-out at the Works.'

We dressed and washed, for every civilized convenience was at hand. The door, however, was fastened, and it was clear that we were prisoners for the time. In spite of the apparent absence of any ventilation, the atmosphere kept perfectly sweet, and we found that this was due to a current of air which came through small holes in the wall. There was some source of central heating, too, for though no stove was visible, the temperature was pleasantly warm. Presently I observed a knob upon one of the walls, and pressed it. This was, as I expected, a bell, for the door instantly opened, and a small, dark man, dressed in a yellow robe, appeared in the aperture. He looked at us inquiringly, with large brown, kindly eyes.

'We are hungry,' said Maracot; 'can you get us some food?'

The man shook his head and smiled. It was clear that the words were incomprehensible to him.

Scanlan tried his luck with a flow of American slang, which

was received with the same blank smile. When, however, I opened my mouth and thrust my finger into it, our visitor nodded vigorously and hurried away.

Ten minutes later the door opened and two of the yellow attendants appeared, rolling a small table before them. Had we been at the Biltmore Hotel we could not have had better fare. There were coffee, hot milk, rolls, delicious flat fish, and honey. For half an hour we were far too busy to discuss what we ate or whence it was obtained. At the end of that time the two servants appeared once more, rolled out the tray, and closed the door carefully behind them.

'I'm fair black and blue with pinching myself,' said Scanlan. 'Is this a pipe dream or what? Say, Doc, you got us down here, and I guess it is up to you to tell us just how you size it all up.'

The Doctor shook his head.

'It is like a dream to me also, but it is a glorious dream! What a story for the world if we could but get it to them!'

'One thing is clear,' said I, 'there was certainly truth in this legend of Atlantis, and some of the folk have in a marvellous way managed to carry on.'

'Well, even if they carried on,' cried Bill Scanlan, scratching his bullet head, 'I am darned if I can understand how they could get air and fresh water and the rest. Maybe if that queer duck with the beard that we saw last night comes to give us a once-over he will put us wise to it.'

'How can he do that when we have no common language?'

'Well, we shall use our own observation,' said Maracot. 'One thing I can already understand. I learned it from the honey at breakfast. That was clearly synthetic honey, such as we have already learned to make upon the earth. But if synthetic honey, why not synthetic coffee, or flour? The molecules of the elements are like bricks, and these bricks lie all around us. We have only to learn how to pull out certain bricks—sometimes just a single brick—in order to make a fresh substance. Sugar becomes starch, or either becomes alcohol, just by a shifting of the bricks. What is it that shifts them? Heat. Electricity. Other things perhaps of which we know nothing. Some of them will shift themselves, and radium becomes lead or uranium becomes radium without our touching them.'

'You think, then, that they have an advanced chemistry?'

'I'm sure of it. After all there is no elemental brick which is not ready to their hands. Hydrogen and oxygen come readily from the sea water. There are nitrogen and carbon in those masses of sea vegetation, and there are phosphorus and calcium in the *bathybic* deposit. With skilful management and adequate knowledge, what is there which could not be produced?'

The Doctor had launched upon a chemical lecture when the door opened and Manda entered, giving us a friendly greeting. There came with him the same old gentleman of venerable appearance whom we had met the night before. He may have had a reputation for learning, for he tried several sentences, which were probably different languages, upon us, but all were equally unintelligible. Then he shrugged his shoulders and spoke to Manda, who gave an order to the two yellow-clad servants, still waiting at the door. They vanished, but returned presently with a curious screen, supported by two side posts. It was exactly like one of our cinema screens, but it was coated with some sparkling material which glittered and shimmered in the light. This was placed against one of the walls. The old man then paced out very carefully a certain distance, and marked it upon the floor. Standing at this point he turned to Maracot and touched his forehead, pointing to the screen.

'Clean dippy,' said Scanlan. 'Bats in the belfry.'

Maracot shook his head to show that we were nonplussed. So was the old man for a moment. An idea struck him, however, and he pointed to his own figure. Then he turned towards the screen, fixed his eyes upon it, and seemed to concentrate his attention. In an instant a reflection of himself appeared on the screen before us. Then he pointed to us, and a moment later our own little group took the place of his image. It was not particularly like us. Scanlan looked like a comic Chinaman and Maracot like a decayed corpse, but it was clearly meant to be ourselves as we appeared in the eyes of the operator.

'It's a reflection of thought,' I cried.

'Exactly,' said Maracot. 'This is certainly a most marvellous invention, and yet it is but a combination of such telepathy and television as we dimly comprehend upon earth.'

'I never thought I'd live to see myself on the movies, if that cheese-faced Chink is really meant for me,' said Scanlan. 'Say, if we could get all this news to the editor of the Ledger he'd cough up enough to keep me for life. We've sure got the goods if we could deliver them.'

'That's the trouble,' said I. 'By George, we could stir the whole world if we could only get back to it. But what is he beckoning about?'

'The old guy wants you to try your hand at it, Doc.'

Maracot took the place indicated, and his strong, clear-cut brain focused his picture to perfection. We saw an image of Manda, and then another one of the *Stratford* as we had left her.

Both Manda and the old scientist nodded their great approval at the sight of the ship, and Manda made a sweeping gesture with his hands, pointing first to us and then to the screen.

'To tell them all about it—that's the idea,' I cried. 'They want to know in pictures who we are, and how we got here.'

Maracot nodded to Manda to show that he understood, and had begun to throw an image of our voyage, when Manda held up his hand and stopped him. At an order the attendants re-moved the screen, and the two Atlanteans beckoned that we should follow them.

It was a huge building, and we proceeded down corridor after corridor until we came at last to a large hall with seats arranged in tiers like a lecture room. At one side was a broad screen of the same nature as that which we had seen. Facing it there was as-sembled an audience of at least a thousand people, who set up a murmur of welcome as we entered. They were of both sexes and of all ages, the men dark and bearded, the women beautiful in youth and dignified in age. We had little time to observe them, for we were led to seats in the front row, and Maracot was then placed on a stand opposite the screen, the lights were in some fashion turned down, and he had the signal to begin.

And excellently well he played his part. We first saw our vessel sailing forth from the Thames, and a buzz of excitement went up from the tense audience at this authentic glimpse of a real modern city. Then a map appeared which marked her course. Then was seen the steel shell with its fittings, which was greeted with a murmur of recognition. We saw ourselves once more descending, and reaching the edge of the abyss. Then came the appearance of the monster who had wrecked us. '*Marax! Marax!*' cried the people, as the beast appeared. It was clear that they had learned to know and to fear it. There was a terrified hush as the creature fumbled with our hawser, and a groan of horror as the wires parted and we dropped into the gulf. In a month of explanation we could not have made our plight so clear as in that half-hour of visible demonstration.

As the audience broke up they showered every sign of sympathy upon us, crowding round us and patting our backs to show that we were welcome. We were presented in turn to some of the chiefs, but the chieftainship seemed to lie in wisdom alone, for all appeared to be on the same social scale, and were dressed in much the same way. The men wore tunics of a saffron colour coming down to the knees, with belts and high boots of a scaly tough material which must have been the hide of some sea beast. The women were beautifully draped in classical style, their flowing robes of every tint of pink and blue and green, ornamented with clusters of pearl or opalescent sheets of shell. Many of them were lovely beyond any earthly comparison. There was one—but why should I mix my private feelings up with this public narrative? Let me say only that Mona is the only daughter of Manda, one of the leaders of the people, and that from that first day of meeting I read in her dark eyes a message of sympathy and of understanding which went home to my heart, as my gratitude and admiration may have gone to hers. I need not say more at present about this exquisite lady. Suffice it that a new and strong influence had come into my life. When I saw Maracot gesticulating with unwonted animation to one kindly lady, while Scanlan stood conveying his admiration in pantomime in the centre of a group of laughing girls, I realized that my companions also had begun to find that there was a lighter side to our tragic position. If we were dead to the world we had at least found a life beyond, which promised some compensation for what we had lost.

Later in the day we were guided by Manda and other friends round some portions of the immense building. It had been so embedded in the sea-floor by the accumulations of ages that it was only through the roof that it could be entered, and from this point the passages led down and down until the floor level was reached several hundred feet below the entrance chamber. The floor in turn had been excavated, and we saw in all directions passages which sloped downwards into the bowels of the earth. We were shown the air-making apparatus with the pumps which circulated it through the building. Maracot pointed out with wonder and admiration that not only was the oxygen united with the nitrogen, but that smaller retorts supplied other gases which could only be the argon, neon, and other little-known constituents of the atmosphere which we are only just beginning to understand. The distilling vats for making fresh water and the enormous electrical instalments were other objects of interest, but much of the machinery was so intricate that it was difficult for us to follow the details. I can only say that I saw with my own eyes, and tested with my own palate, that chemicals in gaseous and liquid forms were poured into various machines, that they were treated by heat, by pressure, and by electricity, and that flour, tea, coffee, or wine was collected as the product.

There was one consideration which was very quickly forced upon us by our examination, on various occasions, of as much of this building as was open to our inspection. This was that the exposure to the sea had been foreseen and the protection against the inrush of the water had been prepared long before the land sank beneath the waves. Of course, it stood to reason, and needed no proof, that such precautions could not have been taken after the event, but we were witnesses now of the signs that the whole great building had from the first been constructed with the one idea of being an enduring ark of refuge. The huge retorts and vats in which the air, the food, the distilled water, and the other necessary products were made were all built into the walls, and were evidently integral parts of the original construction. So, too, with the exit chambers, the silica works where the vitrine bells were constructed, and the huge pumps which controlled the water. Every one of these things had been prepared by the skill and the foresight of that wonderful far-away people who seemed, from what we could learn, to have thrown out one arm to Central America and one to Egypt, and so left traces of themselves even upon this earth when their own land went down into the Atlantic. As to these, their descendants, we judged that they had probably degenerated, as was but natural, and that at the most they had been stagnant and only preserved some of the science and knowledge of their ancestors without having the energy to add to it. They possessed wonderful powers and yet seemed to us to be strangely wanting in initiative, and had added nothing to that wonderful legacy which they had inherited. I am sure that Maracot, using this knowledge, would very soon have attained greater results. As to Scanlan, with his quick brain and mechanical skill, he was continually putting in touches which probably seemed as remarkable to them as their powers to us. He had a beloved mouth-organ in his coat-pocket when we made our descent, and his use of this was a perpetual joy to our companions, who sat around in entranced groups, as we might listen to a Mozart, while he handed out to them the crooning coon songs of his native land.

I have said that the whole building was not open to our inspection, and I might give a little further detail upon that subject. There was one well-worn corridor down which we saw folk continually passing, but which was always avoided by our guides in our excursions. As was natural our curiosity was aroused, and we determined one evening that we would take a chance and do a little exploring upon our own account. We slipped out of our room, therefore, and made our way to the unknown quarter at a time when few people were about.

The passage led us to a high arched door, which appeared to be made of solid gold. When we pushed it open we found ourselves in a huge room, forming a square of not less than two hundred feet. All around, the walls were painted with vivid colours and adorned with extraordinary pictures and statues of grotesque creatures with enormous head-dresses, like the full dress regalia of our American Indians. At the end of this great hall there was one huge seated figure, the legs crossed like a Buddha, but with none of the benignity of aspect which is seen on the Buddha's placid features. On the contrary, this was a creature of Wrath, open-mouthed and fierce-eyed, the latter being red, and their effect exaggerated by two electric lights which shone through them. On his lap was a great oven, which we observed, as we approached it, to be filled with ashes.

'Moloch!' said Maracot. 'Moloch or Baal—the old god of the Phoenician races.'

'Good heavens!' I cried, with recollections of old Carthage before me. 'Don't tell me that these gentle folk could go in for human sacrifice.'

'Look it here, Bo!' said Scanlan, anxiously. 'I hope they keep it in the family, anyhow. We don't want them to pull no such dope on us.'

'No, I guess they have learned their lesson,' said I. 'It's misfortune that teaches folk to have pity for others.'

'That's right,' Maracot remarked, poking about among the ashes, 'it is the old hereditary god, but it is surely a gentler cult. These are burned loaves and the like. But perhaps there was a time—'

But our speculations were interrupted by a stern voice at our elbow, and we found several men in yellow garments and high hats, who were clearly the priests of the Temple. From the expression on their faces I should judge that we were very near to being the last victims to Baal, and one of them had actually drawn a knife from his girdle. With fierce gestures and cries they drove us roughly out of their sacred shrine.

'By gosh!' cried Scanlan, 'I'll sock that duck if he keeps crowding me! Look it here, you Bindlestiff, keep your hands off my coat.'

For a moment I feared that we should have had what Scanlan called a 'rough house' within the sacred precincts. However, we got the angry mechanic away without blows and regained the shelter of our room, but we could tell from the demeanour of Manda and others of our friends that our escapade was known and resented.

But there was another shrine which was freely shown to us and which had a very unexpected result, for it opened up a slow and imperfect method of communication between our companions and ourselves. This was a room in the lower quarter of the Temple, with no decorations or distinction save that at one end there stood a statue of ivory yellow with age, representing a woman holding a spear, with an owl perched upon her shoulder. A very old man was the guardian of the room, and in spite of his age it was clear to us that he was of a very different race, and one of a finer, larger type than the men of the Temple. As we stood gazing at the ivory statue, Maracot and I, both wondering where we had seen something like it, the old man addressed us.

'Thea,' said he, pointing to the figure.

'By George!' I cried, 'he is speaking Greek.'

'Thea! Athena!' repeated the man.

There was not a doubt of it. 'Goddess—Athena,' the words were unmistakable. Maracot, whose wonderful brain had absorbed something from every branch of human knowledge, began at once to ask questions in Classical Greek which were only partly understood and were answered in a dialect so archaic that it was almost incomprehensible. Still, he acquired some knowledge, and he found an intermediary through whom he could dimly convey something to our companions.

'It is a remarkable proof,' said Maracot that evening, in his high neighing voice and in the tones of one addressing a large class, 'of the reliability of legend. There is always a basis of fact even if in the course of the years it should become distorted. You are aware—or probably you are not aware'—('Bet your life!' from Scanlan)—'that a war was going on between the primitive Greeks and, the Atlanteans at the time of the destruction of the great island. The fact is recorded in Solon's description of what he learned from the priests of Sais. We may conjecture that there were Greek prisoners in the hands of the Atlanteans at the time, that some of them were in the service of the Temple, and that they carried their own religion with them. That man was, so far as I could understand, the old hereditary priest of the cult, and perhaps when we know more we shall see something of these ancient people.'

'Well, I hand it to them for good sense,' said Scanlan. 'I guess if you want a plaster god it is better to have a fine woman than that blatherskite with the red eyes and the coal-bunker on his knees.'

'Lucky they can't understand your views,' I remarked. 'If they did you might end up as a Christian martyr.'

'Not so long as I can play them jazz,' he answered, 'I guess they've got used to me now, and they couldn't do without me.'

They were a cheerful crowd, and it was a happy life, but there were and are times when one's whole heart goes out to the homelands which we have lost, and visions of the dear old quadrangles of Oxford, or of the ancient elms and the familiar campus of Harvard, came up before my mind. In those early days they seemed as far from me as some landscape in the moon, and only now in a dim uncertain fashion does the hope of seeing them once more begin to grow in my soul.

Chapter 4

It was a few days after our arrival that our hosts or our captors—we were dubious sometimes as to which to call them—took us out for an expedition upon the bottom of the ocean. Six of them came with us, including Manda, the chief. We assembled in the same exit chamber in which we had originally been received, and we were now in a condition to examine it a little more closely. It was a very large place, at least a hundred feet each way, and its low walls and ceiling were green with marine growths and dripping with moisture. A long row of pegs, with marks which I presume were numbers, ran round the whole room, and on each was hung one of the semi-transparent bells of vitrine and a pair of the shoulder batteries which ensured respiration. The floor was of flagged stone worn into concavities, the footsteps of many generations, these hollows now lying as pools of shallow water. The whole was highly illuminated by fluor tubes round the cornice. We were fastened into our vitrine coverings, and a stout pointed staff made of some light metal was handed to each of us. Then, by signals, Manda ordered us to take a grip of a rail which ran round the room, he and his friends setting us an example. The object of this soon became evident, for as the outer door swung slowly open the sea water came pouring in with such force that we should have been swept from our feet but for this precaution. It rose rapidly, however, to above the level of our heads, and the pressure upon us was eased. Manda led the way to the door, and an instant afterwards we were out on the ocean bed once more, leaving the portal open behind us ready for our return.

Looking round us in the cold, flickering, spectral light which illuminates the *bathybian* plain, we could see for a radius of at least a quarter of a mile in every direction.

What amazed us was to observe, on the very limit of what was visible, a very brilliant glow of radiance. It was towards this that our leader turned his steps, our party walking in single file behind him. It was slow going, for there was the resistance of the water, and our feet were buried deeply in the soft slush with every step; but soon we were able to see clearly what the beacon was which had attracted us. It was our own shell, our last reminder of terrestrial life, which lay tilted upon one of the cupolas of the far-flung building, with all its lights still blazing. It was three-quarters full of water, but the imprisoned air still preserved that portion in which our electric instalment lay. It was strange indeed as we gazed into it to see the familiar interior with our settees and instruments still in position, while several good-sized fish like minnows in a bottle swam round and round inside it. One after the other our party clambered in through the open flap, Maracot to rescue a book of notes which floated on the surface, Scanlan and I to pick up some personal belongings. Manda came also with one or two of his comrades, examining with the greatest interest the bathometer and thermometer with the other instruments which were attached to the wall. The latter we detached and took away with us. It may interest scientists to know that forty degrees Fahrenheit represents the temperature at the greatest sea depths to which man has ever descended, and that it is higher, on account of the chemical decomposition of the ooze, than the upper strata of the sea.

Our little expedition had, it seems, a definite object besides that of allowing us a little exercise upon the bed of the ocean. We were hunting for food. Every now and then I saw our comrades strike sharply down with their pointed sticks, impaling each time a large brown flat fish, not unlike a turbot, which was numerous, but lay so closely in the ooze that it took practised eyes to detect it. Soon each of the little men had two or three of these dangling at his side. Scanlan and I soon got the knack of it, and captured a couple each, but Maracot walked as one in a dream, quite lost in his wonder at the ocean beauties around him and making long and excited speeches which were lost to the ear, but visible to the eyes from the contortion of his features.

Our first impression had been one of monotony, but we soon found that the grey plains were broken up into varied formations by the action of the deep-sea currents which flowed like submarine rivers across them. These streams cut channels in the soft slime and exposed the beds which lay beneath. The floor of these banks consisted of red clay which forms the base of all things on the surface of the bed of the ocean, and they were thickly studded with white objects which I imagined to be shells, but which proved, when we examined them, to be the ear bones of whales and the teeth of sharks and the other sea monsters. One of these teeth which I picked up was fifteen inches long, and we could but be thankful that so fearful a monster frequented the higher levels of ocean. It belonged, according to Maracot, to a giant-killing grampus or Orca gladiator. It recalled the observation of Mitchell Hedges that even the most terrible sharks that he had caught bore upon their bodies the marks which showed that they had encountered creatures larger and more formidable than themselves.

There was one peculiarity of the ocean depths which impresses itself upon the observer. There is, as I have said, a constant cold light rising up from the slow phosphorescent decay of the great masses of organic matter. But above, all is black as night. The effect is that of a dim winter day, with a heavy black thundercloud lying low above the earth. Out of this black canopy there falls slowly an incessant snowstorm of tiny white flakes, which glimmer against the sombre background. These are the shells of sea snails and other small creatures who live and die in the five miles of water which separate us from the surface, and though many of these are dissolved as they fall and add to the lime salts in the ocean, the rest go in the course of ages to form that deposit which had entombed the great city in the upper part of which we now dwelt.

Leaving our last link with earth beneath us, we pushed on

into the gloom of the submarine world and soon we were met by a completely new development. A moving patch appeared in front of us, which broke up as we approached it into a crowd of men, each in his vitrine envelope, who were dragging behind them broad sledges heaped with coal. It was heavy work, and the poor devils were bending and straining, tugging hard at the sharkskin ropes which served as traces. With each gang of men there was one who appeared to be in authority, and it interested us to see that the leaders and the workers were clearly of a different race. The latter were tall men, fair, with blue eyes and powerful bodies. The others were, as already described, dark and almost negroid, with squat, broad frames. We could not inquire into the mystery at that moment, but the impression was left upon my mind that the one race represented the hereditary slaves of the other, and Maracot was of the opinion that they may have been the descendants of those Greek prisoners whose goddess we had seen in the Temple.

Several droves of these men, each drawing its load of coal, were met by us before we came to the mine itself. At this point the deep-sea deposits and the sandy formations which lay beneath them had been cut away, and a great pit exposed, which consisted of alternate layers of clay and coal, representing strata in the old perished world of long ago which now lay at the bottom of the Atlantic. At the various levels of this huge excavation we could see gangs of men at work hewing the coal, while others gathered it into loads and placed it in baskets, by means of which it was hoisted up to the level above. The whole mine was on so vast a scale that we could not see the other side of the enormous pit which so many generations of workers had scooped in the bed of the ocean. This, then, transmuted into electric force, was the source of the motive power by which the whole machinery of Atlantis was run. It is interesting, by the way, to record that the name of the old city had been correctly preserved in the legends, for when we had mentioned it to Manda and others they first looked greatly surprised that we should know it, and then nodded their heads vigorously to show that they understood.

Passing the great coal pit—or, rather, branching away from it to the right—we came on a line of low cliffs of basalt, their surface as clear and shining as on the day when they were shot up from the bowels of the earth, while their summit; some hundreds of feet above us, loomed up against the dark background. The base of these volcanic cliffs was draped in a deep jungle of high seaweed, growing out of tangled masses of *crinoid* corals laid down in the old terrestrial days. Along the edge of this thick undergrowth we wandered for some time, our companions beating it with their sticks and driving out for our amusement an extraordinary assortment of strange fishes and *crustacea*, now and again securing a specimen for their own tables. For a mile or more we wandered along in this happy fashion, when I saw Manda stop suddenly and look round him with gestures of alarm and surprise. These submarine gestures formed a language in themselves, for in a moment his companions understood the cause of his trouble, and then with a shock we realized it also. Dr. Maracot had disappeared.

He had certainly been with us at the coal pit, and he had come as far as the basalt cliffs. It was inconceivable that he had got ahead of us, so it was evident that he must be somewhere along the line of jungle in our rear. Though our friends were disturbed, Scanlan and I, who knew something of the good man's absent-minded eccentricities were confident that there was no cause for alarm, and that we should soon find him loitering over some sea form which had attracted him. We all turned to retrace our steps, and had hardly gone a hundred yards before we caught sight of him.

But he was running—running with an agility which I should have thought impossible for a man of his habits. Even the least athletic can run, however, when fear is the pacemaker. His hands were outstretched for help, and he stumbled and blundered forward with clumsy energy. He had good cause to exert himself, for three horrible creatures were close at his heels. They were tiger crabs, striped black and white, each about the size of a Newfoundland dog. Fortunately they were themselves not very swift travellers, and were scurrying along the soft sea bottom in a curious sidelong fashion which was little faster than that of the terrified fugitive.

Their wind was better, however, and they would probably have had their horrible claws upon him in a very few minutes had not our friends intervened. They dashed forward with their pointed sticks, and Manda flashed a power electric lantern, which he carried in his belt, in the face of the loathsome monsters, who scuttled into the jungle and were lost to view. Our comrade sat down on a lump of coral and his face showed that he was exhausted by his adventure. He told us afterwards that he had penetrated the jungle in the hope of securing what seemed to him to be a rare specimen of the deep-sea Chimoera, and that he had blundered into the nest of these fierce tiger crabs, who had instantly dashed after him. It was only after a long rest that he was able to resume the journey.

Our next stage after skirting the basalt cliffs led us to our goal. The grey plain in front of us was covered at this point by irregular hummocks and tall projections which told us that the great city of old lay beneath it. It would all have been completely buried for ever by the ooze, as Herculaneum has been by lava or Pompeii by ashes, had an entrance to it not been excavated by the survivors of the Temple. This entrance was a long, downward cutting, which ended up in a broad street with buildings exposed on either side. The walls of these buildings were occasionally cracked and shattered, for they were not of the solid construction which had preserved the Temple, but the interiors were in most cases exactly as they had been when the catastrophe occurred, save that sea changes of all sorts, beautiful and rare in some cases and horrifying in others, had modified the appearances of the rooms. Our guides did not encourage us to examine the first ones which we reached, but hurried us onwards until we came to that which had clearly been the great central citadel or palace round which the whole town centred. The pillars and columns and vast sculptured cornices and friezes and staircases of this building exceeded anything which I have ever seen upon earth.

Its nearest approach seemed to me to be the remains of the

Temple of Karnack at Luxor in Egypt, and, strange to say, the decorations and half-effaced engravings resembled in detail those of the great ruin beside the Nile, and the lotus-shaped capitals of the columns were the same. It was an amazing experience to stand on the marble tessellated floors of those vast halls, with great statues looming high above one on every side, and to see, as we saw that day, huge silvery eels gliding above our heads and frightened fish darting away in every direction from the light which was projected before us. From room to room we wandered, marking every sign of luxury and occasionally of that lascivious folly which is said, by the lingering legend, to have drawn God's curse upon the people. One small room was wonderfully enamelled with mother-of-pearl, so that even now it gleamed with brilliant opalescent tints when the light played across it. An ornamented platform of yellow metal and a similar couch lay in one corner, and one felt that it may well have been the bedchamber of a queen, but beside the couch there lay now a loathsome black squid, its foul body rising and falling in a slow, stealthy rhythm so that it seemed like some evil heart which still beat in the very centre of the wicked palace. I was glad, and so, I learned, were my companions, when our guides led the way out once more, glancing for a moment at a ruined amphitheatre and again at a pier with a lighthouse at the end, which showed that the city had been a seaport. Soon we had emerged from these places of ill omen and were out on the familiar *bathybian* plain once more.

Our adventures were not quite over, for there was one more which was as alarming to our companions as to ourselves. We had nearly made our way home when one of our guides pointed upwards with alarm. Gazing in that direction we saw an extraordinary sight. Out of the black gloom of the waters a huge, dark figure was emerging, falling rapidly downwards. At first it seemed a shapeless mass, but as it came more clearly into the light we could see that it was the dead body of a monstrous fish, which had burst so that the entrails were streaming up behind it as it fell. No doubt the gases had buoyed it up in the higher reaches of the ocean until, having been released by putrefaction or by the ravages of sharks, there was nothing left but dead weight, which sent it hurtling down to the bottom of the sea. Already in our walk we had observed several of these great skeletons picked clean by the fish, but this creature was still, save for its disembowelment, even as it had lived. Our guides seized us with the intention of dragging us out of the path of the falling mass, but presently they were reassured and stood still, for it was clear that it would miss us. Our vitrine helmets prevented our hearing the thud, but it must have been prodigious when the huge body struck the floor of the ocean, and we saw the globigerina ooze fly upwards as the mud splashes when a heavy stone is hurled into it. It was a sperm whale, some seventy feet long, and from the excited and joyful gestures of the submarine folk I gathered that they would find plenty of use for the spermaceti and the fat. For the moment, however, we left the derelict creature, and with joyful hearts, for we unpractised visitors were weary and aching, found ourselves once more in front of the engraved portal of the roof, and finally standing safe and sound, divested of our vitrine bells, on the sloppy floor of the entrance chamber.

A few days—as we reckon time—after the occasion when we had given the community a cinema view of our own pro-ceedings, we were present at a very much more solemn and august exhibition of the same sort, which gave us in a clear and wonderful way the past history of this remarkable people. I cannot flatter myself that it was given entirely on our behalf, for I rather think that the events were publicly rehearsed from time to time in order to carry on the record, and that the part to which we were admitted was only some intermezzo of a long religious ceremony. However that may be, I will describe it exactly as it occurred.

We were led to the same great hall or theatre where Dr. Mara-cot had thrown our own adventures upon the screen. There the whole community was assembled, and we were given, as before, places of honour in front of the great luminous screen. Then, after a long song, which may have been some sort of patriotic chant, a very old white-haired man, the historian or chronicler of the nation, advanced amid much applause to the focus point and threw upon the bright surface before him a series of pictures to represent the rise and fall of his own people. I wish I could convey to you their vividness and drama. My two companions and I lost all sense of time and place, so absorbed were we in the contemplation, while the audience was moved to its depths and groaned or wept as the tragedy unfolded, which depicted the ruin of their fatherland, the destruction of their race.

In the first series of scenes we saw the old continent in its glory, as its memory had been handed down by these historical records passed from fathers to sons. We had a bird's-eye view of a glorious rolling country, enormous in extent, well watered and cleverly irrigated, with great fields of grain, waving orchards, lovely streams and woody hills, still lakes and occasional picturesque mountains. It was studded with villages and covered with farm-houses and beautiful private residences. Then our attention was carried to the capital, a wonderful and gorgeous city upon the sea-shore, the harbour crammed with galleys, her quays piled with merchandise, and her safety assured by high walls with towering battlements and circular moats, all on the most gigantic scale. The houses stretched inland for many miles, and in the centre of the city was a crenellated castle or citadel, so widespread and commanding that it was like some creation of a dream. We were then shown the faces of those who lived in that golden age, wise and venerable old men, virile warriors, saintly priests, beautiful and dignified women, lovely children, an apotheosis of the human race.

Then came pictures of another sort. We saw wars, constant wars, war by land and war by sea. We saw naked and defenceless races trampled down and over-ridden by great chariots or the rush of mailed horsemen. We saw treasures heaped upon the victors, but even as the riches increased the faces upon the screen became more animal and more cruel. Down, down they sank from one generation to another. We were shown signs of lascivious dissipation or moral degeneracy, of the accretion of matter and decline of spirit. Brutal sports at the expense of others had taken the place of the manly exercises of old. There was no longer the quiet and simple family life, nor the cultivation of the mind, but we had a glimpse of a people who were restless and shallow, rushing from one pursuit to another, grasping ever at pleasure, for ever missing it, and yet imagining always that in some more complex and unnatural form it might still be found. There had arisen on the one hand an over-rich class who sought only sensual gratification, and on the other hand an over-poor residue whose whole function in life was to minister to the wants of their masters, however evil those wants might be.

And now once again a new note was struck. There were reformers at work who were trying to turn the nation from its evil ways, and to direct it back into those higher paths which it had forsaken. We saw them, grave and earnest men, reasoning and pleading with the people, but we saw them scorned and jeered at by those whom they were trying to save. Especially we could see that it was the priests of Baal, priests who had gradually allowed forms and show and outward ceremonies to take the place of unselfish spiritual development, who led the opposition to the reformers. But the latter were not to be bullied or browbeaten. They continued to try for the salvation of the people, and their faces assumed a graver and even a terror-inspiring aspect, as those of men who had a fearsome warning to give which was like some dreadful vision before their own minds. Of their auditors some few seemed to heed and be terrified at the words, but others turned away laughing and plunged ever deeper into their morass of sin. There came a time at last when the reformers turned away also as men who could do no more, and left this degenerate people to its fate.

Then we saw a strange sight. There was one reformer, a man of singular strength of mind and body, who gave a lead to all the others. He had wealth and influence and powers, which latter seemed to be not entirely of this earth. We saw him in what seemed to be a trance, communing with higher spirits. It was he who brought all the science of his land—science which far outshone anything known by us moderns—to the task of building an ark of refuge against the coming troubles. We saw myriads of workmen at work, and the walls rising while crowds of careless citizens looked on and made merry at such elaborate and useless precautions. We saw others who seemed to reason with him and to say to him that if he had fears it would be easier for him to fly to some safer land. His answer, so far as we could follow it, was that there were some who must be saved at the last moment, and that for their sake he must remain in the new Temple of safety. Meanwhile he collected in it those who had followed him, and he held them there, for he did not himself know the day nor the hour, though forces beyond mortal had assured him of the coming fact. So when the ark was ready and the water-tight doors were finished and tested, he waited upon doom, with his family, his friends, his followers, and his servants.

And doom came. It was a terrible thing even in a picture. God knows what it could be like in reality. We first saw a huge sleek mountain of water rise to an incredible height out of a calm ocean. Then we saw it travel, sweeping on and on, mile after mile, a great glistening hill, topped with foam, at an ever-increasing rate. Two little ships tossing among the snowy fringe upon the summit became, as the wave rolled towards us, a couple of shattered galleys. Then we saw it strike the shore and sweep over the city, while the houses went down before it like a field of corn before a tornado. We saw the folk upon the house-tops glaring out at the approaching death, their faces twisted with horror, their eyes staring, their mouths contorted, gnawing at their hands and gibbering in an insanity of terror. The very men and women who had mocked at the warning were now screaming to Heaven for mercy, grovelling with their faces on the ground, or kneeling with frenzied arms raised in wild appeal. There was no time now to reach the ark, which stood beyond the city, but thousands dashed up to the Citadel, which stood upon higher ground, and the battlement walls were black with people. Then suddenly the Castle began to sink. Everything began to sink. The water had poured down into the remote recesses of the earth, the central fires had expanded it into steam, and the very foundations of the land were blown apart. Down went the city and ever down, while a cry went up from ourselves and the audience at the terrible sight. The pier broke in two and vanished. The high Pharus collapsed under the waves. The roofs looked for a while like successive reefs of rock forming lines of spouting breakers until they, too, went under.

The Citadel was left alone upon the surface, like some monstrous ship, and then it also slid sideways down into the abyss, with a fringe of helpless waving hands upon its summit. The awful drama was over, and an unbroken sea lay across the whole continent, a sea which bore no life upon it, but which among its huge smoking swirls and eddies showed all the wrack of the tragedy tossed hither and thither, dead men and animals, chairs, tables, articles of clothing, floating hats and bales of goods, all bobbing and heaving in one huge liquid fermentation. Slowly we saw it die away, and a great wide expanse as smooth and bright as quicksilver, with a murky sun low on the horizon, showed us the grave of the land that God had weighed and found wanting.

The story was complete. We could ask for no more, since our own brains and imagination could supply the rest. We realized the slow remorseless descent of that great land lower and lower into the abyss of the ocean amid volcanic convulsions which threw up submarine peaks around it. We saw it in our mind's eye stretched out, over miles of what was now the bed of the Atlantic, the shattered city lying alongside of the ark or refuge in which the handful of nerve-shattered survivors were assembled. And then finally we understood how these had carried on their lives, how they had used the various devices with which the foresight and science of their great leader had endowed them, how he had taught them all his arts before he passed away, and how some fifty or sixty survivors had grown now into a large community, which had to dig its way into the bowels of the earth in order to get room to expand. No library of information could make it clearer than that series of pictures and the inferences which we could draw from them. Such was the fate, and such the causes of the fate, which overwhelmed the great land of Atlantis. Some day far distant, when this *bathybian* ooze has turned to chalk, this great city will be thrown up once more by some fresh expiration of Nature, and the geologist of the future, delving in the quarry, will exhume not flints nor shells, but the remains of a vanished civilization, and the traces of an old-world catastrophe.

Only one point had remained undecided, and that was the length of time since the tragedy had occurred. Dr. Maracot discovered a rough method of making an estimate. Among the many annexes of the great building there was one huge vault, which was the burial-place of the chiefs. As in Egypt and in Yucatan, the practice of mummifying had been usual, and in niches in the walls there were endless rows of these grim relics of the past. Manda pointed proudly to the next one in the succession, and gave us to understand that it was specially arranged for himself.

'If you take an average of the European kings,' said Maracot, in his best professional manner, 'you will find that they run to above five in the century. We may adopt the same figure here. We cannot hope for scientific accuracy, but it will give us an approximation. I have counted the mummies, and they are four hundred in number.'

'Then it would be eight thousand years?'

'Exactly. And this agrees to some extent with Plato's estimate. It certainly occurred before the Egyptian written records begin, and they go back between six and seven thousand years from the present date. Yes, I think we may say that our eyes have seen the reproduction of a tragedy which occurred at least eight thousand years ago. But, of course, to build up such a civilization as we see the traces of, must in itself have taken many thousands of years.

'Thus,' he concluded—and I pass the claim on to you—we have extended the horizon of ascertained human history as no men have ever done since history began.'

Chapter 5

It was about a month, according to our calculations, after our visit to the buried city that the most amazing and unexpected thing of all occurred. We had thought by this time that we were immune to shocks and that nothing new could really stagger us, but this actual fact went far beyond anything for which our imagination might have prepared us.

It was Scanlan who brought the news that something momentous had happened. You must realize that by this time we were, to some extent, at home in the great building; that we knew where the common rest rooms and recreation rooms were situated; that we attended concerts (their music was very strange and elaborate) and theatrical entertainments, where the unintelligible words were translated by very vivid and dramatic gestures; and that, speaking generally, we were part of the community. We visited various families in their own private rooms, and our lives—I can speak for my own, at any rate— were made the brighter by the glamour of these strange people, especially of that one dear young lady whose name I have already mentioned. Mona was the daughter of one of the leaders of the tribe, and I found in his family a warm and kindly welcome which rose above all differences of race or language. When it comes to the most tender language of all, I did not find that there was so much between old Atlantis and modern America. I guess that what would please a Massachusetts girl of Brown's College is just about what would please my lady under the waves.

But I must get back to the fact that Scanlan came into our room with news of some great happening.

'Say, there is one of them just blown in, and he's that excited that he clean forgot to take his glass lid off, and he was jabbering for some minutes before he understood that no one could hear him. Then it was *blah blah blah* as long as his breath would hold, and they are all following him now to the jumping-off place. It's me for the water, for there is sure something worth our seeing.'

Running out, we found our friends all hurrying down the corridor with excited gestures, and we, joining the procession, soon formed part of the crowd who were hurrying across the sea bottom, led by the excited messenger. They drove along at a rate which made it no easy matter for us to keep up, but they carried their electric lanterns with them, and even though we fell behind we were able to follow the gleam. The route lay as before, along the base of the basalt cliffs until we came to a spot where a set of steps, concave from long usage, led up to the top. Ascending these, we found ourselves in broken country, with many jagged pinnacles of rock and deep crevasses which made it difficult travelling. Emerging from this tangle of ancient lava, we came out on a circular plain, brilliant by the phosphorescent light, and there in the very centre of it lay an object which set me gasping. As I looked at my companions I could see from their amazed expression how fully they shared my emotion.

Half embedded in the slime there lay a good-sized steamer. It was tilted upon its side, the funnel had broken and was hanging at a strange angle, and the foremast had snapped off short, but otherwise the vessel was intact and as clean and fresh as if she had just left the dock. We hurried towards her and found ourselves under the stern. You can imagine how we felt when we read the name '*Stratford*, London'. Our ship had followed ourselves into the Maracot Deep.

Of course, after the first shock the affair did not seem so incomprehensible. We remembered the falling glass, the reefed sails of the experienced Norwegian skipper, the strange black cloud upon the horizon. Clearly there had been a sudden cyclone of phenomenal severity and the *Stratford* had been blown over. It was too evident that all her people were dead, for most of the boats were trailing in different states of destruction from the davits, and in any case what boat could live in such a hurricane? The tragedy had occurred, no doubt, within an hour or two of our own disaster. Perhaps the sounding-line which we had seen had only just been wound in before the blow fell. It was terrible, but whimsical, that we should be still alive, while those who were mourning our destruction had themselves been destroyed. We had no means of telling whether the ship had drifted in the upper levels of the ocean or whether she had lain for some time where we found her before she was discovered by the Atlantean.

Poor Howie, the captain, or what was left of him, was still at his post upon the bridge, the rail grasped firmly in his stiffened hands. His body and that of three stokers in the engine-room were the only ones which had sunk with the ship. They were each removed under our direction and buried under the ooze with a wreath of sea-flowers over their remains. I give this detail in the hope that it may be some comfort to Mrs. Howie in her bereavement. The names of the stokers were unknown to us.

Whilst we had been performing this duty the little men had swarmed over the ship. Looking up, we saw them everywhere, like mice upon a cheese. Their excitement and curiosity made it clear to us that it was the first modern ship—possibly the first steamer—which had ever come down to them. We found out later that their oxygen apparatus inside their vitrine bells would not allow of a longer absence from the recharging station than a few hours, and so their chances of learning anything of what was on the sea-bed were limited to so many miles from their central base. They set to work at once breaking up the wreck and removing all that would be of use to them, a very long process, which is hardly accomplished yet. We were glad also to make our way to our cabins and to get many of those articles of clothing and books which were not ruined beyond redemption.

Among the other things which we rescued from the *Stratford* was the ship's log, which had been written up to the last day by the captain in view of our own catastrophe. It was strange indeed that we should be reading it and that he should be dead. The day's entry ran thus:

Oct. 3. The three brave but foolhardy adventurers have today, against my will and advice, descended in their apparatus to the bottom of the ocean, and the accident which I had foreseen has occurred. God rest their souls. They went down at eleven a.m. and I had some doubts about permitting them, as a squall seemed to be coming up. I would that I had acted upon my impulse, but it would only have postponed the inevitable tragedy. I bade each of them farewell with the conviction that I would see them no more. For a time all was well, and at eleven forty-five they had reached a depth of three hundred fathoms, where they had found bottom. Dr. Maracot sent several messages to me and all seemed to be in order, when suddenly I heard his voice in agitation, and there was considerable agitation of the wire hawser. An instant later it snapped. It would appear that they were by this time over a deep chasm, for at the Doctor's request the ship had steamed very slowly forwards. The air tubes continued to run out for a distance which I should estimate at half a mile, and then they also snapped. It is the last which we can ever hope to hear of Dr. Maracot, Mr. Headley, or Mr. Scanlan.

And yet a most extraordinary thing must be recorded, the meaning of which I have not had time to weigh, for with this foul weather coming up there is much to distract me. A deep-sea sounding was taken at the same time, and the depth recorded was twenty-six thousand six hundred feet. The weight was, of course, left at the bottom, but the wire has just been drawn in and, incredible as it may seem, above the porcelain sample cup there was found Mr. Headley's handkerchief with his name marked upon it. The ship's company were all amazed, and no one can suggest how such a thing could have occurred. In my next entry I may have more to say about this. We have lingered a few hours in the hope of something coming to the surface, and we have pulled up the hawser, which shows a jagged end. Now I must look to the ship, for I have never seen a worse sky and the barometer is at 8.5 and sinking fast.

So it was that we got the final news of our former companions. A terrific cyclone must have struck her and destroyed her immediately afterwards.

We stayed at the wreck until a certain stuffiness within our vitrine bells and a feeling of increasing weight upon our chests warned us that it was high time to begin our return. Then it was, on our homeward journey, that we had an adventure which showed us the sudden dangers to which these submarine folk are exposed, and which may explain why their numbers, in spite of the lapse of time, were not greater than they were. Including the Grecian slaves we cannot reckon those numbers at more than four or five thousand at the most. We had descended the staircase and were making our way along the edge of the jungle which skirts the basalt cliffs, when Manda pointed excitedly upwards and beckoned furiously to one of our party who was some distance out in the open. At the same time he and those around him ran to the side of some high boulders, pulling us along with them. It was only when we were in their shelter that we saw the cause of the alarm. Some distance above us, but descending rapidly, was a huge fish of a most peculiar shape. It might have been a great floating feather-bed, soft and bulging, with a white under-surface and a long red fringe, the vibration of which propelled it through the water. It appeared to have neither mouth nor eyes, but it soon showed that it was formidably alert. The member of our party who was out in the open ran for the same shelter that we had taken, but he was too late. I saw his face convulsed with terror as he realized his fate.

The horrible creature descended upon him, enveloped him on all sides, and lay upon him, pulsing in a dreadful way as if it were thrusting his body against the coral rocks and grinding it to pieces. The tragedy was taking place within a few yards of us, and yet our companions were so overcome by the suddenness of it that they seemed to be bereft of all power of action. It was

Scanlan who rushed out and, jumping on the creature's broad back, blotched with red and brown markings, dug the sharp end of his metal staff into its soft tissues.

I had followed Scanlan's example, and finally Maracot and all of them attacked the monster, which glided slowly off, leaving a trail of oily and glutinous excretion behind it. Our help had come too late, however, for the impact of the great fish had broken the vitrine bell of the Atlantean and he had been drowned. It was a day of mourning when we carried his body back into the Refuge, but it was also a day of triumph for us, for our prompt action had raised us greatly in the estimation of our companions. As to the strange fish, we had Dr. Maracot's assurance that it was a specimen of the blanket fish, well known to ichthyologists, but of a size such as had never entered into his dreams.

I speak of this creature because it chanced to bring about a tragedy, but I could, and perhaps will, write a book upon the wonderful life which we have seen here. Red and black are the prevailing colours in deep-sea life, while the vegetation is of the palest olive, and is of so tough a fibre that it is seldom dragged up by our trawls, so that Science has come to believe that the bed of the ocean is bare. Many of the marine forms are of surpassing loveliness, and others so grotesque in their horror that they are like the images of delirium and of a danger such as no land animal can rival. I have seen a black sting-ray thirty feet long with a horrible fang upon its tail, one blow of which would kill any living creature. I have seen, too, a frog-like beast with protruding green eyes, which is simply a gaping mouth with a huge stomach behind it. To meet it is death unless one has an electric flash with which to repel it. I have seen the blind red eel which lies among the rocks and kills by the emission of poison, and I have seen also the giant sea-scorpion, one of the terrors of the deep, and the hag fish, which lurks among the sea jungle.

Once, too, it was my privilege to see the real sea-serpent, a creature which has seldom appeared before the human eye, for it lives in the extreme depths and is seen on the surface only when some submarine convulsion has driven it out of its haunts. Two of them swam, or rather glided, past us one day while Mona and I cowered among the bunches of *lamellaria*. They were enormous—some ten feet in height and two hundred in length, black above, silver-white below, with a high fringe upon the back, and small eyes no larger than those of an ox. Of these and many other such things an account will be found in the paper of Dr. Maracot, should it ever reach your hands.

Week glided into week in our new life. It had become a very pleasant one, and we were slowly picking up enough of this long-forgotten tongue to enable us to converse a little with our companions. There were endless subjects both for study and for amusement in the Refuge, and already Maracot has mastered so much of the old chemistry that he declares that he can revolutionize all worldly ideas if he can only transmit his knowledge. Among other things they have learned to split the atom, and though the energy released is less than our scientists had anticipated, it is still sufficient to supply them with a great reservoir of power. Their acquaintance with the power and nature of the ether is also far ahead of ours, and indeed that strange translation of thought into pictures, by which we had told them our story and they theirs, was due to an etheric impression translated back into terms of matter.

And yet, in spite of their knowledge, there were points connected with modern scientific developments which had been overlooked by their ancestors.

It was left to Scanlan to demonstrate the fact. For weeks he was in a state of suppressed excitement, bursting with some great secret, and chuckling continually at his own thoughts. We only saw him occasionally during this time, for he was extremely busy and his one friend and confidant was a fat and jovial Atlantean named Berbrix, who was in charge of some of the machinery. Scanlan and Berbrix, though their intercourse was carried on chiefly by signs and mutual back-slapping, had become very close friends, and were now continually closeted together. One evening Scanlan came in radiant.

'Look here, Doc,' he said to Maracot, 'I've a dope of my own that I want to hand to these folk. They've shown us a thing or two and I figure that it is up to us to return it. What's the matter with calling them together tomorrow night for a show?'

'Jazz or the Charleston?' I asked.

'Charleston nothing. Wait till you see it. Man, it's the greatest stunt—but there, I won't say a word more. Just this, Bo. I won't let you down, for I've got the goods, and I mean to deliver them.'

Accordingly, the community were assembled next evening in the familiar hall. Scanlan and Berbrix were on the platform, beaming with pride. One or other of them touched a button, and then—well, to use Scanlan's own language, 'I hand it to him, for he did surprise us some!'

'2L.O. calling,' cried a clear voice. 'London calling the British Isles. Weather forecast.' Then followed the usual sentence about depressions and anticyclones. 'First News Bulletin. His Majesty the King this morning opened the new wing of the Children's Hospital in Hammersmith—' and so on and on, in the familiar strain. For the first time we were back in a workaday England once more, plodding bravely through its daily task, with its stout back bowed under its war debts. Then we heard the foreign news, the sporting news. The old world was droning on the same as ever. Our friends the Atlanteans listened in amazement, but without comprehension. When, however, as the first item after the news, the Guards' band struck up the march from Lohengrin a positive shout of delight broke from the people, and it was funny to see them rush upon the platform, and turn over the curtains, and look behind the screens to find the source of the music. Yes, we have left our mark for ever upon the submarine civilization.

'No, sir,' said Scanlan, afterwards. 'I could not make an issuing station. They have not the material, and I have not the brains. But down at home I rigged a two-valve set of my own with the aerial beside the clothes line in the yard, and I learned to handle it, and to pick up any station in the States. It seemed to me funny if, with all this electricity to hand, and with their glasswork ahead of ours, we couldn't vamp up something that would catch an ether wave, and a wave would sure travel through water just as easy as through air. Old Berbrix nearly threw a fit when we got the first call, but he is wise to it now, and I guess it's a permanent institution.'

Among the discoveries of the Atlantean chemists is a gas which is nine times lighter than hydrogen and which Maracot has named levigen. It was his experiments with this which gave us the idea of sending glass balls with information as to our fate to the surface of the ocean.

'I have made Manda understand the idea,' said he. 'He has given orders to the silica workers, and in a day or two the globes will be ready.'

'But how can we get our news inside?' I asked.

'There is a small aperture left through which the gas is inserted. Into this we can push the papers. Then these skilful workers can seal up the hole. I am assured that when we release them they will shoot up to the surface.'

'And bob about unseen for a year.'

'That might be. But the ball would reflect the sun's rays. It would surely attract attention. We were on the line of shipping between Europe and South America. I see no reason why, if we send several, one at least may not be found.'

And this, my dear Talbot, or you others who read this narrative, is how it comes into your hands. But a far more fateful scheme may lie behind it. The idea came from the fertile brain of the American mechanic.

'Say friends,' said he, as we sat alone in our chamber, 'it's dandy down here, and the drink is good and the eats are good, and I've met a wren that makes anything in Philadelphia look like two cents, but all the same there are times when I want to feel that I might see God's own country once more.'

'We may all feel that way,' said I, 'but I don't see how you can hope to make it.'

'Look it here, Bo! If these balls of gas could carry up our message, maybe they could carry us up also. Don't think I'm joshing, for I've figured it out to. rights. We will suppose we put three or four of them together so as to get a good lift. See? Then we have our vitrine bells on and harness ourselves on to the balls. When the bell rings we cut loose and up we go. What is going to stop us between here and the surface?'

'A shark, maybe.'

'Blah! Sharks nothing! We would streak past any shark so's he'd hardly know we was there. He'd think we was three flashes of light and we'd get such a lick on that we'd shoot fifty feet up in the air at the other end. I tell you the goof that sees us come up is going to say his prayers over it.'

'But suppose it is possible, what will happen afterwards!'

'For Pete's sake, leave afterwards out of it! Let us chance our luck, or we are here for keeps. It's me for cutting loose and having a dash at it.'

'I certainly greatly desire to return to the world, if only to lay our results before the learned societies,' said Maracot. 'It is only my personal influence which can make them realize the fund of new knowledge which I have acquired. I should be quite in favour of any such attempt as Scanlan has indicated.'

There were good reasons, as I will tell later, which made me the least eager of the three.

'It would be perfect madness as you propose it. Unless we had someone expecting us on the surface we should infallibly drift about and perish from hunger and thirst.'

'Shucks, man, how could we have someone expecting us?'

'Perhaps even that could be managed,' said Maracot. 'We can give within a mile or two the exact latitude and longitude of our position.'

'And they would let down a ladder,' said I, with bitterness.

'Ladder nothing! The boss is right. See here, Mr. Headley, you put in that letter that you are going to send the universe— my! don't I see the scare lines in the journals!—that we are at 27 North Latitude and 28.14 West Longitude, or whatever other figure is the right one, Got that? Then you say that three of the most important folk in history, the great man of Science, Maracot, and the rising-star bug-collector, Headley, and Bob Scanlan, a peach of a mechanic and the pride of Merribank's; are all yellin' and whoopin' for help from the bottom of the sea. Follow my idea?'

'Well, what then?'

'Well, then it's up to them, you see. It's kind of a challenge that they can't forget. Same as I've read of Stanley finding Livingstone and the like. It's for them to find some way to yank us out or to catch us at the other end if we can take the jump ourselves.'

'We could suggest the way ourselves,' said the Professor. 'Let them drop a deep-sea line into these waters and we will look out for it. When it comes we can tie a message to it and bid them stand by for us.'

'You've said a mouthful!' cried Bob Scanlan. 'That is sure the way to do it.'

'And if any lady cared to share our fortunes four would be as easy as three,' said Maracot, with a roguish smile at me.

'For that matter, five is as easy as four,' said Scanlan. 'But you've got it now, Mr. Headley. You write that down, and in six months we shall be back in London River once more.'

So now we launch our two balls into that water which is to us what the air is to you. Our two little balloons will go aloft. Will both be lost on the way? It is possible. Or may we hope that one will get through? We leave it on the knees of the gods. If nothing can be done for us, then let those who care for us know that in any case we are safe and happy. If, on the other hand, this suggestion could be carried out and the money and energy for our rescue should be forthcoming, we have given you the means by which it can be done. Meanwhile, good-bye—or is it *au revoir?*

****

So ended the narrative in the vitrine ball.

The preceding narrative covers the facts so far as they were available when the account was first drawn up. While the script was in the hands of the printer there came an epilogue of the most unexpected and sensational description. I refer to the rescue of the adventurers by Mr. Faverger's steam yacht *Marion* and the account sent out by the wireless transmitter of that vessel, and picked up by the cable station at the Cape de Verde Islands, which has just forwarded it to Europe and America. This account was drawn up by Mr. Key Osborne, the well-known representative of the Associated Press.

It would appear that immediately upon the first narrative of the plight of Dr. Maracot and his friends reaching Europe an expedition was quietly and effectively fitted up in the hope of bringing about a rescue. Mr. Faverger generously placed his famous steam yacht at the disposal of the party, which he accompanied in person. The *Marion* sailed from Cherbourg in June, picked up Mr. Key Osborne and a motion-picture operator at Southampton, and set forth at once for the tract of ocean which was indicated in the original document. This was reached upon the first of July.

A deep-sea piano-wire line was lowered, and was dragged slowly along the bottom of the ocean. At the end of this line, beside the heavy lead, there was suspended a bottle containing a message. The message ran:

> Your account has been received by the world, and we are here to help you. We duplicate this message by our wireless transmitter in the hope that it may reach you. We will slowly traverse your region. When you have detached this bottle, please replace your own message in it. We will act upon your instructions.

For two days the *Marion* cruised slowly to and fro without result. On the third a very great surprise awaited the rescue party. A small, highly luminous ball shot out of the water a few hundred yards from the ship, and proved to be a vitreous message-bearer of the sort which had been described in the original document. Having been broken with some difficulty, the following message was read:

> Thanks, dear friends. We greatly appreciate your grand loyalty and energy. We receive your wireless messages with facility, and are in a position to answer you in this fashion. We have endeavoured to get possession of your line, but the currents lift it high, and it sweeps along rather faster than even the most active of us can move against the resistance of the water. We propose to make our venture at six tomorrow morning, which should, according to our

reckoning, be Tuesday, July 5th. We will come one at a time, so that any advice arising from our experience can be wirelessed back to those who come later. Once again heartfelt thanks.

Maracot. Headley. Scanlan.

Mr. Key Osborne now takes up the narrative.

****

'It was a perfect morning, and the deep sapphire sea lay as smooth as a lake, with the glorious arch of the deep blue sky unbroken by the smallest cloud. The whole crew of the *Marion* was early astir, and awaited events with the most tense interest. As the hour of six drew near our anticipation was painful. A look-out had been placed upon our signal mast, and it was just five minutes to the hour when we heard him shouting, and saw him pointing to the water on our port bow. We all crowded to that side of the deck, and I was able to perch myself on one of the boats, from which I had a clear view. I saw through the still water something which looked like a silver bubble ascending with great rapidity from the depths of the ocean. It broke the surface about two hundred yards from the ship, and soared straight up into the air, a beautiful shining globe some three feet in diameter, rising to a great height and then drifting away in some slight current of wind exactly as a toy balloon would do. It was a marvellous sight, but it filled us with apprehension, for it seemed as if the harness might have come loose, and the burden which this tractor should have borne through the waters had been shaken loose upon the way. A wireless was at once dispatched:

'*Your messenger has appeared close to the vessel. It had nothing attached and has flown away.* Meanwhile we lowered a boat so as to be ready for any development.

'Just after six o'clock there was another signal from our watchman, and an instant later I caught sight of another silver globe, which was swimming up from the depths very much more slowly than the last. On reaching the surface it floated in the air, but its burden was supported upon the water. This burden proved upon examination to be a great bundle of books, papers, and miscellaneous objects all wrapped in a casing of fish skin. It was hoisted dripping upon the deck, and was acknowledged by wireless, while we eagerly awaited the next arrival.

'This was not long in coming. Again the silver bubble, again the breaking of the surface, but this time the glistening ball shot high into the air, suspending under it, to our amazement, the slim figure of a woman. It was but the impetus which had carried her into the air, and an instant later she had been towed to the side of the vessel. A leather circlet had been firmly fastened round the upper curve of the glass ball, and from this long straps depended which were attached to a broad leather belt round her dainty waist. The upper part of her body was covered by a peculiar pear-shaped glass shade—I call it glass, but it was of the same tough light material as the vitreous ball. It was almost transparent, with silvery veins running through its substance. This glass covering had tight elastic attachments at the waist and shoulders, which made it perfectly watertight, while it was provided within, as has been described in Headley's original manuscript, with novel but very light and practical chemical apparatus for the renovation of air. With some difficulty the breathing bell was removed and the lady hoisted upon deck. She lay there in a deep faint, but her regular breathing encouraged us to think that she would soon recover from the effects of her rapid journey and from the change of pressure, which had been minimized by the fact that the density of the air inside the protective sheath was considerably higher than our atmosphere, so that it may be said to have represented that half-way point at which human divers are wont to pause.

'Presumably this is the Atlantean woman referred to in the first message as Mona, and if we may take her as a sample they are indeed a race worth reintroducing to earth. She is dark in complexion, beautifully clear-cut and high-bred in feature, with long black hair, and magnificently hazel eyes which looked round her presently in a charming amazement. Sea-shells and mother-of-pearl were worked into her cream-coloured tunic, and tangled in her dark hair. A more perfect Naiad of the Deep could not be imagined, the very personification of the mystery and the glamour of the sea. We could see complete consciousness coming back into those marvellous eyes, and then she sprang suddenly to her feet with the activity of a young doe and ran to the side of the vessel. "Cyrus! Cyrus!" she cried.

'We had already removed the anxiety of those below by a wireless. But now in quick succession each of them arrived, shooting thirty or forty feet into the air, and then falling back into the sea, from which we quickly raised them. All three were unconscious, and Scanlan was bleeding at the nose and ears, but within an hour all were able to totter to their feet: The first action of each was, I imagine, characteristic. Scanlan was led off by a laughing group to the bar, from which shouts of merriment are now resounding, much to the detriment of this composition. Dr. Maracot seized the bundle of papers, tore out one which consisted entirely, so far as I could judge, of algebraic symbols, and disappeared downstairs, while Cyrus Headley ran to the side of his strange maiden, and looks, by last reports, as if he had no intention of ever quitting it. Thus the matter stands, and we trust our weak wireless will carry our message as far as the Cape de Verde station. The fuller details of this wonderful adventure will come later, as is fitting, from the adventurers themselves.'

Chapter 6

There are very many people who have written both to me, Cyrus Headley, Rhodes Scholar of Oxford, and to Professor Maracot, and even to Bill Scanlan, since our very remarkable experience at the bottom of the Atlantic, where we were able at a point 200 miles south-west of the Canaries to make a submarine descent which has not only led to a revision of our views concerning deep-sea life and pressures, but has also established the survival of an old civilization under incredibly difficult conditions. In these letters we have been continually asked to give further details about our experiences. It will be understood that my original document was a very superficial one, and yet it covered most of the facts. There were some, however, which were withheld, and above all the tremendous episode of the Lords of the Dark Face. This involved some facts and some conclusions of so utterly extraordinary a nature that we all thought it was best to suppress it entirely for the present. Now, however, that Science has accepted our conclusions—and I may add since Society has accepted my bride—our general veracity is established and we may perhaps venture upon a narrative which might have repulsed public sympathy in the first instance.

Before I get to the one tremendous happening I would lead up to it by some reminiscences of those wonderful months in the buried home of the Atlanteans, who by means of their vitrine oxygen bells are able to walk the ocean floor with the same ease as those Londoners whom I see now from my windows in the Hyde Park Hotel are strolling among the flower-beds.

When first we were taken in by these people after our dreadful fall from the surface we were in the position of prisoners rather than of guests. I wish now to set upon record how this came to change and how through the splendour of Dr. Maracot we have left such a name down there that the memory of us will go down in their annals as of some celestial visitation. They knew nothing of our leaving, which they would certainly have prevented if they could, so that no doubt there is already a legend that we have returned to some heavenly sphere, taking with us the sweetest and choicest flower of their flock.

I would wish now to set down in their order some of the strange things of this wonderful world, and also some of the adventures which befell us until I came to the supreme adventure of all—one which will leave a mark upon each of us for ever—the coming of the Lord of the Dark Face. In some ways I wish that we could have stayed longer in the Maracot Deep for there were many mysteries there, and up to the end there were things which we could not understand. Also we were rapidly learning something of their language, so that soon we should have had much more information.

Experience had taught these people what was terrible and what was innocent. One day, I remember, that there was a sudden alarm and that we all ran out in our oxygen bells on to the ocean bed, though why we ran or what we meant to do was a mystery to us. There could be no mistake, however, as to the horror and distraction upon the faces of those around us. When we got out on to the plain we met a number of the Greek coal-workers who were hastening towards the door of our Colony. They had come at such a pace, and were so weary that they kept falling down in the ooze, and it was clear that we were really a rescue party for the purpose of picking up these cripples, and hurrying up the laggards. We saw no sign of weapons and no show of resistance against the coming danger. Soon the colliers were hustled along, and when the last one had been shoved through the door we looked back along the line that they had traversed. All that we could see was a couple of greenish wisp-like clouds, luminous in the centre and ragged at the edges, which were drifting rather than moving in our direction. At the clear sight of them, though they were quite half a mile away, my companions were filled with panic and beat at the door so as to get in the sooner. It was surely nervous work to see these mysterious centres of trouble draw nearer, but the pumps acted swiftly and we were soon in safety once more. There was a great block of transparent crystal, ten feet long and two feet broad, above the lintel of the door, with lights so arranged that they threw a strong glare outside. Mounted on the ladders kept for the purpose, several of us, including myself, looked through this rude window. I saw the strange shimmering green circles of light pause before the door. As they did so the Atlanteans on either side of me simply gibbered with fear. Then one of the shadowy creatures outside came flicking up through the water and made for our crystal window. Instantly my companions pulled me down below the level of vision, but it seems that in my carelessness some of my hair did not get clear from whatever the maleficent influence may be which these strange creatures send forth. There is a patch there which is withered and white to this day.

It was not for a long time that the Atlanteans dared to open their door, and when at last a scout was sent forth he went amid hand-shakings and slaps on the back as one who does a gallant deed. His report was that all was clear, and soon joy had returned to the community, and this strange visitation seemed to have been forgotten. We only gathered from the word 'Praxa', repeated in various tones of horror, that this was the name of the creature. The only person who derived real joy from the incident was Professor Maracot, who could hardly be restrained from sallying out with a small net and a glass vase. 'A new order of life, partly organic, partly gaseous, but clearly intelligent,' was his general comment. 'A freak out of Hell,' was Scanlan's less scientific description.

Two days afterwards, when we were out on what we called a shrimping expedition, when we walked among the deep-sea foliage and captured in our hand-nets specimens of the smaller fish, we came suddenly upon the body of one of the coal-workers, who had no doubt been overtaken in his flight by these strange creatures. The glass bell had been broken—a matter which called for enormous strength, for this vitrine substance is extraordinarily tough, as you realized when you attempted to reach my first documents. The man's eyes had been torn out, but otherwise he had been uninjured.

'A dainty feeder!' said the Professor after our return. 'There is a hawk parrot in New Zealand which will kill the lamb in order to get at a particular morsel of fat above the kidney. So this creature will slay the man for his eyes. In the heavens above and in the waters below Nature knows but one law, and it is, alas! remorseless cruelty.'

We had many examples of that terrible law down there in the depths of the ocean. I can remember, for example, that many times we observed a curious groove upon the soft *bathybian* mud, as if a barrel had been rolled along it. We pointed it out to our Atlantean companions, and when we could interrogate them we tried to get from them some account of what this creature could be. As to its name our friends gave some of those peculiar click-ing sounds which come into the Atlantean speech, and which cannot be reproduced either by the European tongue or by the European alphabet. *Krixchok* is, perhaps, an approximation to it. But as to its appearance we could always in such cases make use of the Atlantean thought reflector by which our friends were able to give a very clear vision of whatever was in their own minds. By this means they conveyed to us a picture of a very strange marine creature which the Professor could only classify as a gigantic sea slug. It seemed to be of great size, sausage shaped with eyes at the ends of stems, and a thick coating of coarse hair or bristles. When showing this apparition, our friends by their gestures expressed the greatest horror and repulsion.

But this, as anyone could predicate who knew Maracot, only served to inflame his scientific passions and to make him the more eager to determine the exact species and sub-species of this unknown monster. Accordingly I was not surprised when, on the occasion of our next excursion, he stopped at the point where we clearly saw the mark of the brute upon the slime, and turned deliberately towards the tangle of seaweed and basaltic blocks out of which it seemed to have come. The moment we left the plain the traces of course ceased, and yet there seemed to be a natural gully amid the rocks which clearly led to the den of the monster. We were all three armed with the pikes which the Atlanteans usually carried, but they seemed to me to be frail things with which to face unknown dangers. The Professor trudged ahead, however, and we could but follow after.

The rocky gorge ran upwards, its sides formed of huge clusters of volcanic debris and draped with a profusion of the long red and black forms of *lamellaria* which are characteristic of the extreme depths of Ocean. A thousand beautiful *ascidians* and *echinoderms* of every joyous colour and fantastic shape peeped out from amid this herbage, which was alive with strange *crustaceans* and low forms of creeping life. Our progress was slow, for walking is never easy in the depths, and the angle up which we toiled was an acute one. Suddenly, however, we saw the creature whom we hunted, and the sight was not a reassuring one.

It was half protruded from its lair, which was a hollow in a basaltic pile. About five feet of hairy body was visible, and we perceived its eyes, which were as large as saucers, yellow in colour, and glittering like agates, moving round slowly upon their long pedicles as it heard the sound of our approach. Then slowly it began to unwind itself from its burrow, waving its heavy body along in caterpillar fashion. Once it reared up its head some four feet from the rocks, so as to have a better look at us, and I observed, as it did so, that it had what looked like the corrugated soles of tennis shoes fastened on either side of its neck, the same colour, size, and striped appearance. What this might mean I could not conjecture, but we were soon to have an object lesson in their use.

The Professor had braced himself with his pike projecting forward and a most determined expression upon his face. It was clear that the hope of a rare specimen had swept all fear from his mind. Scanlan and I were by no means so sure of ourselves, but we could not abandon the old man, so we stood our ground on either side of him.

The creature, after that one long stare, began slowly and clumsily to make its way down the slope, worming its path among the rocks, and raising its pedicled eyes from time to time to see what we were about. It came so slowly that we seemed safe enough, since we could always out-distance it. And yet, had we only known it, we were standing very near to death.

It was surely Providence that sent us our warning. The beast was still making its lumbering approach, and may have been sixty yards from us, when a very large fish, a deep-sea groper, shot out from the algae-jungle on our side of the gorge and swam slowly across it. It had reached the centre, and was about midway between the creature and ourselves when it gave a convulsive leap, turned belly upwards, and sank dead to the bottom of the ravine. At the same moment each of us felt an extraordinary and most unpleasant tingling pass over our whole bodies, while our knees seemed to give way beneath us. Old Maracot was as wary as he was audacious, and in an instant he had sized up the situation and realized that the game was up. We were faced by some creature which threw out electric waves to kill its prey, and our pikes were of no more use against it than against a machine-gun. Had it not been for the lucky chance that the fish drew its fire, we should have waited until it was near enough to loose off its full battery, which would infallibly have destroyed us. We blundered off as swiftly as we could, with the resolution to leave the giant electric sea-worm severely alone for the future.

These were some of the more terrible of the dangers of the deep.. Yet another was the little black *Hydrops ferox*, as the Professor named him. He was a red fish not much longer than a herring, with a large mouth and a formidable row of teeth. He was harmless in ordinary circumstances, but the shedding of blood, even the very smallest amount of it, attracted him in an instant, and there was no possible salvation for the victim, who was torn to pieces by swarms of attackers. We saw a horrible sight once at the colliery pits, where a slave worker had the misfortune to cut his hand. In an instant, coming from all quarters, thousands of these fish were on to him. In vain he threw himself down and struggled; in vain his horrified companions beat them away with their picks and shovels. The lower part of him, beneath his bell, dissolved before our eyes amid the cloud of vibrant life which surrounded him. One instant we saw a man. The next there was a red mass with white protruding bones. A minute later the bones only were left below the waist and half a clean-picked skeleton was lying at the bottom of the sea. The sight was so horrifying that we were all ill, and the hard-boiled Scanlan actually fell down in a faint and we had some difficulty in getting him home.

But the strange sights which we saw were not always horrifying. I have in mind one which will never fade from our memory. It was on one of those excursions which we delighted to take, sometimes with an Atlantean guide, and sometimes by ourselves when our hosts had learned that we did not need constant attendance and nursing. We were passing over a portion of the plain with which we were quite familiar, when we perceived, to our surprise, that a great patch of light yellow sand, half an acre or so in extent, had been laid down or uncovered since our last visit. We were standing in some surprise, wondering what submarine current or seismic movement could have brought this about, when to our absolute amazement the whole thing rose up and swam with slow undulations immediately above our heads. It was so huge that the great canopy took some appreciable time, a minute or two, to pass from over us. It was a gigantic flat fish, not different, so far as the Professor could observe, from one of our own little dabs, but grown to this enormous size upon the nutritious food which the *bathybian* deposits provide. It vanished away into the darkness above us, a great, glimmering, flickering white—and yellow expanse, and we saw it no more.

There was one other phenomenon of the deep sea which was very unexpected. That was the tornadoes which frequently occur. They seem to be caused by the periodical arrival of violent submarine currents which set in with little warning and are terrific while they last, causing as much confusion and destruction as the highest wind would do upon land. No doubt without these visitations there would be that putridity and stagnation which absolute immobility must give, so that, as in all Nature's processes, there was an excellent object in view; but the experience none the less was an alarming one.

On the first occasion when I was caught in such a watery cyclone, I had gone out with that very dear lady to whom I have alluded, Mona, the daughter of Manda. There was a very beautiful bank loaded with algae of a thousand varied colours which lay a mile or so from the Colony. This was Mona's very special garden which she greatly loved, a tangle of pink *serpularia*, purple *ophiurids* and red *holothurians*. On this day she had taken me to see it, and it was while we were standing before it that the storm burst. So strong was the current which suddenly flowed upon us that it was only by holding together and getting behind the shelter of rocks that we could save ourselves from being washed away. I observed that this rushing stream of water was quite warm, almost as warm as one could bear, which may show that there is a volcanic origin in these disturbances and that they are the wash from some submarine disturbance in some far-off region of the ocean bed. The mud of the great plain was stirred up by the rush of the current, and the light was darkened by the thick cloud of matter suspended in the water around us. To find our way back was impossible, for we had lost all sense of direction, and in any case could hardly move against the rush of the water. Then on the top of all else a slowly increasing heaviness of the chest and difficulty in breathing warned me that our oxygen supply was beginning to fail us.

It is at such times, when we are in the immediate presence of death, that the great primitive passions float to the surface and submerge all our lesser emotions. It was only at that moment that I knew that I loved my gentle companion, loved her with all my heart and soul, loved her with a love which was rooted deep down and was part of my very self. How strange a thing is a love like that! How impossible to analyse! It was not for her face or figure, lovely as they were. It was not for her voice, though it was more musical than any I have known, nor was it for mental communion, since I could only learn her thoughts from her sensitive ever-changing face. No, it was something at the back of her dark dreamy eyes, something in the very depths of her soul as of mine which made us mates for all time. I held out my hand and clasped her own, reading in her face that there was no thought or emotion of mine which was not flooding her own receptive mind and flushing her lovely cheek. Death at my side would present no terror to her, and as for myself my heart throbbed at the very thought.

But it was not to be. One would think that our glass coverings excluded sounds, but as a matter of fact the throb of certain air vibrations penetrated them easily, or by their impact started similar vibrations within. There was a loud beat, a reverberating clang, like that of a distant gong. I had no idea what it might mean, but my companion was in no doubt. Still holding my hand, she rose from our shelter, and after listening intently she crouched down and began to make her way against the storm. It was a race against death, for every instant the terrible oppression on my chest became more unbearable. I saw her dear face peering most anxiously into mine, and I staggered on in the direction to which she led me. Her appearance and her movements showed that her oxygen supply was less exhausted than mine. I held on as long as Nature would allow, and then suddenly everything swam around me. I threw out my arms and fell senseless upon the soft ocean floor.

When I came to myself I was lying on my own couch inside the Atlantean Palace. The old yellow—clad priest was standing beside me, a phial of some stimulant in his hand. Maracot and Scanlan, with distressed faces, were bending over me, while Mona knelt at the bottom of the bed with tender anxiety upon her features. It seems that the brave girl had hastened on to the community door, from which on occasions of this sort it was the custom to beat a great gong as a guide to any wanderers who might be lost. There she had explained my position and had guided back the rescue party, including my two comrades who had brought me back in their arms. Whatever I may do in life, it is truly Mona who will do it, for that life has been a gift from her.

Now that by a miracle she has come to join me in the upper world, the human world under the sky, it is strange to reflect upon the fact that my love was such that I was willing, most willing, to remain for ever in the depths so long as she should be all my own. For long I could not understand that deep, deep intimate bond which held us together, and which was felt, as I could see, as strongly by her as by me. It was Manda, her father, who gave me an explanation which was as unexpected as it was satisfying.

He had smiled gently over our love affair—smiled with the indulgent, half-amused air of one who sees that come to pass which he had already anticipated. Then one day he led me aside and in his own chamber he placed that silver screen upon which his thoughts and knowledge could be reflected. Never while the breath of life is in my body can I forget that which he showed me—and her. Seated side by side, our hands clasped together, we watched entranced while the pictures flickered up before our eyes, formed and projected by that racial memory of the past which these Atlanteans possess.

There was a rocky peninsula jutting out into a lovely blue ocean. I may not have told you before that in these thought cinemas, if I may use the expression, colour is produced as well as form. On this headland was a house of quaint design, wide-spread, red-roofed, white-walled, and beautiful. A grove of palm trees surrounded it. In this grove there appeared to be a camp, for we could see the white sheen of tents and here and there the glimmer of arms as of some sentinel keeping ward. Out of this grove there walked a middle-aged man clad in mail armour, with a round light shield on his arm. He carried something in his other hand, but whether sword or javelin I could not see. He turned his face towards us once, and I saw at once that he was of the same breed as the Atlantean men who were around me. Indeed, he might have been the twin brother of Manda, save that his features were harsh and menacing—a brute man, but one who was brutal not from ignorance but from the trend of his own nature. The brute and the brain are surely the most dangerous of all combinations. In this high forehead and sardonic, bearded mouth one sensed the very essence of evil. If this were indeed some previous incarnation of Manda himself, and by his gestures he seemed to wish us to understand that it was, then in soul, if not in mind, he has risen far since then.

As he approached the house, we saw in the picture that a young woman came out to meet him. She was clad as the old

Greeks were clad, in a long clinging white garment, the simplest and yet the most beautiful and dignified dress that woman has ever yet devised. Her manner as she approached the man was one of submission and reverence—the manner of a dutiful daughter to a father. He repulsed her savagely, however, raising his hand as if to strike her As she shrank back from him, the sun lit up her beautiful, tearful face and I saw that it was my Mona.

The silver screen blurred, and an instant later another scene was forming. It was a rock-bound cove, which I sensed to belong to that very peninsula which I had already seen. A strange-shaped boat with high pointed ends was in the foreground. It was night, but the moon shone very brightly on the water. The familiar stars, the same to Atlantis as to us, glittered in the sky. Slowly and cautiously the boat drew in. There were two rowers, and in the bows a man enveloped in a dark cloak. As he came close to the shore he stood up and looked eagerly around him. I saw his pale, earnest face in the clear moonlight. It did not need the convulsive clasp of Mona or the ejaculation of Manda to explain that strange intimate thrill which shot over me as I looked. The man was myself.

Yes, I, Cyrus Headley, now of New York and of Oxford; I, the latest product of modern culture, had myself once been part of this mighty civilization of old. I understood now why many of the symbols and hieroglyphs which I had seen around had impressed me with a vague familiarity. Again and again I had felt like a man who strains his memory because he feels that he is on the edge of some great discovery, which is always awaiting him, and yet is always just outside his grasp. Now, too, I understood that deep soul thrill which I had encountered when my eyes met those of Mona. They came from the depths of my own subconscious self where the memories of twelve thousand years still lingered.

Now the boat had touched the shore, and out of the bushes above there had come a glimmering white figure. My arms were outstretched to enfold it. After one hurried embrace I had half lifted, half carried her into the boat. But now there was a sudden alarm. With frantic gestures I beckoned to the rowers to push out. It was too late. Men swarmed out of the bushes. Eager hands scized the side of the boat. In vain I tried to beat them off. An axe gleamed in the air and crashed down upon my head. I fell forward dead upon the lady bathing her white robe in my blood. I saw her screaming, wild-eyed and open-mouthed, while her father dragged her by her long black hair from underneath my body. Then the curtain closed down.

Once again a picture flickered up upon the silver screen. It was inside the house of refuge which had been built by the wise Atlantean for a place of refuge on the day of doom—that very house in which we now stood. I saw its crowded, terrified inmates at the moment of the catastrophe. Then I saw my Mona once again, and there also was her father who had learned better and wiser ways so that he was now included among those who might be saved. We saw the great hall rocking like a ship in a storm, while the awestruck refugees clung to the pillars or fell upon the floor. Then we saw the lurch and fall as it descended through the waves. Once more the scene died away, and Manda turned smiling to show that all was over.

Yes, we had lived before, the whole group of us, Manda and Mona and I, and perhaps shall live again, acting and reacting down the long chain of our lives. I had died in the upper world, and so my own reincarnations had been upon that plane. Manda and Mona had died under, the waves, and so it was there that their cosmic destiny had been worked out. We had for a moment seen a corner lifted in the great dark veil of Nature and had one passing gleam of truth amid the mysteries which surround us. Each life is but one chapter in a story which God has designed. You cannot judge its wisdom or its justice until in some supreme day, from some pinnacle of knowledge, you look back and see at last the cause and the effect, acting and reacting, down all the long chronicles of Time.

This new-found and delightful relationship of mine may have saved us all a little later when the only serious quarrel which we ever had broke out between us and the community with which we dwelt. As it was, it might have gone ill with us had not a far greater matter come to engage the attention of all, and to place us on a pinnacle in their estimation. It came about thus.

One morning, if such a term can be used where the time of day could only be judged by our occupations, the Professor and I were seated in our large common room. He had fitted one corner of it as a laboratory and was busily engaged in dissecting a *gastrostomus* which he had netted the day before. On his table were scattered a litter of amphipods and copepods with specimens of *Valella*, *Ianthina*, Physalia, and a hundred other creatures whose smell was by no means as attractive as their appearance. I was seated near him studying an Atlantean grammar, for our friends had plenty of books, printed in curious right to left fashion upon what I thought was parchment but which proved to be the bladders of fishes, pressed and preserved. I was bent on getting the key which would unlock all this knowledge, and therefore I spent much of my time over the alphabet and the elements of the language.

Suddenly, however, our peaceful pursuits were rudely interrupted by an extraordinary procession which rushed into the room. First came Bill Scanlan, very red and excited, one arm waving in the air, and, to our amazement, a plump and noisy baby under the other. Behind him was Berbrix, the Atlantean engineer who had helped Scanlan to erect the wireless receiver. He was a large stout jovial man as a rule, but now his big fat face was convulsed with grief. Behind him again was a woman whose straw-coloured hair and blue eyes showed that she was no Atlantean but one of the subordinate race which we traced to the ancient Greeks.

'Look it here, boss,' cried the excited Scanlan. 'This guy Berbrix, who is a regular fellar, is going clean goofie and so is this skirt whom he has married, and I guess it is up to us to see that they get a square deal. Far as I understand it she is like a nigger would be down South, and he said a mouthful when he asked her to marry him, but I reckon that's the guy's own affair and nothing to us.'

'Of course it is his own affair,' said I. 'What on earth has bitten you, Scanlan?'

'It's like this, boss. Here ha! a baby come along. It seems the folk here don't want a breed of that sort nohow, and the Priests are out to offer up the baby to that darn image down yonder. The chief high muck-a-muck got hold of the baby and was sailin' off with it but Berbrix yanked it away, and I threw him down on his ear-hole, and now the whole pack are at our heels and—'

Scanlan got no further with his explanation, for there was a shouting and a rush of feet in the passage, our door was flung open, and several of the yellow-clad attendants of the Temple rushed into the room. Behind them, fierce and austere, came the high-nosed formidable Priest. He, beckoned with his hand, and his servants rushed forward to seize the child. They halted, however, in indecision as they saw Scanlan throw the baby down among the specimens on the table behind him, and pick up a pike with which he confronted his assailants. They had drawn their knives, so I also ran with a pike to Scanlan's aid, while Berbrix did the same. So menacing were we that the Temple servants shrank back and things seemed to have come to a deadlock.

'Mr. Headley, sir, you speak a bit of their lingo,' cried: Scanlan. 'Tell them there ain't no soft pickings here. Tell them we ain't givin' away no babies this morning, thank you. Tell them there will be such a rough house as they never saw if they don't *vamose* the *ranche*. There now, you asked for it and you've got it good and plenty and I wish you joy.'

The latter part of Scanlan's speech was caused by the fact that Dr. Maracot had suddenly plunged the scalpel with which he was performing his dissection into the arm of one of the attendants who had crept round and had raised his knife to stab Scanlan. The man howled and danced about in fear and pain while his comrades, incited by the old Priest, prepared to make a rush. Heaven only knows what would have happened if Manda and Mona had not entered the room. He stared with amazement at the scene and asked a number of eager questions of the High Priest. Mona had come over to me, and with a happy inspiration I picked up the baby and placed it in her arms, where it settled down and cooed most contentedly.

Manda's brow was overcast and it was clear that he was greatly puzzled what to do. He sent the Priest and his satellites back to the

Temple, and then he entered into a long explanation, only a part of which I could understand and pass on to my companions.

'You are to give up the baby,' I said to Scanlan.

'Give it up! No, sir. Nothin' doing!'

'This lady is to take charge of mother and child.'

'That's another matter. If Miss Mona takes it on, I am contented. But if that bindlestiff of a priest—'

'No, no, he cannot interfere. The matter is to be referred to the Council. It is very serious, for I understand Manda to say that the Priest is within his rights and that it is an old-established custom of the nation. They could never, he says, distinguish between the upper and lower races if they had all sorts of intermediates in between. If children are born they must die. That is the law.'

'Well, this baby won't die anyhow.'

'I hope not. He said he would do all he could with the Council. But it will be a week or two before they meet. So it's safe up to then, and who knows what may happen in the meantime.'

Yes, who knew what might happen. Who could have dreamed what did happen. Out of this is fashioned the next chapter of our adventures.

Chapter 7

I have already said that within a short distance of the underground dwelling of the Atlanteans, prepared beforehand to meet the catastrophe which overwhelmed their native land, there lay the ruins of that great city of which their dwelling had once been part. I have described also how with the vitrine bells charged with oxygen upon our heads we were taken to visit this place, and I tried to convey how deep were our emotions as we viewed it. No words can describe the tremendous impression produced by those colossal ruins, the huge carved pillars and gigantic buildings, all lying stark and silent in the grey phosphorescent light of the *bathybian* deeps, with no movement save the slow wash of the giant fronds in the deep-sea currents, or the flickering shadows of the great fish which passed through the gaping doors or flitted round the dismantled chambers. It was a favourite haunt of ours, and under the guidance of our friend Manda we passed many an hour examining the strange architecture and all the other remains of that vanished civilization which bore every sign of having been, so far as material knowledge goes, far ahead of our own.

I have said material knowledge. Soon we were to have proof that in spiritual culture there was a vast chasm which separated them from us. The lesson which we carry from their rise and their fall is that the greatest danger which can come to a state is when its intellect outruns its soul. It destroyed this old civilization, and it may yet be the ruin of our own.

We had observed that in one part of the ancient city there

was a large building which must have stood upon a hill, for it was still considerably elevated above the general level. A long flight of broad steps constructed from black marble led up to it, and the same material had been used in most of the building, but it was nearly obscured now by a horrible yellow fungus, a fleshy leprous mass, which hung down from every cornice and projection. Above the main doorway, carved also in black marble, was a terrible Medusa-like head with radiating serpents, and the same symbol was repeated here and there upon the walls. Several times we had wished to explore this sinister building, but on each occasion our friend Manda had shown the greatest agitation and by frantic gestures had implored us to turn away. It was clear that so long as he was in our company we should never have our way, and yet a great curiosity urged us to penetrate the secret of this ominous place. We held a council on the matter one morning, Bill Scanlan and I.

'Look it here, Bo,' said he, 'there is something there that this guy does not want us to see, and the more he hides it the more of a hunch have I that I want to be set wise to it. We don't need no guides any more, you or I. I guess we can put on our own glass tops and walk out of the front door same as any other citizen. Let us go down and explore.'

'Why not?' said I, for I was as curious about the matter as Scanlan. 'Do you see any objection, sir?' I asked, for Dr. Maracot had entered the room. 'Perhaps you would care to come down with us and fathom the mystery of the Palace of Black Marble.'

'It may be the Palace of Black Magic as well,' said he. 'Did you ever hear of the Lord of the Dark Face?'

I confessed that I never did. I forget if I have said before that the Professor was a world-famed specialist on Comparative Religions and ancient primitive beliefs. Even the distant Atlantis was not beyond the range of his learning.

'Our knowledge of the conditions there came to us chiefly by way of Egypt,' said he. 'It is what the Priests of the Temple at Sais told Solon which is the solid nucleus round which all the rest, part fact and part fiction, has gathered.'

'And what wisecracks did the priests say?' asked Scanlan.

'Well, they said a good deal. But among other things they handed down a legend of the Lord of the Dark Face. I can't help thinking that he may have been the Master of the Black Marble Palace. Some say that there were several Lords of the Dark Face—but one at least is on record.'

'And what sort of a duck was he?' asked Scanlan.,

'Well, by all accounts, he was more than a man, both in his power and in his wickedness. Indeed, it was on account of these things, and on account of the utter corruption which he had brought upon the people, that the whole land was destroyed.'

'Like Sodom and Gomorrah.'

'Exactly. There would seem to be a point where things become impossible. Nature's patience is exhausted, and the only course open is to smear it all out and begin again. This creature, one can hardly call him a man, had trafficked in unholy arts and had acquired magic powers of the most far—reaching sort which he turned to evil ends. That is the legend of the Lord of the Dark Face. It would explain why his house is still a thing of horror to these poor people and why they dread that we should go near it.'

'Which makes me the more eager to do so,' I cried.

'Same here, Bo,' Bill added.

'I confess that I, too, should be interested to examine it,' said the Professor. 'I cannot see that our kind hosts here will be any the worse if we make a little expedition of our own, since their superstition makes it difficult for them to accompany us. We will take our opportunity and do so.'

It was some little time before that opportunity came, for our small community was so closely knit that there was little privacy in life. It chanced, however, one morning—so far as we could with our rough calendar reckon night and morning— there was some religious observance which assembled them all and took up all their attention. The chance was too good for us to miss and having assured the two janitors who worked the great pumps of the entrance chamber that all was right we soon found ourselves alone upon the ocean bed and bound for the old city. Progress is slow through the heavy medium of salt water, and even a short walk is wearying, but within an hour we found ourselves in front of the huge black building which had excited our curiosity. With no friendly guide to check us, and no presentiment of danger, we ascended the marble stair and passed through the huge carved portals of this palace of evil.

It was far better preserved than the other buildings of the old city—so much so, indeed, that the stone shell was in no way altered, and only the furniture and the hangings had long decayed and vanished. Nature, however, had brought her own hangings, and very horrible they were. It was a gloomy shadowy place at the best, but in those hideous shadows lurked the obscene shapes of monstrous polyps and strange, misformed fish which were like the creations of a nightmare. Especially I remember an enormous purple sea-slug which crawled, in great numbers, everywhere and large black flat fish which lay like mats upon the floor, with long waving tentacles tipped with flame vibrating above them in the water. We had to step carefully, for the whole building was filled with hideous creatures which might well prove to be as poisonous as they looked.

There were richly ornamented passages with small side rooms leading out from them, but the centre of the building was taken up by one magnificent hall, which in the days of its grandeur must have been one of the most wonderful chambers ever erected by human hands. In that gloomy light we could see neither the roof nor the full sweep of the walls, but as we walked round, our lamps casting tunnels of light before us, we appreciated its huge proportions and the marvellous decorations of the walls. These decorations took the form of statues and ornaments, carved with the highest perfection of art, but horrible and revolting in their subjects. All that the most depraved human mind could conceive of Sadic cruelty and bestial lust was reproduced upon the walls. Through the shadows monstrous images and horrible imaginings loomed round us on every side. If ever the devil had a Temple erected in his honour, it was there. So too was the devil himself, for at one end of the room, under a canopy of discoloured metal which may well have been gold, and on a high throne of red marble, there was seated a dreadful deity, the very impersonation of evil, savage, scowling and relentless, modelled upon the same lines as the Baal whom we had seen in the Atlantean Colony, but infinitely stranger and more repulsive. There was a fascination in the wonderful vigour of that terrible countenance, and we were standing with our lamps playing upon it, absorbed in our reflections, when the most amazing, the most incredible thing came to break in upon our reflections. From behind us there came the sound of a loud, derisive human laugh.

Our heads were, as I have explained, enclosed in our glass bells, from which all sound was excluded, nor was it possible for anyone wearing a bell to utter any sound. And yet that mocking laugh fell clear upon the ears of each of us. We sprang round and stood amazed at what was before us.

Against one of the pillars of the hall a man was leaning, his arms folded upon his chest, and his malevolent eyes fixed with a threatening glare upon ourselves. I have called him a man, but he was unlike any man whom I have ever seen, and the fact that he both breathed and talked as no man could breathe or talk, and made his voice carry as no human voice could carry, told us that he had that in him which made him very different from ourselves. Outwardly he was a magnificent creature, not less than seven feet in height and built upon the lines of a perfect athlete, which was more noticeable as he wore a costume which fitted tightly upon his figure, and seemed to consist of black glazed leather. His face was that of a bronze statue—a statue wrought by some master craftsman in order to depict all the power and also all the evil which the human features could por-tray. It was not bloated or sensual, for such characteristics would have meant weakness and there was no trace of weakness there. On the contrary, it was extraordinarily clean-cut and aquiline, with an eagle nose, dark bristling brows, and smouldering black eyes which flashed and glowed with an inner fire. It was those remorseless, malignant eyes, and the beautiful but cruel straight hard-lipped mouth, set like fate, which gave the terror to his face. One felt, as one looked at him, that magnificent as he was in his person, he was evil to the very marrow, his glance a threat, his smile a sneer, his laugh a mockery:

'Well, gentlemen,' he said, talking excellent English in a voice which sounded as clear as if we were all back upon earth, 'you have had a remarkable adventure in the past and are likely to have an even more exciting one in the future, though it may be my pleasant task to bring it to a sudden end. This, I fear, is a rather one-sided conversation, but as I am perfectly well able to read your thoughts, and as I know all about you, you need not fear any misunderstanding. But you have a great deal—a very great deal to learn.'

We looked at each other in helpless amazement. It was hard, indeed, to be prevented from comparing notes as to our reactions to this amazing development. Again we heard that rasping laugh.

'Yes, it is indeed hard. But you can talk when you return, for I wish you to return and to take a message with you. If it were not for that message, I think that this visit to my home would have been your end. But first of all I have a few things which I wished to say to you. I will address you, Dr. Maracot, as the oldest and presumably the wisest of the party, though none could have been very wise to make such an excursion as this. You hear me very well, do you not? That is right, a nod or a shake is all I ask.

'Of course you know who I am. I fancy you discovered me lately. No one can speak or think of me that I do not know it. No one can come into this my old home, my innermost intimate shrine, that I am not summoned. That is why these poor wretches down yonder avoid it, and wanted you to avoid it also. You would have been wiser if you had followed their advice. You have brought me to you, and when once I am brought I do not readily leave.

'Your mind with its little grain of earth science is worrying itself over the problems which I present. How is it that I can live here without oxygen? I do not live here. I live in the great world of men under the light of the sun. I only come here when I am called as you have called me. But I am an ether-breathing creature. There is as much ether here as on a mountain top. Some of your own people can live without air. The cataleptic lies for months and never breathes. I'm even as he, but I remain, as you see me, conscious and active.

104

'Now you worry as to how you can hear me. Is it not the very essence of wireless transmission that it turns from the ether to the air? So I, too, can turn my words from my etheric utterance to impinge upon your ears through the air which fills those clumsy bells of yours.

'And my English? Well, I hope it is fairly good. I have lived some time on earth, oh a weary, weary time. How long is it? Is this the eleventh thousand or the twelfth thousand year? The latter, I think. I have had time to learn all human tongues. My English is no better than the rest.

'Have I resolved some of your doubts? That is right. I can see if I cannot hear you. But now I have something more serious to say.

'I am Baal-seepa. I am the Lord of the Dark Face. I am he who went so far into the inner secrets of Nature that I could defy death himself. I have so handled things that I could not die if I would. Some will stronger than my own is to be found if I am ever to die. Oh, mortals, never pray to be delivered from death. It may seem terrible, but eternal life is infinitely more so. To go on and on and on while the endless procession of humanity goes past you. To sit ever at the wayside of history and to see it go, ever moving onwards and leaving you behind. Is it a wonder that my heart is black and bitter, and that I curse the whole foolish drove of them? I injure them when I can. Why should I not?

'You wonder how I can injure them. I have powers, and they are not small ones. I can sway the minds of men. I am the master of the mob. Where evil has been planned there have I ever been. I was with the Huns when they laid half Europe in ruins. I was with the Saracens when under the name of religion they put to the sword all who gainsayed them. I was out on Bartholomew's night. I lay behind the slave trade. It was my whisper which burned ten thousand old crones whom the fools called witches. I was the tall dark man who led the mob in Paris when the streets swam in blood. Rare times those, but they have been even better of late in Russia. That is whence I have come. I had half forgotten this colony of sea-rats who burrow under the mud and carry on a few of the arts and legends of that grand land where life flourished as never since. It is you who reminded me of them, for this old home of mine is still united, by personal vibrations of which your science knows nothing, to the man who built and loved it. I knew that strangers had entered it. I inquired, and here I am. So now since I am here—and it is the first time for a thousand years—it has reminded me of these people. They have lingered long enough. It is time for them to go. They are sprung from the power of one who defied me in his life, and who built up this means of escape from the catastrophe which engulfed all but his people and myself. His wisdom saved them and my powers saved me. But now my powers will crush those whom he saved, and the story will be complete.'

He put his hand into his breast and he took out a piece of script. 'You will give this to the chief of the water-rats,' said he. 'I regret that you gentlemen should share their fate, but since you are the primary cause of their misfortune it is only justice, after all. I will see you again later. Meanwhile I would commend a study of these pictures and carvings, which will give you some idea of the height to which I had raised Atlantis during the days of my rule. Here you will find some record of the manners and customs of the people when under my influence. Life was very varied, very highly coloured, very many-sided. In these drab days they would call it an orgy of wickedness. Well, call it what you will, I brought it about, I rejoiced in it, and I have no regrets. Had I my time again, I would do even so and more, save only for this fatal gift of eternal life. Warda, whom I curse and whom I should have killed before he grew strong enough to turn people against me, was wiser than I in this. He still revisits earth, but it is as a spirit, not a man. And now I go. You came here from curiosity, my friends. I can but trust that that curiosity is satisfied.'

And then we saw him disappear. Yes, before our very eyes he vanished. It was not done in an instant. He stood clear of the pillar against which he had been leaning. His splendid towering figure seemed blurred at the edges. The light died out of his eyes and his features grew indistinct. Then in a moment he had become a dark whirling cloud which swept upwards through the stagnant water of this dreadful hall. Then he was gone, and we stood gazing at each other and marvelling at the strange possibilities of life.

We did not linger in that horrible palace. It was not a safe place in which to loiter. As it was, I picked one of those noxious purple slugs off the shoulder of Bill Scanlan, and I was myself badly stung in the hand by the venom spat at me by a great yellow *lamelli* branch. As we staggered out I had one last impression of those dreadful carvings, the devil's own handiwork, upon the walls, and then we almost ran down the darksome passage, cursing the day that ever we had been fools enough to enter it. It was joy indeed to be out in the phosphorescent light of the *bathybian* plain, and to see the clear translucent water once again around us. Within an hour we were back in our home once more. With our helmets removed, we met in consultation in our own chamber. The Professor and I were too overwhelmed with it all to be able to put our thoughts into words. It was only the irrepressible vitality of Bill Scanlan which rose superior.

'Holy smoke!' said he. 'We are up against it now. I guess this guy is the big noise out of hell. Seems to me, with his pictures and statues and the rest, he would make the wardsman of a red light precinct look like two cents. How to handle him—that's the question.'

Dr. Maracot was lost in thought. Then he rang the bell and summoned our yellow-clad attendant. 'Manda,' said he. A minute later our friend was in the room. Maracot handed him the fateful letter.

Never have I admired a man as I did Manda at that moment. We had brought threatened ruin upon his people and himself by our unjustifiable curiosity—we, the strangers whom he had rescued when everything was hopelessly lost. And yet, though he turned a ghastly colour as he read the message, there was no touch of reproach upon the sad brown eyes which turned upon us. He shook his head, and despair was in every gesture. 'Baal-seepa! Baal-seepa!' he cried, and pressed his hands convulsively to his eyes, as if shutting out some horrible vision. He ran about the room like a man distracted with his grief, and finally rushed away to read the fatal message to the community. We heard a few minutes later the clang of the great bell which summoned them all to conference in the Central Hall.

'Shall we go?' I asked.

Dr. Maracot shook his head.

'What can we do? For that matter, what can they do? What chance have they against one who has the powers of a demon?'

'As much chance as a bunch of rabbits against a weasel,' said Scanlan. 'But, by Gosh, it's up to us to find a way out. I guess we can't go out of our way to raise the devil and then pass the buck to the folk that saved us.'

'What do you suggest?' I asked eagerly, for behind all his slang and his levity I recognized the strong, practical ability of this modern man of his hands.

'Well, you can search me,' said he. 'And yet maybe this guy is not as safe as he thinks. A bit of it may have got worn out with age, and he's getting on in years if we can take his word for it.'

'You think we might attack him?'

'Lunacy!' interjected the doctor.

Scanlan went to his locker. When he faced round he had a big six-shooter in his hand.

'What about this?' he said. 'I laid hold of it when we got our chance at the wreck. I thought maybe it might come useful. I've a dozen shells here. Maybe if I made as many holes in the big stiff it would let out some of his Magic. Lord save us! What is it?'

The revolver clattered down upon the floor, and Scanlan was writhing in agonies of pain, his left hand clasping his right wrist. Terrible cramps had seized his arm, and as we tried to alleviate them we could feel the muscles knotted up as hard as the roots of a tree. The sweat of agony streamed down the poor fellow's brow. Finally, utterly cowed and exhausted, he fell upon his bed.

'That lets me out,' he said. 'I'm through. Yes, thank you, the pain is better. But it is K.O. to William Scanlan. I've learned my lesson. You don't fight hell with six-shooters, and it's no use to try. I give him best from now onwards.'

'Yes, you have had your lesson,' said Maracot, 'and it has been a severe one.'

'Then you think our case is hopeless?'

'What can we do when, as it would seem, he is aware of every word and action? And yet we will not despair.' He sat in thought for a few moments. 'I think,' he resumed, 'that you, Scanlan, had best lie where you are for a time. You have had a shock from which it will take you some time to recover.'

'If there is anything doing, count me in, though I guess we can cut out the rough stuff,' said our comrade bravely, but his drawn face and shaking limbs showed what he had endured.

'There is nothing doing so far as you are concerned. We at least have learned what is the wrong way to go to work. All violence is useless. We are working on another plane—the plane of spirit. Do you remain here, Headley. I am going to the room which I use as a study. Perhaps if I were alone I could see a little more clearly what we should do.'

Both Scanlan and I had learned to have a great confidence in Maracot. If any human brain could solve our difficulties, it would be his. And yet surely we had reached a point which was beyond all human capacity. We were as helpless as children in the face of forces which we could neither understand nor control. Scanlan had fallen into a troubled sleep. My own one thought as I sat beside him was not how we should escape, but rather what form the blow would take and when it would fall. At any moment I was prepared to see the solid roof above us sink in, the walls collapse, and the dark waters of the lowest deep close in upon those who had defied them so long.

Then suddenly the great bell pealed out once more. Its harsh clamour jarred upon every nerve. I sprang to my feet, and Scanlan sat up in bed. It was no ordinary summons which rang through the old palace. The agitated tumultuous ringing, broken and irregular, was calling an alarm. All had to come, and at once. It was menacing and insistent.

'Come now! Come at once! Leave everything and come!' cried the bell.

'Say, Bo, we should be with them,' said Scanlan. 'guess they're up against it now.'

'And yet what can we do?'

'Maybe just the sight of us will give them a bit of heart. Anyhow, they must not think that we are quitters. Where is the Doc?'

'He went to his study. But you are right, Scanlan. We should be with the others and let them see that we are ready to share their fate.'

'The poor boobs seem to lean on us in a way. It may be that they know more than we, but we seem to have more sand in our craw than they. I guess they have taken what was given to them, and we have had to find things for ourselves. Well, it's me for the deluge—if the deluge has got to be.'

But as we approached the door a most unexpected interruption detained us. Dr. Maracot stood before us. But was it indeed the Dr. Maracot whom we had known—this self-assured man with strength and resolution shining from every feature of his masterful face? The quiet scholar had been submerged, and here was a superman, a great leader, a dominant soul who might mould mankind to his desires.

'Yes, friends, we shall be needed. All may yet be well. But come at once, or it may be too late. I will explain everything later—if there is any later for us. Yes, yes, we are coming.'

The latter words, with appropriate gesture, were spoken to some terrified Atlanteans who had appeared at the door and were eagerly beckoning to us to come. It was a fact, as Scanlan had said, that we had shown ourselves several times to be stronger in character and prompter in action than these secluded people, and at this hour of supreme danger they seemed to cling to us. I could hear a subdued murmur of satisfaction and relief as we entered the crowded hall, and took the places reserved for us in the front row.

It was time that we came, if we were indeed to bring any help. The terrible presence was already standing upon the dais and facing with a cruel, thin-lipped, demoniacal smile the cowering folk before him. Scanlan's simile of a bunch of rabbits before a weasel came back to my memory as I looked round at them. They sank together, holding on to each other in their terror, and gazing wide—eyed at the mighty figure which towered above them and the ruthless granite-hewed face which looked

110

down upon them. Never can I forget the impression of those semi-circular rows, tier above tier, of haggard, wide-eyed faces with their horrified gaze all directed towards the central dais. It would seem that he had already pronounced their doom and that they stood in the shadow of death waiting for its fulfilment. Manda was standing in abject submission, pleading in broken accents for his people, but one could see that the words only gave an added zest to the monster who stood sneering before him. The creature interrupted him with a few rasping words, and raised his right hand in the air, while a cry of despair rose from the assembly.

And at that moment Dr. Maracot sprang upon the dais. It was amazing to watch him. Some miracle seemed to have altered the man. He had the gait and the gesture of a youth, and yet upon his face there was a look of such power as I have never seen upon human features yet. He strode up to the swarthy giant, who glared down at him in amazement.

'Well, little man, what have you to say?' he asked.

'I have this to say,' said Maracot. 'Your time has come. You have over-stayed it. Go down! Go down into the Hell that has been waiting for you so long. You are a prince of darkness. Go where the darkness is.'

The demon's eyes shot dark fire as he answered:

'When my time comes, if it should ever come, it will not be from the lips of a wretched mortal that I shall learn it,' said he. 'What power have you that you could oppose for a moment one who is in the secret places of Nature? I could blast you where you stand.'

Maracot looked into those terrible eyes without blenching. It seemed to me that it was the giant who flinched away from his gaze.

'Unhappy being,' said Maracot. 'It is I who have the power and the will to blast you where you stand. Too long have you cursed the world with your presence. You have been a plague-spot infecting all that was beautiful and good. The hearts of men will be lighter when you are gone, and the sun will shine more brightly.'

'What is this? Who are you? What is it that you are saying?' stammered the creature.

'You speak of secret knowledge. Shall I tell you that which is at the very base of it? It is that on every plane the good of that plane can be stronger than the evil. The angel will still beat the devil. For the moment I am on the same plane on which you have so long been, and I hold the power of the conqueror. It has been given to me. So again I say: Down with you! Down to Hell to which you belong! Down, sir! Down, I say! Down!'

And then the miracle occurred. For a minute or more— how can one count time at such moments?—the two beings, the mortal and the demon, faced each other as rigid as statues, glaring into each other's eyes, with inexorable will upon the two faces, the dark one and the fair. Then suddenly the great creature flinched. His face convulsed with rage, he threw two clawing hands up into the air. 'It is you, Warda, you cursed one! I recognize your handiwork. Oh, curse you, Warda. Curse you! Curse you!' His voice died away, his long dark figure became blurred in its outline, his head drooped upon his chest, his knees sagged under him, down he sank and down, and as he sank he changed his shape. At first it was a crouching human being, then it was a dark formless mass, and then with sudden collapse it had become a semi-liquid heap of black and horrible putrescence which stained the dais and poisoned the air. At the same time Scanlan and I dashed forward on to the platform, for Dr. Maracot, with a deep groan, his powers exhausted, had fallen forward in helpless collapse. 'We have won! We have won!' he muttered, and an instant later his senses had left him and he lay half dead upon the floor.

****

Thus it was that the Atlantean colony was saved from the most horrible danger that could threaten it, and that an evil presence was banished for ever from the world. It was not for some days that Dr. Maracot could tell his story, and when he did it was of such a character that if we had not seen the results we should have put it down as the delirium of his illness. I may say that his power had left him with the occasion which had called it forth, and that he was now the same quiet, gentle man of science whom we had known.

'That it should have happened to me!' he cried. 'To me, a materialist, a man so immersed in matter that the invisible did not exist in my philosophy. The theories of a whole lifetime have crumbled about my ears.'

'I guess we have all been to school again,' said Scanlan, 'If ever I get back to the little home town, I shall have something to tell the boys.'

'The less you tell them the better, unless you want to get the name of being the greatest liar that ever came out of America,' said I. 'Would you or I have believed it all if someone else had told us?'

'Maybe not. But say, Doc, you had the dope right enough. That great black stiff got his ten and out as neat as ever I saw. There was no come-back there. You clean pushed him off the map. I don't know on what other map he has found his location, but it is no place for Bill Scanlan anyhow.'

'I will tell you exactly what occurred,' said the Doctor. 'You will remember that I left you and retired into my study. I had little hope in my heart, but I had read a good deal at different times about black magic and occult arts. I was aware that white can always dominate black if it can but reach the same plane. He was on a much stronger—I will not say higher—plane than we. That was the fatal fact.

'I saw no way of getting over it. I flung myself down on the settee and I prayed—yes, I, the hardened materialist, prayed—for help. When one is at the very end of all human power, what can one do save to stretch appealing hands into the mists which gird us round? I prayed—and my prayer was most wonderfully answered.

'I was suddenly aware of the fact that I was not alone in the room. There stood before me a tall figure, as swarthy as the evil presence whom we fought, but with a kindly, bearded face which shone with benevolence and love. The sense of power which he conveyed was not less than the other, but it was the power of good, the power within the influence of which evil would shred away as the mists do before the sun. He looked at me with kindly eyes, and I sat, too amazed to speak, staring up at him. Something within me, some inspiration or intuition, told me that this was the spirit of that great and wise Atlantean who had fought the evil while he lived, and who, when he could not prevent the destruction of his country, took such steps as would ensure that the more worthy should survive even though they should be sunk to the depths of the Ocean. This wondrous being was now interposing to prevent the ruin of his work and the destruction of his children. With a sudden gush of hope I realized all this as clearly as if he had said it. Then, still smiling, he advanced, and he laid his two hands upon my head. It was his own virtue and strength, no doubt, which he was transferring to me. I felt it coursing like fire down my veins. Nothing in the world seemed impossible at that moment. I had the will and the might to do miracles. Then at that moment I heard the bell clang out, which told me that the crisis had come. As I rose from the couch the spirit, smiling his encouragement, vanished before me. Then I joined you, and the rest you know.'

'Well, sir,' said I, 'I think you have made your reputation. If you care to set up as a god down here, I expect you would find no difficulty.'

'You got away with it better than I did, Doc,' said Scanlan in a rueful voice. 'How is it this guy didn't know what you were doing? He was quick enough on to me when I laid hand on a gun. And yet you had him guessing.'

'I suppose that you were on the plane of matter, and that, for the moment, we were upon that of spirit,' said the Doctor thoughtfully. 'Such things teach one humility. It is only when you touch the higher that you realize how low we may be among the possibilities of creation. I have had my lesson. May my future life show that I have learned it.'

So this was the end of our supreme experience. It was but a little time later that we conceived the idea of sending news of ourselves to the surface, and that later by means of vitrine balls filled with levigen, we ascended ourselves to be met in the manner already narrated. Dr. Maracot actually talks of going back. There is some point of Ichthyology upon which he wants more precise information. But Scanlan has, I hear, married his wren in Philadelphia, and has been promoted as works manager of Merribanks, so he seeks no further adventure, while I—well, the deep sea has given me a precious pearl, and I ask for no more.

Short Stories

Lot No. 249

Of the dealings of Edward Bellingham with William Monk-house Lee, and of the cause of the great terror of Abercrombie Smith, it may be that no absolute and final judgment will ever be delivered. It is true that we have the full and clear narrative of Smith himself, and such corroboration as he could look for from Thomas Styles the servant, from the Reverend Plumptree Peterson, Fellow of Old's, and from such other people as chanced to gain some passing glance at this or that incident in a singular chain of events. Yet, in the main, the story must rest upon Smith alone, and the most will think that it is more likely that one brain, however outwardly sane, has some subtle warp in its texture, some strange flaw in its workings, than that the path of Nature has been overstepped in open day in so famed a centre of learning and light as the University of Oxford. Yet when we think how narrow and how devious this path of Nature is, how dimly we can trace it, for all our lamps of science, and how from the darkness which girds it round great and terrible possibilities loom ever shadowly upwards, it is a bold and confident man who will put a limit to the strange by-paths into which the human spirit may wander.

In a certain wing of what we will call Old College in Oxford there is a corner turret of an exceeding great age. The heavy arch which spans the open door has bent downwards in the centre under the weight of its years, and the grey, lichen-blotched blocks of stone are, bound and knitted together with withes and strands of ivy, as though the old mother had set herself to brace them up against wind and weather. From the door a stone stair curves upward spirally, passing two landings, and terminating in a third one, its steps all shapeless and hollowed by the tread of so many generations of the seekers after knowledge. Life has flowed like water down this winding stair, and, water like, has left these smooth-worn grooves behind it. From the long-gowned, pedantic scholars of Plantagenet days down to the young bloods of a later age, how full and strong had been that tide of young English life. And what was left now of all those hopes, those strivings, those fiery energies, save here and there in some old-world churchyard a few scratches upon a stone, and perchance a handful of dust in a mouldering coffin? Yet here were the silent stair and the grey old wall, with bend and saltire and many another heraldic device still to be read upon its surface, like grotesque shadows thrown back from the days that had passed.

In the month of May, in the year 1884, three young men occupied the sets of rooms which opened on to the separate landings of the old stair. Each set consisted simply of a sitting-room and of a bedroom, while the two corresponding rooms upon the ground-floor were used, the one as a coal-cellar, and the other as the living-room of the servant, or gyp, Thomas Styles, whose duty it was to wait upon the three men above him. To right and to left was a line of lecture-rooms and of offices, so that the dwellers in the old turret enjoyed a certain seclusion, which made the chambers popular among the more studious undergraduates. Such were the three who occupied them now—Abercrombie Smith above, Edward Bellingham beneath him, and William Monkhouse Lee upon the lowest storey.

It was ten o'clock on a bright spring night, and Abercrombie Smith lay back in his arm-chair, his feet upon the fender, and his briar-root pipe between his lips. In a similar chair, and equally at his ease, there lounged on the other side of the fireplace his old school friend Jephro Hastie. Both men were in flannels, for they had spent their evening upon the river, but apart from their dress no one could look at their hard-cut, alert faces without seeing that they were open-air men—men whose minds and tastes turned naturally to all that was manly and robust. Hastie, indeed, was stroke of his college boat, and Smith was an even better oar, but a coming examination had already cast its shadow over him and held him to his work, save for the few hours a week which health demanded. A litter of medical books upon the table, with scattered bones, models and anatomical plates, pointed to the extent as well as the nature of his studies, while a couple of single-sticks and a set of boxing-gloves above the mantelpiece hinted at the means by which, with Hastie's help, he might take his exercise in its most compressed and least distant form. They knew each other very well—so well that they could sit now in that soothing silence which is the very highest development of companionship.

"Have some whisky," said Abercrombie Smith at last between two cloudbursts. "Scotch in the jug and Irish in the bottle."

"No, thanks. I'm in for the sculls. I don't liquor when I'm training. How about you?"

"I'm reading hard. I think it best to leave it alone."

Hastie nodded, and they relapsed into a contented silence.

"By-the-way, Smith," asked Hastie, presently, "have you made the acquaintance of either of the fellows on your stair yet?"

"Just a nod when we pass. Nothing more."

"Hum! I should be inclined to let it stand at that. I know something of them both. Not much, but as much as I want. I don't think I should take them to my bosom if I were you. Not that there's much amiss with Monkhouse Lee."

"Meaning the thin one?"

"Precisely. He is a gentlemanly little fellow. I don't think there is any vice in him. But then you can't know him without knowing Bellingham."

"Meaning the fat one?"

"Yes, the fat one. And he's a man whom I, for one, would rather not know."

Abercrombie Smith raised his eyebrows and glanced across at his companion.

"What's up, then?" he asked. "Drink? Cards? Cad? You used not to be censorious."

"Ah! you evidently don't know the man, or you wouldn't

ask. There's something damnable about him—something reptilian. My gorge always rises at him. I should put him down as a man with secret vices—an evil liver. He's no fool, though. They say that he is one of the best men in his line that they have ever had in the college."

"Medicine or classics?"

"Eastern languages. He's a demon at them. Chillingworth met him somewhere above the second cataract last long, and he told me that he just prattled to the Arabs as if he had been born and nursed and weaned among them. He talked Coptic to the Copts, and Hebrew to the Jews, and Arabic to the Bedouins, and they were all ready to kiss the hem of his frock-coat. There are some old hermit Johnnies up in those parts who sit on rocks and scowl and spit at the casual stranger. Well, when they saw this chap Bellingham, before he had said five words they just lay down on their bellies and wriggled. Chillingworth said that he never saw anything like it. Bellingham seemed to take it as his right, too, and strutted about among them and talked down to them like a Dutch uncle. Pretty good for an undergrad. of Old's, wasn't it?"

"Why do you say you can't know Lee without knowing Bellingham?"

"Because Bellingham is engaged to his sister Eveline. Such a bright little girl, Smith! I know the whole family well. It's disgusting to see that brute with her. A toad and a dove, that's what they always remind me of."

Abercrombie Smith grinned and knocked his ashes out against the side of the grate.

"You show every card in your hand, old chap," said he. "What a prejudiced, green-eyed, evil-thinking old man it is! You have really nothing against the fellow except that."

"Well, I've known her ever since she was as long as that cherry-wood pipe, and I don't like to see her taking risks. And it is a risk. He looks beastly. And he has a beastly temper, a venomous temper. You remember his row with Long Norton?"

"No; you always forget that I am a freshman."

"Ah, it was last winter. Of course. Well, you know the towpath along by the river. There were several fellows going along it, Bellingham in front, when they came on an old market-woman coming the other way. It had been raining—you know what those fields are like when it has rained—and the path ran between the river and a great puddle that was nearly as broad. Well, what does this swine do but keep the path, and push the old girl into the mud, where she and her marketings came to terrible grief. It was a blackguard thing to do, and Long Norton, who is as gentle a fellow as ever stepped, told him what he thought of it. One word led to another, and it ended in Norton laying his stick across the fellow's shoulders. There was the deuce of a fuss about it, and it's a treat to see the way in which Bellingham looks at Norton when they meet now. By Jove, Smith, it's nearly eleven o'clock!"

"No hurry. Light your pipe again."

"Not I. I'm supposed to be in training. Here I've been sitting gossiping when I ought to have been safely tucked up. I'll borrow your skull, if you can share it. Williams has had mine for a month. I'll take the little bones of your ear, too, if you are sure you won't need them. Thanks very much. Never mind a bag, I can carry them very well under my arm. Good-night, my son, and take my tip as to your neighbour."

When Hastie, bearing his anatomical plunder, had clattered off down the winding stair, Abercrombie Smith hurled his pipe into the wastepaper basket, and drawing his chair nearer to the lamp, plunged into a formidable green-covered volume, adorned with great coloured maps of that strange internal kingdom of which we are the hapless and helpless monarchs. Though a freshman at Oxford, the student was not so in medicine, for he had worked for four years at Glasgow and at Berlin, and this coming examination would place him finally as a member of his profession. With his firm mouth, broad forehead, and clear-cut, somewhat hard-featured face, he was a man who, if he had no brilliant talent, was yet so dogged, so patient, and so strong that he might in the end overtop a more showy genius. A man who can hold his own among Scotchmen and North Germans is not a man to be easily set back. Smith had left a name at Glasgow and at Berlin, and he was bent now upon doing as much at Oxford, if hard work and devotion could accomplish it.

He had sat reading for about an hour, and the hands of the noisy carriage clock upon the side table were rapidly closing together upon the twelve, when a sudden sound fell upon the student's ear—a sharp, rather shrill sound, like the hissing intake of a man's breath who gasps under some strong emotion. Smith laid down his book and slanted his ear to listen. There was no one on either side or above him, so that the interruption came certainly from the neighbour beneath—the same neighbour of whom Hastie had given so unsavoury an account. Smith knew him only as a flabby, pale-faced man of silent and studious habits, a man, whose lamp threw a golden bar from the old turret even after he had extinguished his own. This community in lateness had formed a certain silent bond between them. It was soothing to Smith when the hours stole on towards dawning to feel that there was another so close who set as small a value upon his sleep as he did. Even now, as his thoughts turned towards him, Smith's feelings were kindly. Hastie was a good fellow, but he was rough, strong-fibred, with no imagination or sympathy. He could not tolerate departures from what he looked upon as the model type of manliness. If a man could not be measured by a public-school standard, then he was beyond the pale with Hastie. Like so many who are themselves robust, he was apt to confuse the constitution with the character, to ascribe to want of principle what was really a want of circulation. Smith, with his stronger mind, knew his friend's habit, and made allowance for it now as his thoughts turned towards the man beneath him.

There was no return of the singular sound, and Smith was about to turn to his work once more, when suddenly there broke out in the silence of the night a hoarse cry, a positive scream—the call of a man who is moved and shaken beyond all control. Smith sprang out of his chair and dropped his book. He was a man of fairly firm fibre, but there was something in this sudden, uncontrollable shriek of horror which chilled his blood and pringled in his skin. Coming in such a place and at such an hour, it brought a thousand fantastic possibilities into his head. Should he rush down, or was it better to wait? He had all the national hatred of making a scene, and he knew so little of his neighbour that he would not lightly intrude upon his affairs. For a moment he stood in doubt and even as he balanced the matter there was a quick rattle of footsteps upon the stairs, and young Monkhouse Lee, half dressed and as white as ashes, burst into his room.

"Come down!" he gasped. "Bellingham's ill."

Abercrombie Smith followed him closely down stairs into the sitting-room which was beneath his own, and intent as he was upon the matter in hand, he could not but take an amazed glance around him as he crossed the threshold. It was such a chamber as he had never seen before—a museum rather than a study. Walls and ceiling were thickly covered with a thousand strange relics from Egypt and the East. Tall, angular figures bearing burdens or weapons stalked in an uncouth frieze round the apartments. Above were bull-headed, stork-headed, cat-headed, owl-headed statues, with viper-crowned, almond-eyed monarchs, and strange, beetle-like deities cut out of the blue Egyptian lapis lazuli. Horus and Isis and Osiris peeped down from every niche and shelf, while across the ceiling a true son of Old Nile, a great, hanging-jawed crocodile, was slung in a double noose.

In the centre of this singular chamber was a large, square table, littered with papers, bottles, and the dried leaves of some graceful, palm-like plant. These varied objects had all been heaped together in order to make room for a mummy case, which had been conveyed from the wall, as was evident from the gap there, and laid across the front of the table. The mummy itself, a horrid, black, withered thing, like a charred head on a gnarled bush, was lying half out of the case, with its claw-like hand and bony forearm resting upon the table. Propped up against the sarcophagus was an old yellow scroll of papyrus, and in front of it, in a wooden armchair, sat the owner of the room, his head thrown back, his widely-opened eyes directed in a horrified stare to the crocodile above him, and his blue, thick lips puffing loudly with every expiration.

"My God! he's dying!" cried Monkhouse Lee distractedly.

He was a slim, handsome young fellow, olive-skinned and dark-eyed, of a Spanish rather than of an English type, with a Celtic intensity of manner which contrasted with the Saxon phlegm of Abercombie Smith.

"Only a faint, I think," said the medical student. "Just give me a hand with him. You take his feet. Now on to the sofa. Can you kick all those little wooden devils off? What a litter it is! Now he will be all right if we undo his collar and give him some water. What has he been up to at all?"

"I don't know. I heard him cry out. I ran up. I know him pretty well, you know. It is very good of you to come down."

"His heart is going like a pair of castanets," said Smith, laying his hand on the breast of the unconscious man. "He seems to me to be frightened all to pieces. Chuck the water over him! What a face he has got on him!"

It was indeed a strange and most repellent face, for colour and outline were equally unnatural. It was white, not with the ordinary pallor of fear but with an absolutely bloodless white, like the under side of a sole. He was very fat, but gave the impression of having at some time been considerably fatter, for his skin hung loosely in creases and folds, and was shot with a meshwork of wrinkles. Short, stubbly brown hair bristled up from his scalp, with a pair of thick, wrinkled ears protruding on either side. His light grey eyes were still open, the pupils dilated and the balls projecting in a fixed and horrid stare. It seemed to Smith as he looked down upon him that he had never seen nature's danger signals flying so plainly upon a man's countenance, and his thoughts turned more seriously to the warning which Hastie had given him an hour before.

"What the deuce can have frightened him so?" he asked.

"It's the mummy."

"The mummy? How, then?"

"I don't know. It's beastly and morbid. I wish he would drop it. It's the second fright he has given me. It was the same last winter. I found him just like this, with that horrid thing in front of him."

"What does he want with the mummy, then?"

"Oh, he's a crank, you know. It's his hobby. He knows more about these things than any man in England. But I wish he wouldn't! Ah, he's beginning to come to."

A faint tinge of colour had begun to steal back into Belling-

126

ham's ghastly cheeks, and his eyelids shivered like a sail after a calm. He clasped and unclasped his hands, drew a long, thin breath between his teeth, and suddenly jerking up his head, threw a glance of recognition around him. As his eyes fell upon the mummy, he sprang off the sofa, seized the roll of papyrus, thrust it into a drawer, turned the key, and then staggered back on to the sofa.

"What's up?" he asked. "What do you chaps want?"

"You've been shrieking out and making no end of a fuss," said Monkhouse Lee. "If our neighbour here from above hadn't come down, I'm sure I don't know what I should have done with you."

"Ah, it's Abercrombie Smith," said Bellingham, glancing up at him. "How very good of you to come in! What a fool I am! Oh, my God, what a fool I am!"

He sunk his head on to his hands, and burst into peal after peal of hysterical laughter.

"Look here! Drop it!" cried Smith, shaking him roughly by the shoulder.

"Your nerves are all in a jangle. You must drop these little midnight games with mummies, or you'll be going off your chump. You're all on wires now."

"I wonder," said Bellingham, "whether you would be as cool as I am if you had seen——"

"What then?"

"Oh, nothing. I meant that I wonder if you could sit up at night with a mummy without trying your nerves. I have no doubt that you are quite right. I dare say that I have been taking it out of myself too much lately. But I am all right now. Please don't go, though. Just wait for a few minutes until I am quite myself."

"The room is very close," remarked Lee, throwing open the window and letting in the cool night air.

"It's balsamic resin," said Bellingham. He lifted up one of the dried palmate leaves from the table and frizzled it over the chimney of the lamp. It broke away into heavy smoke wreaths, and a pungent, biting odour filled the chamber. "It's the sacred plant—the plant of the priests," he remarked. "Do you know anything of Eastern languages, Smith?"

"Nothing at all. Not a word."

The answer seemed to lift a weight from the Egyptologist's mind.

"By-the-way," he continued, "how long was it from the time that you ran down, until I came to my senses?"

"Not long. Some four or five minutes."

"I thought it could not be very long," said he, drawing a long breath. "But what a strange thing unconsciousness is! There is no measurement to it. I could not tell from my own sensations if it were seconds or weeks. Now that gentleman on the table was packed up in the days of the eleventh dynasty, some forty centuries ago, and yet if he could find his tongue he would tell us that this lapse of time has been but a closing of the eyes and a reopening of them. He is a singularly fine mummy, Smith."

Smith stepped over to the table and looked down with a professional eye at the black and twisted form in front of him. The features, though horribly discoloured, were perfect, and two little nut-like eyes still lurked in the depths of the black, hollow sockets. The blotched skin was drawn tightly from bone to bone, and a tangled wrap of black coarse hair fell over the ears. Two thin teeth, like those of a rat, overlay the shrivelled lower lip. In its crouching position, with bent joints and craned head, there was a suggestion of energy about the horrid thing which made Smith's gorge rise. The gaunt ribs, with their parchment-like covering, were exposed, and the sunken, leaden-hued abdomen, with the long slit where the embalmer had left his mark; but the lower limbs were wrapt round with coarse yellow bandages. A number of little clove-like pieces of myrrh and of cassia were sprinkled over the body, and lay scattered on the inside of the case.

"I don't know his name," said Bellingham, passing his hand over the shrivelled head. "You see the outer sarcophagus with the inscriptions is missing. Lot 249 is all the title he has now. You see it printed on his case. That was his number in the auction at which I picked him up."

"He has been a very pretty sort of fellow in his day," remarked Abercrombie Smith.

"He has been a giant. His mummy is six feet seven in length, and that would be a giant over there, for they were never a very robust race. Feel these great knotted bones, too. He would be a nasty fellow to tackle."

"Perhaps these very hands helped to build the stones into the pyramids," suggested Monkhouse Lee, looking down with disgust in his eyes at the crooked, unclean talons.

"No fear. This fellow has been pickled in *natron*, and looked after in the most approved style. They did not serve hodsmen in that fashion. Salt or bitumen was enough for them. It has been calculated that this sort of thing cost about seven hundred and thirty pounds in our money. Our friend was a noble at the least. What do you make of that small inscription near his feet, Smith?"

"I told you that I know no Eastern tongue."

"Ah, so you did. It is the name of the embalmer, I take it. A very conscientious worker he must have been. I wonder how many modern works will survive four thousand years?"

He kept on speaking lightly and rapidly, but it was evident to Abercrombie Smith that he was still palpitating with fear. His hands shook, his lower lip trembled, and look where he would, his eye always came sliding round to his gruesome companion. Through all his fear, however, there was a suspicion of triumph in his tone and manner. His eye shone, and his footstep, as he paced the room, was brisk and jaunty. He gave the impression of a man who has gone through an ordeal, the marks of which he still bears upon him, but which has helped him to his end.

"You're not going yet?" he cried, as Smith rose from the sofa.

At the prospect of solitude, his fears seemed to crowd back upon him, and he stretched out a hand to detain him.

"Yes, I must go. I have my work to do. You are all right now. I think that with your nervous system you should take up some less morbid study."

"Oh, I am not nervous as a rule; and I have unwrapped mummies before."

"You fainted last time," observed Monkhouse Lee.

"Ah, yes, so I did. Well, I must have a nerve tonic or a course of electricity. You are not going, Lee?"

"I'll do whatever you wish, Ned."

"Then I'll come down with you and have a shake-down on your sofa. Good-night, Smith. I am so sorry to have disturbed you with my foolishness."

They shook hands, and as the medical student stumbled up the spiral and irregular stair he heard a key turn in a door, and the steps of his two new acquaintances as they descended to the lower floor.

In this strange way began the acquaintance between Edward Bellingham and Abercrombie Smith, an acquaintance which the latter, at least, had no desire to push further. Bellingham, however, appeared to have taken a fancy to his rough-spoken neighbour, and made his advances in such a way that he could hardly be repulsed without absolute brutality. Twice he called to thank Smith for his assistance, and many times afterwards he looked in with books, papers, and such other civilities as two bachelor neighbours can offer each other. He was, as Smith soon found, a man of wide reading, with catholic tastes and an extraordinary memory. His manner, too, was so pleasing and suave that one came, after a time, to overlook his repellent appearance. For a jaded and wearied man he was no unpleasant companion, and Smith found himself, after a time, looking forward to his visits, and even returning them.

Clever as he undoubtedly was, however, the medical student seemed to detect a dash of insanity in the man. He broke out at times into a high, inflated style of talk which was in contrast with the simplicity of his life.

"It is a wonderful thing," he cried, "to feel that one can command powers of good and of evil—a ministering angel or a demon of vengeance." And again, of Monkhouse Lee, he said,— "Lee is a good fellow, an honest fellow, but he is without strength or ambition. He would not make a fit partner for a man with a great enterprise. He would not make a fit partner for me."

At such hints and innuendoes stolid Smith, puffing solemnly at his pipe, would simply raise his eyebrows and shake his head, with little interjections of medical wisdom as to earlier hours and fresher air.

One habit Bellingham had developed of late which Smith knew to be a frequent herald of a weakening mind. He appeared to be forever talking to himself. At late hours of the night, when there could be no visitor with him, Smith could still hear his voice beneath him in a low, muffled monologue, sunk almost to a whisper, and yet very audible in the silence. This solitary babbling annoyed and distracted the student, so that he spoke more than once to his neighbour about it. Bellingham, however, flushed up at the charge, and denied curtly that he had uttered a sound; indeed, he showed more annoyance over the matter than the occasion seemed to demand.

Had Abercrombie Smith had any doubt as to his own ears he had not to go far to find corroboration. Tom Styles, the little wrinkled man-servant who had attended to the wants of the lodgers in the turret for a longer time than any man's memory could carry him, was sorely put to it over the same matter.

"If you please, sir," said he, as he tidied down the top chamber one morning, "do you think Mr. Bellingham is all right, sir?"

"All right, Styles?"

"Yes sir. Right in his head, sir."

"Why should he not be, then?"

"Well, I don't know, sir. His habits has changed of late. He's not the same man he used to be, though I make free to say that he was never quite one of my gentlemen, like Mr. Hastie or yourself, sir. He's took to talkin' to himself something awful. I wonder it don't disturb you. I don't know what to make of him, sir."

"I don't know what business it is of yours, Styles."

"Well, I takes an interest, Mr. Smith. It may be forward of me, but I can't help it. I feel sometimes as if I was mother and father to my young gentlemen. It all falls on me when things go wrong and the relations come. But Mr. Bellingham, sir. I want to know what it is that walks about his room sometimes when he's out and when the door's locked on the outside."

"Eh! you're talking nonsense, Styles."

"Maybe so, sir; but I heard it more'n once with my own ears."

"Rubbish, Styles."

"Very good, sir. You'll ring the bell if you want me."

Abercrombie Smith gave little heed to the gossip of the old man-servant, but a small incident occurred a few days later which left an unpleasant effect upon his mind, and brought the words of Styles forcibly to his memory.

Bellingham had come up to see him late one night, and was entertaining him with an interesting account of the rock tombs of Beni Hassan in Upper Egypt, when Smith, whose hearing was remarkably acute, distinctly heard the sound of a door opening on the landing below.

"There's some fellow gone in or out of your room," he remarked.

Bellingham sprang up and stood helpless for a moment, with the expression of a man who is half incredulous and half afraid.

"I surely locked it. I am almost positive that I locked it," he stammered. "No one could have opened it."

"Why, I hear someone coming up the steps now," said Smith.

Bellingham rushed out through the door, slammed it loudly behind him, and hurried down the stairs. About half-way down Smith heard him stop, and thought he caught the sound of whispering. A moment later the door beneath him shut, a key creaked in a lock, and Bellingham, with beads of moisture upon his pale face, ascended the stairs once more, and re-entered the room.

"It's all right," he said, throwing himself down in a chair. "It was that fool of a dog. He had pushed the door open. I don't know how I came to forget to lock it."

"I didn't know you kept a dog," said Smith, looking very thoughtfully at the disturbed face of his companion.

"Yes, I haven't had him long. I must get rid of him. He's a great nuisance."

"He must be, if you find it so hard to shut him up. I should have thought that shutting the door would have been enough, without locking it."

"I want to prevent old Styles from letting him out. He's of some value, you know, and it would be awkward to lose him."

"I am a bit of a dog-fancier myself," said Smith, still gazing hard at his companion from the corner of his eyes. "Perhaps you'll let me have a look at it."

132

"Certainly. But I am afraid it cannot be to-night; I have an appointment. Is that clock right? Then I am a quarter of an hour late already. You'll excuse me, I am sure."

He picked up his cap and hurried from the room. In spite of his appointment, Smith heard him re-enter his own chamber and lock his door upon the inside.

This interview left a disagreeable impression upon the medical student's mind. Bellingham had lied to him, and lied so clumsily that it looked as if he had desperate reasons for concealing the truth. Smith knew that his neighbour had no dog. He knew, also, that the step which he had heard upon the stairs was not the step of an animal. But if it were not, then what could it be? There was old Styles's statement about the something which used to pace the room at times when the owner was absent. Could it be a woman? Smith rather inclined to the view. If so, it would mean disgrace and expulsion to Bellingham if it were discovered by the authorities, so that his anxiety and falsehoods might be accounted for. And yet it was inconceivable that an undergraduate could keep a woman in his rooms without being instantly detected. Be the explanation what it might, there was something ugly about it, and Smith determined, as he turned to his books, to discourage all further attempts at intimacy on the part of his soft-spoken and ill-favoured neighbour.

But his work was destined to interruption that night. He had hardly caught tip the broken threads when a firm, heavy footfall came three steps at a time from below, and Hastie, in blazer and flannels, burst into the room.

"Still at it!" said he, plumping down into his wonted armchair. "What a chap you are to stew! I believe an earthquake might come and knock Oxford into a cocked hat, and you would sit perfectly placid with your books among the rains. However, I won't bore you long. Three whiffs of baccy, and I am off."

"What's the news, then?" asked Smith, cramming a plug of bird's-eye into his briar with his forefinger.

"Nothing very much. Wilson made 70 for the freshmen against the eleven. They say that they will play him instead of

Buddicomb, for Buddicomb is clean off colour. He used to be able to bowl a little, but it's nothing but half-vollies and long hops now."

"Medium right," suggested Smith, with the intense gravity which comes upon a 'varsity man when he speaks of athletics.

"Inclining to fast, with a work from leg. Comes with the arm about three inches or so. He used to be nasty on a wet wicket. Oh, by-the-way, have you heard about Long Norton?"

"What's that?"

"He's been attacked."

"Attacked?"

"Yes, just as he was turning out of the High Street, and within a hundred yards of the gate of Old's."

"But who——"

"Ah, that's the rub! If you said 'what,' you would be more grammatical. Norton swears that it was not human, and, indeed, from the scratches on his throat, I should be inclined to agree with him."

"What, then? Have we come down to spooks?"

Abercrombie Smith puffed his scientific contempt.

"Well, no; I don't think that is quite the idea, either. I am inclined to think that if any showman has lost a great ape lately, and the brute is in these parts, a jury would find a true bill against it. Norton passes that way every night, you know, about the same hour. There's a tree that hangs low over the path—the big elm from Rainy's garden. Norton thinks the thing dropped on him out of the tree. Anyhow, he was nearly strangled by two arms, which, he says, were as strong and as thin as steel bands. He saw nothing; only those beastly arms that tightened and tightened on him. He yelled his head nearly off, and a couple of chaps came running, and the thing went over the wall like a cat. He never got a fair sight of it the whole time. It gave Norton a shake up, I can tell you. I tell him it has been as good as a change at the sea-side for him."

"A garrotter, most likely," said Smith.

"Very possibly. Norton says not; but we don't mind what he says. The garrotter had long nails, and was pretty smart at swinging himself over walls. By-the-way, your beautiful neighbour would be pleased if he heard about it. He had a grudge against Norton, and he's not a man, from what I know of him, to forget his little debts. But hallo, old chap, what have you got in your noddle?"

"Nothing," Smith answered curtly.

He had started in his chair, and the look had flashed over his face which comes upon a man who is struck suddenly by some unpleasant idea.

"You looked as if something I had said had taken you on the raw. By-the-way, you have made the acquaintance of Master B. since I looked in last, have you not? Young Monkhouse Lee told me something to that effect."

"Yes; I know him slightly. He has been up here once or twice."

"Well, you're big enough and ugly enough to take care of yourself. He's not what I should call exactly a healthy sort of Johnny, though, no doubt, he's very clever, and all that. But you'll soon find out for yourself. Lee is all right; he's a very decent little fellow. Well, so long, old chap! I row Mullins for the Vice-Chancellor's pot on Wednesday week, so mind you come down, in case I don't see you before."

Bovine Smith laid down his pipe and turned stolidly to his books once more. But with all the will in the world, he found it very hard to keep his mind upon his work. It would slip away to brood upon the man beneath him, and upon the little mystery which hung round his chambers. Then his thoughts turned to this singular attack of which Hastie had spoken, and to the grudge which Bellingham was said to owe the object of it. The two ideas would persist in rising together in his mind, as though there were some close and intimate connection between them. And yet the suspicion was so dim and vague that it could not be put down in words.

"Confound the chap!" cried Smith, as he shied his book on pathology across the room. "He has spoiled my night's reading, and that's reason enough, if there were no other, why I should steer clear of him in the future."

For ten days the medical student confined himself so closely to his studies that he neither saw nor heard anything of either of the men beneath him. At the hours when Bellingham had been accustomed to visit him, he took care to sport his oak, and though he more than once heard a knocking at his outer door, he resolutely refused to answer it. One afternoon, however, he was descending the stairs when, just as he was passing it, Bellingham's door flew open, and young Monkhouse Lee came out with his eyes sparkling and a dark flush of anger upon his olive cheeks. Close at his heels followed Bellingham, his fat, unhealthy face all quivering with malignant passion.

"You fool!" he hissed. "You'll be sorry."

"Very likely," cried the other. "Mind what I say. It's off! I won't hear of it!"

"You've promised, anyhow."

"Oh, I'll keep that! I won't speak. But I'd rather little Eva was in her grave. Once for all, it's off. She'll do what I say. We don't want to see you again."

So much Smith could not avoid hearing, but he hurried on, for he had no wish to be involved in their dispute. There had been a serious breach between them, that was clear enough, and Lee was going to cause the engagement with his sister to be broken off. Smith thought of Hastie's comparison of the toad and the dove, and was glad to think that the matter was at an end. Bellingham's face when he was in a passion was not pleasant to look upon. He was not a man to whom an innocent girl could be trusted for life. As he walked, Smith wondered languidly what could have caused the quarrel, and what the promise might be which Bellingham had been so anxious that Monkhouse Lee should keep.

It was the day of the sculling match between Hastie and Mullins, and a stream of men were making their way down to the banks of the Isis. A May sun was shining brightly, and the yellow path was barred with the black shadows of the tall elm-trees. On either side the grey colleges lay back from the road, the hoary old mothers of minds looking out from their high, mullioned windows at the tide of young life which swept so merrily past them. Black-clad tutors, prim officials, pale reading men, brown-faced, straw-hatted young athletes in white sweaters or many-coloured blazers, all were hurrying towards the blue winding river which curves through the Oxford meadows.

Abercrombie Smith, with the intuition of an old oarsman, chose his position at the point where he knew that the struggle, if there were a struggle, would come. Far off he heard the hum which announced the start, the gathering roar of the approach, the thunder of running feet, and the shouts of the men in the boats beneath him. A spray of half-clad, deep-breathing runners shot past him, and craning over their shoulders, he saw Hastie pulling a steady thirty-six, while his opponent, with a jerky forty, was a good boat's length behind him. Smith gave a cheer for his friend, and pulling out his watch, was starting off again for his chambers, when he felt a touch upon his shoulder, and found that young Monkhouse Lee was beside him.

"I saw you there," he said, in a timid, deprecating way. "I wanted to speak to you, if you could spare me a half-hour. This cottage is mine. I share it with Harrington of King's. Come in and have a cup of tea."

"I must be back presently," said Smith. "I am hard on the grind at present. But I'll come in for a few minutes with pleasure. I wouldn't have come out only Hastie is a friend of mine."

"So he is of mine. Hasn't he a beautiful style? Mullins wasn't in it. But come into the cottage. It's a little den of a place, but it is pleasant to work in during the summer months."

It was a small, square, white building, with green doors and shutters, and a rustic trellis-work porch, standing back some fifty yards from the river's bank. Inside, the main room was roughly fitted up as a study—deal table, unpainted shelves with books, and a few cheap oleographs upon the wall. A kettle sang upon a spirit-stove, and there were tea things upon a tray on the table.

"Try that chair and have a cigarette," said Lee. "Let me pour you out a cup of tea. It's so good of you to come in, for I know that your time is a good deal taken up. I wanted to say to you that, if I were you, I should change my rooms at once."

"Eh?"

Smith sat staring with a lighted match in one hand and his unlit cigarette in the other.

"Yes; it must seem very extraordinary, and the worst of it is that I cannot give my reasons, for I am under a solemn promise—a very solemn promise. But I may go so far as to say that I don't think Bellingham is a very safe man to live near. I intend to camp out here as much as I can for a time."

"Not safe! What do you mean?"

"Ah, that's what I mustn't say. But do take my advice, and move your rooms. We had a grand row to-day. You must have heard us, for you came down the stairs."

"I saw that you had fallen out."

"He's a horrible chap, Smith. That is the only word for him. I have had doubts about him ever since that night when he fainted—you remember, when you came down. I taxed him to-day, and he told me things that made my hair rise, and wanted me to stand in with him. I'm not strait-laced, but I am a clergyman's son, you know, and I think there are some things which are quite beyond the pale. I only thank God that I found him out before it was too late, for he was to have married into my family."

"This is all very fine, Lee," said Abercrombie Smith curtly. "But either you are saying a great deal too much or a great deal too little."

"I give you a warning."

"If there is real reason for warning, no promise can bind you. If I see a rascal about to blow a place up with dynamite no pledge will stand in my way of preventing him."

"Ah, but I cannot prevent him, and I can do nothing but warn you."

"Without saying what you warn me against."

"Against Bellingham."

"But that is childish. Why should I fear him, or any man?"

"I can't tell you. I can only entreat you to change your rooms. You are in danger where you are. I don't even say that Bellingham would wish to injure you. But it might happen, for he is a dangerous neighbour just now."

138

"Perhaps I know more than you think," said Smith, looking keenly at the young man's boyish, earnest face. "Suppose I tell you that some one else shares Bellingham's rooms."

Monkhouse Lee sprang from his chair in uncontrollable excitement.

"You know, then?" he gasped.

"A woman."

Lee dropped back again with a groan.

"My lips are sealed," he said. "I must not speak."

"Well, anyhow," said Smith, rising, "it is not likely that I should allow myself to be frightened out of rooms which suit me very nicely. It would be a little too feeble for me to move out all my goods and chattels because you say that Bellingham might in some unexplained way do me an injury. I think that I'll just take my chance, and stay where I am, and as I see that it's nearly five o'clock, I must ask you to excuse me."

He bade the young student *adieu* in a few curt words, and made his way homeward through the sweet spring evening feeling half-ruffled, half-amused, as any other strong, unimaginative man might who has been menaced by a vague and shadowy danger.

There was one little indulgence which Abercrombie Smith always allowed himself, however closely his work might press upon him. Twice a week, on the Tuesday and the Friday, it was his invariable custom to walk over to Farlingford, the residence of Dr. Plumptree Peterson, situated about a mile and a half out of Oxford. Peterson had been a close friend of Smith's elder brother Francis, and as he was a bachelor, fairly well-to-do, with a good cellar and a better library, his house was a pleasant goal for a man who was in need of a brisk walk. Twice a week, then, the medical student would swing out there along the dark country roads, and spend a pleasant hour in Peterson's comfortable study, discussing, over a glass of old port, the gossip of the 'varsity or the latest developments of medicine or of surgery.

On the day which followed his interview with Monkhouse Lee, Smith shut up his books at a quarter past eight, the hour when he usually started for his friend's house. As he was leaving his room, however, his eyes chanced to fall upon one of the books which Bellingham had lent him, and his conscience pricked him for not having returned it. However repellent the man might be, he should not be treated with discourtesy. Taking the book, he walked downstairs and knocked at his neighbour's door. There was no answer; but on turning the handle he found that it was unlocked. Pleased at the thought of avoiding an interview, he stepped inside, and placed the book with his card upon the table.

The lamp was turned half down, but Smith could see the details of the room plainly enough. It was all much as he had seen it before—the frieze, the animal-headed gods, the banging crocodile, and the table littered over with papers and dried leaves. The mummy case stood upright against the wall, but the mummy itself was missing. There was no sign of any second occupant of the room, and he felt as he withdrew that he had probably done Bellingham an injustice. Had he a guilty secret to preserve, he would hardly leave his door open so that all the world might enter.

The spiral stair was as black as pitch, and Smith was slowly making his way down its irregular steps, when he was suddenly conscious that something had passed him in the darkness. There was a faint sound, a whiff of air, a light brushing past his elbow, but so slight that he could scarcely be certain of it. He stopped and listened, but the wind was rustling among the ivy outside, and he could hear nothing else.

"Is that you, Styles?" he shouted.

There was no answer, and all was still behind him. It must have been a sudden gust of air, for there were crannies and cracks in the old turret. And yet he could almost have sworn that he heard a footfall by his very side. He had emerged into the quadrangle, still turning the matter over in his head, when a man came running swiftly across the smooth-cropped lawn.

"Is that you, Smith?"

"Hullo, Hastie!"

"For God's sake come at once! Young Lee is drowned! Here's Harrington of King's with the news. The doctor is out. You'll do, but come along at once. There may be life in him."

140

"Have you brandy?"

"No."

"I'll bring some. There's a flask on my table."

Smith bounded up the stairs, taking three at a time, seized the flask, and was rushing down with it, when, as he passed Bellingham's room, his eyes fell upon something which left him gasping and staring upon the landing.

The door, which he had closed behind him, was now open, and right in front of him, with the lamp-light shining upon it, was the mummy case. Three minutes ago it had been empty. He could swear to that. Now it framed the lank body of its horrible occupant, who stood, grim and stark, with his black shrivelled face towards the door. The form was lifeless and inert, but it seemed to Smith as he gazed that there still lingered a lurid spark of vitality, some faint sign of consciousness in the little eyes which lurked in the depths of the hollow sockets. So astounded and shaken was he that he had forgotten his errand, and was still staring at the lean, sunken figure when the voice of his friend below recalled him to himself.

"Come on, Smith!" he shouted. "It's life and death, you know. Hurry up! Now, then," he added, as the medical student reappeared, "let us do a sprint. It is well under a mile, and we should do it in five minutes. A human life is better worth running for than a pot."

Neck and neck they dashed through the darkness, and did not pull up until, panting and spent, they had reached the little cottage by the river. Young Lee, limp and dripping like a broken water-plant, was stretched upon the sofa, the green scum of the river upon his black hair, and a fringe of white foam upon his leaden-hued lips. Beside him knelt his fellow-student Harrington, endeavouring to chafe some warmth back into his rigid limbs.

"I think there's life in him," said Smith, with his hand to the lad's side. "Put your watch glass to his lips. Yes, there's dimming on it. You take one arm, Hastie. Now work it as I do, and we'll soon pull him round."

For ten minutes they worked in silence, inflating and depressing the chest of the unconscious man. At the end of that time a shiver ran through his body, his lips trembled, and he opened his eyes. The three students burst out into an irrepressible cheer.

"Wake up, old chap. You've frightened us quite enough."

"Have some brandy. Take a sip from the flask."

"He's all right now," said his companion Harrington. "Heavens, what a fright I got! I was reading here, and he had gone for a stroll as far as the river, when I heard a scream and a splash. Out I ran, and by the time that I could find him and fish him out, all life seemed to have gone. Then Simpson couldn't get a doctor, for he has a game-leg, and I had to run, and I don't know what I'd have done without you fellows. That's right, old chap. Sit up."

Monkhouse Lee had raised himself on his hands, and looked wildly about him.

"What's up?" he asked. "I've been in the water. Ah, yes; I remember."

A look of fear came into his eyes, and he sank his face into his hands.

"How did you fall in?"

"I didn't fall in."

"How, then?"

"I was thrown in. I was standing by the bank, and something from behind picked me up like a feather and hurled me in. I heard nothing, and I saw nothing. But I know what it was, for all that."

"And so do I," whispered Smith.

Lee looked up with a quick glance of surprise. "You've learned, then!" he said. "You remember the advice I gave you?"

"Yes, and I begin to think that I shall take it."

"I don't know what the deuce you fellows are talking about," said Hastie, "but I think, if I were you, Harrington, I should get Lee to bed at once. It will be time enough to discuss the why and the wherefore when he is a little stronger. I think, Smith, you and I can leave him alone now. I am walking back to college; if you are coming in that direction, we can have a chat."

But it was little chat that they had upon their homeward path. Smith's mind was too full of the incidents of the evening, the absence of the mummy from his neighbour's rooms, the step that passed him on the stair, the reappearance—the extraordinary, inexplicable reappearance of the grisly thing—and then this attack upon Lee, corresponding so closely to the previous outrage upon another man against whom Bellingham bore a grudge. All this settled in his thoughts, together with the many little incidents which had previously turned him against his neighbour, and the singular circumstances under which he was first called in to him. What had been a dim suspicion, a vague, fantastic conjecture, had suddenly taken form, and stood out in his mind as a grim fact, a thing not to be denied. And yet, how monstrous it was! how unheard of! how entirely beyond all bounds of human experience. An impartial judge, or even the friend who walked by his side, would simply tell him that his eyes had deceived him, that the mummy had been there all the time, that young Lee had tumbled into the river as any other man tumbles into a river, and that a blue pill was the best thing for a disordered liver. He felt that he would have said as much if the positions had been reversed. And yet he could swear that Bellingham was a murderer at heart, and that he wielded a weapon such as no man had ever used in all the grim history of crime.

Hastie had branched off to his rooms with a few crisp and emphatic comments upon his friend's unsociability, and Abercrombie Smith crossed the quadrangle to his corner turret with a strong feeling of repulsion for his chambers and their associations. He would take Lee's advice, and move his quarters as soon as possible, for how could a man study when his ear was ever straining for every murmur or footstep in the room below? He observed, as he crossed over the lawn, that the light was still shining in Bellingham's window, and as he passed up the staircase the door opened, and the man himself looked out at him. With his fat, evil face he was like some bloated spider fresh from the weaving of his poisonous web.

"Good-evening," said he. "Won't you come in?"

"No," cried Smith, fiercely.

"No? You are busy as ever? I wanted to ask you about Lee. I was sorry to hear that there was a rumour that something was amiss with him."

His features were grave, but there was the gleam of a hidden laugh in his eyes as he spoke. Smith saw it, and he could have knocked him down for it.

"You'll be sorrier still to hear that Monkhouse Lee is doing very well, and is out of all danger," he answered. "Your hellish tricks have not come off this time. Oh, you needn't try to brazen it out. I know all about it."

Bellingham took a step back from the angry student, and half-closed the door as if to protect himself.

"You are mad," he said. "What do you mean? Do you assert that I had anything to do with Lee's accident?"

"Yes," thundered Smith. "You and that bag of bones behind you; you worked it between you. I tell you what it is, Master B., they have given up burning folk like you, but we still keep a hangman, and, by George! if any man in this college meets his death while you are here, I'll have you up, and if you don't swing for it, it won't be my fault. You'll find that your filthy Egyptian tricks won't answer in England."

"You're a raving lunatic," said Bellingham.

"All right. You just remember what I say, for you'll find that I'll be better than my word."

The door slammed, and Smith went fuming up to his chamber, where he locked the door upon the inside, and spent half the night in smoking his old briar and brooding over the strange events of the evening.

Next morning Abercrombie Smith heard nothing of his neighbour, but Harrington called upon him in the afternoon to say that Lee was almost himself again. All day Smith stuck fast to his work, but in the evening he determined to pay the visit to his friend Dr. Peterson upon which he had started upon the night before. A good walk and a friendly chat would be welcome to his jangled nerves.

Bellingham's door was shut as he passed, but glancing back when he was some distance from the turret, he saw his neighbour's head at the window outlined against the lamp-light, his face pressed apparently against the glass as he gazed out into the darkness. It was a blessing to be away from all contact with

144

him, but if for a few hours, and Smith stepped out briskly, and breathed the soft spring air into his lungs. The half-moon lay in the west between two Gothic pinnacles, and threw upon the silvered street a dark tracery from the stone-work above. There was a brisk breeze, and light, fleecy clouds drifted swiftly across the sky. Old's was on the very border of the town, and in five minutes Smith found himself beyond the houses and between the hedges of a May-scented Oxfordshire lane.

It was a lonely and little frequented road which led to his friend's house. Early as it was, Smith did not meet a single soul upon his way. He walked briskly along until he came to the avenue gate, which opened into the long gravel drive leading up to Farlingford. In front of him he could see the cosy red light of the windows glimmering through the foliage. He stood with his hand upon the iron latch of the swinging gate, and he glanced back at the road along which he had come. Something was coming swiftly down it.

It moved in the shadow of the hedge, silently and furtively, a dark, crouching figure, dimly visible against the black background. Even as he gazed back at it, it had lessened its distance by twenty paces, and was fast closing upon him. Out of the darkness he had a glimpse of a scraggy neck, and of two eyes that will ever haunt him in his dreams. He turned, and with a cry of terror he ran for his life up the avenue. There were the red lights, the signals of safety, almost within a stone's throw of him. He was a famous runner, but never had he run as he ran that night.

The heavy gate had swung into place behind him, but he heard it dash open again before his pursuer. As he rushed madly and wildly through the night, he could hear a swift, dry patter behind him, and could see, as he threw back a glance, that this horror was bounding like a tiger at his heels, with blazing eyes and one stringy arm out-thrown. Thank God, the door was ajar. He could see the thin bar of light which shot from the lamp in the hall. Nearer yet sounded the clatter from behind. He heard a hoarse gurgling at his very shoulder. With a shriek he flung himself against the door, slammed and bolted it behind him, and sank half-fainting on to the hall chair.

"My goodness, Smith, what's the matter?" asked Peterson, appearing at the door of his study.

"Give me some brandy!" Peterson disappeared, and came rushing out again with a glass and a decanter.

"You need it," he said, as his visitor drank off what he poured out for him. "Why, man, you are as white as a cheese."

Smith laid down his glass, rose up, and took a deep breath.

"I am my own man again now," said he. "I was never so unmanned before. But, with your leave, Peterson, I will sleep here to-night, for I don't think I could face that road again except by daylight. It's weak, I know, but I can't help it."

Peterson looked at his visitor with a very questioning eye.

"Of course you shall sleep here if you wish. I'll tell Mrs. Burney to make up the spare bed. Where are you off to now?"

"Come up with me to the window that overlooks the door. I want you to see what I have seen."

They went up to the window of the upper hall whence they could look down upon the approach to the house. The drive and the fields on either side lay quiet and still, bathed in the peaceful moonlight.

"Well, really, Smith," remarked Peterson, "it is well that I know you to be an abstemious man. What in the world can have frightened you?"

"I'll tell you presently. But where can it have gone? Ah, now look, look! See the curve of the road just beyond your gate."

"Yes, I see; you needn't pinch my arm off. I saw someone pass. I should say a man, rather thin, apparently, and tall, very tall. But what of him? And what of yourself? You are still shaking like an aspen leaf."

"I have been within hand-grip of the devil, that's all. But come down to your study, and I shall tell you the whole story."

He did so. Under the cheery lamplight, with a glass of wine on the table beside him, and the portly form and florid face of his friend in front, he narrated, in their order, all the events, great and small, which had formed so singular a chain, from the night on which he had found Bellingham fainting in front of the mummy case until his horrid experience of an hour ago.

146

"There now," he said as he concluded, "that's the whole black business. It is monstrous and incredible, but it is true."

Dr. Plumptree Peterson sat for some time in silence with a very puzzled expression upon his face.

"I never heard of such a thing in my life, never!" he said at last. "You have told me the facts. Now tell me your inferences."

"You can draw your own."

"But I should like to hear yours. You have thought over the matter, and I have not."

"Well, it must be a little vague in detail, but the main points seem to me to be clear enough. This fellow Bellingham, in his Eastern studies, has got hold of some infernal secret by which a mummy—or possibly only this particular mummy—can be temporarily brought to life. He was trying this disgusting business on the night when he fainted. No doubt the sight of the creature moving had shaken his nerve, even though he had expected it. You remember that almost the first words he said were to call out upon himself as a fool. Well, he got more hardened afterwards, and carried the matter through without fainting. The vitality which he could put into it was evidently only a passing thing, for I have seen it continually in its case as dead as this table. He has some elaborate process, I fancy, by which he brings the thing to pass. Having done it, he naturally bethought him that he might use the creature as an agent. It has intelligence and it has strength. For some purpose he took Lee into his confidence; but Lee, like a decent Christian, would have nothing to do with such a business. Then they had a row, and Lee vowed that he would tell his sister of Bellingham's true character. Bellingham's game was to prevent him, and he nearly managed it, by setting this creature of his on his track. He had already tried its powers upon another man—Norton—towards whom he had a grudge. It is the merest chance that he has not two murders upon his soul. Then, when I taxed him with the matter, he had the strongest reasons for wishing to get me out of the way before I could convey my knowledge to anyone else. He got his chance when I went out, for he knew my habits, and where I was bound for. I have had a narrow shave, Peterson, and it is mere luck you didn't find me on your doorstep in the morning. I'm not a nervous man as a rule, and I never thought to have the fear of death put upon me as it was to-night."

"My dear boy, you take the matter too seriously," said his companion. "Your nerves are out of order with your work, and you make too much of it. How could such a thing as this stride about the streets of Oxford, even at night, without being seen?"

"It has been seen. There is quite a scare in the town about an escaped ape, as they imagine the creature to be. It is the talk of the place."

"Well, it's a striking chain of events. And yet, my dear fellow, you must allow that each incident in itself is capable of a more natural explanation."

"What! even my adventure of to-night?"

"Certainly. You come out with your nerves all unstrung, and your head full of this theory of yours. Some gaunt, half-famished tramp steals after you, and seeing you run, is emboldened to pursue you. Your fears and imagination do the rest."

"It won't do, Peterson; it won't do."

"And again, in the instance of your finding the mummy case empty, and then a few moments later with an occupant, you know that it was lamplight, that the lamp was half turned down, and that you had no special reason to look hard at the case. It is quite possible that you may have overlooked the creature in the first instance."

"No, no; it is out of the question."

"And then Lee may have fallen into the river, and Norton been garrotted. It is certainly a formidable indictment that you have against Bellingham; but if you were to place it before a police magistrate, he would simply laugh in your face."

"I know he would. That is why I mean to take the matter into my own hands."

"Eh?"

"Yes; I feel that a public duty rests upon me, and, besides, I must do it for my own safety, unless I choose to allow myself to be hunted by this beast out of the college, and that would be a little too feeble. I have quite made up my mind what I shall do. And first of all, may I use your paper and pens for an hour?"

"Most certainly. You will find all that you want upon that side table."

Abercrombie Smith sat down before a sheet of foolscap, and for an hour, and then for a second hour his pen travelled swiftly over it. Page after page was finished and tossed aside while his friend leaned back in his arm-chair, looking across at him with patient curiosity. At last, with an exclamation of satisfaction, Smith sprang to his feet, gathered his papers up into order, and laid the last one upon Peterson's desk.

"Kindly sign this as a witness," he said.

"A witness? Of what?"

"Of my signature, and of the date. The date is the most important. Why, Peterson, my life might hang upon it."

"My dear Smith, you are talking wildly. Let me beg you to go to bed."

"On the contrary, I never spoke so deliberately in my life. And I will promise to go to bed the moment you have signed it."

"But what is it?"

"It is a statement of all that I have been telling you to-night. I wish you to witness it."

"Certainly," said Peterson, signing his name under that of his companion. "There you are! But what is the idea?"

"You will kindly retain it, and produce it in case I am arrested."

"Arrested? For what?"

"For murder. It is quite on the cards. I wish to be ready for every event. There is only one course open to me, and I am determined to take it."

"For Heaven's sake, don't do anything rash!"

"Believe me, it would be far more rash to adopt any other course. I hope that we won't need to bother you, but it will ease my mind to know that you have this statement of my motives. And now I am ready to take your advice and to go to roost, for I want to be at my best in the morning."

Abercrombie Smith was not an entirely pleasant man to have as an enemy. Slow and easy tempered, he was formidable when driven to action. He brought to every purpose in life the same deliberate resoluteness which had distinguished him as a scientific student. He had laid his studies aside for a day, but he intended that the day should not be wasted. Not a word did he say to his host as to his plans, but by nine o'clock he was well on his way to Oxford.

In the High Street he stopped at Clifford's, the gun-maker's, and bought a heavy revolver, with a box of central-fire cartridges. Six of them he slipped into the chambers, and half-cocking the weapon, placed it in the pocket of his coat. He then made his way to Hastie's rooms, where the big oarsman was lounging over his breakfast, with the Sporting Times propped up against the coffeepot.

"Hullo! What's up?" he asked. "Have some coffee?"

"No, thank you. I want you to come with me, Hastie, and do what I ask you."

"Certainly, my boy."

"And bring a heavy stick with you."

"Hullo!" Hastie stared. "Here's a hunting-crop that would fell an ox."

"One other thing. You have a box of amputating knives. Give me the longest of them."

"There you are. You seem to be fairly on the war trail. Anything else?"

"No; that will do." Smith placed the knife inside his coat, and led the way to the quadrangle. "We are neither of us chickens, Hastie," said he. "I think I can do this job alone, but I take you as a precaution. I am going to have a little talk with Bellingham. If I have only him to deal with, I won't, of course, need you. If I shout, however, up you come, and lam out with your whip as hard as you can lick. Do you understand?"

"All right. I'll come if I hear you bellow."

"Stay here, then. It may be a little time, but don't budge until I come down."

"I'm a fixture."

Smith ascended the stairs, opened Bellingham's door and stepped in. Bellingham was seated behind his table, writing. Beside him, among his litter of strange possessions, towered the mummy case, with its sale number 249 still stuck upon its front, and its hideous occupant stiff and stark within it. Smith looked very deliberately round him, closed the door, locked it, took the key from the inside, and then stepping across to the fireplace, struck a match and set the fire alight. Bellingham sat staring, with amazement and rage upon his bloated face.

"Well, really now, you make yourself at home," he gasped.

Smith sat himself deliberately down, placing his watch upon the table, drew out his pistol, cocked it, and laid it in his lap. Then he took the long amputating knife from his bosom, and threw it down in front of Bellingham.

"Now, then," said he, "just get to work and cut up that mummy."

"Oh, is that it?" said Bellingham with a sneer.

"Yes, that is it. They tell me that the law can't touch you. But I have a law that will set matters straight. If in five minutes you have not set to work, I swear by the God who made me that I will put a bullet through your brain!"

"You would murder me?"

Bellingham had half risen, and his face was the colour of putty.

"Yes."

"And for what?"

"To stop your mischief. One minute has gone."

"But what have I done?"

"I know and you know."

"This is mere bullying."

"Two minutes are gone."

"But you must give reasons. You are a madman—a dangerous madman. Why should I destroy my own property? It is a valuable mummy."

"You must cut it up, and you must burn it."

"I will do no such thing."

"Four minutes are gone."

Smith took up the pistol and he looked towards Bellingham with an inexorable face. As the second-hand stole round, he raised his hand, and the finger twitched upon the trigger.

"There! there! I'll do it!" screamed Bellingham.

In frantic haste he caught up the knife and hacked at the

figure of the mummy, ever glancing round to see the eye and the weapon of his terrible visitor bent upon him. The creature crackled and snapped under every stab of the keen blade. A thick yellow dust rose up from it. Spices and dried essences rained down upon the floor. Suddenly, with a rending crack, its backbone snapped asunder, and it fell, a brown heap of sprawling limbs, upon the floor.

"Now into the fire!" said Smith.

The flames leaped and roared as the dried and tinder-like debris was piled upon it. The little room was like the stoke-hole of a steamer and the sweat ran down the faces of the two men; but still the one stooped and worked, while the other sat watching him with a set face. A thick, fat smoke oozed out from the fire, and a heavy smell of burned rosin and singed hair filled the air. In a quarter of an hour a few charred and brittle sticks were all that was left of Lot No. 249.

"Perhaps that will satisfy you," snarled Bellingham, with hate and fear in his little grey eyes as he glanced back at his tormenter.

"No; I must make a clean sweep of all your materials. We must have no more devil's tricks. In with all these leaves! They may have something to do with it."

"And what now?" asked Bellingham, when the leaves also had been added to the blaze.

"Now the roll of papyrus which you had on the table that night. It is in that drawer, I think."

"No, no," shouted Bellingham. "Don't burn that! Why, man, you don't know what you do. It is unique; it contains wisdom which is nowhere else to be found."

"Out with it!"

"But look here, Smith, you can't really mean it. I'll share the knowledge with you. I'll teach you all that is in it. Or, stay, let me only copy it before you burn it!"

Smith stepped forward and turned the key in the drawer. Taking out the yellow, curled roll of paper, he threw it into the fire, and pressed it down with his heel. Bellingham screamed, and grabbed at it; but Smith pushed him back, and stood over it until it was reduced to a formless grey ash.

"Now, Master B.," said he, "I think I have pretty well drawn your teeth. You'll hear from me again, if you return to your old tricks. And now good-morning, for I must go back to my studies."

And such is the narrative of Abercrombie Smith as to the singular events which occurred in Old College, Oxford, in the spring of '84. As Bellingham left the university immediately afterwards, and was last heard of in the Soudan, there is no one who can contradict his statement. But the wisdom of men is small, and the ways of nature are strange, and who shall put a bound to the dark things which may be found by those who seek for them?

John Barrington Cowles

It might seem rash of me to say that I ascribe the death of my poor friend, John Barrington Cowles, to any preternatural agency. I am aware that in the present state of public feeling a chain of evidence would require to be strong indeed before the possibility of such a conclusion could be admitted.

I shall therefore merely state the circumstances which led up to this sad event as concisely and as plainly as I can, and leave every reader to draw his own deductions. Perhaps there may be some one who can throw light upon what is dark to me.

I first met Barrington Cowles when I went up to Edinburgh University to take out medical classes there. My landlady in Northumberland Street had a large house, and, being a widow without children, she gained a livelihood by providing accommodation for several students.

Barrington Cowles happened to have taken a bedroom upon the same floor as mine, and when we came to know each other better we shared a small sitting-room, in which we took our meals. In this manner we originated a friendship which was unmarred by the slightest disagreement up to the day of his death.

Cowles' father was the colonel of a Sikh regiment and had remained in India for many years. He allowed his son a handsome income, but seldom gave any other sign of parental affection—writing irregularly and briefly.

My friend, who had himself been born in India, and whose whole disposition was an ardent tropical one, was much hurt by this neglect. His mother was dead, and he had no other relation in the world to supply the blank.

Thus he came in time to concentrate all his affection upon me, and to confide in me in a manner which is rare among men. Even when a stronger and deeper passion came upon him, it never infringed upon the old tenderness between us.

Cowles was a tall, slim young fellow, with an olive, Velasquez-like face, and dark, tender eyes. I have seldom seen a man who was more likely to excite a woman's interest, or to captivate her imagination. His expression was, as a rule, dreamy, and even languid; but if in conversation a subject arose which interested him he would be all animation in a moment. On such occasions his colour would heighten, his eyes gleam, and he could speak with an eloquence which would carry his audience with him.

In spite of these natural advantages he led a solitary life, avoiding female society, and reading with great diligence. He was one of the foremost men of his year, taking the senior medal for anatomy, and the Neil Arnott prize for physics.

How well I can recollect the first time we met her! Often and often I have recalled the circumstances, and tried to remember what the exact impression was which she produced on my mind at the time.

After we came to know her my judgment was warped, so that I am curious to recollect what my unbiased instincts were. It is hard, however, to eliminate the feelings which reason or prejudice afterwards raised in me.

It was at the opening of the Royal Scottish Academy in the spring of 1879. My poor friend was passionately attached to art in every form, and a pleasing chord in music or a delicate effect upon canvas would give exquisite pleasure to his highly-strung nature. We had gone together to see the pictures, and were standing in the grand central salon, when I noticed an extremely beautiful woman standing at the other side of the room. In my whole life I have never seen such a classically perfect countenance. It was the real Greek type—the forehead broad, very low, and as white as marble, with a cloudlet of delicate locks wreathing round it, the nose straight and clean cut, the lips inclined to thinness, the chin and lower jaw beautifully rounded off, and yet sufficiently developed to promise unusual strength of character.

But those eyes—those wonderful eyes! If I could but give some faint idea of their varying moods, their steely hardness, their feminine softness, their power of command, their penetrating intensity suddenly melting away into an expression of womanly weakness—but I am speaking now of future impressions!

There was a tall, yellow-haired young man with this lady, whom I at once recognised as a law student with whom I had a slight acquaintance.

Archibald Reeves—for that was his name—was a dashing, handsome young fellow, and had at one time been a ringleader in every university escapade; but of late I had seen little of him, and the report was that he was engaged to be married. His companion was, then, I presumed, his fiancée. I seated myself upon the velvet settee in the centre of the room, and furtively watched the couple from behind my catalogue.

The more I looked at her the more her beauty grew upon me. She was somewhat short in stature, it is true; but her figure was perfection, and she bore herself in such a fashion that it was only by actual comparison that one would have known her to be under the medium height.

As I kept my eyes upon them, Reeves was called away for some reason, and the young lady was left alone. Turning her back to the pictures, she passed the time until the return of her escort in taking a deliberate survey of the company, without paying the least heed to the fact that a dozen pair of eyes, attracted by her elegance and beauty, were bent curiously upon her. With one of her hands holding the red silk cord which railed off the pictures, she stood languidly moving her eyes from face to face with as little self-consciousness as if she were looking at the canvas creatures behind her. Suddenly, as I watched her, I saw her gaze become fixed, and, as it were, intense. I followed the direction of her looks, wondering what could have attracted her so strongly.

John Barrington Cowles was standing before a picture—one,

I think, by Noel Paton—I know that the subject was a noble and ethereal one. His profile was turned towards us, and never have I seen him to such advantage. I have said that he was a strikingly handsome man, but at that moment he looked absolutely magnificent. It was evident that he had momentarily forgotten his surroundings, and that his whole soul was in sympathy with the picture before him. His eyes sparkled, and a dusky pink shone through his clear olive cheeks. She continued to watch him fixedly, with a look of interest upon her face, until he came out of his reverie with a start, and turned abruptly round, so that his gaze met hers. She glanced away at once, but his eyes remained fixed upon her for some moments. The picture was forgotten already, and his soul had come down to earth once more.

We caught sight of her once or twice before we left, and each time I noticed my friend look after her. He made no remark, however, until we got out into the open air, and were walking arm-in-arm along Princes Street.

"Did you notice that beautiful woman, in the dark dress, with the white fur?" he asked.

"Yes, I saw her," I answered.

"Do you know her?" he asked eagerly. "Have you any idea who she is?"

"I don't know her personally," I replied. "But I have no doubt I could find out all about her, for I believe she is engaged to young Archie Reeves, and he and I have a lot of mutual friends."

"Engaged!" ejaculated Cowles.

"Why, my dear boy," I said, laughing, "you don't mean to say you are so susceptible that the fact that a girl to whom you never spoke in your life is engaged is enough to upset you?"

"Well, not exactly to upset me," he answered, forcing a laugh. "But I don't mind telling you, Armitage, that I never was so taken by any one in my life. It wasn't the mere beauty of the face—though that was perfect enough—but it was the character and the intellect upon it. I hope, if she is engaged, that it is to some man who will be worthy of her."

"Why," I remarked, "you speak quite feelingly. It is a clear case of love at first sight, Jack. However, to put your perturbed

157

spirit at rest, I'll make a point of finding out all about her whenever I meet any fellow who is likely to know."

Barrington Cowles thanked me, and the conversation drifted off into other channels. For several days neither of us made any allusion to the subject, though my companion was perhaps a little more dreamy and distraught than usual. The incident had almost vanished from my remembrance, when one day young Brodie, who is a second cousin of mine, came up to me on the university steps with the face of a bearer of tidings.

"I say," he began, "you know Reeves, don't you?"

"Yes. What of him?"

"His engagement is off."

"Off!" I cried. "Why, I only learned the other day that it was on."

"Oh, yes—it's all off. His brother told me so. Deucedly mean of Reeves, you know, if he has backed out of it, for she was an uncommonly nice girl."

"I've seen her," I said; "but I don't know her name."

"She is a Miss Northcott, and lives with an old aunt of hers in Abercrombie Place. Nobody knows anything about her people, or where she comes from. Anyhow, she is about the most unlucky girl in the world, poor soul!"

"Why unlucky?"

"Well, you know, this was her second engagement," said young Brodie, who had a marvellous knack of knowing everything about everybody. "She was engaged to Prescott—William Prescott, who died. That was a very sad affair. The wedding day was fixed, and the whole thing looked as straight as a die when the smash came."

"What smash?" I asked, with some dim recollection of the circumstances.

"Why, Prescott's death. He came to Abercrombie Place one night, and stayed very late. No one knows exactly when he left, but about one in the morning a fellow who knew him met him walking rapidly in the direction of the Queen's Park. He bade him good night, but Prescott hurried on without heeding him, and that was the last time he was ever seen alive. Three days afterwards his body was found floating in St. Margaret's Loch, under St. Anthony's Chapel. No one could ever understand it, but of course the verdict brought it in as temporary insanity."

"It was very strange," I remarked.

"Yes, and deucedly rough on the poor girl," said Brodie. "Now that this other blow has come it will quite crush her. So gentle and ladylike she is too!"

"You know her personally, then!" I asked.

"Oh, yes, I know her. I have met her several times. I could easily manage that you should be introduced to her."

"Well," I answered, "it's not so much for my own sake as for a friend of mine. However, I don't suppose she will go out much for some little time after this. When she does I will take advantage of your offer."

We shook hands on this, and I thought no more of the matter for some time.

The next incident which I have to relate as bearing at all upon the question of Miss Northcott is an unpleasant one. Yet I must detail it as accurately as possible, since it may throw some light upon the sequel. One cold night, several months after the conversation with my second cousin which I have quoted above, I was walking down one of the lowest streets in the city on my way back from a case which I had been attending. It was very late, and I was picking my way among the dirty loungers who were clustering round the doors of a great gin-palace, when a man staggered out from among them, and held out his hand to me with a drunken leer. The gaslight fell full upon his face, and, to my intense astonishment, I recognised in the degraded creature before me my former acquaintance, young Archibald Reeves, who had once been famous as one of the most dressy and particular men in the whole college. I was so utterly surprised that for a moment I almost doubted the evidence of my own senses; but there was no mistaking those features, which, though bloated with drink, still retained something of their former comeliness. I was determined to rescue him, for one night at least, from the company into which he had fallen.

159

"Holloa, Reeves!" I said. "Come along with me. I'm going in your direction."

He muttered some incoherent apology for his condition, and took my arm. As I supported him towards his lodgings I could see that he was not only suffering from the effects of a recent debauch, but that a long course of intemperance had affected his nerves and his brain. His hand when I touched it was dry and feverish, and he started from every shadow which fell upon the pavement. He rambled in his speech, too, in a manner which suggested the delirium of disease rather than the talk of a drunkard.

When I got him to his lodgings I partially undressed him and laid him upon his bed. His pulse at this time was very high, and he was evidently extremely feverish. He seemed to have sunk into a doze; and I was about to steal out of the room to warn his landlady of his condition, when he started up and caught me by the sleeve of my coat.

"Don't go!" he cried. "I feel better when you are here. I am safe from her then."

"From her!" I said. "From whom?"

"Her! her!" he answered peevishly. "Ah! you don't know her. She is the devil! Beautiful—beautiful; but the devil!"

"You are feverish and excited," I said. "Try and get a little sleep. You will wake better."

"Sleep!" he groaned. "How am I to sleep when I see her sitting down yonder at the foot of the bed with her great eyes watching and watching hour after hour? I tell you it saps all the strength and manhood out of me. That's what makes me drink. God help me—I'm half drunk now!"

"You are very ill," I said, putting some vinegar to his temples; "and you are delirious. You don't know what you say."

"Yes, I do," he interrupted sharply, looking up at me. "I know very well what I say. I brought it upon myself. It is my own choice. But I couldn't—no, by heaven, I couldn't—accept the alternative. I couldn't keep my faith to her. It was more than man could do."

I sat by the side of the bed, holding one of his burning hands in mine, and wondering over his strange words. He lay still for some time, and then, raising his eyes to me, said in a most plaintive voice—

"Why did she not give me warning sooner? Why did she wait until I had learned to love her so?"

He repeated this question several times, rolling his feverish head from side to side, and then he dropped into a troubled sleep. I crept out of the room, and, having seen that he would be properly cared for, left the house. His words, however, rang in my ears for days afterwards, and assumed a deeper significance when taken with what was to come.

My friend, Barrington Cowles, had been away for his summer holidays, and I had heard nothing of him for several months. When the winter session came on, however, I received a telegram from him, asking me to secure the old rooms in Northumberland Street for him, and telling me the train by which he would arrive. I went down to meet him, and was delighted to find him looking wonderfully hearty and well.

"By the way," he said suddenly, that night, as we sat in our chairs by the fire, talking over the events of the holidays, "you have never congratulated me yet!"

"On what, my boy?" I asked.

"What! Do you mean to say you have not heard of my engagement?"

"Engagement! No!" I answered. "However, I am delighted to hear it, and congratulate you with all my heart."

"I wonder it didn't come to your ears," he said. "It was the queerest thing. You remember that girl whom we both admired so much at the Academy?"

"What!" I cried, with a vague feeling of apprehension at my heart. "You don't mean to say that you are engaged to her?"

"I thought you would be surprised," he answered. "When I was staying with an old aunt of mine in Peterhead, in Aberdeenshire, the Northcotts happened to come there on a visit, and as we had mutual friends we soon met. I found out that it was a false alarm about her being engaged, and then—well, you know what it is when you are thrown into the society of such a girl in a place like Peterhead. Not, mind you," he added, "that I consider I did a foolish or hasty thing. I have never regretted it for a moment. The more I know Kate the more I admire her and love her. However, you must be introduced to her, and then you will form your own opinion."

I expressed my pleasure at the prospect, and endeavoured to speak as lightly as I could to Cowles upon the subject, but I felt depressed and anxious at heart. The words of Reeves and the unhappy fate of young Prescott recurred to my recollection, and though I could assign no tangible reason for it, a vague, dim fear and distrust of the woman took possession of me. It may be that this was foolish prejudice and superstition upon my part, and that I involuntarily contorted her future doings and sayings to fit into some half-formed wild theory of my own. This has been suggested to me by others as an explanation of my narrative. They are welcome to their opinion if they can reconcile it with the facts which I have to tell.

I went round with my friend a few days afterwards to call upon Miss Northcott. I remember that, as we went down Abercrombie Place, our attention was attracted by the shrill yelping of a dog—which noise proved eventually to come from the house to which we were bound. We were shown upstairs, where I was introduced to old Mrs. Merton, Miss Northcott's aunt, and to the young lady herself. She looked as beautiful as ever, and I could not wonder at my friend's infatuation. Her face was a little more flushed than usual, and she held in her hand a heavy dog-whip, with which she had been chastising a small Scotch terrier, whose cries we had heard in the street. The poor brute was cringing up against the wall, whining piteously, and evidently completely cowed.

"So Kate," said my friend, after we had taken our seats, "you have been falling out with Carlo again."

"Only a very little quarrel this time," she said, smiling charmingly. "He is a dear, good old fellow, but he needs correction now and then." Then, turning to me, "We all do that, Mr. Armitage, don't we? What a capital thing if, instead of receiving a collective punishment at the end of our lives, we were to have one at once, as the dogs do, when we did anything wicked. It would make us more careful, wouldn't it?"

I acknowledged that it would.

"Supposing that every time a man misbehaved himself a gigantic hand were to seize him, and he were lashed with a whip until he fainted"—she clenched her white fingers as she spoke, and cut out viciously with the dog-whip—"it would do more to keep him good than any number of high-minded theories of morality."

"Why, Kate," said my friend, "you are quite savage to-day."

"No, Jack," she laughed. "I'm only propounding a theory for Mr. Armitage's consideration."

The two began to chat together about some Aberdeenshire reminiscence, and I had time to observe Mrs. Merton, who had remained silent during our short conversation. She was a very strange-looking old lady. What attracted attention most in her appearance was the utter want of colour which she exhibited. Her hair was snow-white, and her face extremely pale. Her lips were bloodless, and even her eyes were of such a light tinge of blue that they hardly relieved the general pallor. Her dress was a grey silk, which harmonised with her general appearance. She had a peculiar expression of countenance, which I was unable at the moment to refer to its proper cause.

She was working at some old-fashioned piece of ornamental needlework, and as she moved her arms her dress gave forth a dry, melancholy rustling, like the sound of leaves in the autumn. There was something mournful and depressing in the sight of her. I moved my chair a little nearer, and asked her how she liked Edinburgh, and whether she had been there long.

When I spoke to her she started and looked up at me with a scared look on her face. Then I saw in a moment what the expression was which I had observed there. It was one of fear— intense and overpowering fear. It was so marked that I could have staked my life on the woman before me having at some period of her life been subjected to some terrible experience or dreadful misfortune.

"Oh, yes, I like it," she said, in a soft, timid voice; "and we have been here long—that is, not very long. We move about a great deal." She spoke with hesitation, as if afraid of committing herself.

"You are a native of Scotland, I presume?" I said.

"No—that is, not entirely. We are not natives of any place. We are cosmopolitan, you know." She glanced round in the direction of Miss Northcott as she spoke, but the two were still chatting together near the window. Then she suddenly bent forward to me, with a look of intense earnestness upon her face, and said—

"Don't talk to me any more, please. She does not like it, and I shall suffer for it afterwards. Please, don't do it."

I was about to ask her the reason for this strange request, but when she saw I was going to address her, she rose and walked slowly out of the room. As she did so I perceived that the lovers had ceased to talk and that Miss Northcott was looking at me with her keen, grey eyes.

"You must excuse my aunt, Mr. Armitage," she said; "she is odd, and easily fatigued. Come over and look at my album."

We spent some time examining the portraits. Miss Northcott's father and mother were apparently ordinary mortals enough, and I could not detect in either of them any traces of the character which showed itself in their daughter's face. There was one old daguerreotype, however, which arrested my attention. It represented a man of about the age of forty, and strikingly handsome. He was clean shaven, and extraordinary power was expressed upon his prominent lower jaw and firm, straight mouth. His eyes were somewhat deeply set in his head, however, and there was a snake-like flattening at the upper part of his forehead, which detracted from his appearance. I almost involuntarily, when I saw the head, pointed to it, and exclaimed—

"There is your prototype in your family, Miss Northcott."

"Do you think so?" she said. "I am afraid you are paying me a very bad compliment. Uncle Anthony was always considered the black sheep of the family."

"Indeed," I answered; "my remark was an unfortunate one, then."

"Oh, don't mind that," she said; "I always thought myself that he was worth all of them put together. He was an officer in the Forty-first Regiment, and he was killed in action during the Persian War—so he died nobly, at any rate."

"That's the sort of death I should like to die," said Cowles, his dark eyes flashing, as they would when he was excited; "I often wish I had taken to my father's profession instead of this vile pill-compounding drudgery."

"Come, Jack, you are not going to die any sort of death yet," she said, tenderly taking his hand in hers.

I could not understand the woman. There was such an extraordinary mixture of masculine decision and womanly tenderness about her, with the consciousness of something all her own in the background, that she fairly puzzled me. I hardly knew, therefore, how to answer Cowles when, as we walked down the street together, he asked the comprehensive question—

"Well, what do you think of her?"

"I think she is wonderfully beautiful," I answered guardedly.

"That, of course," he replied irritably. "You knew that before you came!"

"I think she is very clever too," I remarked.

Barrington Cowles walked on for some time, and then he suddenly turned on me with the strange question—

"Do you think she is cruel? Do you think she is the sort of girl who would take a pleasure in inflicting pain?"

"Well, really," I answered, "I have hardly had time to form an opinion."

We then walked on for some time in silence.

"She is an old fool," at length muttered Cowles. "She is mad."

"Who is?" I asked.

"Why, that old woman—that aunt of Kate's—Mrs. Merton, or whatever her name is."

Then I knew that my poor colourless friend had been speaking to Cowles, but he never said anything more as to the nature of her communication.

My companion went to bed early that night, and I sat up a long time by the fire, thinking over all that I had seen and heard.

I felt that there was some mystery about the girl—some dark fatality so strange as to defy conjecture. I thought of Prescott's interview with her before their marriage, and the fatal termination of it. I coupled it with poor drunken Reeves' plaintive cry, "Why did she not tell me sooner?" and with the other words he had spoken. Then my mind ran over Mrs. Merton's warning to me, Cowles' reference to her, and even the episode of the whip and the cringing dog.

The whole effect of my recollections was unpleasant to a degree, and yet there was no tangible charge which I could bring against the woman. It would be worse than useless to attempt to warn my friend until I had definitely made up my mind what I was to warn him against. He would treat any charge against her with scorn. What could I do? How could I get at some tangible conclusion as to her character and antecedents? No one in Edinburgh knew them except as recent acquaintances. She was an orphan, and as far as I knew she had never disclosed where her former home had been. Suddenly an idea struck me. Among my father's friends there was a Colonel Joyce, who had served a long time in India upon the staff, and who would be likely to know most of the officers who had been out there since the Mutiny. I sat down at once, and, having trimmed the lamp, proceeded to write a letter to the Colonel. I told him that I was very curious to gain some particulars about a certain Captain Northcott, who had served in the Forty-first Foot, and who had fallen in the Persian War. I described the man as well as I could from my recollection of the daguerreotype, and then, having directed the letter, posted it that very night, after which, feeling that I had done all that could be done, I retired to bed, with a mind too anxious to allow me to sleep.

Part 2

I got an answer from Leicester, where the Colonel resided, within two days. I have it before me as I write, and copy it verbatim.

Dear Bob,

I remember the man well. I was with him at Calcutta, and afterwards at Hyderabad. He was a curious, solitary sort of mortal; but a gallant soldier enough, for he distinguished himself at Sobraon, and was wounded, if I remember right. He was not popular in his corps—they said he was a pitiless, cold-blooded fellow, with no geniality in him. There was a rumour, too, that he was a devil-worshipper, or something of that sort, and also that he had the evil eye, which, of course, was all nonsense. He had some strange theories, I remember, about the power of the human will and the effects of mind upon matter.

How are you getting on with your medical studies? Never forget, my boy, that your father's son has every claim upon me, and that if I can serve you in any way I am always at your command.

Ever affectionately yours,

Edward Joyce

P.S.—By the way, Northcott did not fall in action. He was killed after peace was declared in a crazy attempt to get some of the eternal fire from the sun-worshippers' temple. There was considerable mystery about his death.

I read this epistle over several times—at first with a feeling of satisfaction, and then with one of disappointment. I had come on some curious information, and yet hardly what I wanted. He was an eccentric man, a devil-worshipper, and rumoured to have the power of the evil eye. I could believe the young lady's eyes, when endowed with that cold, grey shimmer which I had noticed in them once or twice, to be capable of any evil which human eye ever wrought; but still the superstition was an effete one. Was there not more meaning in that sentence which followed—"He had theories of the power of the human will and of the effect of mind upon matter"? I remember having once read a quaint treatise, which I had imagined to be mere charlatanism at the time, of the power of certain human minds, and of effects produced by them at a distance.

Was Miss Northcott endowed with some exceptional power of the sort?

The idea grew upon me, and very shortly I had evidence which convinced me of the truth of the supposition.

It happened that at the very time when my mind was dwelling upon this subject, I saw a notice in the paper that our town was to be visited by Dr. Messinger, the well-known medium and mesmerist. Messinger was a man whose performance, such as it was, had been again and again pronounced to be genuine by competent judges. He was far above trickery, and had the reputation of being the soundest living authority upon the strange pseudo-sciences of animal magnetism and electro-biology. Determined, therefore, to see what the human will could do, even against all the disadvantages of glaring footlights and a public platform, I took a ticket for the first night of the performance, and went with several student friends.

We had secured one of the side boxes, and did not arrive until after the performance had begun. I had hardly taken my seat before I recognised Barrington Cowles, with his fiancée and old Mrs. Merton, sitting in the third or fourth row of the stalls. They caught sight of me at almost the same moment, and we bowed to each other. The first portion of the lecture was somewhat commonplace, the lecturer giving tricks of pure legerdemain, with one or two manifestations of mesmerism, performed upon a subject whom he had brought with him. He gave us an exhibition of clairvoyance too, throwing his subject into a trance, and then demanding particulars as to the movements of absent friends, and the whereabouts of hidden objects all of which appeared to be answered satisfactorily. I had seen all this before, however. What I wanted to see now was the effect of the lecturer's will when exerted upon some independent member of the audience.

He came round to that as the concluding exhibition in his performance. "I have shown you," he said, "that a mesmerised subject is entirely dominated by the will of the mesmeriser. He loses all power of volition, and his very thoughts are such as are suggested to him by the master-mind. The same end may be attained without any preliminary process. A strong will can, simply by virtue of its strength, take possession of a weaker one, even at a distance, and can regulate the impulses and the actions of the owner of it. If there was one man in the world who had a very much more highly-developed will than any of the rest of the human family, there is no reason why he should not be able to rule over them all, and to reduce his fellow-creatures to the condition of automatons. Happily there is such a dead level of mental power, or rather of mental weakness, among us that such a catastrophe is not likely to occur; but still within our small compass there are variations which produce surprising effects. I shall now single out one of the audience, and endeavour 'by the mere power of will' to compel him to come upon the platform, and do and say what I wish. Let me assure you that there is no collusion, and that the subject whom I may select is at perfect liberty to resent to the uttermost any impulse which I may communicate to him."

With these words the lecturer came to the front of the platform, and glanced over the first few rows of the stalls. No doubt Cowles' dark skin and bright eyes marked him out as a man of a highly nervous temperament, for the mesmerist picked him out in a moment, and fixed his eyes upon him. I saw my friend give a start of surprise, and then settle down in his chair, as if to express his determination not to yield to the influence of the operator. Messinger was not a man whose head denoted any great brain-power, but his gaze was singularly intense and penetrating. Under the influence of it Cowles made one or two spasmodic motions of his hands, as if to grasp the sides of his seat, and then half rose, but only to sink down again, though with an evident effort. I was watching the scene with intense interest, when I happened to catch a glimpse of Miss Northcott's face. She was sitting with her eyes fixed intently upon the mesmerist, and with such an expression of concentrated power upon her features as I have never seen on any other human countenance. Her jaw was firmly set, her lips compressed, and her face as hard as if it were a beautiful sculpture cut out of the whitest marble. Her eyebrows were drawn down, however, and from beneath them her grey eyes seemed to sparkle and gleam with a cold light.

I looked at Cowles again, expecting every moment to see him rise and obey the mesmerist's wishes, when there came from the platform a short, gasping cry as of a man utterly worn out and prostrated by a prolonged struggle. Messinger was leaning against the table, his hand to his forehead, and the perspiration pouring down his face. "I won't go on," he cried, addressing the audience. "There is a stronger will than mine acting against me. You must excuse me for to-night." The man was evidently ill, and utterly unable to proceed, so the curtain was lowered, and the audience dispersed, with many comments upon the lecturer's sudden indisposition.

I waited outside the hall until my friend and the ladies came out. Cowles was laughing over his recent experience.

"He didn't succeed with me, Bob," he cried triumphantly, as he shook my hand. "I think he caught a Tartar that time."

"Yes," said Miss Northcott, "I think that Jack ought to be very proud of his strength of mind; don't you! Mr. Armitage?"

"It took me all my time, though," my friend said seriously. "You can't conceive what a strange feeling I had once or twice. All the strength seemed to have gone out of me—especially just before he collapsed himself."

I walked round with Cowles in order to see the ladies home. He walked in front with Mrs. Merton, and I found myself behind with the young lady. For a minute or so I walked beside her without making any remark, and then I suddenly blurted out, in a manner which must have seemed somewhat brusque to her—

"You did that, Miss Northcott."

"Did what?" she asked sharply.

"Why, mesmerised the mesmeriser—I suppose that is the best way of describing the transaction."

"What a strange idea!" she said, laughing. "You give me credit for a strong will then?"

"Yes," I said. "For a dangerously strong one."

"Why dangerous?" she asked, in a tone of surprise.

"I think," I answered, "that any will which can exercise such power is dangerous—for there is always a chance of its being turned to bad uses."

"You would make me out a very dreadful individual, Mr. Armitage," she said; and then looking up suddenly in my face— "You have never liked me. You are suspicious of me and distrust me, though I have never given you cause."

The accusation was so sudden and so true that I was unable to find any reply to it. She paused for a moment, and then said in a voice which was hard and cold—

"Don't let your prejudice lead you to interfere with me, however, or say anything to your friend, Mr. Cowles, which might lead to a difference between us. You would find that to be very bad policy."

There was something in the way she spoke which gave an indescribable air of a threat to these few words.

"I have no power," I said, "to interfere with your plans for the future. I cannot help, however, from what I have seen and heard, having fears for my friend."

"Fears!" she repeated scornfully. "Pray what have you seen and heard. Something from Mr. Reeves, perhaps—I believe he is another of your friends?"

"He never mentioned your name to me," I answered, truthfully enough. "You will be sorry to hear that he is dying." As I said it we passed by a lighted window, and I glanced down to see what effect my words had upon her. She was laughing—there was no doubt of it; she was laughing quietly to herself. I could see merriment in every feature of her face. I feared and mistrusted the woman from that moment more than ever.

We said little more that night.

When we parted she gave me a quick, warning glance, as if to remind me of what she had said about the danger of interference. Her cautions would have made little difference to me could I have seen my way to benefiting Barrington Cowles by anything which I might say. But what could I say? I might say that her former suitors had been unfortunate.

I might say that I believed her to be a cruel-hearted woman. I might say that I considered her to possess wonderful, and almost preternatural powers. What impression would any of these accusations make upon an ardent lover—a man with my friend's enthusiastic temperament? I felt that it would be useless to advance them, so I was silent.

And now I come to the beginning of the end. Hitherto much has been surmise and inference and hearsay. It is my painful task to relate now, as dispassionately and as accurately as I can, what actually occurred under my own notice, and to reduce to writing the events which preceded the death of my friend.

Towards the end of the winter Cowles remarked to me that he intended to marry Miss Northcott as soon as possible—probably some time in the spring. He was, as I have already remarked, fairly well off, and the young lady had some money of her own, so that there was no pecuniary reason for a long engagement. "We are going to take a little house out at Corstorphine," he said, "and we hope to see your face at our table, Bob, as often as you can possibly come." I thanked him, and tried to shake off my apprehensions, and persuade myself that all would yet be well.

It was about three weeks before the time fixed for the marriage, that Cowles remarked to me one evening that he feared he would be late that night. "I have had a note from Kate," he said, "asking me to call about eleven o'clock to-night, which seems rather a late hour, but perhaps she wants to talk over something quietly after old Mrs. Merton retires."

It was not until after my friend's departure that I suddenly recollected the mysterious interview which I had been told of as preceding the suicide of young Prescott. Then I thought of the ravings of poor Reeves, rendered more tragic by the fact that I had heard that very day of his death. What was the meaning of it all? Had this woman some baleful secret to disclose which must be known before her marriage? Was it some reason which forbade her to marry? Or was it some reason which forbade others to marry her? I felt so uneasy that I would have followed Cowles, even at the risk of offending him, and endeavoured to dissuade him from keeping his appointment, but a glance at the clock showed me that I was too late.

I was determined to wait up for his return, so I piled some coals upon the fire and took down a novel from the shelf. My thoughts proved more interesting than the book, however, and

I threw it on one side. An indefinable feeling of anxiety and depression weighed upon me. Twelve o'clock came, and then half-past, without any sign of my friend. It was nearly one when I heard a step in the street outside, and then a knocking at the door. I was surprised, as I knew that my friend always carried a key—however, I hurried down and undid the latch. As the door flew open I knew in a moment that my worst apprehensions had been fulfilled. Barrington Cowles was leaning against the railings outside with his face sunk upon his breast, and his whole attitude expressive of the most intense despondency. As he passed in he gave a stagger, and would have fallen had I not thrown my left arm around him. Supporting him with this, and holding the lamp in my other hand, I led him slowly upstairs into our sitting-room. He sank down upon the sofa without a word. Now that I could get a good view of him, I was horrified to see the change which had come over him. His face was deadly pale, and his very lips were bloodless. His cheeks and forehead were clammy, his eyes glazed, and his whole expression altered. He looked like a man who had gone through some terrible ordeal, and was thoroughly unnerved.

"My dear fellow, what is the matter?" I asked, breaking the silence. "Nothing amiss, I trust? Are you unwell?"

"Brandy!" he gasped. "Give me some brandy!"

I took out the decanter, and was about to help him, when he snatched it from me with a trembling hand, and poured out nearly half a tumbler of the spirit. He was usually a most abstemious man, but he took this off at a gulp without adding any water to it.

It seemed to do him good, for the colour began to come back to his face, and he leaned upon his elbow.

"My engagement is off, Bob," he said, trying to speak calmly, but with a tremor in his voice which he could not conceal. "It is all over."

"Cheer up!" I answered, trying to encourage him. "Don't get down on your luck. How was it? What was it all about?"

"About?" he groaned, covering his face with his hands. "If I

173

did tell you, Bob, you would not believe it. It is too dreadful—too horrible—unutterably awful and incredible! O Kate, Kate!" and he rocked himself to and fro in his grief; "I pictured you an angel and I find you a——"

"A what?" I asked, for he had paused.

He looked at me with a vacant stare, and then suddenly burst out, waving his arms: "A fiend!" he cried. "A ghoul from the pit! A vampire soul behind a lovely face! Now, God forgive me!" he went on in a lower tone, turning his face to the wall; "I have said more than I should. I have loved her too much to speak of her as she is. I love her too much now."

He lay still for some time, and I had hoped that the brandy had had the effect of sending him to sleep, when he suddenly turned his face towards me.

"Did you ever read of werewolves?" he asked.

I answered that I had.

"There is a story," he said thoughtfully, "in one of Marryat's books, about a beautiful woman who took the form of a wolf at night and devoured her own children. I wonder what put that idea into Marryat's head?"

He pondered for some minutes, and then he cried out for some more brandy. There was a small bottle of laudanum upon the table, and I managed, by insisting upon helping him myself, to mix about half a *drachm* with the spirits. He drank it off, and sank his head once more upon the pillow. "Anything better than that," he groaned. "Death is better than that. Crime and cruelty; cruelty and crime. Anything is better than that," and so on, with the monotonous refrain, until at last the words became indistinct, his eyelids closed over his weary eyes, and he sank into a profound slumber. I carried him into his bedroom without arousing him; and making a couch for myself out of the chairs, I remained by his side all night.

In the morning Barrington Cowles was in a high fever. For weeks he lingered between life and death. The highest medical skill of Edinburgh was called in, and his vigorous constitution slowly got the better of his disease. I nursed him during this anxious time; but through all his wild delirium and ravings he

174

never let a word escape him which explained the mystery connected with Miss Northcott. Sometimes he spoke of her in the tenderest words and most loving voice. At others he screamed out that she was a fiend, and stretched out his arms, as if to keep her off. Several times he cried that he would not sell his soul for a beautiful face, and then he would moan in a most piteous voice, "But I love her—I love her for all that; I shall never cease to love her."

When he came to himself he was an altered man. His severe illness had emaciated him greatly, but his dark eyes had lost none of their brightness. They shone out with startling brilliancy from under his dark, overhanging brows. His manner was eccentric and variable—sometimes irritable, sometimes recklessly mirthful, but never natural. He would glance about him in a strange, suspicious manner, like one who feared something, and yet hardly knew what it was he dreaded. He never mentioned Miss Northcott's name—never until that fatal evening of which I have now to speak.

In an endeavour to break the current of his thoughts by frequent change of scene, I travelled with him through the highlands of Scotland, and afterwards down the east coast. In one of these peregrinations of ours we visited the Isle of May, an island near the mouth of the Firth of Forth, which, except in the tourist season, is singularly barren and desolate. Beyond the keeper of the lighthouse there are only one or two families of poor fisher-folk, who sustain a precarious existence by their nets, and by the capture of cormorants and solan geese. This grim spot seemed to have such a fascination for Cowles that we engaged a room in one of the fishermen's huts, with the intention of passing a week or two there. I found it very dull, but the loneliness appeared to be a relief to my friend's mind. He lost the look of apprehension which had become habitual to him, and became something like his old self.

He would wander round the island all day, looking down from the summit of the great cliffs which gird it round, and watching the long green waves as they came booming in and burst in a shower of spray over the rocks beneath.

One night—I think it was our third or fourth on the island—Barrington Cowles and I went outside the cottage before retiring to rest, to enjoy a little fresh air, for our room was small, and the rough lamp caused an unpleasant odour. How well I remember every little circumstance in connection with that night! It promised to be tempestuous, for the clouds were piling up in the north-west, and the dark wrack was drifting across the face of the moon, throwing alternate belts of light and shade upon the rugged surface of the island and the restless sea beyond.

We were standing talking close by the door of the cottage, and I was thinking to myself that my friend was more cheerful than he had been since his illness, when he gave a sudden, sharp cry, and looking round at him I saw, by the light of the moon, an expression of unutterable horror come over his features. His eyes became fixed and staring, as if riveted upon some approaching object, and he extended his long thin forefinger, which quivered as he pointed.

"Look there!" he cried. "It is she! It is she! You see her there coming down the side of the brae." He gripped me convulsively by the wrist as he spoke. "There she is, coming towards us!"

"Who?" I cried, straining my eyes into the darkness.

"She—Kate—Kate Northcott!" he screamed. "She has come for me. Hold me fast, old friend. Don't let me go!"

"Hold up, old man," I said, clapping him on the shoulder. "Pull yourself together; you are dreaming; there is nothing to fear."

"She is gone!" he cried, with a gasp of relief. "No, by heaven! there she is again, and nearer—coming nearer. She told me she would come for me, and she keeps her word."

"Come into the house," I said. His hand, as I grasped it, was as cold as ice.

"Ah, I knew it!" he shouted. "There she is, waving her arms. She is beckoning to me. It is the signal. I must go. I am coming, Kate; I am coming!"

I threw my arms around him, but he burst from me with superhuman strength, and dashed into the darkness of the night. I followed him, calling to him to stop, but he ran the more swiftly. When the moon shone out between the clouds I could catch a glimpse of his dark figure, running rapidly in a straight line, as if to reach some definite goal. It may have been imagination, but it seemed to me that in the flickering light I could distinguish a vague something in front of him—a shimmering form which eluded his grasp and led him onwards. I saw his outlines stand out hard against the sky behind him as he surmounted the brow of a little hill, then he disappeared, and that was the last ever seen by mortal eye of Barrington Cowles.

The fishermen and I walked round the island all that night with lanterns, and examined every nook and corner without seeing a trace of my poor lost friend. The direction in which he had been running terminated in a rugged line of jagged cliffs overhanging the sea. At one place here the edge was somewhat crumbled, and there appeared marks upon the turf which might have been left by human feet. We lay upon our faces at this spot, and peered with our lanterns over the edge, looking down on the boiling surge two hundred feet below. As we lay there, suddenly, above the beating of the waves and the howling of the wind, there rose a strange wild screech from the abyss below. The fishermen—a naturally superstitious race—averred that it was the sound of a woman's laughter, and I could hardly persuade them to continue the search. For my own part I think it may have been the cry of some sea-fowl startled from its nest by the flash of the lantern. However that may be, I never wish to hear such a sound again.

And now I have come to the end of the painful duty which I have undertaken. I have told as plainly and as accurately as I could the story of the death of John Barrington Cowles, and the train of events which preceded it. I am aware that to others the sad episode seemed commonplace enough. Here is the prosaic account which appeared in the Scotsman a couple of days afterwards:

Sad Occurrence on the Isle of May

The Isle of May has been the scene of a sad disaster. Mr. John Barrington Cowles, a gentleman well known in University circles as a most distinguished student, and the present holder of the Neil Arnott prize for physics, has been recruiting his health in this quiet retreat. The night before last he suddenly left his friend, Mr. Robert Armitage, and he has not since been heard of. It is almost certain that he has met his death by falling over the cliffs which surround the island. Mr. Cowles' health has been failing for some time, partly from over study and partly from worry connected with family affairs. By his death the University loses one of her most promising alumni.

I have nothing more to add to my statement. I have unburdened my mind of all that I know. I can well conceive that many, after weighing all that I have said, will see no ground for an accusation against Miss Northcott. They will say that, because a man of a naturally excitable disposition says and does wild things, and even eventually commits self-murder after a sudden and heavy disappointment, there is no reason why vague charges should be advanced against a young lady. To this, I answer that they are welcome to their opinion. For my own part, I ascribe the death of William Prescott, of Archibald Reeves, and of John Barrington Cowles to this woman with as much confidence as if I had seen her drive a dagger into their hearts.

You ask me, no doubt, what my own theory is which will explain all these strange facts. I have none, or, at best, a dim and vague one. That Miss Northcott possessed extraordinary powers over the minds, and through the minds over the bodies, of others, I am convinced, as well as that her instincts were to use this power for base and cruel purposes. That some even more fiendish and terrible phase of character lay behind this—some horrible trait which it was necessary for her to reveal before marriage—is to be inferred from the experience of her three lovers, while the dreadful nature of the mystery thus revealed can only be surmised from the fact that the very mention of it drove from her those who had loved her so passionately. Their subsequent fate was, in my opinion, the result of her vindictive remembrance of their desertion of her, and that they were forewarned of it at the time was shown by the words of both Reeves and Cowles. Above this, I can say nothing. I lay the facts soberly before the public as they came under my notice. I have never seen Miss Northcott since, nor do I wish to do so. If by the words I have written I can save any one human being from the snare of those bright eyes and that beautiful face, then I can lay down my pen with the assurance that my poor friend has not died altogether in vain.

The Jew's Breastplate

My particular friend, Ward Mortimer, was one of the best men of his day at everything connected with Oriental archaeology. He had written largely upon the subject, he had lived two years in a tomb at Thebes, while he excavated in the Valley of the Kings, and finally he had created a considerable sensation by his exhumation of the alleged mummy of Cleopatra in the inner room of the Temple of Horus, at Philae. With such a record at the age of thirty-one, it was felt that a considerable career lay before him, and no one was surprised when he was elected to the curatorship of the Belmore Street Museum, which carries with it the lectureship at the Oriental College, and an income which has sunk with the fall in land, but which still remains at that ideal sum which is large enough to encourage an investigator, but not so large as to enervate him.

There was only one reason which made Ward Mortimer's position a little difficult at the Belmore Street Museum, and that was the extreme eminence of the man whom he had to succeed. Professor Andreas was a profound scholar and a man of European reputation. His lectures were frequented by students from every part of the world, and his admirable management of the collection entrusted to his care was a commonplace in all learned societies. There was, therefore, considerable surprise when, at the age of fifty-five, he suddenly resigned his position and retired from those duties which had been both his livelihood and his pleasure. He and his daughter left the comfortable suite of rooms which had formed his official residence in connection with the museum, and my friend, Mortimer, who was a bachelor, took up his quarters there.

On hearing of Mortimer's appointment Professor Andreas had written him a very kindly and flattering congratulatory letter. I was actually present at their first meeting, and I went with Mortimer round the museum when the Professor showed us the admirable collection which he had cherished so long. The Professor's beautiful daughter and a young man, Captain Wilson, who was, as I understood, soon to be her husband, accompanied us in our inspection. There were fifteen rooms, but the Babylonian, the Syrian, and the central hall, which contained the Jewish and Egyptian collection, were the finest of all. Professor Andreas was a quiet, dry, elderly man, with a clean-shaven face and an impassive manner, but his dark eyes sparkled and his features quickened into enthusiastic life as he pointed out to us the rarity and the beauty of some of his specimens. His hand lingered so fondly over them, that one could read his pride in them and the grief in his heart now that they were passing from his care into that of another.

He had shown us in turn his mummies, his papyri, his rare scarabs, his inscriptions, his Jewish relics, and his duplication of the famous seven-branched candlestick of the Temple, which was brought to Rome by Titus, and which is supposed by some to be lying at this instant in the bed of the Tiber. Then he approached a case which stood in the very centre of the hall, and he looked down through the glass with reverence in his attitude and manner.

"This is no novelty to an expert like yourself, Mr. Mortimer," said he; "but I daresay that your friend, Mr. Jackson, will be interested to see it."

Leaning over the case I saw an object, some five inches square, which consisted of twelve precious stones in a framework of gold, with golden hooks at two of the corners. The stones were all varying in sort and colour, but they were of the same size. Their shapes, arrangement, and gradation of tint made me think of a box of water-colour paints. Each stone had some hieroglyphic scratched upon its surface.

"You have heard, Mr. Jackson, of the *urim* and *thummim*?"

I had heard the term, but my idea of its meaning was exceedingly vague.

"The *urim* and *thummim* was a name given to the jewelled plate which lay upon the breast of the high priest of the Jews. They had a very special feeling of reverence for it—something of the feeling which an ancient Roman might have for the Sibylline books in the Capitol. There are, as you see, twelve magnificent stones, inscribed with mystical characters. Counting from the left-hand top corner, the stones are carnelian, peridot, emerald, ruby, lapis lazuli, onyx, sapphire, agate, amethyst, topaz, beryl, and jasper."

I was amazed at the variety and beauty of the stones.

"Has the breastplate any particular history?" I asked.

"It is of great age and of immense value," said Professor Andreas. "Without being able to make an absolute assertion, we have many reasons to think that it is possible that it may be the original *urim* and *thummim* of Solomon's Temple. There is certainly nothing so fine in any collection in Europe. My friend, Captain Wilson, here, is a practical authority upon precious stones, and he would tell you how pure these are."

Captain Wilson, a man with a dark, hard, incisive face, was standing beside his fiancée at the other side of the case.

"Yes," said he, curtly, "I have never seen finer stones."

"And the gold-work is also worthy of attention. The ancients excelled in——"—he was apparently about to indicate the setting of the stones, when Captain Wilson interrupted him.

"You will see a finer example of their gold-work in this candlestick," said he, turning to another table, and we all joined him in his admiration of its embossed stem and delicately ornamented branches. Altogether it was an interesting and a novel experience to have objects of such rarity explained by so great an expert; and when, finally, Professor Andreas finished our inspection by formally handing over the precious collection to the care of my friend, I could not help pitying him and envying his successor whose life was to pass in so pleasant a duty. Within a week, Ward Mortimer was duly installed in his new set of rooms, and had become the autocrat of the Belmore Street Museum.

About a fortnight afterwards my friend gave a small dinner to half a dozen bachelor friends to celebrate his promotion. When his guests were departing he pulled my sleeve and signalled to me that he wished me to remain.

"You have only a few hundred yards to go," said he—I was living in chambers in the Albany. "You may as well stay and have a quiet cigar with me. I very much want your advice."

I relapsed into an arm-chair and lit one of his excellent Matronas. When he had returned from seeing the last of his guests out, he drew a letter from his dress-jacket and sat down opposite to me.

"This is an anonymous letter which I received this morning," said he. "I want to read it to you and to have your advice."

"You are very welcome to it for what it is worth."

"This is how the note runs: 'Sir,—I should strongly advise you to keep a very careful watch over the many valuable things which are committed to your charge. I do not think that the present system of a single watchman is sufficient. Be upon your guard, or an irreparable misfortune may occur.'"

"Is that all?"

"Yes, that is all."

"Well," said I, "it is at least obvious that it was written by one of the limited number of people who are aware that you have only one watchman at night."

Ward Mortimer handed me the note, with a curious smile. "Have you an eye for handwriting?" said he. "Now, look at this!" He put another letter in front of me. "Look at the c in 'congratulate' and the c in 'committed.' Look at the capital I. Look at the trick of putting in a dash instead of a stop!"

"They are undoubtedly from the same hand—with some attempt at disguise in the case of this first one."

"The second," said Ward Mortimer, "is the letter of congratulation which was written to me by Professor Andreas upon my obtaining my appointment."

I stared at him in amazement. Then I turned over the letter in my hand, and there, sure enough, was "Martin Andreas" signed upon the other side. There could be no doubt, in the mind of anyone who had the slightest knowledge of the science of graphology, that the Professor had written an anonymous letter, warning his successor against thieves. It was inexplicable, but it was certain.

"Why should he do it?" I asked.

"Precisely what I should wish to ask you. If he had any such misgivings, why could he not come and tell me direct?"

"Will you speak to him about it?"

"There again I am in doubt. He might choose to deny that he wrote it."

"At any rate," said I, "this warning is meant in a friendly spirit, and I should certainly act upon it. Are the present precautions enough to insure you against robbery?"

"I should have thought so. The public are only admitted from ten till five, and there is a guardian to every two rooms. He stands at the door between them, and so commands them both."

"But at night?"

"When the public are gone, we at once put up the great iron shutters, which are absolutely burglar-proof. The watchman is a capable fellow. He sits in the lodge, but he walks round every three hours. We keep one electric light burning in each room all night."

"It is difficult to suggest anything more—short of keeping your day watches all night."

"We could not afford that."

"At least, I should communicate with the police, and have a special constable put on outside in Belmore Street," said I. "As to the letter, if the writer wishes to be anonymous, I think he has a right to remain so. We must trust to the future to show some reason for the curious course which he has adopted."

So we dismissed the subject, but all that night after my return to my chambers I was puzzling my brain as to what possible motive Professor Andreas could have for writing an anonymous warning letter to his successor—for that the writing was his was as certain to me as if I had seen him actually doing it. He foresaw some danger to the collection. Was it because he foresaw it that he abandoned his charge of it? But if so, why should he hesitate to warn Mortimer in his own name? I puzzled and puzzled until at last I fell into a troubled sleep, which carried me beyond my usual hour of rising.

I was aroused in a singular and effective method, for about nine o'clock my friend Mortimer rushed into my room with an expression of consternation upon his face. He was usually one of the most tidy men of my acquaintance, but now his collar was undone at one end, his tie was flying, and his hat at the back of his head. I read his whole story in his frantic eyes.

"The museum has been robbed!" I cried, springing up in bed.

"I fear so! Those jewels! The jewels of the *urim* and *thummim*!" he gasped, for he was out of breath with running. "I'm going on to the police-station. Come to the museum as soon as you can, Jackson! Good-bye!" He rushed distractedly out of the room, and I heard him clatter down the stairs.

I was not long in following his directions, but I found when I arrived that he had already returned with a police inspector, and another elderly gentleman, who proved to be Mr. Purvis, one of the partners of Morson and Company, the well-known diamond merchants. As an expert in stones he was always prepared to advise the police. They were grouped round the case in which the breastplate of the Jewish priest had been exposed. The plate had been taken out and laid upon the glass top of the case, and the three heads were bent over it.

"It is obvious that it has been tampered with," said Mortimer. "It caught my eye the moment that I passed through the room this morning. I examined it yesterday evening, so that it is certain that this has happened during the night."

It was, as he had said, obvious that someone had been at work upon it. The settings of the uppermost row of four stones—the carnelian, peridot, emerald, and ruby—were rough and jagged as if someone had scraped all round them. The stones were in their places, but the beautiful gold-work which we had admired only a few days before had been very clumsily pulled about.

"It looks to me," said the police inspector, "as if someone had been trying to take out the stones."

"My fear is," said Mortimer, "that he not only tried, but succeeded. I believe these four stones to be skilful imitations which have been put in the place of the originals."

The same suspicion had evidently been in the mind of the expert, for he had been carefully examining the four stones with the aid of a lens. He now submitted them to several tests, and finally turned cheerfully to Mortimer.

"I congratulate you, sir," said he, heartily. "I will pledge my reputation that all four of these stones are genuine, and of a most unusual degree of purity."

The colour began to come back to my poor friend's frightened face, and he drew a long breath of relief.

"Thank God!" he cried. "Then what in the world did the thief want?"

"Probably he meant to take the stones, but was interrupted."

"In that case one would expect him to take them out one at a time, but the setting of each of these has been loosened, and yet the stones are all here."

"It is certainly most extraordinary," said the inspector. "I never remember a case like it. Let us see the watchman."

The commissionaire was called—a soldierly, honest-faced man, who seemed as concerned as Ward Mortimer at the incident.

"No, sir, I never heard a sound," he answered, in reply to the questions of the inspector. "I made my rounds four times, as usual, but I saw nothing suspicious. I've been in my position ten years, but nothing of the kind has ever occurred before."

"No thief could have come through the windows?"

"Impossible, sir."

"Or passed you at the door?"

"No, sir; I never left my post except when I walked my rounds."

"What other openings are there in the museum?"

"There is the door into Mr. Ward Mortimer's private rooms."

"That is locked at night," my friend explained, "and in order to reach it anyone from the street would have to open the outside door as well."

"Your servants?"

"Their quarters are entirely separate."

"Well, well," said the inspector, "this is certainly very obscure. However, there has been no harm done, according to Mr. Purvis."

"I will swear that those stones are genuine."

"So that the case appears to be merely one of malicious damage. But none the less, I should be very glad to go carefully round the premises, and to see if we can find any trace to show us who your visitor may have been."

His investigation, which lasted all the morning, was careful and intelligent, but it led in the end to nothing. He pointed out to us that there were two possible entrances to the museum which we had not considered. The one was from the cellars by a trap-door opening in the passage. The other through a sky-light from the lumber-room, overlooking that very chamber to which the intruder had penetrated. As neither the cellar nor the lumber-room could be entered unless the thief was already within the locked doors, the matter was not of any practical importance, and the dust of cellar and attic assured us that no one had used either one or the other. Finally, we ended as we began, without the slightest clue as to how, why, or by whom the setting of these four jewels had been tampered with.

There remained one course for Mortimer to take, and he took it. Leaving the police to continue their fruitless researches, he asked me to accompany him that afternoon in a visit to Professor Andreas. He took with him the two letters, and it was his intention to openly tax his predecessor with having written the anonymous warning, and to ask him to explain the fact that he should have anticipated so exactly that which had actually occurred. The Professor was living in a small villa in Upper Norwood, but we were informed by the servant that he was away from home. Seeing our disappointment, she asked us if we should like to see Miss Andreas, and showed us into the modest drawing-room.

I have mentioned incidentally that the Professor's daughter was a very beautiful girl. She was a blonde, tall and graceful, with a skin of that delicate tint which the French call "mat," the colour of old ivory, or of the lighter petals of the sulphur rose. I was shocked, however, as she entered the room to see how much she had changed in the last fortnight. Her young face was haggard and her bright eyes heavy with trouble.

"Father has gone to Scotland," she said. "He seems to be tired, and has had a good deal to worry him. He only left us yesterday."

"You look a little tired yourself, Miss Andreas," said my friend.

"I have been so anxious about father."

"Can you give me his Scotch address?"

"Yes, he is with his brother, the Rev. David Andreas, 1, Arran Villas, Ardrossan."

Ward Mortimer made a note of the address, and we left without saying anything as to the object of our visit. We found ourselves in Belmore Street in the evening in exactly the same position in which we had been in the morning. Our only clue was the Professor's letter, and my friend had made up his mind to start for Ardrossan next day, and to get to the bottom of the anonymous letter, when a new development came to alter our plans.

Very early on the following morning I was aroused from my sleep by a tap upon my bedroom door. It was a messenger with a note from Mortimer.

"Do come round," it said; "the matter is becoming more and more extraordinary."

When I obeyed his summons I found him pacing excitedly up and down the central room, while the old soldier who guarded the premises stood with military stiffness in a corner.

"My dear Jackson," he cried, "I am so delighted that you have come, for this is a most inexplicable business."

"What has happened, then?"

He waved his hand towards the case which contained the breastplate.

"Look at it," said he.

I did so, and could not restrain a cry of surprise. The setting of the middle row of precious stones had been profaned in the same manner as the upper ones. Of the twelve jewels eight had been now tampered with in this singular fashion. The setting of the lower four was neat and smooth. The others jagged and irregular.

"Have the stones been altered?" I asked.

"No, I am certain that these upper four are the same which the expert pronounced to be genuine, for I observed yesterday that little discoloration on the edge of the emerald. Since they have not extracted the upper stones, there is no reason to think the lower have been transposed. You say that you heard nothing, Simpson?"

"No, sir," the commissionaire answered. "But when I made my round after daylight I had a special look at these stones, and I saw at once that someone had been meddling with them. Then I called you, sir, and told you. I was backwards and forwards all night, and I never saw a soul or heard a sound."

"Come up and have some breakfast with me," said Mortimer, and he took me into his own chambers.—"Now, what DO you think of this, Jackson?" he asked.

"It is the most objectless, futile, idiotic business that ever I heard of. It can only be the work of a monomaniac."

"Can you put forward any theory?"

A curious idea came into my head. "This object is a Jewish relic of great antiquity and sanctity," said I. "How about the anti-Semitic movement? Could one conceive that a fanatic of that way of thinking might desecrate——"

"No, no, no!" cried Mortimer. "That will never do! Such a man might push his lunacy to the length of destroying a Jewish relic, but why on earth should he nibble round every stone so carefully that he can only do four stones in a night? We must have a better solution than that, and we must find it for ourselves, for I do not think that our inspector is likely to help us. First of all, what do you think of Simpson, the porter?"

"Have you any reason to suspect him?"

"Only that he is the one person on the premises."

"But why should he indulge in such wanton destruction? Nothing has been taken away. He has no motive."

"Mania?"

"No, I will swear to his sanity."

"Have you any other theory?"

"Well, yourself, for example. You are not a somnambulist, by any chance?"

"Nothing of the sort, I assure you."

"Then I give it up."

"But I don't—and I have a plan by which we will make it all clear."

"To visit Professor Andreas?"

"No, we shall find our solution nearer than Scotland. I will tell you what we shall do. You know that skylight which overlooks the central hall? We will leave the electric lights in the hall, and we will keep watch in the lumber-room, you and I, and solve the mystery for ourselves. If our mysterious visitor is doing four stones at a time, he has four still to do, and there is every reason to think that he will return tonight and complete the job."

"Excellent!" I cried.

"We will keep our own secret, and say nothing either to the police or to Simpson. Will you join me?"

"With the utmost pleasure," said I; and so it was agreed.

It was ten o'clock that night when I returned to the Belmore Street Museum. Mortimer was, as I could see, in a state of suppressed nervous excitement, but it was still too early to begin our vigil, so we remained for an hour or so in his chambers, discussing all the possibilities of the singular business which we had met to solve. At last the roaring stream of hansom cabs and the rush of hurrying feet became lower and more intermittent as the pleasure-seekers passed on their way to their stations or their homes. It was nearly twelve when Mortimer led the way to the lumber-room which overlooked the central hall of the museum.

He had visited it during the day, and had spread some sacking so that we could lie at our ease, and look straight down into the museum. The skylight was of unfrosted glass, but was so covered with dust that it would be impossible for anyone looking up from below to detect that he was overlooked. We cleared a small piece at each corner, which gave us a complete view of the room beneath us. In the cold white light of the electric lamps everything stood out hard and clear, and I could see the smallest detail of the contents of the various cases.

Such a vigil is an excellent lesson, since one has no choice but to look hard at those objects which we usually pass with such half-hearted interest. Through my little peep hole I employed the hours in studying every specimen, from the huge mummy-case which leaned against the wall to those very jewels which had brought us there, gleaming and sparkling in their glass case immediately beneath us. There was much precious gold-work and many valuable stones scattered through the numerous cases, but those wonderful twelve which made up the *urim* and *thummim* glowed and burned with a radiance which far eclipsed the others. I studied in turn the tomb-pictures of Sicara, the friezes from Karnak, the statues of Memphis, and the inscriptions of Thebes, but my eyes would always come back to that wonderful Jewish relic, and my mind to the singular mystery which surrounded it. I was lost in the thought of it when my companion suddenly drew his breath sharply in, and seized my arm in a convulsive grip. At the same instant I saw what it was which had excited him.

I have said that against the wall—on the right-hand side of the doorway (the right-hand side as we looked at it, but the left as one entered)—there stood a large mummy-case. To our unutterable amazement it was slowly opening. Gradually, gradually the lid was swinging back, and the black slit which marked the opening was becoming wider and wider. So gently and carefully was it done that the movement was almost imperceptible. Then, as we breathlessly watched it, a white thin hand appeared at the opening, pushing back the painted lid, then another hand, and finally a face—a face which was familiar to us both, that of Professor Andreas. Stealthily he slunk out of the mummy-case, like a fox stealing from its burrow, his head turning incessantly to left and to right, stepping, then pausing, then stepping again, the very image of craft and of caution. Once some sound in the street struck him motionless, and he stood listening, with his ear turned, ready to dart back to the shelter behind him. Then he crept onwards again upon tiptoe, very, very softly and slowly, until he had reached the case in the centre of the room. There he took a bunch of keys from his pocket, unlocked the case, took out the Jewish breastplate, and, laying it upon the glass in front of him, began to work upon it with some sort of small, glistening tool. He was so directly underneath us that his bent head covered his work, but we could guess from the movement of his hand that he was engaged in finishing the strange disfigurement which he had begun.

I could realize from the heavy breathing of my companion, and the twitchings of the hand which still clutched my wrist, the furious indignation which filled his heart as he saw this vandalism in the quarter of all others where he could least have expected it. He, the very man who a fortnight before had reverently bent over this unique relic, and who had impressed its antiquity and its sanctity upon us, was now engaged in this outrageous profanation. It was impossible, unthinkable—and yet there, in the white glare of the electric light beneath us, was that dark figure with the bent grey head, and the twitching elbow. What inhuman hypocrisy, what hateful depth of malice against his successor must underlie these sinister nocturnal labours. It was painful to think of and dreadful to watch. Even I, who had none of the acute feelings of a virtuoso, could not bear to look on and see this deliberate mutilation of so ancient a relic. It was a relief to me when my companion tugged at my sleeve as a signal that I was to follow him as he softly crept out of the room. It was not until we were within his own quarters that he opened his lips, and then I saw by his agitated face how deep was his consternation.

"The abominable Goth!" he cried. "Could you have believed it?"

"It is amazing."

"He is a villain or a lunatic—one or the other. We shall very soon see which. Come with me, Jackson, and we shall get to the bottom of this black business."

A door opened out of the passage which was the private entrance from his rooms into the museum. This he opened softly with his key, having first kicked off his shoes, an example which I followed. We crept together through room after room, until the large hall lay before us, with that dark figure still stooping and working at the central case. With an advance as cautious as his own we closed in upon him, but softly as we went we could not take him entirely unawares. We were still a dozen yards from him when he looked round with a start, and uttering a husky cry of terror, ran frantically down the museum.

"Simpson! Simpson!" roared Mortimer, and far away down the vista of electric lighted doors we saw the stiff figure of the old soldier suddenly appear. Professor Andreas saw him also, and stopped running, with a gesture of despair. At the same instant we each laid a hand upon his shoulder.

"Yes, yes, gentlemen," he panted, "I will come with you. To your room, Mr. Ward Mortimer, if you please! I feel that I owe you an explanation."

My companion's indignation was so great that I could see that he dared not trust himself to reply. We walked on each side of the old Professor, the astonished commissionaire bringing up the rear. When we reached the violated case, Mortimer stopped and examined the breastplate. Already one of the stones of the lower row had had its setting turned back in the same manner as the others. My friend held it up and glanced furiously at his prisoner.

"How could you!" he cried. "How could you!"

"It is horrible—horrible!" said the Professor. "I don't wonder at your feelings. Take me to your room."

"But this shall not be left exposed!" cried Mortimer. He picked the breastplate up and carried it tenderly in his hand, while I walked beside the Professor, like a policeman with a malefactor. We passed into Mortimer's chambers, leaving the amazed old soldier to understand matters as best he could. The Professor sat down in Mortimer's arm-chair, and turned so ghastly a colour that for the instant all our resentment was changed to concern. A stiff glass of brandy brought the life back to him once more.

"There, I am better now!" said he. "These last few days have been too much for me. I am convinced that I could not stand it any longer. It is a nightmare—a horrible nightmare—that I should be arrested as a burglar in what has been for so long my own museum. And yet I cannot blame you. You could not have done otherwise. My hope always was that I should get it all over before I was detected. This would have been my last night's work."

"How did you get in?" asked Mortimer.

"By taking a very great liberty with your private door. But the object justified it. The object justified everything. You will not be angry when you know everything—at least, you will not be angry with me. I had a key to your side door and also to the museum door. I did not give them up when I left. And so you see it was not difficult for me to let myself into the museum. I used to come in early before the crowd had cleared from the street. Then I hid myself in the mummy-case, and took refuge there whenever Simpson came round. I could always hear him coming. I used to leave in the same way as I came."

"You ran a risk."

"I had to."

"But why? What on earth was your object—*you* to do a thing like that!" Mortimer pointed reproachfully at the plate which lay before him on the table.

"I could devise no other means. I thought and thought, but there was no alternate except a hideous public scandal, and a private sorrow which would have clouded our lives. I acted for the best, incredible as it may seem to you, and I only ask your attention to enable me to prove it."

"I will hear what you have to say before I take any further steps," said Mortimer, grimly.

"I am determined to hold back nothing, and to take you both completely into my confidence. I will leave it to your own generosity how far you will use the facts with which I supply you."

"We have the essential facts already."

"And yet you understand nothing. Let me go back to what passed a few weeks ago, and I will make it all clear to you. Believe me that what I say is the absolute and exact truth.

"You have met the person who calls himself Captain Wilson. I say 'calls himself' because I have reason now to believe that it is not his correct name. It would take me too long if I were to describe all the means by which he obtained an introduction to me and ingratiated himself into my friendship and the affection of my daughter. He brought letters from foreign colleagues which compelled me to show him some attention. And then, by his own attainments, which are considerable, he succeeded in making himself a very welcome visitor at my rooms. When I learned that my daughter's affections had been gained by him, I may have thought it premature, but I certainly was not surprised, for he had a charm of manner and of conversation which would have made him conspicuous in any society.

"He was much interested in Oriental antiquities, and his knowledge of the subject justified his interest. Often when he spent the evening with us he would ask permission to go down into the museum and have an opportunity of privately inspecting the various specimens. You can imagine that I, as an enthusiast, was in sympathy with such a request, and that I felt no surprise at the constancy of his visits. After his actual engagement to Elise, there was hardly an evening which he did not pass with us, and an hour or two were generally devoted to the museum. He had the free run of the place, and when I have been away for the evening I had no objection to his doing whatever he wished here. This state of things was only terminated by the fact of my resignation of my official duties and my retirement to Norwood, where I hoped to have the leisure to write a considerable work which I had planned.

"It was immediately after this—within a week or so—that I first realized the true nature and character of the man whom I had so imprudently introduced into my family. The discovery came to me through letters from my friends abroad, which showed me that his introductions to me had been forgeries. Aghast at the revelation, I asked myself what motive this man could originally have had in practising this elaborate deception upon me. I was too poor a man for any fortune-hunter to have marked me down. Why, then, had he come? I remembered that some of the most precious gems in Europe had been under my charge, and I remembered also the ingenious excuses by which this man had made himself familiar with the cases in which they were kept. He was a rascal who was planning some gigantic robbery. How could I, without striking my own daughter, who was infatuated about him, prevent him from carrying out any plan which he might have formed? My device was a clumsy one, and yet I could think of nothing more effective. If I had written a letter under my own name, you would naturally have turned to me for details which I did not wish to give. I resorted to an anonymous letter, begging you to be upon your guard.

"I may tell you that my change from Belmore Street to Norwood had not affected the visits of this man, who had, I believe, a real and overpowering affection for my daughter. As to her, I could not have believed that any woman could be so completely under the influence of a man as she was. His stronger nature seemed to entirely dominate her. I had not realized how far this was the case, or the extent of the confidence which existed between them, until that very evening when his true character for the first time was made clear to me. I had given orders that when he called he should be shown into my study instead of to the drawing-room. There I told him bluntly that I knew all about him, that I had taken steps to defeat his designs, and that neither I nor my daughter desired ever to see him again. I added that I thanked God that I had found him out before he had time to harm those precious objects which it had been the work of my life-time to protect.

"He was certainly a man of iron nerve. He took my remarks without a sign either of surprise or of defiance, but listened gravely and attentively until I had finished. Then he walked across the room without a word and struck the bell.

"'Ask Miss Andreas to be so kind as to step this way,' said he to the servant.

"My daughter entered, and the man closed the door behind her. Then he took her hand in his.

"'Elise,' said he, 'your father has just discovered that I am a villain. He knows now what you knew before.'

"She stood in silence, listening.

"'He says that we are to part for ever,' said he.

"She did not withdraw her hand.

"'Will you be true to me, or will you remove the last good influence which is ever likely to come into my life?'

"'John,' she cried, passionately. 'I will never abandon you! Never, never, not if the whole world were against you.'

"In vain I argued and pleaded with her. It was absolutely useless. Her whole life was bound up in this man before me. My daughter, gentlemen, is all that I have left to love, and it filled me with agony when I saw how powerless I was to save her from her ruin. My helplessness seemed to touch this man who was the cause of my trouble.

"'It may not be as bad as you think, sir,' said he, in his quiet, inflexible way. 'I love Elise with a love which is strong enough to rescue even one who has such a record as I have. It was but yesterday that I promised her that never again in my whole life would I do a thing of which she should be ashamed. I have made up my mind to it, and never yet did I make up my mind to a thing which I did not do.'

"He spoke with an air which carried conviction with it. As he concluded he put his hand into his pocket and he drew out a small cardboard box.

"'I am about to give you a proof of my determination,' said he. 'This, Elise, shall be the first-fruits of your redeeming influence over me. You are right, sir, in thinking that I had designs upon the jewels in your possession. Such ventures have had a charm for me, which depended as much upon the risk run as upon the value of the prize. Those famous and antique stones of the Jewish priest were a challenge to my daring and my ingenuity. I determined to get them.'

"'I guessed as much.'

"'There was only one thing that you did not guess.'

"'And what is that?'

"'That I got them. They are in this box.'

"He opened the box, and tilted out the contents upon the corner of my desk. My hair rose and my flesh grew cold as I looked. There were twelve magnificent square stones engraved with mystical characters. There could be no doubt that they were the jewels of the *urim* and *thummim*.

"'Good God!' I cried. 'How have you escaped discovery?'

"'By the substitution of twelve others, made especially to my order, in which the originals are so carefully imitated that I defy the eye to detect the difference.'

"'Then the present stones are false?' I cried.

"'They have been for some weeks.'

"We all stood in silence, my daughter white with emotion, but still holding this man by the hand.

"'You see what I am capable of, Elise,' said he.

"'I see that you are capable of repentance and restitution,' she answered.

"'Yes, thanks to your influence! I leave the stones in your hands, sir. Do what you like about it. But remember that whatever you do against me, is done against the future husband of your only daughter. You will hear from me soon again, Elise. It is the last time that I will ever cause pain to your tender heart,' and with these words he left both the room and the house.

"My position was a dreadful one. Here I was with these precious relics in my possession, and how could I return them without a scandal and an exposure? I knew the depth of my daughter's nature too well to suppose that I would ever be able to detach her from this man now that she had entirely given him her heart. I was not even sure how far it was right to detach her if she had such an ameliorating influence over him. How could I expose him without injuring her—and how far was I justified in exposing him when he had voluntarily put himself into my power? I thought and thought until at last I formed a resolution which may seem to you to be a foolish one, and yet, if I had to do it again, I believe it would be the best course open to me.

"My idea was to return the stones without anyone being the wiser. With my keys I could get into the museum at any time, and I was confident that I could avoid Simpson, whose hours and methods were familiar to me. I determined to take no one into my confidence—not even my daughter—whom I told that I was about to visit my brother in Scotland. I wanted a free hand for a few nights, without inquiry as to my comings and goings. To this end I took a room in Harding Street that very night, with an intimation that I was a Pressman, and that I should keep very late hours.

"That night I made my way into the museum, and I replaced four of the stones. It was hard work, and took me all night. When Simpson came round I always heard his footsteps, and concealed myself in the mummy-case. I had some knowledge of gold-work, but was far less skilful than the thief had been. He had replaced the setting so exactly that I defy anyone to see the difference. My work was rude and clumsy. However, I hoped that the plate might not be carefully examined, or the roughness of the setting observed, until my task was done. Next night I replaced four more stones. And tonight I should have finished my task had it not been for the unfortunate circumstance which has caused me to reveal so much which I should have wished to keep concealed. I appeal to you, gentlemen, to your sense of honour and of compassion, whether what I have told you should go any farther or not. My own happiness, my daughter's future, the hopes of this man's regeneration, all depend upon your decision.

"Which is," said my friend, "that all is well that ends well and that the whole matter ends here and at once. Tomorrow the loose settings shall be tightened by an expert goldsmith, and so passes the greatest danger to which, since the destruction of the Temple, the *urim* and *thummim* has been exposed. Here is my hand, Professor Andreas, and I can only hope that under such difficult circumstances I should have carried myself as unselfishly and as well."

Just one footnote to this narrative. Within a month Elise Andreas was married to a man whose name, had I the indiscretion to mention it, would appeal to my readers as one who is now widely and deservedly honoured. But if the truth were known that honour is due not to him, but to the gentle girl who plucked him back when he had gone so far down that dark road along which few return.

Cyprian Overbeck Wells
A Literary Mosaic

From my boyhood I have had an intense and overwhelming conviction that my real vocation lay in the direction of literature. I have, however, had a most unaccountable difficulty in getting any responsible person to share my views. It is true that private friends have sometimes, after listening to my effusions, gone the length of remarking, "Really, Smith, that's not half bad!" or, "You take my advice, old boy, and send that to some magazine!" but I have never on these occasions had the moral courage to inform my adviser that the article in question had been sent to well-nigh every publisher in London, and had come back again with a rapidity and precision which spoke well for the efficiency of our postal arrangements.

Had my manuscripts been paper boomerangs they could not have returned with greater accuracy to their unhappy dispatch-er. Oh, the vileness and utter degradation of the moment when the stale little cylinder of closely written pages, which seemed so fresh and full of promise a few days ago, is handed in by a remorseless postman! And what moral depravity shines through the editor's ridiculous plea of "want of space!" But the subject is a painful one, and a digression from the plain statement of facts which I originally contemplated.

From the age of seventeen to that of three-and-twenty I was a literary volcano in a constant state of eruption. Poems and tales, articles and reviews, nothing came amiss to my pen. From the great sea-serpent to the nebular hypothesis, I was ready to write on anything or everything, and I can safely say that I seldom handled a subject without throwing new lights upon it. Poetry and romance, however, had always the greatest attractions for me. How I have wept over the pathos of my heroines, and laughed at the comicalities of my buffoons! Alas! I could find no one to join me in my appreciation, and solitary admiration for one's self, however genuine, becomes satiating after a time. My father remonstrated with me too on the score of expense and loss of time, so that I was finally compelled to relinquish my dreams of literary independence and to become a clerk in a wholesale mercantile firm connected with the West African trade.

Even when condemned to the prosaic duties which fell to my lot in the office, I continued faithful to my first love. I have introduced pieces of word-painting into the most commonplace business letters which have, I am told, considerably astonished the recipients. My refined sarcasm has made defaulting creditors writhe and wince. Occasionally, like the great Silas Wegg, I would drop into poetry, and so raise the whole tone of the correspondence. Thus what could be more elegant than my rendering of the firm's instructions to the captain of one of their vessels. It ran in this way:—

"From England, Captain, you must steer a Course directly to Madeira, Land the casks of salted beef, Then away to Tenerife. Pray be careful, cool, and wary With the merchants of Canary. When you leave them make the most Of the trade winds to the coast. Down it you shall sail as far As the land of Calabar, And from there you'll onward go To Bonny and Fernando Po"——

and so on for four pages. The captain, instead of treasuring up this little gem, called at the office next day, and demanded with quite unnecessary warmth what the thing meant, and I was compelled to translate it all back into prose. On this, as on other similar occasions, my employer took me severely to task—for he was, you see, a man entirely devoid of all pretensions to literary taste!

All this, however, is a mere preamble, and leads up to the fact that after ten years or so of drudgery I inherited a legacy which, though small, was sufficient to satisfy my simple wants. Finding myself independent, I rented a quiet house removed from the uproar and bustle of London, and there I settled down with the intention of producing some great work which should single me out from the family of the Smiths, and render my name immortal. To this end I laid in several quires of foolscap, a box of quill pens, and a sixpenny bottle of ink, and having given my housekeeper injunctions to deny me to all visitors, I proceeded to look round for a suitable subject.

I was looking round for some weeks. At the end of that time I found that I had by constant nibbling devoured a large number of the quills, and had spread the ink out to such advantage, what with blots, spills, and abortive commencements, that there appeared to be some everywhere except in the bottle. As to the story itself, however, the facility of my youth had deserted me completely, and my mind remained a complete blank; nor could I, do what I would, excite my sterile imagination to conjure up a single incident or character.

In this strait I determined to devote my leisure to running rapidly through the works of the leading English novelists, from Daniel Defoe to the present day, in the hope of stimulating my latent ideas and of getting a good grasp of the general tendency of literature. For some time past I had avoided opening any work of fiction because one of the greatest faults of my youth had been that I invariably and unconsciously mimicked the style of the last author whom I had happened to read. Now, however, I made up my mind to seek safety in a multitude, and by consulting ALL the English classics to avoid?? the danger of imitating any one too closely. I had just accomplished the task of reading through the majority of the standard novels at the time when my narrative commences.

It was, then, about twenty minutes to ten on the night of the fourth of June, eighteen hundred and eighty-six, that, after disposing of a pint of beer and a Welsh rarebit for my supper, I seated myself in my arm-chair, cocked my feet upon a stool, and lit my pipe, as was my custom. Both my pulse and my temperature were, as far as I know, normal at the time. I would give the state of the barometer, but that unlucky instrument had experienced an unprecedented fall of forty-two inches—from a nail to the ground—and was not in a reliable condition. We live in a scientific age, and I flatter myself that I move with the times.

Whilst in that comfortable lethargic condition which accompanies both digestion and poisoning by nicotine, I suddenly became aware of the extraordinary fact that my little drawing-room had elongated into a great salon, and that my humble table had increased in proportion. Round this colossal mahogany were seated a great number of people who were talking earnestly together, and the surface in front of them was strewn with books and pamphlets. I could not help observing that these persons were dressed in a most extraordinary mixture of costumes, for those at the end nearest to me wore peruke wigs, swords, and all the fashions of two centuries back; those about the centre had tight knee-breeches, high cravats, and heavy bunches of seals; while among those at the far side the majority were dressed in the most modern style, and among them I saw, to my surprise, several eminent men of letters whom I had the honour of knowing. There were two or three women in the company. I should have risen to my feet to greet these unexpected guests, but all power of motion appeared to have deserted me, and I could only lie still and listen to their conversation, which I soon perceived to be all about myself.

"Egad!" exclaimed a rough, weather-beaten man, who was smoking a long churchwarden pipe at my end of the table, "my heart softens for him. Why, gossips, we've been in the same straits ourselves. Gadzooks, never did mother feel more concern for her eldest born than I when Rory Random went out to make his own way in the world."

"Right, Tobias, right!" cried another man, seated at my very elbow.

"By my troth, I lost more flesh over poor Robin on his island, than had I the sweating sickness twice told. The tale was well-nigh done when in swaggers my Lord of Rochester—a merry gallant, and one whose word in matters literary might make or mar. 'How now, Defoe,' quoth he, 'hast a tale on hand?' 'Even so, your lordship,' I returned. 'A right merry one, I trust,' quoth he.

'Discourse unto me concerning thy heroine, a comely lass, Dan, or I mistake.' 'Nay,' I replied, 'there is no heroine in the matter.' 'Split not your phrases,' quoth he; 'thou weighest every word like a scald attorney. Speak to me of thy principal female character, be she heroine or no.' 'My lord,' I answered, 'there is no female character.' 'Then out upon thyself and thy book too!' he cried. 'Thou hadst best burn it!'—and so out in great dudgeon, whilst I fell to mourning over my poor romance, which was thus, as it were, sentenced to death before its birth. Yet there are a thousand now who have read of Robin and his man Friday, to one who has heard of my Lord of Rochester."

"Very true, Defoe," said a genial-looking man in a red waistcoat, who was sitting at the modern end of the table. "But all this won't help our good friend Smith in making a start at his story, which, I believe, was the reason why we assembled."

"The Dickens it is!" stammered a little man beside him, and everybody laughed, especially the genial man, who cried out, "Charley Lamb, Charley Lamb, you'll never alter. You would make a pun if you were hanged for it."

"That would be a case of haltering," returned the other, on which everybody laughed again.

By this time I had begun to dimly realise in my confused brain the enormous honour which had been done me. The greatest masters of fiction in every age of English letters had apparently made a rendezvous beneath my roof, in order to assist me in my difficulties. There were many faces at the table whom I was unable to identify; but when I looked hard at others I often found them to be very familiar to me, whether from paintings or from mere description. Thus between the first two speakers, who had betrayed themselves as Defoe and Smollett, there sat a dark, saturnine corpulent old man, with harsh prominent features, who I was sure could be none other than the famous author of Gulliver. There were several others of whom I was not so sure, sitting at the other side of the table, but I conjecture that both Fielding and Richardson were among them, and I could swear to the lantern-jaws and cadaverous visage of Lawrence Sterne. Higher up I could see among the crowd the high forehead of Sir Walter

Scott, the masculine features of George Eliott, and the flattened nose of Thackeray; while amongst the living I recognised James Payn, Walter Besant, the lady known as "Ouida," Robert Louis Stevenson, and several of lesser note. Never before, probably, had such an assemblage of choice spirits gathered under one roof.

"Well," said Sir Walter Scott, speaking with a pronounced accent, "ye ken the auld proverb, sirs, 'Ower mony cooks,' or as the Border minstrel sang—

"Black Johnstone wi' his troopers ten
"Might mak' the heart turn cauld,
"But Johnstone when he's a' alane
"Is waur ten thoosand fauld.

"The Johnstones were one of the Redesdale families, second cousins of the Armstrongs, and connected by marriage to——"

"Perhaps, Sir Walter," interrupted Thackeray, "you would take the responsibility off our hands by yourself dictating the commencement of a story to this young literary aspirant."

"Na, na!" cried Sir Walter; "I'll do my share, but there's Chairlie over there as full o' wut as a Radical's full o' treason. He's the laddie to give a cheery opening to it."

Dickens was shaking his head, and apparently about to refuse the honour, when a voice from among the moderns—I could not see who it was for the crowd—said:

"Suppose we begin at the end of the table and work round, any one contributing a little as the fancy seizes him?"

"Agreed! agreed!" cried the whole company; and every eye was turned on Defoe, who seemed very uneasy, and filled his pipe from a great tobacco-box in front of him.

"Nay, gossips," he said, "there are others more worthy——" But he was interrupted by loud cries of "No! no!" from the whole table; and Smollett shouted out, "Stand to it, Dan—stand to it! You and I and the Dean here will make three short tacks just to fetch her out of harbour, and then she may drift where she pleases." Thus encouraged, Defoe cleared his throat, and began in this way, talking between the puffs of his pipe:—

"My father was a well-to-do yeoman of Cheshire, named Cyprian Overbeck, but, marrying about the year 1617, he assumed the name of his wife's family, which was Wells; and thus I, their eldest son, was named Cyprian Overbeck Wells. The farm was a very fertile one, and contained some of the best grazing land in those parts, so that my father was enabled to lay by money to the extent of a thousand crowns, which he laid out in an adventure to the Indies with such surprising success that in less than three years it had increased fourfold. Thus encouraged, he bought a part share of the trader, and, fitting her out once more with such commodities as were most in demand (*viz.*, old muskets, hangers and axes, besides glasses, needles, and the like), he placed me on board as supercargo to look after his interests, and despatched us upon our voyage.

"We had a fair wind as far as Cape de Verde, and there, getting into the north-west trade-winds, made good progress down the African coast. Beyond sighting a Barbary rover once, whereat our mariners were in sad distress, counting themselves already as little better than slaves, we had good luck until we had come within a hundred leagues of the Cape of Good Hope, when the wind veered round to the southward and blew exceeding hard, while the sea rose to such a height that the end of the mainyard dipped into the water, and I heard the master say that though he had been at sea for five-and-thirty years he had never seen the like of it, and that he had little expectation of riding through it. On this I fell to wringing my hands and bewailing myself, until the mast going by the board with a crash, I thought that the ship had struck, and swooned with terror, falling into the scuppers and lying like one dead, which was the saving of me, as will appear in the sequel. For the mariners, giving up all hope of saving the ship, and being in momentary expectation that she would founder, pushed off in the long-boat, whereby I fear that they met the fate which they hoped to avoid, since I have never from that day heard anything of them. For my own part, on recovering from the swoon into which I had fallen, I found that, by the mercy of Providence, the sea had gone down, and that I was alone in the vessel. At which last discovery I was so terror-struck that I could but stand wringing my hands and bewailing my sad fate, until at last taking heart, I fell to comparing my lot with that of my unhappy *camerados*, on which I became more cheerful, and descending to the cabin, made a meal off such dainties as were in the captain's locker."

Having got so far, Defoe remarked that he thought he had given them a fair start, and handed over the story to Dean Swift, who, after premising that he feared he would find himself as much at sea as Master Cyprian Overbeck Wells, continued in this way:

"For two days I drifted about in great distress, fearing that there should be a return of the gale, and keeping an eager lookout for my late companions. Upon the third day, towards evening, I observed to my extreme surprise that the ship was under the influence of a very powerful current, which ran to the northeast with such violence that she was carried, now bows on, now stern on, and occasionally drifting sideways like a crab, at a rate which I cannot compute at less than twelve or fifteen knots an hour. For several weeks I was borne away in this manner, until one morning, to my inexpressible joy, I sighted an island upon the starboard quarter. The current would, however, have carried me past it had I not made shift, though single-handed, to set the flying-jib so as to turn her bows, and then clapping on the sprit-sail, studding-sail, and fore-sail, I clewed up the halliards upon the port side, and put the wheel down hard a-starboard, the wind being at the time north-east-half-east."

At the description of this nautical manoeuvre I observed that Smollett grinned, and a gentleman who was sitting higher up the table in the uniform of the Royal Navy, and who I guessed to be Captain Marryat, became very uneasy and fidgeted in his seat.

"By this means I got clear of the current and was able to steer within a quarter of a mile of the beach, which indeed I might have approached still nearer by making another tack, but being an excellent swimmer, I deemed it best to leave the vessel, which was almost waterlogged, and to make the best of my way to the shore.

"I had had my doubts hitherto as to whether this new-found country was inhabited or no, but as I approached nearer to it, being on the summit of a great wave, I perceived a number of figures on the beach, engaged apparently in watching me and my vessel. My joy, however, was considerably lessened when on reaching the land I found that the figures consisted of a vast concourse of animals of various sorts who were standing about in groups, and who hurried down to the water's edge to meet me. I had scarce put my foot upon the sand before I was surrounded by an eager crowd of deer, dogs, wild boars, buffaloes, and other creatures, none of whom showed the least fear either of me or of each other, but, on the contrary, were animated by a common feeling of curiosity, as well as, it would appear, by some degree of disgust."

"A second edition," whispered Lawrence Sterne to his neighbour; "Gulliver served up cold."

"Did you speak, sir?" asked the Dean very sternly, having evidently overheard the remark.

"My words were not addressed to you, sir," answered Sterne, looking rather frightened.

"They were none the less insolent," roared the Dean. "Your reverence would fain make a Sentimental Journey of the narrative, I doubt not, and find pathos in a dead donkey—though faith, no man can blame thee for mourning over thy own kith and kin."

"Better that than to wallow in all the filth of Yahoo-land," returned Sterne warmly, and a quarrel would certainly have ensued but for the interposition of the remainder of the company. As it was, the Dean refused indignantly to have any further hand in the story, and Sterne also stood out of it, remarking with a sneer that he was loth to fit a good blade on to a poor handle. Under these circumstances some further unpleasantness might have occurred had not Smollett rapidly taken up the narrative, continuing it in the third person instead of the first:

"Our hero, being considerably alarmed at this strange reception, lost little time in plunging into the sea again and regaining his vessel, being convinced that the worst which might befall him from the elements would be as nothing compared to the dangers of this mysterious island. It was as well that he took this course, for before nightfall his ship was overhauled and he himself picked up by a British man-of-war, the Lightning, then returning from the West Indies, where it had formed part of the fleet under the command of Admiral Benbow. Young Wells, being a likely lad enough, well-spoken and high-spirited, was at once entered on the books as officer's servant, in which capacity he both gained great popularity on account of the freedom of his manners, and found an opportunity for indulging in those practical pleasantries for which he had all his life been famous.

"Among the quartermasters of the Lightning there was one named Jedediah Anchorstock, whose appearance was so remarkable that it quickly attracted the attention of our hero. He was a man of about fifty, dark with exposure to the weather, and so tall that as he came along the 'tween decks he had to bend himself nearly double. The most striking peculiarity of this individual was, however, that in his boyhood some evil-minded person had tattooed eyes all over his countenance with such marvellous skill that it was difficult at a short distance to pick out his real ones among so many counterfeits. On this strange personage Master Cyprian determined to exercise his talents for mischief, the more so as he learned that he was extremely superstitious, and also that he had left behind him in Portsmouth a strong-minded spouse of whom he stood in mortal terror. With this object he secured one of the sheep which were kept on board for the officers' table, and pouring a can of *rumbo* down its throat, reduced it to a state of utter intoxication. He then conveyed it to Anchorstock's berth, and with the assistance of some other imps, as mischievous as himself, dressed it up in a high nightcap and gown, and covered it over with the bedclothes.

"When the quartermaster came down from his watch our hero met him at the door of his berth with an agitated face. 'Mr. Anchorstock,' said he, 'can it be that your wife is on board?' 'Wife!' roared the astonished sailor. 'Ye white-faced swab, what d'ye mean?' 'If she's not here in the ship it must be her ghost,' said Cyprian, shaking his head gloomily. 'In the ship! How in thunder could she get into the ship? Why, master, I believe as how you're weak in the upper works, d'ye see? to as much as think o' such a thing. My Poll is moored head and starn, behind the point at Portsmouth, more'n two thousand mile away.' 'Upon my word,' said our hero, very earnestly, 'I saw a female look out of your cabin not five minutes ago.' 'Ay, ay, Mr. Anchorstock,' joined in several of the conspirators. 'We all saw her—a spanking-looking craft with a dead-light mounted on one side.' 'Sure enough,' said Anchorstock, staggered by this accumulation of evidence, 'my Polly's starboard eye was doused for ever by long Sue Williams of the Hard. But if so be as she be there I must see her, be she ghost or quick;' with which the honest sailor, in much perturbation and trembling in every limb, began to shuffle forward into the cabin, holding the light well in front of him. It chanced, however, that the unhappy sheep, which was quietly engaged in sleeping off the effects of its unusual potations, was awakened by the noise of this approach, and finding herself in such an unusual position, sprang out of the bed and rushed furiously for the door, bleating wildly, and rolling about like a brig in a tornado, partly from intoxication and partly from the night-dress which impeded her movements. As Anchorstock saw this extraordinary apparition bearing down upon him, he uttered a yell and fell flat upon his face, convinced that he had to do with a supernatural visitor, the more so as the confederates heightened the effect by a chorus of most ghastly groans and cries.

"The joke had nearly gone beyond what was originally intended, for the quartermaster lay as one dead, and it was only with the greatest difficulty that he could be brought to his senses. To the end of the voyage he stoutly asserted that he had seen the distant Mrs. Anchorstock, remarking with many oaths that though he was too woundily scared to take much note of the features, there was no mistaking the strong smell of rum which was characteristic of his better half.

"It chanced shortly after this to be the king's birthday, an event which was signalised aboard the Lightening by the death of the commander under singular circumstances. This officer, who was a real fair-weather Jack, hardly knowing the ship's keel from her ensign, had obtained his position through parliamentary interest, and used it with such tyranny and cruelty that he was universally execrated. So unpopular was he that when a plot was entered into by the whole crew to punish his misdeeds with death, he had not a single friend among six hundred souls to warn him of his danger. It was the custom on board the king's ships that upon his birthday the entire ship's company should be drawn up upon deck, and that at a signal they should discharge their muskets into the air in honour of his Majesty. On this occasion word had been secretly passed round for every man to slip a slug into his firelock, instead of the blank cartridge provided. On the boatswain blowing his whistle the men mustered upon deck and formed line, whilst the captain, standing well in front of them, delivered a few words to them. 'When I give the word,' he concluded, 'you shall discharge your pieces, and by thunder, if any man is a second before or a second after his fellows I shall trice him up to the weather rigging!' With these words he roared 'Fire!' on which every man levelled his musket straight at his head and pulled the trigger. So accurate was the aim and so short the distance, that more than five hundred bullets struck him simultaneously, blowing away his head and a large portion of his body. There were so many concerned in this matter, and it was so hopeless to trace it to any individual, that the officers were unable to punish any one for the affair—the more readily as the captain's haughty ways and heartless conduct had made him quite as hateful to them as to the men whom they commanded.

"By his pleasantries and the natural charm of his manners our hero so far won the good wishes of the ship's company that they parted with infinite regret upon their arrival in England. Filial duty, however, urged him to return home and report himself to his father, with which object he posted from Portsmouth to London, intending to proceed thence to Shropshire. As it chanced, however, one of the horses sprained his off foreleg while passing through Chichester, and as no change could be obtained, Cyprian found himself compelled to put up at the Crown and Bull for the night.

"Ods bodikins!" continued Smollett, laughing, "I never could pass a comfortable hostel without stopping, and so, with your permission, I'll e'en stop here, and whoever wills may lead friend Cyprian to his further adventures. Do you, Sir Walter, give us a touch of the Wizard of the North."

With these words Smollett produced a pipe, and filling it at Defoe's tobacco-pot, waited patiently for the continuation of the story.

"If I must, I must," remarked the illustrious Scotchman, taking a pinch of snuff; "but I must beg leave to put Mr. Wells back a few hundred years, for of all things I love the true mediaeval smack. To proceed then:—

"Our hero, being anxious to continue his journey, and learning that it would be some time before any conveyance would be ready, determined to push on alone mounted on his gallant grey steed. Travelling was particularly dangerous at that time, for besides the usual perils which beset wayfarers, the southern parts of England were in a lawless and disturbed state which bordered on insurrection. The young man, however, having loosened his sword in his sheath, so as to be ready for every eventuality, galloped cheerily upon his way, guiding himself to the best of his ability by the light of the rising moon.

"He had not gone far before he realised that the cautions which had been impressed upon him by the landlord, and which he had been inclined to look upon as self-interested advice, were only too well justified. At a spot where the road was particularly rough, and ran across some marsh land, he perceived a short distance from him a dark shadow, which his practised eye detected at once as a body of crouching men. Reining up his horse within a few yards of the ambuscade, he wrapped his cloak round his bridle-arm and summoned the party to stand forth.

"'What ho, my masters!' he cried. 'Are beds so scarce, then, that ye must hamper the high road of the king with your bodies? Now, by St. Ursula of Alpuxerra, there be those who might think that birds who fly o' nights were after higher game than the moorhen or the woodcock!'

"'Blades and targets, comrades!' exclaimed a tall powerful man, springing into the centre of the road with several companions, and standing in front of the frightened horse. 'Who is this swashbuckler who summons his Majesty's lieges from their repose? A very *soldado*, o' truth. Hark ye, sir, or my lord, or thy grace, or whatsoever title your honour's honour may be pleased to approve, thou must curb thy tongue play, or by the seven witches of Gambleside thou may find thyself in but a sorry plight.'

"'I prythee, then, that thou wilt expound to me who and what ye are,' quoth our hero, 'and whether your purpose be such as an honest man may approve of. As to your threats, they turn from my mind as your caitiffly weapons would shiver upon my hauberk from Milan.'

"'Nay, Allen,' interrupted one of the party, addressing him who seemed to be their leader; 'this is a lad of mettle, and such a one as our honest Jack longs for. But we lure not hawks with empty hands. Look ye, sir, there is game afoot which it may need such bold hunters as thyself to follow. Come with us and take a firkin of canary, and we will find better work for that glaive of thine than getting its owner into broil and bloodshed; for, by my troth! Milan or no Milan, if my curtel axe do but ring against that morion of thine it will be an ill day for thy father's son.'

"For a moment our hero hesitated as to whether it would best become his knightly traditions to hurl himself against his enemies, or whether it might not be better to obey their requests. Prudence, mingled with a large share of curiosity, eventually carried the day, and dismounting from his horse, he intimated that he was ready to follow his captors.

"'Spoken like a man!' cried he whom they addressed as Allen. 'Jack Cade will be right glad of such a recruit. Blood and carrion! but thou hast the thews of a young ox; and I swear, by the haft of my sword, that it might have gone ill with some of us hadst thou not listened to reason!'

"'Nay, not so, good Allen—not so,' squeaked a very small man, who had remained in the background while there was any prospect of a fray, but who now came pushing to the front. 'Hadst thou been alone it might indeed have been so, perchance, but an expert swordsman can disarm at pleasure such a one as this young knight. Well I remember in the Palatinate how I clove to the chine even such another—the Baron von Slogstaff. He struck at me, look ye, so; but I, with buckler and blade, did, as one might say, deflect it; and then, countering in carte, I returned in tierce, and so—St. Agnes save us! who comes here?'

"The apparition which frightened the loquacious little man was sufficiently strange to cause a qualm even in the bosom of the knight. Through the darkness there loomed a figure which appeared to be of gigantic size, and a hoarse voice, issuing apparently some distance above the heads of the party, broke roughly on the silence of the night.

"'Now out upon thee, Thomas Allen, and foul be thy fate if thou hast abandoned thy post without good and sufficient cause. By St. Anselm of the Holy Grove, thou hadst best have never been born than rouse my spleen this night. Wherefore is it that you and your men are trailing over the moor like a flock of geese when Michaelmas is near?'

"'Good captain,' said Allen, doffing his bonnet, an example followed by others of the band, 'we have captured a goodly youth who was pricking it along the London road. Methought that some word of thanks were meet reward for such service, rather than taunt or threat.'

"'Nay, take it not to heart, bold Allen,' exclaimed their leader, who was none other than the great Jack Cade himself. 'Thou knowest of old that my temper is somewhat choleric, and my tongue not greased with that unguent which oils the mouths of the lip-serving lords of the land. And you,' he continued, turning suddenly upon our hero, 'are you ready to join the great cause which will make England what it was when the learned Alfred reigned in the land? Zounds, man, speak out, and pick not your phrases.'

"'I am ready to do aught which may become a knight and a gentleman,' said the soldier stoutly.

"'Taxes shall be swept away!' cried Cade excitedly—'the impost and the anpost—the tithe and the hundred-tax. The poor man's salt-box and flour-bin shall be as free as the nobleman's cellar. Ha! what sayest thou?'

"'It is but just,' said our hero.

"'Ay, but they give us such justice as the falcon gives the

leveret!' roared the orator. 'Down with them, I say—down with every man of them! Noble and judge, priest and king, down with them all!'

"'Nay,' said Sir Overbeck Wells, drawing himself up to his full height, and laying his hand upon the hilt of his sword, 'there I cannot follow thee, but must rather defy thee as traitor and *faineant*, seeing that thou art no true man, but one who would usurp the rights of our master the king, whom may the Virgin protect!'

"At these bold words, and the defiance which they conveyed, the rebels seemed for a moment utterly bewildered; but, encouraged by the hoarse shout of their leader, they brandished their weapons and prepared to fall upon the knight, who placed himself in a posture for defence and awaited their attack.

"There now!" cried Sir Walter, rubbing his hands and chuckling, "I've put the *chiel* in a pretty warm corner, and we'll see which of you moderns can take him oot o't. Ne'er a word more will ye get frae me to help him one way or the other."

"You try your hand, James," cried several voices, and the author in question had got so far as to make an allusion to a solitary horseman who was approaching, when he was interrupted by a tall gentleman a little farther down with a slight stutter and a very nervous manner.

"Excuse me," he said, "but I fancy that I may be able to do something here. Some of my humble productions have been said to excel Sir Walter at his best, and I was undoubtedly stronger all round. I could picture modern society as well as ancient; and as to my plays, why Shakespeare never came near 'The Lady of Lyons' for popularity. There is this little thing——" (Here he rummaged among a great pile of papers in front of him). "Ah! that's a report of mine, when I was in India! Here it is. No, this is one of my speeches in the House, and this is my criticism on Tennyson. Didn't I warm him up? I can't find what I wanted, but of course you have read them all—*Rienzi*, and *Harold*, and *The Last of the Barons*. Every schoolboy knows them by heart, as poor Macaulay would have said. Allow me to give you a sample:—

"In spite of the gallant knight's valiant resistance the combat was too unequal to be sustained. His sword was broken by a slash from a brown bill, and he was borne to the ground. He expected immediate death, but such did not seem to be the intention of the ruffians who had captured him. He was placed upon the back of his own charger and borne, bound hand and foot, over the trackless moor, in the fastnesses of which the rebels secreted themselves.

"In the depths of these wilds there stood a stone building which had once been a farm-house, but having been for some reason abandoned had fallen into ruin, and had now become the headquarters of Cade and his men. A large cow house near the farm had been utilised as sleeping quarters, and some rough attempts had been made to shield the principal room of the main building from the weather by stopping up the gaping apertures in the walls. In this apartment was spread out a rough meal for the returning rebels, and our hero was thrown, still bound, into an empty outhouse, there to await his fate."

Sir Walter had been listening with the greatest impatience to Bulwer Lytton's narrative, but when it had reached this point he broke in impatiently.

"We want a touch of your own style, man," he said. "The animal-magnetico-electro-hysterical-biological-mysterious sort of story is all your own, but at present you are just a poor copy of myself, and nothing more."

There was a murmur of assent from the company, and Defoe remarked, "Truly, Master Lytton, there is a plaguey resemblance in the style, which may indeed be but a chance, and yet methinks it is sufficiently marked to warrant such words as our friend hath used."

"Perhaps you will think that this is an imitation also," said Lytton bitterly, and leaning back in his chair with a morose countenance, he continued the narrative in this way:—

"Our unfortunate hero had hardly stretched himself upon the straw with which his dungeon was littered, when a secret door opened in the wall and a venerable old man swept majestically into the apartment. The prisoner gazed upon him with astonishment not unmixed with awe, for on his broad brow was printed the seal of much knowledge—such knowledge as it is not granted to the son of man to know. He was clad in a long white robe, crossed and chequered with mystic devices in the Arabic character, while a high scarlet tiara marked with the square and circle enhanced his venerable appearance. 'My son,' he said, turning his piercing and yet dreamy gaze upon Sir Overbeck, 'all things lead to nothing, and nothing is the foundation of all things. Cosmos is impenetrable. Why then should we exist?'

"Astounded at this weighty query, and at the philosophic demeanour of his visitor, our hero made shift to bid him welcome and to demand his name and quality. As the old man answered him his voice rose and fell in musical cadences, like the sighing of the east wind, while an ethereal and aromatic vapour pervaded the apartment.

"'I am the eternal non-ego,' he answered. 'I am the concentrated negative—the everlasting essence of nothing. You see in me that which existed before the beginning of matter many years before the commencement of time. I am the algebraic x which represents the infinite divisibility of a finite particle.'

"Sir Overbeck felt a shudder as though an ice-cold hand had been placed upon his brow. 'What is your message?' he whispered, falling prostrate before his mysterious visitor.

"'To tell you that the eternities beget chaos, and that the immensities are at the mercy of the divine *ananke*. Infinitude crouches before a personality. The mercurial essence is the prime mover in spirituality, and the thinker is powerless before the pulsating inanity. The cosmical procession is terminated only by the unknowable and unpronounceable——'

"May I ask, Mr. Smollett, what you find to laugh at?"

"Gad zooks, master," cried Smollett, who had been sniggering for some time back. "It seems to me that there is little danger of any one venturing to dispute that style with you."

"It's all your own," murmured Sir Walter.

"And very pretty, too," quoth Lawrence Sterne, with a malignant grin. "Pray sir, what language do you call it?"

Lytton was so enraged at these remarks, and at the favour with which they appeared to be received, that he endeavoured to stutter out some reply, and then, losing control of himself completely, picked up all his loose papers and strode out of the room, dropping pamphlets and speeches at every step. This incident amused the company so much that they laughed for several minutes without cessation. Gradually the sound of their laughter sounded more and more harshly in my ears, the lights on the table grew dim and the company more misty, until they and their symposium vanished away altogether. I was sitting before the embers of what had been a roaring fire, but was now little more than a heap of grey ashes, and the merry laughter of the august company had changed to the recriminations of my wife, who was shaking me violently by the shoulder and exhorting me to choose some more seasonable spot for my slumbers. So ended the wondrous adventures of Master Cyprian Overbeck Wells, but I still live in the hopes that in some future dream the great masters may themselves finish that which they have begun.

The Terror of Blue John Gap

The following narrative was found among the papers of Dr. James Hardcastle, who died of phthisis on February 4th, 1908, at 36, Upper Coventry Flats, South Kensington. Those who knew him best, while refusing to express an opinion upon this particular statement, are unanimous in asserting that he was a man of a sober and scientific turn of mind, absolutely devoid of imagination, and most unlikely to invent any abnormal series of events. The paper was contained in an envelope, which was docketed, *A Short Account of the Circumstances which occurred near Miss Allerton's Farm in North-West Derbyshire in the Spring of Last Year.* The envelope was sealed, and on the other side was written in pencil—

Dear Seaton,
It may interest, and perhaps pain you, to know that the incredulity with which you met my story has prevented me from ever opening my mouth upon the subject again. I leave this record after my death, and perhaps strangers may be found to have more confidence in me than my friend.

Inquiry has failed to elicit who this Seaton may have been. I may add that the visit of the deceased to Allerton's Farm, and the general nature of the alarm there, apart from his particular explanation, have been absolutely established. With this foreword I append his account exactly as he left it. It is in the form of a diary, some entries in which have been expanded, while a few have been erased.

April 17.—Already I feel the benefit of this wonderful up-land air. The farm of the Allertons lies fourteen hundred and twenty feet above sea-level, so it may well be a bracing climate. Beyond the usual morning cough I have very little discomfort, and, what with the fresh milk and the home-grown mutton, I have every chance of putting on weight. I think Saunderson will be pleased.

The two Miss Allertons are charmingly quaint and kind, two dear little hard-working old maids, who are ready to lavish all the heart which might have gone out to husband and to children upon an invalid stranger. Truly, the old maid is a most useful person, one of the reserve forces of the community. They talk of the superfluous woman, but what would the poor superfluous man do without her kindly presence? By the way, in their simplicity they very quickly let out the reason why Saunderson recommended their farm. The Professor rose from the ranks himself, and I believe that in his youth he was not above scaring crows in these very fields.

It is a most lonely spot, and the walks are picturesque in the extreme. The farm consists of grazing land lying at the bottom of an irregular valley. On each side are the fantastic limestone hills, formed of rock so soft that you can break it away with your hands. All this country is hollow. Could you strike it with some gigantic hammer it would boom like a drum, or possibly cave in altogether and expose some huge subterranean sea. A great sea there must surely be, for on all sides the streams run into the mountain itself, never to reappear. There are gaps everywhere amid the rocks, and when you pass through them you find yourself in great caverns, which wind down into the bowels of the earth. I have a small bicycle lamp, and it is a perpetual joy to me to carry it into these weird solitudes, and to see the wonderful silver and black effect when I throw its light upon the stalactites which drape the lofty roofs. Shut off the lamp, and you are in the blackest darkness. Turn it on, and it is a scene from the Arabian Nights.

But there is one of these strange openings in the earth which has a special interest, for it is the handiwork, not of nature, but of man. I had never heard of Blue John when I came to these parts. It is the name given to a peculiar mineral of a beautiful purple shade, which is only found at one or two places in the world. It is so rare that an ordinary vase of Blue John would be valued at a great price. The Romans, with that extraordinary instinct of theirs, discovered that it was to be found in this valley, and sank a horizontal shaft deep into the mountain side. The opening of their mine has been called Blue John Gap, a clean-cut arch in the rock, the mouth all overgrown with bushes. It is a goodly passage which the Roman miners have cut, and it intersects some of the great water-worn caves, so that if you enter Blue John Gap you would do well to mark your steps and to have a good store of candles, or you may never make your way back to the daylight again. I have not yet gone deeply into it, but this very day I stood at the mouth of the arched tunnel, and peering down into the black recesses beyond, I vowed that when my health returned I would devote some holiday to exploring those mysterious depths and finding out for myself how far the Roman had penetrated into the Derbyshire hills.

Strange how superstitious these countrymen are! I should have thought better of young Armitage, for he is a man of some education and character, and a very fine fellow for his station in life. I was standing at the Blue John Gap when he came across the field to me.

"Well, doctor," said he, "you're not afraid, anyhow."

"Afraid!" I answered. "Afraid of what?"

"Of it," said he, with a jerk of his thumb towards the black vault, "of the Terror that lives in the Blue John Cave."

How absurdly easy it is for a legend to arise in a lonely countryside! I examined him as to the reasons for his weird belief. It seems that from time to time sheep have been missing from the fields, carried bodily away, according to Armitage. That they could have wandered away of their own accord and disappeared among the mountains was an explanation to which he would not listen. On one occasion a pool of blood had been found, and some tufts of wool. That also, I pointed out, could be explained in a perfectly natural way. Further, the nights upon which sheep disappeared were invariably very dark, cloudy nights with no moon. This I met with the obvious retort that those were the nights which a commonplace sheep-stealer would naturally choose for his work. On one occasion a gap had been made in a wall, and some of the stones scattered for a considerable distance. Human agency again, in my opinion. Finally, Armitage clinched all his arguments by telling me that he had actually heard the Creature—indeed, that anyone could hear it who remained long enough at the Gap. It was a distant roaring of an immense volume. I could not but smile at this, knowing, as I do, the strange reverberations which come out of an underground water system running amid the chasms of a limestone formation. My incredulity annoyed Armitage so that he turned and left me with some abruptness.

And now comes the queer point about the whole business. I was still standing near the mouth of the cave turning over in my mind the various statements of Armitage, and reflecting how readily they could be explained away, when suddenly, from the depth of the tunnel beside me, there issued a most extraordinary sound. How shall I describe it? First of all, it seemed to be a great distance away, far down in the bowels of the earth. Secondly, in spite of this suggestion of distance, it was very loud. Lastly, it was not a boom, nor a crash, such as one would associate with falling water or tumbling rock, but it was a high whine, tremulous and vibrating, almost like the whinnying of a horse. It was certainly a most remarkable experience, and one which for a moment, I must admit, gave a new significance to Armitage's words. I waited by the Blue John Gap for half an hour or more, but there was no return of the sound, so at last I wandered back to the farmhouse, rather mystified by what had occurred. Decidedly I shall explore that cavern when my strength is restored. Of course, Armitage's explanation is too absurd for discussion, and yet that sound was certainly very strange. It still rings in my ears as I write.

April 20.—In the last three days I have made several expeditions to the Blue John Gap, and have even penetrated some short distance, but my bicycle lantern is so small and weak that I dare not trust myself very far. I shall do the thing more systematically. I have heard no sound at all, and could almost believe that I had been the victim of some hallucination suggested, perhaps, by Armitage's conversation. Of course, the whole idea is absurd, and yet I must confess that those bushes at the entrance of the cave do present an appearance as if some heavy creature had forced its way through them. I begin to be keenly interested. I have said nothing to the Miss Allertons, for they are quite superstitious enough already, but I have bought some candles, and mean to investigate for myself.

I observed this morning that among the numerous tufts of sheep's wool which lay among the bushes near the cavern there was one which was smeared with blood. Of course, my reason tells me that if sheep wander into such rocky places they are likely to injure themselves, and yet somehow that splash of crimson gave me a sudden shock, and for a moment I found myself shrinking back in horror from the old Roman arch. A fetid breath seemed to ooze from the black depths into which I peered. Could it indeed be possible that some nameless thing, some dreadful presence, was lurking down yonder? I should have been incapable of such feelings in the days of my strength, but one grows more nervous and fanciful when one's health is shaken.

For the moment I weakened in my resolution, and was ready to leave the secret of the old mine, if one exists, for ever unsolved. But tonight my interest has returned and my nerves grown more steady. Tomorrow I trust that I shall have gone more deeply into this matter.

April 22.—Let me try and set down as accurately as I can my extraordinary experience of yesterday. I started in the afternoon, and made my way to the Blue John Gap. I confess that my misgivings returned as I gazed into its depths, and I wished that I had brought a companion to share my exploration. Finally, with a return of resolution, I lit my candle, pushed my way through the briars, and descended into the rocky shaft.

It went down at an acute angle for some fifty feet, the floor being covered with broken stone. Thence there extended a long, straight passage cut in the solid rock. I am no geologist, but the lining of this corridor was certainly of some harder material than limestone, for there were points where I could actually see the tool-marks which the old miners had left in their excavation, as fresh as if they had been done yesterday. Down this strange, old-world corridor I stumbled, my feeble flame throwing a dim circle of light around me, which made the shadows beyond the more threatening and obscure. Finally, I came to a spot where the Roman tunnel opened into a water-worn cavern—a huge hall, hung with long white icicles of lime deposit. From this central chamber I could dimly perceive that a number of passages worn by the subterranean streams wound away into the depths of the earth. I was standing there wondering whether I had better return, or whether I dare venture farther into this dangerous labyrinth, when my eyes fell upon something at my feet which strongly arrested my attention.

The greater part of the floor of the cavern was covered with boulders of rock or with hard incrustations of lime, but at this particular point there had been a drip from the distant roof, which had left a patch of soft mud. In the very centre of this there was a huge mark—an ill-defined blotch, deep, broad and irregular, as if a great boulder had fallen upon it. No loose stone lay near, however, nor was there anything to account for the impression. It was far too large to be caused by any possible animal, and besides, there was only the one, and the patch of mud was of such a size that no reasonable stride could have covered it. As I rose from the examination of that singular mark and then looked round into the black shadows which hemmed me in, I must confess that I felt for a moment a most unpleasant sinking of my heart, and that, do what I could, the candle trembled in my outstretched hand.

I soon recovered my nerve, however, when I reflected how absurd it was to associate so huge and shapeless a mark with the track of any known animal. Even an elephant could not have produced it. I determined, therefore, that I would not be scared by vague and senseless fears from carrying out my exploration. Before proceeding, I took good note of a curious rock formation in the wall by which I could recognize the entrance of the Roman tunnel. The precaution was very necessary, for the great cave, so far as I could see it, was intersected by passages. Having made sure of my position, and reassured myself by examining my spare candles and my matches, I advanced slowly over the rocky and uneven surface of the cavern.

And now I come to the point where I met with such sudden and desperate disaster. A stream, some twenty feet broad, ran across my path, and I walked for some little distance along the bank to find a spot where I could cross dry-shod. Finally, I came to a place where a single flat boulder lay near the centre, which I could reach in a stride. As it chanced, however, the rock had been cut away and made top-heavy by the rush of the stream, so that it tilted over as I landed on it and shot me into the ice-cold water. My candle went out, and I found myself floundering about in utter and absolute darkness.

I staggered to my feet again, more amused than alarmed by my adventure. The candle had fallen from my hand, and was lost in the stream, but I had two others in my pocket, so that it was of no importance. I got one of them ready, and drew out my box of matches to light it. Only then did I realize my position. The box had been soaked in my fall into the river. It was impossible to strike the matches.

A cold hand seemed to close round my heart as I realized my position. The darkness was opaque and horrible. It was so utter, one put one's hand up to one's face as if to press off something solid. I stood still, and by an effort I steadied myself. I tried to reconstruct in my mind a map of the floor of the cavern as I had last seen it. Alas! the bearings which had impressed themselves upon my mind were high on the wall, and not to be found by touch. Still, I remembered in a general way how the sides were situated, and I hoped that by groping my way along them I should at last come to the opening of the Roman tunnel. Moving very slowly, and continually striking against the rocks, I set out on this desperate quest.

But I very soon realized how impossible it was. In that black, velvety darkness one lost all one's bearings in an instant. Before I had made a dozen paces, I was utterly bewildered as to my whereabouts. The rippling of the stream, which was the one sound audible, showed me where it lay, but the moment that I left its bank I was utterly lost. The idea of finding my way back in absolute darkness through that limestone labyrinth was clearly an impossible one.

I sat down upon a boulder and reflected upon my unfortunate plight. I had not told anyone that I proposed to come to the Blue John mine, and it was unlikely that a search party would come after me. Therefore I must trust to my own resources to get clear of the danger. There was only one hope, and that was that the matches might dry. When I fell into the river, only half of me had got thoroughly wet. My left shoulder had remained above the water. I took the box of matches, therefore, and put it into my left armpit. The moist air of the cavern might possibly be counteracted by the heat of my body, but even so, I knew that I could not hope to get a light for many hours. Meanwhile there was nothing for it but to wait.

By good luck I had slipped several biscuits into my pocket before I left the farm-house. These I now devoured, and washed them down with a draught from that wretched stream which had been the cause of all my misfortunes. Then I felt about for a comfortable seat among the rocks, and, having discovered a place where I could get a support for my back, I stretched out my legs and settled myself down to wait. I was wretchedly damp and cold, but I tried to cheer myself with the reflection that modern science prescribed open windows and walks in all weather for my disease. Gradually, lulled by the monotonous gurgle of the stream, and by the absolute darkness, I sank into an uneasy slumber.

How long this lasted I cannot say. It may have been for an hour, it may have been for several. Suddenly I sat up on my rock couch, with every nerve thrilling and every sense acutely on the alert. Beyond all doubt I had heard a sound—some sound very distinct from the gurgling of the waters. It had passed, but the reverberation of it still lingered in my ear. Was it a search party? They would most certainly have shouted, and vague as this sound was which had wakened me, it was very distinct from the human voice. I sat palpitating and hardly daring to breathe. There it was again! And again! Now it had become continuous. It was a tread—yes, surely it was the tread of some living creature. But what a tread it was! It gave one the impression of enormous weight carried upon sponge-like feet, which gave forth a muffled but ear-filling sound. The darkness was as complete as ever, but the tread was regular and decisive. And it was coming beyond all question in my direction.

My skin grew cold, and my hair stood on end as I listened to that steady and ponderous footfall. There was some creature there, and surely by the speed of its advance, it was one which could see in the dark. I crouched low on my rock and tried to blend myself into it. The steps grew nearer still, then stopped, and presently I was aware of a loud lapping and gurgling. The creature was drinking at the stream. Then again there was silence, broken by a succession of long sniffs and snorts of tremendous volume and energy. Had it caught the scent of me? My own nostrils were filled by a low fetid odour, mephitic and abominable. Then I heard the steps again. They were on my side of the stream now. The stones rattled within a few yards of where I lay. Hardly daring to breathe, I crouched upon my rock. Then the steps drew away. I heard the splash as it returned across the river, and the sound died away into the distance in the direction from which it had come.

For a long time I lay upon the rock, too much horrified to move. I thought of the sound which I had heard coming from the depths of the cave, of Armitage's fears, of the strange impression in the mud, and now came this final and absolute proof that there was indeed some inconceivable monster, something utterly unearthly and dreadful, which lurked in the hollow of the mountain. Of its nature or form I could frame no conception, save that it was both light-footed and gigantic. The combat between my reason, which told me that such things could not be, and my senses, which told me that they were, raged within me as I lay. Finally, I was almost ready to persuade myself that this experience had been part of some evil dream, and that my abnormal condition might have conjured up an hallucination. But there remained one final experience which removed the last possibility of doubt from my mind.

I had taken my matches from my armpit and felt them. They seemed perfectly hard and dry. Stooping down into a crevice of the rocks, I tried one of them. To my delight it took fire at once. I lit the candle, and, with a terrified backward glance into the obscure depths of the cavern, I hurried in the direction of the Roman passage. As I did so I passed the patch of mud on which I had seen the huge imprint. Now I stood astonished before it, for there were three similar imprints upon its surface, enormous in size, irregular in outline, of a depth which indicated the ponderous weight which had left them. Then a great terror surged over me. Stooping and shading my candle with my hand, I ran in a frenzy of fear to the rocky archway, hastened up it, and never stopped until, with weary feet and panting lungs, I rushed up the final slope of stones, broke through the tangle of briars, and flung myself exhausted upon the soft grass under the peaceful light of the stars. It was three in the morning when I reached the farm-house, and today I am all unstrung and quivering after my terrific adventure. As yet I have told no one. I must move warily in the matter. What would the poor lonely women, or the uneducated yokels here think of it if I were to tell them my experience? Let me go to someone who can understand and advise.

April 25.—I was laid up in bed for two days after my incredible adventure in the cavern. I use the adjective with a very definite meaning, for I have had an experience since which has shocked me almost as much as the other. I have said that I was looking round for someone who could advise me. There is a Dr. Mark Johnson who practices some few miles away, to whom I had a note of recommendation from Professor Saunderson. To him I drove, when I was strong enough to get about, and I recounted to him my whole strange experience. He listened intently, and then carefully examined me, paying special attention to my reflexes and to the pupils of my eyes. When he had finished, he refused to discuss my adventure, saying that it was entirely beyond him, but he gave me the card of a Mr. Picton at Castleton, with the advice that I should instantly go to him and tell him the story exactly as I had done to himself. He was, according to my adviser, the very man who was pre-eminently suited to help me. I went on to the station, therefore, and made my way to the little town, which is some ten miles away. Mr. Picton appeared to be a man of importance, as his brass plate was displayed upon the door of a considerable building on the outskirts of the town. I was about to ring his bell, when some misgiving came into my mind, and, crossing to a neighbouring shop, I asked the man behind the counter if he could tell me anything of Mr. Picton. "Why," said he, "he is the best mad doctor in Derbyshire, and yonder is his asylum." You can imagine that it was not long before I had shaken the dust of Castleton from my feet and returned to the farm, cursing all unimaginative pedants who cannot conceive that there may be things in creation which have never yet chanced to come across their mole's vision. After all, now that I am cooler, I can afford to admit that I have been no more sympathetic to Armitage than Dr. Johnson has been to me.

April 27. When I was a student I had the reputation of being a man of courage and enterprise. I remember that when there was a ghost-hunt at Coltbridge it was I who sat up in the haunted house. Is it advancing years (after all, I am only thirty-five), or is it this physical malady which has caused degeneration? Certainly my heart quails when I think of that horrible cavern in the hill, and the certainty that it has some monstrous occupant. What shall I do? There is not an hour in the day that I do not debate the question. If I say nothing, then the mystery remains unsolved. If I do say anything, then I have the alternative of mad alarm over the whole countryside, or of absolute incredulity which may end in consigning me to an asylum. On the whole, I think that my best course is to wait, and to prepare for some expedition which shall be more deliberate and better thought out than the last. As a first step I have been to Castleton and obtained a few essentials—a large acetylene lantern for one thing, and a good double-barrelled sporting rifle for another. The latter I have hired, but I have bought a dozen heavy game cartridges, which would bring down a rhinoceros. Now I am ready for my troglodyte friend. Give me better health and a little spate of energy, and I shall try conclusions with him yet. But who and what is he? Ah! there is the question which stands between me and my sleep. How many theories do I form, only to discard each in turn! It is all so utterly unthinkable. And yet the cry, the footmark, the tread in the cavern—no reasoning can get past these I think of the old-world legends of dragons and of other monsters. Were they, perhaps, not such fairy-tales as we have thought? Can it be that there is some fact which underlies them, and am I, of all mortals, the one who is chosen to expose it?

May 3.—For several days I have been laid up by the vagaries of an English spring, and during those days there have been developments, the true and sinister meaning of which no one can appreciate save myself. I may say that we have had cloudy and moonless nights of late, which according to my information were the seasons upon which sheep disappeared. Well, sheep have disappeared. Two of Miss Allerton's, one of old Pearson's of the Cat Walk, and one of Mrs. Moulton's. Four in all during three nights. No trace is left of them at all, and the countryside is buzzing with rumours of gipsies and of sheep-stealers.

But there is something more serious than that. Young Armitage has disappeared also. He left his moorland cottage early on Wednesday night and has never been heard of since. He was an unattached man, so there is less sensation than would otherwise be the case. The popular explanation is that he owes money, and has found a situation in some other part of the country, whence he will presently write for his belongings. But I have grave misgivings. Is it not much more likely that the recent tragedy of the sheep has caused him to take some steps which may have ended in his own destruction? He may, for example, have lain in wait for the creature and been carried off by it into the recesses of the mountains. What an inconceivable fate for a civilized Englishman of the twentieth century! And yet I feel that it is possible and even probable. But in that case, how far am I answerable both for his death and for any other mishap which may occur? Surely with the knowledge I already possess it must be my duty to see that something is done, or if necessary to do it myself. It must be the latter, for this morning I went down to the local police-station and told my story. The inspector entered it all in a large book and bowed me out with commendable gravity, but I heard a burst of laughter before I had got down his garden path. No doubt he was recounting my adventure to his family.

June 10.—I am writing this, propped up in bed, six weeks after my last entry in this journal. I have gone through a terrible shock both to mind and body, arising from such an experience as has seldom befallen a human being before. But I have attained my end. The danger from the Terror which dwells in the Blue John Gap has passed never to return. Thus much at least I, a broken invalid, have done for the common good. Let me now recount what occurred as clearly as I may.

The night of Friday, May 3rd, was dark and cloudy—the very night for the monster to walk. About eleven o'clock I went from the farm-house with my lantern and my rifle, having first left a note upon the table of my bedroom in which I said that, if I were missing, search should be made for me in the direction of the Gap. I made my way to the mouth of the Roman shaft, and, having perched myself among the rocks close to the opening, I shut off my lantern and waited patiently with my loaded rifle ready to my hand.

It was a melancholy vigil. All down the winding valley I could see the scattered lights of the farm-houses, and the church clock of Chapel-le-Dale tolling the hours came faintly to my ears. These tokens of my fellow-men served only to make my own position seem the more lonely, and to call for a greater effort to overcome the terror which tempted me continually to get back to the farm, and abandon for ever this dangerous quest.

And yet there lies deep in every man a rooted self-respect which makes it hard for him to turn back from that which he has once undertaken. This feeling of personal pride was my salvation now, and it was that alone which held me fast when every instinct of my nature was dragging me away. I am glad now that I had the strength. In spite of all that is has cost me, my manhood is at least above reproach.

Twelve o'clock struck in the distant church, then one, then two. It was the darkest hour of the night. The clouds were drifting low, and there was not a star in the sky. An owl was hooting somewhere among the rocks, but no other sound, save the gentle sough of the wind, came to my ears. And then suddenly I heard it! From far away down the tunnel came those muffled steps, so soft and yet so ponderous. I heard also the rattle of stones as they gave way under that giant tread. They drew nearer. They were close upon me. I heard the crashing of the bushes round the entrance, and then dimly through the darkness I was conscious of the loom of some enormous shape, some monstrous inchoate creature, passing swiftly and very silently out from the tunnel. I was paralysed with fear and amazement. Long as I had waited, now that it had actually come I was unprepared for the shock. I lay motionless and breathless, whilst the great dark mass whisked by me and was swallowed up in the night.

But now I nerved myself for its return. No sound came from the sleeping countryside to tell of the horror which was loose. In no way could I judge how far off it was, what it was doing, or when it might be back. But not a second time should my nerve fail me, not a second time should it pass unchallenged. I swore it between my clenched teeth as I laid my cocked rifle across the rock.

And yet it nearly happened. There was no warning of approach now as the creature passed over the grass. Suddenly, like a dark, drifting shadow, the huge bulk loomed up once more before me, making for the entrance of the cave. Again came that paralysis of volition which held my crooked forefinger impotent upon the trigger. But with a desperate effort I shook it off. Even as the brushwood rustled, and the monstrous beast blended with the shadow of the Gap, I fired at the retreating form. In the blaze of the gun I caught a glimpse of a great shaggy mass, something with rough and bristling hair of a withered grey colour, fading away to white in its lower parts, the huge body supported upon short, thick, curving legs. I had just that glance, and then I heard the rattle of the stones as the creature tore down into its burrow. In an instant, with a triumphant revulsion of feeling, I had cast my fears to the wind, and uncovering my powerful lantern, with my rifle in my hand, I sprang down from my rock and rushed after the monster down the old Roman shaft.

My splendid lamp cast a brilliant flood of vivid light in front of me, very different from the yellow glimmer which had aided me down the same passage only twelve days before. As I ran, I saw the great beast lurching along before me, its huge bulk filling up the whole space from wall to wall. Its hair looked like coarse faded oakum, and hung down in long, dense masses which swayed as it moved. It was like an enormous unclipped sheep in its fleece, but in size it was far larger than the largest elephant, and its breadth seemed to be nearly as great as its height. It fills me with amazement now to think that I should have dared to follow such a horror into the bowels of the earth, but when one's blood is up, and when one's quarry seems to be flying, the old primeval hunting-spirit awakes and prudence is cast to the wind. Rifle in hand, I ran at the top of my speed upon the trail of the monster.

I had seen that the creature was swift. Now I was to find out to my cost that it was also very cunning. I had imagined that it was in panic flight, and that I had only to pursue it. The idea that it might turn upon me never entered my excited brain. I have already explained that the passage down which I was racing opened into a great central cave. Into this I rushed, fearful lest I should lose all trace of the beast. But he had turned upon his own traces, and in a moment we were face to face.

That picture, seen in the brilliant white light of the lantern, is etched for ever upon my brain. He had reared up on his hind legs as a bear would do, and stood above me, enormous, menacing—such a creature as no nightmare had ever brought to my imagination. I have said that he reared like a bear, and there was something bear-like—if one could conceive a bear which was ten-fold the bulk of any bear seen upon earth—in his whole pose and attitude, in his great crooked forelegs with their ivory-white claws, in his rugged skin, and in his red, gaping mouth, fringed with monstrous fangs. Only in one point did he differ from the bear, or from any other creature which walks the earth, and even at that supreme moment a shudder of horror passed over me as I observed that the eyes which glistened in the glow of my lantern were huge, projecting bulbs, white and sightless. For a moment his great paws swung over my head. The next he fell forward upon me, I and my broken lantern crashed to the earth, and I remember no more.

When I came to myself I was back in the farm-house of the Allertons. Two days had passed since my terrible adventure in the Blue John Gap. It seems that I had lain all night in the cave insensible from concussion of the brain, with my left arm and two ribs badly fractured. In the morning my note had been found, a search party of a dozen farmers assembled, and I had been tracked down and carried back to my bedroom, where I had lain in high delirium ever since. There was, it seems, no sign of the creature, and no bloodstain which would show that my bullet had found him as he passed. Save for my own plight and the marks upon the mud, there was nothing to prove that what I said was true.

Six weeks have now elapsed, and I am able to sit out once more in the sunshine. Just opposite me is the steep hillside, grey with shaley rock, and yonder on its flank is the dark cleft which marks the opening of the Blue John Gap. But it is no longer a source of terror. Never again through that ill-omened tunnel shall any strange shape flit out into the world of men. The educated and the scientific, the Dr. Johnsons and the like, may smile at my narrative, but the poorer folk of the countryside had never a doubt as to its truth. On the day after my recovering consciousness they assembled in their hundreds round the Blue John Gap. As the Castleton *Courier* said:

It was useless for our correspondent, or for any of the adventurous gentlemen who had come from Matlock, Buxton, and other parts, to offer to descend, to explore the cave to the end, and to finally test the extraordinary narrative of Dr. James Hardcastle. The country people had taken the matter into their own hands, and from an early hour of the morning they had worked hard in stopping up the entrance of the tunnel. There is a sharp slope where the shaft begins, and great boulders, rolled along by many willing hands, were thrust down it until the Gap was absolutely sealed. So ends the episode which has caused such excitement throughout the country. Local opinion is fiercely divided upon the subject. On the one hand are those who point to Dr. Hardcastle's impaired health, and to the possibility of cerebral lesions of tubercular origin giving rise to strange hallucinations. Some *idee fixe*, according to these gentlemen, caused the doctor to wander down the tunnel, and a fall among the rocks was sufficient to account for his injuries. On the other hand, a legend of a strange creature in the Gap has existed for some months back, and the farmers look upon Dr. Hardcastle's narrative and his personal injuries as a final corroboration. So the matter stands, and so the matter will continue to stand, for no definite solution seems to us to be now possible. It transcends human wit to give any scientific explanation which could cover the alleged facts.

Perhaps before the *Courier* published these words they would have been wise to send their representative to me. I have thought the matter out, as no one else has occasion to do, and it is possible that I might have removed some of the more obvious difficulties of the narrative and brought it one degree nearer to scientific acceptance. Let me then write down the only explanation which seems to me to elucidate what I know to my cost to have been a series of facts. My theory may seem to be wildly improbable, but at least no one can venture to say that it is impossible.

My view is—and it was formed, as is shown by my diary, before my personal adventure—that in this part of England there is a vast subterranean lake or sea, which is fed by the great number of streams which pass down through the limestone. Where there is a large collection of water there must also be some evaporation, mists or rain, and a possibility of vegetation. This in turn suggests that there may be animal life, arising, as the vegetable life would also do, from those seeds and types which had been introduced at an early period of the world's history, when communication with the outer air was more easy. This place had then developed a fauna and flora of its own, including such monsters as the one which I had seen, which may well have been the old cave-bear, enormously enlarged and modified by its new environment. For countless aeons the internal and the external creation had kept apart, growing steadily away from each other. Then there had come some rift in the depths of the mountain which had enabled one creature to wander up and, by means of the Roman tunnel, to reach the open air. Like all subterranean life, it had lost the power of sight, but this had no doubt been compensated for by nature in other directions. Certainly it had some means of finding its way about, and of hunting down the sheep upon the hillside. As to its choice of dark nights, it is part of my theory that light was painful to those great white eyeballs, and that it was only a pitch-black world which it could tolerate. Perhaps, indeed, it was the glare of my lantern which saved my life at that awful moment when we were face to face. So I read the riddle. I leave these facts behind me, and if you can explain them, do so; or if you choose to doubt them, do so. Neither your belief nor your incredulity can alter them, nor affect one whose task is nearly over.

****

So ended the strange narrative of Dr. James Hardcastle.

F. Habakuk Jephson's Statement

In the month of December in the year 1873, the British ship *Dei Gratia* steered into Gibraltar, having in tow the derelict brigantine *Marie Celeste*, which had been picked up in latitude 38 degrees 40', longitude 17 degrees 15' W. There were several circumstances in connection with the condition and appearance of this abandoned vessel which excited considerable comment at the time, and aroused a curiosity which has never been satisfied. What these circumstances were was summed up in an able article which appeared in the *Gibraltar Gazette*. The curious can find it in the issue for January 4, 1874, unless my memory deceives me. For the benefit of those, however, who may be unable to refer to the paper in question, I shall subjoin a few extracts which touch upon the leading features of the case.

"We have ourselves," says the anonymous writer in the *Gazette*, "been over the derelict *Marie Celeste*, and have closely questioned the officers of the *Dei Gratia* on every point which might throw light on the affair. They are of opinion that she had been abandoned several days, or perhaps weeks, before being picked up. The official log, which was found in the cabin, states that the vessel sailed from Boston to Lisbon, starting upon October 16. It is, however, most imperfectly kept, and affords little information. There is no reference to rough weather, and, indeed, the state of the vessel's paint and rigging excludes the idea that she was abandoned for any such reason. She is perfectly watertight. No signs of a struggle or of violence are to be detected, and there is absolutely nothing to account for the disappearance of the crew.

There are several indications that a lady was present on board, a sewing-machine being found in the cabin and some articles of female attire. These probably belonged to the captain's wife, who is mentioned in the log as having accompanied her husband. As an instance of the mildness of the weather, it may be remarked that a bobbin of silk was found standing upon the sewing-machine, though the least roll of the vessel would have precipitated it to the floor. The boats were intact and slung upon the davits; and the cargo, consisting of tallow and American clocks, was untouched. An old-fashioned sword of curious workmanship was discovered among some lumber in the forecastle, and this weapon is said to exhibit a longitudinal striation on the steel, as if it had been recently wiped. It has been placed in the hands of the police, and submitted to Dr. Monaghan, the analyst, for inspection. The result of his examination has not yet been published. We may remark, in conclusion, that Captain Dalton, of the *Dei Gratia*, an able and intelligent seaman, is of opinion that the *Marie Celeste* may have been abandoned a considerable distance from the spot at which she was picked up, since a powerful current runs up in that latitude from the African coast. He confesses his inability, however, to advance any hypothesis which can reconcile all the facts of the case. In the utter absence of a clue or grain of evidence, it is to be feared that the fate of the crew of the *Marie Celeste* will be added to those numerous mysteries of the deep which will never be solved until the great day when the sea shall give up its dead. If crime has been committed, as is much to be suspected, there is little hope of bringing the perpetrators to justice."

I shall supplement this extract from the *Gibraltar Gazette* by quoting a telegram from Boston, which went the round of the English papers, and represented the total amount of information which had been collected about the *Marie Celeste*. "She was," it said, "a brigantine of 170 tons burden, and belonged to White, Russell & White, wine importers, of this city. Captain J. W. Tibbs was an old servant of the firm, and was a man of known ability and tried probity. He was accompanied by his wife, aged thirty-one, and their youngest child, five years old. The crew consisted of seven hands, including two coloured seamen, and a boy. There were three passengers, one of whom was the well-known Brooklyn specialist on consumption, Dr. Habakuk Jephson, who was a distinguished advocate for Abolition in the early days of the movement, and whose pamphlet, entitled *Where is thy Brother?* exercised a strong influence on public opinion before the war. The other passengers were Mr. J. Harton, a writer in the employ of the firm, and Mr. Septimius Goring, a half-caste gentleman, from New Orleans. All investigations have failed to throw any light upon the fate of these fourteen human beings. The loss of Dr. Jephson will be felt both in political and scientific circles."

I have here epitomised, for the benefit of the public, all that has been hitherto known concerning the *Marie Celeste* and her crew, for the past ten years have not in any way helped to elucidate the mystery. I have now taken up my pen with the intention of telling all that I know of the ill-fated voyage. I consider that it is a duty which I owe to society, for symptoms which I am familiar with in others lead me to believe that before many months my tongue and hand may be alike incapable of conveying information. Let me remark, as a preface to my narrative, that I am Joseph Habakuk Jephson, Doctor of Medicine of the University of Harvard, and ex-Consulting Physician of the Samaritan Hospital of Brooklyn.

Many will doubtless wonder why I have not proclaimed myself before, and why I have suffered so many conjectures and surmises to pass unchallenged. Could the ends of justice have been served in any way by my revealing the facts in my possession I should unhesitatingly have done so. It seemed to me, however, that there was no possibility of such a result; and when I attempted, after the occurrence, to state my case to an English official, I was met with such offensive incredulity that I determined never again to expose myself to the chance of such an indignity. I can excuse the discourtesy of the Liverpool magistrate, however, when I reflect upon the treatment which I received at the hands of my own relatives, who, though they knew my unimpeachable character, listened to my statement with an indulgent smile as if humouring the delusion of a monomaniac.

This slur upon my veracity led to a quarrel between myself and John Vanburger, the brother of my wife, and confirmed me in my resolution to let the matter sink into oblivion—a determination which I have only altered through my son's solicitations. In order to make my narrative intelligible, I must run lightly over one or two incidents in my former life which throw light upon subsequent events.

My father, William K. Jephson, was a preacher of the sect called Plymouth Brethren, and was one of the most respected citizens of Lowell. Like most of the other Puritans of New England, he was a determined opponent to slavery, and it was from his lips that I received those lessons which tinged every action of my life. While I was studying medicine at Harvard University, I had already made a mark as an advanced Abolitionist; and when, after taking my degree, I bought a third share of the practice of Dr. Willis, of Brooklyn, I managed, in spite of my professional duties, to devote a considerable time to the cause which I had at heart, my pamphlet, *Where is thy Brother?*" (Swarburgh, Lister & Co., 1859) attracting considerable attention.

When the war broke out I left Brooklyn and accompanied the 113th New York Regiment through the campaign. I was present at the second battle of Bull's Run and at the battle of Gettysburg. Finally, I was severely wounded at Antietam, and would probably have perished on the field had it not been for the kindness of a gentleman named Murray, who had me carried to his house and provided me with every comfort. Thanks to his charity, and to the nursing which I received from his black domestics, I was soon able to get about the plantation with the help of a stick. It was during this period of convalescence that an incident occurred which is closely connected with my story.

Among the most assiduous of the negresses who had watched my couch during my illness there was one old crone who appeared to exert considerable authority over the others. She was exceedingly attentive to me, and I gathered from the few words that passed between us that she had heard of me, and that she was grateful to me for championing her oppressed race.

One day as I was sitting alone in the veranda, basking in the sun, and debating whether I should rejoin Grant's army, I was surprised to see this old creature hobbling towards me. After looking cautiously around to see that we were alone, she fumbled in the front of her dress and produced a small chamois leather bag which was hung round her neck by a white cord.

"Massa," she said, bending down and croaking the words into my ear, "me die soon. Me very old woman. Not stay long on Massa Murray's plantation."

"You may live a long time yet, Martha," I answered. "You know I am a doctor. If you feel ill let me know about it, and I will try to cure you."

"No wish to live—wish to die. I'm gwine to join the heavenly host." Here she relapsed into one of those half-heathenish rhapsodies in which negroes indulge. "But, massa, me have one thing must leave behind me when I go. No able to take it with me across the Jordan. That one thing very precious, more precious and more holy than all thing else in the world. Me, a poor old black woman, have this because my people, very great people, 'spose they was back in the old country. But you cannot understand this same as black folk could. My fader give it me, and his fader give it him, but now who shall I give it to? Poor Martha hab no child, no relation, nobody. All round I see black man very bad man. Black woman very stupid woman. Nobody worthy of the stone. And so I say, Here is Massa Jephson who write books and fight for coloured folk—he must be good man, and he shall have it though he is white man, and nebber can know what it mean or where it came from." Here the old woman fumbled in the chamois leather bag and pulled out a flattish black stone with a hole through the middle of it. "Here, take it," she said, pressing it into my hand; "take it. No harm nebber come from anything good. Keep it safe—nebber lose it!" and with a warning gesture the old crone hobbled away in the same cautious way as she had come, looking from side to side to see if we had been observed.

I was more amused than impressed by the old woman's earnestness, and was only prevented from laughing during her oration by the fear of hurting her feelings. When she was gone I took a good look at the stone which she had given me. It was intensely black, of extreme hardness, and oval in shape—just such a flat stone as one would pick up on the seashore if one wished to throw a long way. It was about three inches long, and an inch and a half broad at the middle, but rounded off at the extremities. The most curious part about it were several well-marked ridges which ran in semicircles over its surface, and gave it exactly the appearance of a human ear. Altogether I was rather interested in my new possession, and determined to submit it, as a geological specimen, to my friend Professor Shroeder of the New York Institute, upon the earliest opportunity. In the meantime I thrust it into my pocket, and rising from my chair started off for a short stroll in the shrubbery, dismissing the incident from my mind.

As my wound had nearly healed by this time, I took my leave of Mr. Murray shortly afterwards. The Union armies were everywhere victorious and converging on Richmond, so that my assistance seemed unnecessary, and I returned to Brooklyn. There I resumed my practice, and married the second daughter of Josiah Vanburger, the well-known wood engraver. In the course of a few years I built up a good connection and acquired considerable reputation in the treatment of pulmonary complaints. I still kept the old black stone in my pocket, and frequently told the story of the dramatic way in which I had become possessed of it. I also kept my resolution of showing it to Professor Shroeder, who was much interested both by the anecdote and the specimen. He pronounced it to be a piece of meteoric stone, and drew my attention to the fact that its resemblance to an ear was not accidental, but that it was most carefully worked into that shape. A dozen little anatomical points showed that the worker had been as accurate as he was skilful. "I should not wonder," said the Professor, "if it were broken off from some larger statue, though how such hard material could be so perfectly worked is more than I can understand. If there is a statue to correspond I should like to see it!" So I thought at the time, but I have changed my opinion since.

The next seven or eight years of my life were quiet and uneventful.

Summer followed spring, and spring followed winter, without any variation in my duties. As the practice increased I admitted J. S. Jackson as partner, he to have one-fourth of the profits. The continued strain had told upon my constitution, however, and I became at last so unwell that my wife insisted upon my consulting Dr. Kavanagh Smith, who was my colleague at the Samaritan Hospital.

That gentleman examined me, and pronounced the apex of my left lung to be in a state of consolidation, recommending me at the same time to go through a course of medical treatment and to take a long sea-voyage.

My own disposition, which is naturally restless, predisposed me strongly in favour of the latter piece of advice, and the matter was clinched by my meeting young Russell, of the firm of White, Russell & White, who offered me a passage in one of his father's ships, the *Marie Celeste*, which was just starting from Boston. "She is a snug little ship," he said, "and Tibbs, the captain, is an excellent fellow. There is nothing like a sailing ship for an invalid." I was very much of the same opinion myself, so I closed with the offer on the spot.

My original plan was that my wife should accompany me on my travels. She has always been a very poor sailor, however, and there were strong family reasons against her exposing herself to any risk at the time, so we determined that she should remain at home. I am not a religious or an effusive man; but oh, thank God for that! As to leaving my practice, I was easily reconciled to it, as Jackson, my partner, was a reliable and hard-working man.

I arrived in Boston on October 12, 1873, and proceeded immediately to the office of the firm in order to thank them for their courtesy. As I was sitting in the counting-house waiting until they should be at liberty to see me, the words *Marie Celeste* suddenly attracted my attention. I looked round and saw a very tall, gaunt man, who was leaning across the polished mahogany counter asking some questions of the clerk at the other side. His face was turned half towards me, and I could see that he had a strong dash of negro blood in him, being probably a quadroon or even nearer akin to the black. His curved aquiline nose and straight lank hair showed the white strain; but the dark restless eye, sensuous mouth, and gleaming teeth all told of his African origin. His complexion was of a sickly, unhealthy yellow, and as his face was deeply pitted with small-pox, the general impression was so unfavourable as to be almost revolting. When he spoke, however, it was in a soft, melodious voice, and in well-chosen words, and he was evidently a man of some education.

"I wished to ask a few questions about the *Marie Celeste*," he repeated, leaning across to the clerk. "She sails the day after to-morrow, does she not?"

"Yes, sir," said the young clerk, awed into unusual politeness by the glimmer of a large diamond in the stranger's shirt front.

"Where is she bound for?"

"Lisbon."

"How many of a crew?"

"Seven, sir."

"Passengers?"

"Yes, two. One of our young gentlemen, and a doctor from New York."

"No gentleman from the South?" asked the stranger eagerly.

"No, none, sir."

"Is there room for another passenger?"

"Accommodation for three more," answered the clerk.

"I'll go," said the quadroon decisively; "I'll go, I'll engage my passage at once. Put it down, will you—Mr. Septimius Goring, of New Orleans."

The clerk filled up a form and handed it over to the stranger, pointing to a blank space at the bottom. As Mr. Goring stooped over to sign it I was horrified to observe that the fingers of his right hand had been lopped off, and that he was holding the pen between his thumb and the palm. I have seen thousands slain in battle, and assisted at every conceivable surgical operation, but I cannot recall any sight which gave me such a thrill of disgust as that great brown sponge-like hand with the single member protruding from it. He used it skilfully enough, however, for, dashing off his signature, he nodded to the clerk and strolled out of the office just as Mr. White sent out word that he was ready to receive me.

I went down to the *Marie Celeste* that evening, and looked over my berth, which was extremely comfortable considering the small size of the vessel. Mr. Goring, whom I had seen in the morning, was to have the one next mine. Opposite was the captain's cabin and a small berth for Mr. John Harton, a gentleman who was going out in the interests of the firm. These little rooms were arranged on each side of the passage which led from the main-deck to the saloon. The latter was a comfortable room, the panelling tastefully done in oak and mahogany, with a rich Brussels carpet and luxurious settees. I was very much pleased with the accommodation, and also with Tibbs the captain, a bluff, sailor-like fellow, with a loud voice and hearty manner, who welcomed me to the ship with effusion, and insisted upon our splitting a bottle of wine in his cabin. He told me that he intended to take his wife and youngest child with him on the voyage, and that he hoped with good luck to make Lisbon in three weeks. We had a pleasant chat and parted the best of friends, he warning me to make the last of my preparations next morning, as he intended to make a start by the midday tide, having now shipped all his cargo. I went back to my hotel, where I found a letter from my wife awaiting me, and, after a refreshing night's sleep, returned to the boat in the morning. From this point I am able to quote from the journal which I kept in order to vary the monotony of the long sea-voyage. If it is somewhat bald in places I can at least rely upon its accuracy in details, as it was written conscientiously from day to day.

October 16.—Cast off our warps at half-past two and were towed out into the bay, where the tug left us, and with all sail set we bowled along at about nine knots an hour. I stood upon the poop watching the low land of America sinking gradually upon the horizon until the evening haze hid it from my sight. A single red light, however, continued to blaze balefully behind us, throwing a long track like a trail of blood upon the water, and it is still visible as I write, though reduced to a mere speck. The Captain is in a bad humour, for two of his hands disappointed him at the last moment, and he was compelled to ship a couple of negroes who happened to be on the quay. The missing men were steady, reliable fellows, who had been with him several voyages, and their non-appearance puzzled as well as irritated him. Where a crew of seven men have to work a fair-sized ship the loss of two experienced seamen is a serious one, for though the negroes may take a spell at the wheel or swab the decks, they are of little or no use in rough weather. Our cook is also a black man, and Mr. Septimius Goring has a little darkie servant, so that we are rather a piebald community. The accountant, John Harton, promises to be an acquisition, for he is a cheery, amusing young fellow. Strange how little wealth has to do with happiness! He has all the world before him and is seeking his fortune in a far land, yet he is as transparently happy as a man can be. Goring is rich, if I am not mistaken, and so am I; but I know that I have a lung, and Goring has some deeper trouble still, to judge by his features. How poorly do we both contrast with the careless, penniless clerk!

October 17.—Mrs. Tibbs appeared upon deck for the first time this morning—a cheerful, energetic woman, with a dear little child just able to walk and prattle. Young Harton pounced on it at once, and carried it away to his cabin, where no doubt he will lay the seeds of future dyspepsia in the child's stomach. Thus medicine doth make cynics of us all! The weather is still all that could be desired, with a fine fresh breeze from the west-sou'-west. The vessel goes so steadily that you would hardly know that she was moving were it not for the creaking of the cordage, the bellying of the sails, and the long white furrow in our wake. Walked the quarter-deck all morning with the Captain, and I think the keen fresh air has already done my breathing good, for the exercise did not fatigue me in any way. Tibbs is a remarkably intelligent man, and we had an interesting argument about Maury's observations on ocean currents, which we terminated by going down into his cabin to consult the original work. There we found Goring, rather to the Captain's surprise, as it is not usual for passengers to enter that sanctum unless specially invited. He apologised for his intrusion, however, pleading his ignorance of the usages of ship life; and the good-natured sailor simply laughed at the incident, begging him to remain and favour us with his company. Goring pointed to the chronometers, the case of which he had opened, and remarked that he had been admiring them. He has evidently some practical knowledge of mathematical instruments, as he told at a glance which was the most trustworthy of the three, and also named their price within a few dollars. He had a discussion with the Captain too upon the variation of the compass, and when we came back to the ocean currents he showed a thorough grasp of the subject. Altogether he rather improves upon acquaintance, and is a man of decided culture and refinement. His voice harmonises with his conversation, and both are the very antithesis of his face and figure.

The noonday observation shows that we have run two hundred and twenty miles. Towards evening the breeze freshened up, and the first mate ordered reefs to be taken in the topsails and top-gallant sails in expectation of a windy night. I observe that the barometer has fallen to twenty-nine. I trust our voyage will not be a rough one, as I am a poor sailor, and my health would probably derive more harm than good from a stormy trip, though I have the greatest confidence in the Captain's seamanship and in the soundness of the vessel. Played cribbage with Mrs. Tibbs after supper, and Harton gave us a couple of tunes on the violin.

October 18.—The gloomy prognostications of last night were not fulfilled, as the wind died away again, and we are lying now in a long greasy swell, ruffled here and there by a fleeting catspaw which is insufficient to fill the sails. The air is colder than it was yesterday, and I have put on one of the thick woollen jerseys which my wife knitted for me. Harton came into my cabin in the morning, and we had a cigar together. He says that he remembers having seen Goring in Cleveland, Ohio, in '69. He was, it appears, a mystery then as now, wandering about without any visible employment, and extremely reticent on his own affairs. The man interests me as a psychological study. At breakfast this morning I suddenly had that vague feeling of uneasiness which comes over some people when closely stared at, and, looking quickly up, I met his eyes bent upon me with an intensity which amounted to ferocity, though their expression instantly softened as he made some conventional remark upon the weather. Curiously enough, Harton says that he had a very similar experience yesterday upon deck. I observe that Goring frequently talks to the coloured seamen as he strolls about—a trait which I rather admire, as it is common to find half-breeds ignore their dark strain and treat their black kinsfolk with greater intolerance than a white man would do. His little page is devoted to him, apparently, which speaks well for his treatment of him. Altogether, the man is a curious mixture of incongruous qualities, and unless I am deceived in him will give me food for observation during the voyage.

The Captain is grumbling about his chronometers, which do not register exactly the same time. He says it is the first time that they have ever disagreed. We were unable to get a noonday observation on account of the haze. By dead reckoning, we have done about a hundred and seventy miles in the twenty-four hours. The dark seamen have proved, as the skipper prophesied, to be very inferior hands, but as they can both manage the wheel well they are kept steering, and so leave the more experienced men to work the ship. These details are trivial enough, but a small thing serves as food for gossip aboard ship. The appearance of a whale in the evening caused quite a flutter among us. From its sharp back and forked tail, I should pronounce it to have been a rorqual, or "finner," as they are called by the fishermen.

October 19.—Wind was cold, so I prudently remained in my cabin all day, only creeping out for dinner. Lying in my bunk I can, without moving, reach my books, pipes, or anything else I may want, which is one advantage of a small apartment. My old wound began to ache a little to-day, probably from the cold. Read *Montaigne's Essays* and nursed myself. Harton came in in the afternoon with Doddy, the Captain's child, and the skipper himself followed, so that I held quite a reception.

October 20 and 21.—Still cold, with a continual drizzle of rain, and I have not been able to leave the cabin. This confinement makes me feel weak and depressed. Goring came in to see me, but his company did not tend to cheer me up much, as he hardly uttered a word, but contented himself with staring at me in a peculiar and rather irritating manner. He then got up and stole out of the cabin without saying anything. I am beginning to suspect that the man is a lunatic. I think I mentioned that his cabin is next to mine. The two are simply divided by a thin wooden partition which is cracked in many places, some of the cracks being so large that I can hardly avoid, as I lie in my bunk, observing his motions in the adjoining room. Without any wish to play the spy, I see him continually stooping over what appears to be a chart and working with a pencil and compasses. I have remarked the interest he displays in matters connected with navigation, but I am surprised that he should take the trouble to work out the course of the ship. However, it is a harmless amusement enough, and no doubt he verifies his results by those of the Captain.

I wish the man did not run in my thoughts so much. I had a nightmare on the night of the 20th, in which I thought my bunk was a coffin, that I was laid out in it, and that Goring was endeavouring to nail up the lid, which I was frantically pushing away. Even when I woke up, I could hardly persuade myself that I was not in a coffin. As a medical man, I know that a nightmare is simply a vascular derangement of the cerebral hemispheres, and yet in my weak state I cannot shake off the morbid impression which it produces.

October 22.—A fine day, with hardly a cloud in the sky, and a fresh breeze from the sou'-west which wafts us gaily on our way. There has evidently been some heavy weather near us, as there is a tremendous swell on, and the ship lurches until the end of the fore-yard nearly touches the water. Had a refreshing walk up and down the quarter-deck, though I have hardly found my sea-legs yet. Several small birds—chaffinches, I think—perched in the rigging.

4.40 p.m.—While I was on deck this morning I heard a sudden explosion from the direction of my cabin, and, hurrying down, found that I had very nearly met with a serious accident. Goring was cleaning a revolver, it seems, in his cabin, when one of the barrels which he thought was unloaded went off. The ball passed through the side partition and imbedded itself in the bulwarks in the exact place where my head usually rests. I have been under fire too often to magnify trifles, but there is no doubt that if I had been in the bunk it must have killed me. Goring, poor fellow, did not know that I had gone on deck that day, and must therefore have felt terribly frightened. I never saw such emotion in a man's face as when, on rushing out of his cabin with the smoking pistol in his hand, he met me face to face as I came down from deck. Of course, he was profuse in his apologies, though I simply laughed at the incident.

11 p.m.—A misfortune has occurred so unexpected and so horrible that my little escape of the morning dwindles into insignificance. Mrs. Tibbs and her child have disappeared—utterly and entirely disappeared. I can hardly compose myself to write the sad details.

About half-past eight Tibbs rushed into my cabin with a very white face and asked me if I had seen his wife. I answered that I had not. He then ran wildly into the saloon and began groping about for any trace of her, while I followed him, endeavouring vainly to persuade him that his fears were ridiculous. We hunted over the ship for an hour and a half without coming on any sign of the missing woman or child. Poor Tibbs lost his voice completely from calling her name. Even the sailors, who are generally stolid enough, were deeply affected by the sight of him as he roamed bareheaded and dishevelled about the deck, searching with feverish anxiety the most impossible places, and returning to them again and again with a piteous pertinacity. The last time she was seen was about seven o'clock, when she took Doddy on to the poop to give him a breath of fresh air before putting him to bed. There was no one there at the time except the black seaman at the wheel, who denies having seen her at all. The whole affair is wrapped in mystery. My own theory is that while Mrs. Tibbs was holding the child and standing near the bulwarks it gave a spring and fell overboard, and that in her convulsive attempt to catch or save it, she followed it. I cannot account for the double disappearance in any other way. It is quite feasible that such a tragedy should be enacted without the knowledge of the man at the wheel, since it was dark at the time, and the peaked skylights of the saloon screen the greater part of the quarter-deck. Whatever the truth may be it is a terrible catastrophe, and has cast the darkest gloom upon our voyage. The mate has put the ship about, but of course there is not the slightest hope of picking them up. The Captain is lying in a state of stupor in his cabin. I gave him a powerful dose of opium in his coffee that for a few hours at least his anguish may be deadened.

October 23.—Woke with a vague feeling of heaviness and misfortune, but it was not until a few moments' reflection that I was able to recall our loss of the night before. When I came on deck I saw the poor skipper standing gazing back at the waste of waters behind us which contains everything dear to him upon earth. I attempted to speak to him, but he turned brusquely away, and began pacing the deck with his head sunk upon his breast. Even now, when the truth is so clear, he cannot pass a boat or an unbent sail without peering under it. He looks ten years older than he did yesterday morning. Harton is terribly cut up, for he was fond of little Doddy, and Goring seems sorry too. At least he has shut himself up in his cabin all day, and when I got a casual glance at him his head was resting on his two hands as if in a melancholy reverie. I fear we are about as dismal a crew as ever sailed. How shocked my wife will be to hear of our disaster! The swell has gone down now, and we are doing about eight knots with all sail set and a nice little breeze. Hyson is practically in command of the ship, as Tibbs, though he does his best to bear up and keep a brave front, is incapable of applying himself to serious work.

October 24.—Is the ship accursed? Was there ever a voyage which began so fairly and which changed so disastrously? Tibbs shot himself through the head during the night. I was awakened about three o'clock in the morning by an explosion, and immediately sprang out of bed and rushed into the Captain's cabin to find out the cause, though with a terrible presentiment in my heart. Quickly as I went, Goring went more quickly still, for he was already in the cabin stooping over the dead body of the Captain. It was a hideous sight, for the whole front of his face was blown in, and the little room was swimming in blood. The pistol was lying beside him on the floor, just as it had dropped from his hand. He had evidently put it to his mouth before pulling the trigger. Goring and I picked him reverently up and laid him on his bed. The crew had all clustered into his cabin, and the six white men were deeply grieved, for they were old hands who had sailed with him many years. There were dark looks and murmurs among them too, and one of them openly declared that the ship was haunted. Harton helped to lay the poor skipper out, and we did him up in canvas between us. At twelve o'clock the foreyard was hauled aback, and we committed his body to the deep, Goring reading the Church of England burial service. The breeze has freshened up, and we have done ten knots all day and sometimes twelve. The sooner we reach Lisbon and get away from this accursed ship the better pleased shall I be. I feel as though we were in a floating coffin.

Little wonder that the poor sailors are superstitious when I, an educated man, feel it so strongly.

October 25.—Made a good run all day. Feel listless and depressed.

October 26.—Goring, Harton, and I had a chat together on deck in the morning. Harton tried to draw Goring out as to his profession, and his object in going to Europe, but the quadroon parried all his questions and gave us no information. Indeed, he seemed to be slightly offended by Harton's pertinacity, and went down into his cabin. I wonder why we should both take such an interest in this man! I suppose it is his striking appearance, coupled with his apparent wealth, which piques our curiosity. Harton has a theory that he is really a detective, that he is after some criminal who has got away to Portugal, and that he chooses this peculiar way of travelling that he may arrive unnoticed and pounce upon his quarry unawares. I think the supposition is rather a far-fetched one, but Harton bases it upon a book which Goring left on deck, and which he picked up and glanced over. It was a sort of scrap-book it seems, and contained a large number of newspaper cuttings. All these cuttings related to murders which had been committed at various times in the States during the last twenty years or so. The curious thing which Harton observed about them, however, was that they were invariably murders the authors of which had never been brought to justice. They varied in every detail, he says, as to the manner of execution and the social status of the victim, but they uniformly wound up with the same formula that the murderer was still at large, though, of course, the police had every reason to expect his speedy capture. Certainly the incident seems to support Harton's theory, though it may be a mere whim of Gorings, or, as I suggested to Harton, he may be collecting materials for a book which shall outvie De Quincey. In any case it is no business of ours.

October 27, 28.—Wind still fair, and we are making good progress. Strange how easily a human unit may drop out of its place and be forgotten! Tibbs is hardly ever mentioned now; Hyson has taken possession of his cabin, and all goes on as before. Were it not for Mrs. Tibbs's sewing-machine upon a side-table we might forget that the unfortunate family had ever existed. Another accident occurred on board to-day, though fortunately not a very serious one. One of our white hands had gone down the afterhold to fetch up a spare coil of rope, when one of the hatches which he had removed came crashing down on the top of him. He saved his life by springing out of the way, but one of his feet was terribly crushed, and he will be of little use for the remainder of the voyage. He attributes the accident to the carelessness of his negro companion, who had helped him to shift the hatches. The latter, however, puts it down to the roll of the ship. Whatever be the cause, it reduces our short-handed crew still further. This run of ill-luck seems to be depressing Harton, for he has lost his usual good spirits and joviality. Goring is the only one who preserves his cheerfulness. I see him still working at his chart in his own cabin. His nautical knowledge would be useful should anything happen to Hyson—which God forbid!

October 29, 30.—Still bowling along with a fresh breeze. All quiet and nothing of note to chronicle.

October 31.—My weak lungs, combined with the exciting episodes of the voyage, have shaken my nervous system so much that the most trivial incident affects me. I can hardly believe that I am the same man who tied the external iliac artery, an operation requiring the nicest precision, under a heavy rifle fire at Antietam. I am as nervous as a child. I was lying half dozing last night about four bells in the middle watch trying in vain to drop into a refreshing sleep. There was no light inside my cabin, but a single ray of moonlight streamed in through the port hole, throwing a silvery flickering circle upon the door. As I lay I kept my drowsy eyes upon this circle, and was conscious that it was gradually becoming less well-defined as my senses left me, when I was suddenly recalled to full wakefulness by the appearance of a small dark object in the very centre of the luminous disc. I lay quietly and breathlessly watching it. Gradually it grew larger and plainer, and then I perceived that it was a human hand which had been cautiously inserted through the chink of the half-closed door—a hand which, as I observed with a thrill of horror, was not provided with fingers. The door swung cautiously backwards, and Goring's head followed his hand. It appeared in the centre of the moonlight, and was framed as it were in a ghastly uncertain halo, against which his features showed out plainly. It seemed to me that I had never seen such an utterly fiendish and merciless expression upon a human face. His eyes were dilated and glaring, his lips drawn back so as to show his white fangs, and his straight black hair appeared to bristle over his low forehead like the hood of a cobra. The sudden

255

and noiseless apparition had such an effect upon me that I sprang up in bed trembling in every limb, and held out my hand towards my revolver. I was heartily ashamed of my hastiness when he explained the object of his intrusion, as he immediately did in the most courteous language. He had been suffering from toothache, poor fellow! and had come in to beg some laudanum, knowing that I possessed a medicine chest. As to a sinister expression he is never a beauty, and what with my state of nervous tension and the effect of the shifting moonlight it was easy to conjure up something horrible. I gave him twenty drops, and he went off again with many expressions of gratitude. I can hardly say how much this trivial incident affected me. I have felt unstrung all day.

****

A week's record of our voyage is here omitted, as nothing eventful occurred during the time, and my log consists merely of a few pages of unimportant gossip.

****

November 7.—Harton and I sat on the poop all the morning, for the weather is becoming very warm as we come into southern latitudes. We reckon that we have done two-thirds of our voyage. How glad we shall be to see the green banks of the Tagus, and leave this unlucky ship for ever! I was endeavouring to amuse Harton to-day and to while away the time by telling him some of the experiences of my past life. Among others I related to him how I came into the possession of my black stone, and as a finale I rummaged in the side pocket of my old shooting coat and produced the identical object in question. He and I were bending over it together, I pointing out to him the curious ridges upon its surface, when we were conscious of a shadow falling between us and the sun, and looking round saw Goring standing behind us glaring over our shoulders at the stone. For some reason or other he appeared to be powerfully excited, though he was evidently trying to control himself and to conceal his emotion. He pointed once or twice at my relic with his stubby thumb before he could recover himself sufficiently to ask what it was and how I obtained it—a question put in such a brusque manner that I should have been offended had I not known the man to be an eccentric. I told him the story very much as I had told it to Harton. He listened with the deepest interest, and then asked me if I had any idea what the stone was. I said I had not, beyond that it was meteoric. He asked me if I had ever tried its effect upon a negro. I said I had not. "Come," said he, "we'll see what our black friend at the wheel thinks of it." He took the stone in his hand and went across to the sailor, and the two examined it carefully. I could see the man gesticulating and nodding his head excitedly as if making some assertion, while his face betrayed the utmost astonishment, mixed I think with some reverence. Goring came across the deck to us presently, still holding the stone in his hand. "He says it is a worthless, useless thing," he said, "and fit only to be chucked overboard," with which he raised his hand and would most certainly have made an end of my relic, had the black sailor behind him not rushed forward and seized him by the wrist. Finding himself secured Goring dropped the stone and turned away with a very bad grace to avoid my angry remonstrances at his breach of faith. The black picked up the stone and handed it to me with a low bow and every sign of profound respect. The whole affair is inexplicable. I am rapidly coming to the conclusion that Goring is a maniac or something very near one. When I compare the effect produced by the stone upon the sailor, however, with the respect shown to Martha on the plantation, and the surprise of Goring on its first production, I cannot but come to the conclusion that I have really got hold of some powerful talisman which appeals to the whole dark race. I must not trust it in Goring's hands again.

November 8, 9.—What splendid weather we are having! Beyond one little blow, we have had nothing but fresh breezes the whole voyage. These two days we have made better runs than any hitherto. It is a pretty thing to watch the spray fly up from our prow as it cuts through the waves. The sun shines through it and breaks it up into a number of miniature rainbows—"sun-dogs," the sailors call them. I stood on the fo'csle-head for several hours to-day watching the effect, and surrounded by a halo of prismatic colours. The steersman has evidently told the other blacks about my wonderful stone, for I am treated by them all with the greatest respect. Talking about optical phenomena, we had a curious one yesterday evening which was pointed out to me by Hyson. This was the appearance of a triangular well-defined object high up in the heavens to the north of us. He explained that it was exactly like the Peak of Teneriffe as seen from a great distance—the peak was, however, at that moment at least five hundred miles to the south. It may have been a cloud, or it may have been one of those strange reflections of which one reads. The weather is very warm. The mate says that he never knew it so warm in these latitudes. Played chess with Harton in the evening.

November 10.—It is getting warmer and warmer. Some land birds came and perched in the rigging today, though we are still a considerable way from our destination. The heat is so great that we are too lazy to do anything but lounge about the decks and smoke. Goring came over to me to-day and asked me some more questions about my stone; but I answered him rather shortly, for I have not quite forgiven him yet for the cool way in which he attempted to deprive me of it.

November 11, 12.—Still making good progress. I had no idea Portugal was ever as hot as this, but no doubt it is cooler on land. Hyson himself seemed surprised at it, and so do the men.

November 13.—A most extraordinary event has happened, so extraordinary as to be almost inexplicable. Either Hyson has blundered wonderfully, or some magnetic influence has disturbed our instruments. Just about daybreak the watch on the fo'csle-head shouted out that he heard the sound of surf ahead, and Hyson thought he saw the loom of land. The ship was put about, and, though no lights were seen, none of us doubted that we had struck the Portuguese coast a little sooner than we had expected. What was our surprise to see the scene which was revealed to us at break of day! As far as we could look on either side was one long line of surf, great, green billows rolling in and breaking into a cloud of foam. But behind the surf what was there! Not the green banks nor the high cliffs of the shores of Portugal, but a great sandy waste which stretched away and away until it blended with the skyline. To right and left, look where you would, there was nothing but yellow sand, heaped in some places into fantastic mounds, some of them several hundred feet high, while in other parts were long stretches as level apparently as a billiard board. Harton and I, who had come on deck together, looked at each other in astonishment, and Harton burst out laughing. Hyson is exceedingly mortified at the occurrence, and protests that the instruments have been tampered with. There is no doubt that this is the mainland of Africa, and that it was really the Peak of Teneriffe which we saw some days ago upon the northern horizon. At the time when we saw the land birds we must have been passing some of the Canary Islands. If we continued on the same course, we are now to the north of Cape Blanco, near the unexplored country which skirts the great Sahara. All we can do is to rectify our instruments as far as possible and start afresh for our destination.

8.30 p.m.—Have been lying in a calm all day. The coast is now about a mile and a half from us. Hyson has examined the instruments, but cannot find any reason for their extraordinary deviation.

****

This is the end of my private journal, and I must make the remainder of my statement from memory. There is little chance of my being mistaken about facts which have seared themselves into my recollection. That very night the storm which had been brewing so long burst over us, and I came to learn whither all those little incidents were tending which I had recorded so aimlessly. Blind fool that I was not to have seen it sooner! I shall tell what occurred as precisely as I can.

I had gone into my cabin about half-past eleven, and was preparing to go to bed, when a tap came at my door. On opening it I saw Goring's little black page, who told me that his master would like to have a word with me on deck. I was rather surprised that he should want me at such a late hour, but I went up without hesitation. I had hardly put my foot on the quarter-deck before I was seized from behind, dragged down upon my back, and a handkerchief slipped round my mouth. I struggled as hard as I could, but a coil of rope was rapidly and firmly wound round me, and I found myself lashed to the davit of one of the boats, utterly powerless to do or say anything, while the point of a knife pressed to my throat warned me to cease my struggles. The night was so dark that I had been unable hitherto to recognise my assailants, but as my eyes became accustomed to the gloom, and the moon broke out through the clouds that obscured it, I made out that I was surrounded by the two negro sailors, the black cook, and my fellow-passenger Goring. Another man was crouching on the deck at my feet, but he was in the shadow and I could not recognise him.

All this occurred so rapidly that a minute could hardly have elapsed from the time I mounted the companion until I found myself gagged and powerless. It was so sudden that I could scarce bring myself to realise it, or to comprehend what it all meant. I heard the gang round me speaking in short, fierce whispers to each other, and some instinct told me that my life was the question at issue. Goring spoke authoritatively and angrily—the others doggedly and all together, as if disputing his commands. Then they moved away in a body to the opposite side of the deck, where I could still hear them whispering, though they were concealed from my view by the saloon skylights.

All this time the voices of the watch on deck chatting and laughing at the other end of the ship were distinctly audible, and I could see them gathered in a group, little dreaming of the dark doings which were going on within thirty yards of them. Oh! that I could have given them one word of warning, even though I had lost my life in doing it I but it was impossible. The moon was shining fitfully through the scattered clouds, and I could see the silvery gleam of the surge, and beyond it the vast weird desert with its fantastic sand-hills. Glancing down, I saw that the man who had been crouching on the deck was still lying there, and as I gazed at him, a flickering ray of moonlight fell full upon his upturned face. Great Heaven! even now, when more than twelve years have elapsed, my hand trembles as I write that, in spite of distorted features and projecting eyes, I recognised the face of Harton, the cheery young clerk who had been my companion during the voyage. It needed no medical eye to see that he was quite dead, while the twisted handkerchief round the neck, and the gag in his mouth, showed the silent way in which the hell-hounds had done their work. The clue which explained every event of our voyage came upon me like a flash of light as I gazed on poor Harton's corpse. Much was dark and unexplained, but I felt a great dim perception of the truth.

I heard the striking of a match at the other side of the sky-lights, and then I saw the tall, gaunt figure of Goring standing up on the bulwarks and holding in his hands what appeared to be a dark lantern. He lowered this for a moment over the side of the ship, and, to my inexpressible astonishment, I saw it answered instantaneously by a flash among the sand-hills on shore, which came and went so rapidly, that unless I had been following the direction of Goring's gaze, I should never have detected it. Again he lowered the lantern, and again it was answered from the shore. He then stepped down from the bulwarks, and in doing so slipped, making such a noise, that for a moment my heart bounded with the thought that the attention of the watch would be directed to his proceedings. It was a vain hope. The night was calm and the ship motionless, so that no idea of duty kept them vigilant. Hyson, who after the death of Tibbs was in command of both watches, had gone below to snatch a few hours' sleep, and the boatswain who was left in charge was standing with the other two men at the foot of the foremast. Powerless, speechless, with the cords cutting into my flesh and the murdered man at my feet, I awaited the next act in the tragedy.

The four ruffians were standing up now at the other side of the deck. The cook was armed with some sort of a cleaver, the others had knives, and Goring had a revolver. They were all leaning against the rail and looking out over the water as if watching for something. I saw one of them grasp another's arm and point as if at some object, and following the direction I made out the loom of a large moving mass making towards the ship. As it emerged from the gloom I saw that it was a great canoe crammed with men and propelled by at least a score of paddles. As it shot under our stern the watch caught sight of it also, and raising a cry hurried aft. They were too late, however. A swarm of gigantic negroes clambered over the quarter, and led by Goring swept down the deck in an irresistible torrent. All opposition was overpowered in a moment, the unarmed watch were knocked over and bound, and the sleepers dragged out of their bunks and secured in the same manner.

Hyson made an attempt to defend the narrow passage leading to his cabin, and I heard a scuffle, and his voice shouting for assistance. There was none to assist, however, and he was brought on to the poop with the blood streaming from a deep cut in his forehead. He was gagged like the others, and a council was held upon our fate by the negroes. I saw our black seamen pointing towards me and making some statement, which was received with murmurs of astonishment and incredulity by the savages. One of them then came over to me, and plunging his hand into my pocket took out my black stone and held it up. He then handed it to a man who appeared to be a chief, who examined it as minutely as the light would permit, and muttering a few words passed it on to the warrior beside him, who also scrutinised it and passed it on until it had gone from hand to hand round the whole circle. The chief then said a few words to Goring in the native tongue, on which the quadroon addressed me in English. At this moment I seem to see the scene. The tall masts of the ship with the moonlight streaming down, silvering the yards and bringing the network of cordage into hard relief; the group of dusky warriors leaning on their spears; the dead man at my feet; the line of white-faced prisoners, and in front of me the loathsome half-breed, looking in his white linen and elegant clothes a strange contrast to his associates.

"You will bear me witness," he said in his softest accents, "that I am no party to sparing your life. If it rested with me you would die as these other men are about to do. I have no personal grudge against either you or them, but I have devoted my life to the destruction of the white race, and you are the first that has ever been in my power and has escaped me. You may thank that stone of yours for your life. These poor fellows reverence it, and indeed if it really be what they think it is they have cause. Should it prove when we get ashore that they are mistaken, and that its shape and material is a mere chance, nothing can save your life. In the meantime we wish to treat you well, so if there are any of your possessions which you would like to take with you, you are at liberty to get them." As he finished he gave a sign, and a couple of the negroes unbound me, though without removing the gag. I was led down into the cabin, where I put a few valuables into my pockets, together with a pocket-compass and my journal of the voyage. They then pushed me over the side into a small canoe, which was lying beside the large one, and my guards followed me, and shoving off began paddling for the shore. We had got about a hundred yards or so from the ship when our steersman held up his hand, and the paddlers paused for a moment and listened. Then on the silence of the night I heard a sort of dull, moaning sound, followed by a succession of splashes in the water. That is all I know of the fate of my poor shipmates. Almost immediately afterwards the large canoe followed us, and the deserted ship was left drifting about—a dreary, spectre-like hulk. Nothing was taken from her by the savages. The whole fiendish transaction was carried through as decorously and temperately as though it were a religious rite.

The first grey of daylight was visible in the east as we passed through the surge and reached the shore. Leaving half-a-dozen men with the canoes, the rest of the negroes set off through the sand-hills, leading me with them, but treating me very gently and respectfully. It was difficult walking, as we sank over our ankles into the loose, shifting sand at every step, and I was nearly dead beat by the time we reached the native village, or town rather, for it was a place of considerable dimensions. The houses were conical structures not unlike bee-hives, and were made of compressed seaweed cemented over with a rude form of mortar, there being neither stick nor stone upon the coast nor anywhere within many hundreds of miles. As we entered the town an enormous crowd of both sexes came swarming out to meet us, beating tom-toms and howling and screaming. On seeing me they redoubled their yells and assumed a threatening attitude, which was instantly quelled by a few words shouted by my escort. A buzz of wonder succeeded the war-cries and yells of the moment before, and the whole dense mass proceeded down the broad central street of the town, having my escort and myself in the centre.

My statement hitherto may seem so strange as to excite doubt in the minds of those who do not know me, but it was the fact which I am now about to relate which caused my own brother-in-law to insult me by disbelief. I can but relate the occurrence in the simplest words, and trust to chance and time to prove their truth. In the centre of this main street there was a large building, formed in the same primitive way as the others, but towering high above them; a stockade of beautifully polished ebony rails was planted all round it, the framework of the door was formed by two magnificent elephant's tusks sunk in the ground on each side and meeting at the top, and the aperture was closed by a screen of native cloth richly embroidered with gold. We made our way to this imposing-looking structure, but, on reaching the opening in the stockade, the multitude stopped and squatted down upon their hams, while I was led through into the enclosure by a few of the chiefs and elders of the tribe, Goring accompanying us, and in fact directing the proceedings. On reaching the screen which closed the temple—for such it evidently was—my hat and my shoes were removed, and I was then led in, a venerable old negro leading the way carrying in his hand my stone, which had been taken from my pocket. The building was only lit up by a few long slits in the roof, through which the tropical sun poured, throwing broad golden bars upon the clay floor, alternating with intervals of darkness.

The interior was even larger than one would have imagined from the outside appearance. The walls were hung with native mats, shells, and other ornaments, but the remainder of the great space was quite empty, with the exception of a single object in the centre. This was the figure of a colossal negro, which I at first thought to be some real king or high priest of titanic size, but as I approached it I saw by the way in which the light was reflected from it that it was a statue admirably cut in jet-black stone. I was led up to this idol, for such it seemed to be, and looking at it closer I saw that though it was perfect in every other respect, one of its ears had been broken short off. The grey-haired negro who held my relic mounted upon a small stool, and stretching up his arm fitted Martha's black stone on to the jagged surface on the side of the statue's head. There could not be a doubt that the one had been broken off from the other. The parts dove-tailed together so accurately that when the old man removed his hand the ear stuck in its place for a few seconds before dropping into his open palm. The group round me prostrated themselves upon the ground at the sight with a cry of reverence, while the crowd outside, to whom the result was communicated, set up a wild whooping and cheering.

In a moment I found myself converted from a prisoner into a demi-god. I was escorted back through the town in triumph, the people pressing forward to touch my clothing and to gather up the dust on which my foot had trod. One of the largest huts was put at my disposal, and a banquet of every native delicacy was served me. I still felt, however, that I was not a free man, as several spearmen were placed as a guard at the entrance of my hut. All day my mind was occupied with plans of escape, but none seemed in any way feasible. On the one side was the great arid desert stretching away to Timbuctoo, on the other was a sea untraversed by vessels. The more I pondered over the problem the more hopeless did it seem.

I little dreamed how near I was to its solution.

Night had fallen, and the clamour of the negroes had died gradually away. I was stretched on the couch of skins which had been provided for me, and was still meditating over my future, when Goring walked stealthily into the hut. My first idea was that he had come to complete his murderous holocaust by making away with me, the last survivor, and I sprang up upon my feet, determined to defend myself to the last. He smiled when he saw the action, and motioned me down again while he seated himself upon the other end of the couch.

"What do you think of me?" was the astonishing question with which he commenced our conversation.

"Think of you!" I almost yelled. "I think you the vilest, most unnatural renegade that ever polluted the earth. If we were away from these black devils of yours I would strangle you with my hands!"

"Don't speak so loud," he said, without the slightest appearance of irritation. "I don't want our chat to be cut short. So you would strangle me, would you!" he went on, with an amused smile. "I suppose I am returning good for evil, for I have come to help you to escape."

"You!" I gasped incredulously.

"Yes, I," he continued.

"Oh, there is no credit to me in the matter. I am quite consistent. There is no reason why I should not be perfectly candid with you. I wish to be king over these fellows—not a very high ambition, certainly, but you know what Caesar said about being first in a village in Gaul. Well, this unlucky stone of yours has not only saved your life, but has turned all their heads so that they think you are come down from heaven, and my influence will be gone until you are out of the way. That

266

is why I am going to help you to escape, since I cannot kill you"—this in the most natural and dulcet voice, as if the desire to do so were a matter of course.

"You would give the world to ask me a few questions," he went on, after a pause; "but you are too proud to do it. Never mind, I'll tell you one or two things, because I want your fellow white men to know them when you go back—if you are lucky enough to get back. About that cursed stone of yours, for instance. These negroes, or at least so the legend goes, were Mahometans originally. While Mahomet himself was still alive, there was a schism among his followers, and the smaller party moved away from Arabia, and eventually crossed Africa. They took away with them, in their exile, a valuable relic of their old faith in the shape of a large piece of the black stone of Mecca. The stone was a meteoric one, as you may have heard, and in its fall upon the earth it broke into two pieces. One of these pieces is still at Mecca. The larger piece was carried away to Barbary, where a skilful worker modelled it into the fashion which you saw to-day. These men are the descendants of the original seceders from Mahomet, and they have brought their relic safely through all their wanderings until they settled in this strange place, where the desert protects them from their enemies."

"And the ear?" I asked, almost involuntarily.

"Oh, that was the same story over again. Some of the tribe wandered away to the south a few hundred years ago, and one of them, wishing to have good luck for the enterprise, got into the temple at night and carried off one of the ears. There has been a tradition among the negroes ever since that the ear would come back some day. The fellow who carried it was caught by some slaver, no doubt, and that was how it got into America, and so into your hands—and you have had the honour of fulfilling the prophecy."

He paused for a few minutes, resting his head upon his hands, waiting apparently for me to speak. When he looked up again, the whole expression of his face had changed. His features were firm and set, and he changed the air of half levity with which he had spoken before for one of sternness and almost ferocity.

267

"I wish you to carry a message back," he said, "to the white race, the great dominating race whom I hate and defy. Tell them that I have battened on their blood for twenty years, that I have slain them until even I became tired of what had once been a joy, that I did this unnoticed and unsuspected in the face of every precaution which their civilisation could suggest. There is no satisfaction in revenge when your enemy does not know who has struck him. I am not sorry, therefore, to have you as a messenger. There is no need why I should tell you how this great hate became born in me. See this," and he held up his mutilated hand; "that was done by a white man's knife. My father was white, my mother was a slave. When he died she was sold again, and I, a child then, saw her lashed to death to break her of some of the little airs and graces which her late master had encouraged in her. My young wife, too, oh, my young wife!" a shudder ran through his whole frame. "No matter! I swore my oath, and I kept it. From Maine to Florida, and from Boston to San Francisco, you could track my steps by sudden deaths which baffled the police. I warred against the whole white race as they for centuries had warred against the black one. At last, as I tell you, I sickened of blood. Still, the sight of a white face was abhorrent to me, and I determined to find some bold free black people and to throw in my lot with them, to cultivate their latent powers, and to form a nucleus for a great coloured nation. This idea possessed me, and I travelled over the world for two years seeking for what I desired. At last I almost despaired of finding it. There was no hope of regeneration in the slave-dealing Sudanese, the debased Fantee, or the Americanised negroes of Liberia. I was returning from my quest when chance brought me in contact with this magnificent tribe of dwellers in the desert, and I threw in my lot with them. Before doing so, however, my old instinct of revenge prompted me to make one last visit to the United States, and I returned from it in the *Marie Celeste*.

"As to the voyage itself, your intelligence will have told you by this time that, thanks to my manipulation, both compasses and chronometers were entirely untrustworthy. I alone worked out the course with correct instruments of my own, while the steering was done by my black friends under my guidance. I pushed Tibbs's wife overboard. What! You look surprised and shrink away. Surely you had guessed that by this time. I would have shot you that day through the partition, but unfortunately you were not there. I tried again afterwards, but you were awake. I shot Tibbs. I think the idea of suicide was carried out rather neatly. Of course when once we got on the coast the rest was simple. I had bargained that all on board should die; but that stone of yours upset my plans. I also bargained that there should be no plunder. No one can say we are pirates. We have acted from principle, not from any sordid motive."

I listened in amazement to the summary of his crimes which this strange man gave me, all in the quietest and most composed of voices, as though detailing incidents of every-day occurrence. I still seem to see him sitting like a hideous nightmare at the end of my couch, with the single rude lamp flickering over his cadaverous features.

"And now," he continued, "there is no difficulty about your escape. These stupid adopted children of mine will say that you have gone back to heaven from whence you came. The wind blows off the land. I have a boat all ready for you, well stored with provisions and water. I am anxious to be rid of you, so you may rely that nothing is neglected. Rise up and follow me."

I did what he commanded, and he led me through the door of the hut.

The guards had either been withdrawn, or Goring had arranged matters with them. We passed unchallenged through the town and across the sandy plain. Once more I heard the roar of the sea, and saw the long white line of the surge. Two figures were standing upon the shore arranging the gear of a small boat. They were the two sailors who had been with us on the voyage.

"See him safely through the surf," said Goring. The two men sprang in and pushed off, pulling me in after them. With mainsail and jib we ran out from the land and passed safely over the bar. Then my two companions without a word of farewell sprang overboard, and I saw their heads like black dots on the white foam as they made their way back to the shore, while I scudded away into the blackness of the night. Looking back I caught my last glimpse of Goring. He was standing upon the summit of a sand-hill, and the rising moon behind him threw his gaunt angular figure into hard relief. He was waving his arms frantically to and fro; it may have been to encourage me on my way, but the gestures seemed to me at the time to be threatening ones, and I have often thought that it was more likely that his old savage instinct had returned when he realised that I was out of his power. Be that as it may, it was the last that I ever saw or ever shall see of Septimius Goring.

****

There is no need for me to dwell upon my solitary voyage. I steered as well as I could for the Canaries, but was picked up upon the fifth day by the British and African Steam Navigation Company's boat Monrovia. Let me take this opportunity of tendering my sincerest thanks to Captain Stornoway and his officers for the great kindness which they showed me from that time till they landed me in Liverpool, where I was enabled to take one of the Guion boats to New York.

****

From the day on which I found myself once more in the bosom of my family I have said little of what I have undergone. The subject is still an intensely painful one to me, and the little which I have dropped has been discredited. I now put the facts before the public as they occurred, careless how far they may be believed, and simply writing them down because my lung is growing weaker, and I feel the responsibility of holding my peace longer. I make no vague statement. Turn to your map of Africa. There above Cape Blanco, where the land trends away north and south from the westernmost point of the continent, there it is that Septimius Goring still reigns over his dark subjects, unless retribution has overtaken him; and there, where the long green ridges run swiftly in to roar and hiss upon the hot yellow sand, it is there that Harton lies with Hyson and the other poor fellows who were done to death in the *Marie Celeste*.

The Beetle-Hunter

A curious experience? said the Doctor. Yes, my friends, I have had one very curious experience. I never expect to have another, for it is against all doctrines of chances that two such events would befall any one man in a single lifetime. You may believe me or not, but the thing happened exactly as I tell it.

I had just become a medical man, but I had not started in practice, and I lived in rooms in Gower Street. The street has been renumbered since then, but it was in the only house which has a bow-window, upon the left-hand side as you go down from the Metropolitan Station. A widow named Murchison kept the house at that time, and she had three medical students and one engineer as lodgers. I occupied the top room, which was the cheapest, but cheap as it was it was more than I could afford. My small resources were dwindling away, and every week it became more necessary that I should find something to do. Yet I was very unwilling to go into general practice, for my tastes were all in the direction of science, and especially of zoology, towards which I had always a strong leaning. I had almost given the fight up and resigned myself to being a medical drudge for life, when the turning-point of my struggles came in a very extraordinary way.

One morning I had picked up the *Standard* and was glancing over its contents. There was a complete absence of news, and I was about to toss the paper down again, when my eyes were caught by an advertisement at the head of the personal column. It was worded in this way:

"Wanted for one or more days the services of a medical man. It is essential that he should be a man of strong physique, of steady nerves, and of a resolute nature. Must be an *entomologist—coleopterist* preferred. Apply, in person, at 77B, Brook Street. Application must be made before twelve o'clock today."

Now, I have already said that I was devoted to zoology. Of all branches of zoology, the study of insects was the most attractive to me, and of all insects beetles were the species with which I was most familiar. Butterfly collectors are numerous, but beetles are far more varied, and more accessible in these islands than are butterflies. It was this fact which had attracted my attention to them, and I had myself made a collection which numbered some hundred varieties. As to the other requisites of the advertisement, I knew that my nerves could be depended upon, and I had won the weight-throwing competition at the inter-hospital sports. Clearly, I was the very man for the vacancy. Within five minutes of my having read the advertisement I was in a cab and on my was to Brook Street.

As I drove, I kept turning the matter over in my head and trying to make a guess as to what sort of employment it could be which needed such curious qualifications. A strong physique, a resolute nature, a medical training, and a knowledge of beetles—what connection could there be between these various requisites? And then there was the disheartening fact that the situation was not a permanent one, but terminable from day to day, according to the terms of the advertisement. The more I pondered over it the more unintelligible did it become; but at the end of my meditations I always came back to the ground fact that, come what might, I had nothing to lose, that I was completely at the end of my resources, and that I was ready for any adventure, however desperate, which would put a few honest sovereigns into my pocket. The man fears to fail who has to pay for his failure, but there was no penalty which Fortune could exact from me. I was like the gambler with empty pockets, who is still allowed to try his luck with the others.

No. 77B, Brook Street, was one of those dingy and yet imposing houses, dun-coloured and flat-faced, with the intensely respectable and solid air which marks the Georgian builder. As I alighted from the cab, a young man came out of the door and walked swiftly down the street. In passing me, I noticed that he cast an inquisitive and somewhat malevolent glance at me, and I took the incident as a good omen, for his appearance was that of a rejected candidate, and if he resented my application it meant that the vacancy was not yet filled up. Full of hope, I ascended the broad steps and rapped with the heavy knocker.

A footman in powder and livery opened the door. Clearly I was in touch with the people of wealth and fashion.

"Yes, sir?" said the footman.

"I came in answer to—"

"Quite so, sir," said the footman. "Lord Linchmere will see you at once in the library."

Lord Linchmere! I had vaguely heard the name, but could not for the instant recall anything about him. Following the footman, I was shown into a large, book-lined room in which there was seated behind a writing-desk a small man with a pleasant, clean-shaven, mobile face, and long hair shot with grey, brushed back from his forehead. He looked me up and down with a very shrewd, penetrating glance, holding the card which the footman had given him in his right hand. Then he smiled pleasantly, and I felt that externally at any rate I possessed the qualifications which he desired.

"You have come in answer to my advertisement, Dr. Hamilton?" he asked.

"Yes, sir."

"Do you fulfil the conditions which are there laid down?"

"I believe that I do."

"You are a powerful man, or so I should judge from your appearance.

"I think that I am fairly strong."

"And resolute?"

"I believe so."

"Have you ever known what it was to be exposed to imminent danger?"

"No, I don't know that I ever have."

273

"But you think you would be prompt and cool at such a time?"

"I hope so."

"Well, I believe that you would. I have the more confidence in you because you do not pretend to be certain as to what you would do in a position that was new to you. My impression is that, so far as personal qualities go, you are the very man of whom I am in search. That being settled, we may pass on to the next point."

"Which is?"

"To talk to me about beetles."

I looked across to see if he was joking, but, on the contrary, he was leaning eagerly forward across his desk, and there was an expression of something like anxiety in his eyes.

"I am afraid that you do not know about beetles," he cried.

"On the contrary, sir, it is the one scientific subject about which I feel that I really do know something."

"I am overjoyed to hear it. Please talk to me about beetles."

I talked. I do not profess to have said anything original upon the subject, but I gave a short sketch of the characteristics of the beetle, and ran over the more common species, with some allusions to the specimens in my own little collection and to the article upon "Burying Beetles" which I had contributed to the *Journal of Entomological Science*.

"What! not a collector?" cried Lord Linchmere. "You don't mean that you are yourself a collector?" His eyes danced with pleasure at the thought.

"You are certainly the very man in London for my purpose. I thought that among five millions of people there must be such a man, but the difficulty is to lay one's hands upon him. I have been extraordinarily fortunate in finding you."

He rang a gong upon the table, and the footman entered.

"Ask Lady Rossiter to have the goodness to step this way," said his lordship, and a few moments later the lady was ushered into the room. She was a small, middle-aged woman, very like Lord Linchmere in appearance, with the same quick, alert features and grey-black hair. The expression of anxiety, however, which I had observed upon his face was very much more marked upon hers. Some great grief seemed to have cast its shadow over her features. As Lord Linchmere presented me she turned her face full upon me, and I was shocked to observe a half-healed scar extending for two inches over her right eyebrow. It was partly concealed by plaster, but none the less I could see that it had been a serious wound and not long inflicted.

"Dr. Hamilton is the very man for our purpose, Evelyn," said Lord Linchmere. "He is actually a collector of beetles, and he has written articles upon the subject."

"Really!" said Lady Rossiter. "Then you must have heard of my husband. Everyone who knows anything about beetles must have heard of Sir Thomas Rossiter."

For the first time a thin little ray of light began to break into the obscure business. Here, at last, was a connection between these people and beetles. Sir Thomas Rossiter—he was the greatest authority upon the subject in the world. He had made it his lifelong study, and had written a most exhaustive work upon it. I hastened to assure her that I had read and appreciated it.

"Have you met my husband?" she asked.

"No, I have not."

"But you shall," said Lord Linchmere, with decision.

The lady was standing beside the desk, and she put her hand upon his shoulder. It was obvious to me as I saw their faces together that they were brother and sister.

"Are you really prepared for this, Charles? It is noble of you, but you fill me with fears." Her voice quavered with apprehension, and he appeared to me to be equally moved, though he was making strong efforts to conceal his agitation.

"Yes, yes, dear; it is all settled, it is all decided; in fact, there is no other possible way, that I can see."

"There is one obvious way."

"No, no, Evelyn, I shall never abandon you—never. It will come right—depend upon it; it will come right, and surely it looks like the interference of Providence that so perfect an instrument should be put into our hands."

My position was embarrassing, for I felt that for the instant

275

they had forgotten my presence. But Lord Linchmere came back suddenly to me and to my engagement.

"The business for which I want you, Dr. Hamilton, is that you should put yourself absolutely at my disposal. I wish you to come for a short journey with me, to remain always at my side, and to promise to do without question whatever I may ask you, however unreasonable it may appear to you to be."

"That is a good deal to ask," said I.

"Unfortunately I cannot put it more plainly, for I do not myself know what turn matters may take. You may be sure, however, that you will not be asked to do anything which your conscience does not approve; and I promise you that, when all is over, you will be proud to have been concerned in so good a work."

"If it ends happily," said the lady.

"Exactly; if it ends happily," his lordship repeated.

"And terms?" I asked.

"Twenty pounds a day."

I was amazed at the sum, and must have showed my surprise upon my features.

"It is a rare combination of qualities, as must have struck you when you first read the advertisement," said Lord Linchmere; "such varied gifts may well command a high return, and I do not conceal from you that your duties might be arduous or even dangerous. Besides, it is possible that one or two days may bring the matter to an end."

"Please God!" sighed his sister.

"So now, Dr. Hamilton, may I rely upon your aid?"

"Most undoubtedly," said I. "You have only to tell me what my duties are."

"Your first duty will be to return to your home. You will pack up whatever you may need for a short visit to the country. We start together from Paddington Station at 3:40 this afternoon."

"Do we go far?"

"As far as Pangbourne. Meet me at the bookstall at 3:30. I shall have the tickets. Goodbye, Dr. Hamilton! And, by the way, there are two things which I should be very glad if you would bring with you, in case you have them. One is your case for collecting beetles, and the other is a stick, and the thicker and heavier the better."

You may imagine that I had plenty to think of from the time that I left Brook Street until I set out to meet Lord Linchmere at Paddington. The whole fantastic business kept arranging and rearranging itself in kaleidoscopic forms inside my brain, until I had thought out a dozen explanations, each of them more grotesquely improbable than the last. And yet I felt that the truth must be something grotesquely improbable also. At last I gave up all attempts at finding a solution, and contented myself with exactly carrying out the instructions which I had received. With a hand valise, specimen-case, and a loaded cane, I was waiting at the Paddington bookstall when Lord Linchmere arrived. He was an even smaller man than I had thought—frail and peaky, with a manner which was more nervous than it had been in the morning. He wore a long, thick travelling Ulster, and I observed that he carried a heavy blackthorn cudgel in his hand.

"I have the tickets," said he, leading the way up the platform.

"This is our train. I have engaged a carriage, for I am particularly anxious to impress one or two things upon you while we travel down."

And yet all that he had to impress upon me might have been said in a sentence, for it was that I was to remember that I was there as a protection to himself, and that I was not on any consideration to leave him for an instant. This he repeated again and again as our journey drew to a close, with an insistence which showed that his nerves were thoroughly shaken.

"Yes," he said at last, in answer to my looks rather than to my words, "I AM nervous, Dr. Hamilton. I have always been a timid man, and my timidity depends upon my frail physical health. But my soul is firm, and I can bring myself up to face a danger which a less-nervous man might shrink from. What I am doing now is done from no compulsion, but entirely from a sense of duty, and yet it is, beyond doubt, a desperate risk. If things should go wrong, I will have some claims to the title of martyr."

This eternal reading of riddles was too much for me. I felt that I must put a term to it.

"I think it would very much better, sir, if you were to trust me entirely," said I. "It is impossible for me to act effectively, when I do not know what are the objects which we have in view, or even where we are going."

"Oh, as to where we are going, there need be no mystery about that," said he; "we are going to Delamere Court, the residence of Sir Thomas Rossiter, with whose work you are so conversant. As to the exact object of our visit, I do not know that at this stage of the proceedings anything would be gained, Dr. Hamilton, by taking you into my complete confidence. I may tell you that we are acting—I say 'we,' because my sister, Lady Rossiter, takes the same view as myself—with the one object of preventing anything in the nature of a family scandal. That being so, you can understand that I am loth to give any explanations which are not absolutely necessary. It would be a different matter, Dr. Hamilton, if I were asking your advice. As matters stand, it is only your active help which I need, and I will indicate to you from time to time how you can best give it."

There was nothing more to be said, and a poor man can put up with a good deal for twenty pounds a day, but I felt none the less that Lord Linchmere was acting rather scurvily towards me. He wished to convert me into a passive tool, like the blackthorn in his hand. With his sensitive disposition I could imagine, however, that scandal would be abhorrent to him, and I realized that he would not take me into his confidence until no other course was open to him. I must trust to my own eyes and ears to solve the mystery, but I had every confidence that I should not trust to them in vain.

Delamere Court lies a good five miles from Pangbourne Station, and we drove for that distance in an open fly. Lord Linchmere sat in deep thought during the time, and he never opened his mouth until we were close to our destination. When he did speak it was to give me a piece of information which surprised me.

"Perhaps you are not aware," said he, "that I am a medical man like yourself?"

"No, sir, I did not know it."

"Yes, I qualified in my younger days, when there were several lives between me and the peerage. I have not had occasion to practise, but I have found it a useful education, all the same. I never regretted the years which I devoted to medical study. These are the gates of Delamere Court."

We had come to two high pillars crowned with heraldic monsters which flanked the opening of a winding avenue. Over the laurel bushes and rhododendrons, I could see a long, many-gabled mansion, girdled with ivy, and toned to the warm, cheery, mellow glow of old brick-work. My eyes were still fixed in admiration upon this delightful house when my companion plucked nervously at my sleeve.

"Here's Sir Thomas," he whispered. "Please talk beetle all you can."

A tall, thin figure, curiously angular and bony, had emerged through a gap in the hedge of laurels. In his hand he held a spud, and he wore gauntleted gardener's gloves. A broad-brimmed, grey hat cast his face into shadow, but it struck me as exceedingly austere, with an ill-nourished beard and harsh, irregular features. The fly pulled up and Lord Linchmere sprang out.

"My dear Thomas, how are you?" said he, heartily.

But the heartiness was by no means reciprocal. The owner of the grounds glared at me over his brother-in-law's shoulder, and I caught broken scraps of sentences—"well-known wishes . . . hatred of strangers . . . unjustifiable intrusion . . . perfectly inexcusable." Then there was a muttered explanation, and the two of them came over together to the side of the fly.

"Let me present you to Sir Thomas Rossiter, Dr. Hamilton," said Lord Linchmere. "You will find that you have a strong community of tastes."

I bowed. Sir Thomas stood very stiffly, looking at me severely from under the broad brim of his hat.

"Lord Linchmere tells me that you know something about beetles," said he. "What do you know about beetles?"

"I know what I have learned from your work upon the *coleoptera*, Sir Thomas," I answered.

"Give me the names of the better-known species of the British *scarabaei*," said he.

I had not expected an examination, but fortunately I was ready for one. My answers seemed to please him, for his stern features relaxed.

"You appear to have read my book with some profit, sir," said he. "It is a rare thing for me to meet anyone who takes an intelligent interest in such matters. People can find time for such trivialities as sport or society, and yet the beetles are overlooked. I can assure you that the greater part of the idiots in this part of the country are unaware that I have ever written a book at all—I, the first man who ever described the true function of the elytra. I am glad to see you, sir, and I have no doubt that I can show you some specimens which will interest you." He stepped into the fly and drove up with us to the house, expounding to me as we went some recent researches which he had made into the anatomy of the lady-bird.

I have said that Sir Thomas Rossiter wore a large hat drawn down over his brows. As he entered the hall he uncovered himself, and I was at once aware of a singular characteristic which the hat had concealed. His forehead, which was naturally high, and higher still on account of receding hair, was in a continual state of movement. Some nervous weakness kept the muscles in a constant spasm, which sometimes produced a mere twitching and sometimes a curious rotary movement unlike anything which I had ever seen before. It was strikingly visible as he turned towards us after entering the study, and seemed the more singular from the contrast with the hard, steady, grey eyes which looked out from underneath those palpitating brows.

"I am sorry," said he, "that Lady Rossiter is not here to help me to welcome you. By the way, Charles, did Evelyn say anything about the date of her return?"

"She wished to stay in town for a few more days," said Lord Linchmere. "You know how ladies' social duties accumulate if they have been for some time in the country. My sister has many old friends in London at present."

"Well, she is her own mistress, and I should not wish to alter her plans, but I shall be glad when I see her again. It is very lonely here without her company."

"I was afraid that you might find it so, and that was partly why I ran down. My young friend, Dr. Hamilton, is so much interested in the subject which you have made your own, that I thought you would not mind his accompanying me."

"I lead a retired life, Dr. Hamilton, and my aversion to strangers grows upon me," said our host. "I have sometimes thought that my nerves are not so good as they were. My travels in search of beetles in my younger days took me into many malarious and unhealthy places. But a brother *coleopterist* like yourself is always a welcome guest, and I shall be delighted if you will look over my collection, which I think that I may without exaggeration describe as the best in Europe."

And so no doubt it was. He had a huge, oaken cabinet arranged in shallow drawers, and here, neatly ticketed and classified, were beetles from every corner of the earth, black, brown, blue, green, and mottled. Every now and then as he swept his hand over the lines and lines of impaled insects he would catch up some rare specimen, and, handling it with as much delicacy and reverence as if it were a precious relic, he would hold forth upon its peculiarities and the circumstances under which it came into his possession. It was evidently an unusual thing for him to meet with a sympathetic listener, and he talked and talked until the spring evening had deepened into night, and the gong announced that it was time to dress for dinner. All the time Lord Linchmere said nothing, but he stood at his brother-in-law's elbow, and I caught him continually shooting curious little, questioning glances into his face. And his own features expressed some strong emotion, apprehension, sympathy, expectation: I seemed to read them all. I was sure that Lord Linchmere was fearing something and awaiting something, but what that something might be I could not imagine.

The evening passed quietly but pleasantly, and I should have been entirely at my ease if it had not been for that continual sense of tension upon the part of Lord Linchmere. As to our host, I found that he improved upon acquaintance. He spoke constantly with affection of his absent wife, and also of his little son, who had recently been sent to school. The house, he said, was not the same without them. If it were not for his scientific studies, he did not know how he could get through the days. After dinner we smoked for some time in the billiard-room, and finally went early to bed.

And then it was that, for the first time, the suspicion that Lord Linchmere was a lunatic crossed my mind. He followed me into my bedroom, when our host had retired.

"Doctor," said he, speaking in a low, hurried voice, "you must come with me. You must spend the night in my bedroom."

"What do you mean?"

"I prefer not to explain. But this is part of your duties. My room is close by, and you can return to your own before the servant calls you in the morning."

"But why?" I asked.

"Because I am nervous of being alone," said he. "That's the reason, since you must have a reason."

It seemed rank lunacy, but the argument of those twenty pounds would overcome many objections. I followed him to his room.

"Well," said I, "there's only room for one in that bed."

"Only one shall occupy it," said he.

"And the other?"

"Must remain on watch."

"Why?" said I. "One would think you expected to be attacked."

"Perhaps I do."

"In that case, why not lock your door?"

"Perhaps I *want* to be attacked."

It looked more and more like lunacy. However, there was nothing for it but to submit. I shrugged my shoulders and sat down in the arm-chair beside the empty fireplace.

"I am to remain on watch, then?" said I, ruefully.

"We will divide the night. If you will watch until two, I will watch the remainder."

"Very good."

"Call me at two o'clock, then."

"I will do so."

"Keep your ears open, and if you hear any sounds wake me instantly—instantly, you hear?"

"You can rely upon it." I tried to look as solemn as he did.

"And for God's sake don't go to sleep," said he, and so, taking off only his coat, he threw the coverlet over him and settled down for the night.

It was a melancholy vigil, and made more so by my own sense of its folly. Supposing that by any chance Lord Linchmere had cause to suspect that he was subject to danger in the house of Sir Thomas Rossiter, why on earth could he not lock his door and so protect himself?" His own answer that he might wish to be attacked was absurd. Why should he possibly wish to be attacked? And who would wish to attack him? Clearly, Lord Linchmere was suffering from some singular delusion, and the result was that on an imbecile pretext I was to be deprived of my night's rest. Still, however absurd, I was determined to carry out his injunctions to the letter as long as I was in his employment. I sat, therefore, beside the empty fireplace, and listened to a sonorous chiming clock somewhere down the passage which gurgled and struck every quarter of an hour. It was an endless vigil. Save for that single clock, an absolute silence reigned throughout the great house. A small lamp stood on the table at my elbow, throwing a circle of light round my chair, but leaving the corners of the room draped in shadow. On the bed Lord Linchmere was breathing peacefully. I envied him his quiet sleep, and again and again my own eyelids drooped, but every time my sense of duty came to my help, and I sat up, rubbing my eyes and pinching myself with a determination to see my irrational watch to an end.

And I did so. From down the passage came the chimes of two o'clock, and I laid my hand upon the shoulder of the sleeper. Instantly he was sitting up, with an expression of the keenest interest upon his face.

"You have heard something?"

"No, sir. It is two o'clock."

"Very good. I will watch. You can go to sleep."

I lay down under the coverlet as he had done and was soon unconscious. My last recollection was of that circle of lamplight, and of the small, hunched-up figure and strained, anxious face of Lord Linchmere in the centre of it.

How long I slept I do not know; but I was suddenly aroused by a sharp tug at my sleeve. The room was in darkness, but a hot smell of oil told me that the lamp had only that instant been extinguished.

"Quick! Quick!" said Lord Linchmere's voice in my ear.

I sprang out of bed, he still dragging at my arm.

"Over here!" he whispered, and pulled me into a corner of the room. "Hush! Listen!"

In the silence of the night I could distinctly hear that some-one was coming down the corridor. It was a stealthy step, faint and intermittent, as of a man who paused cautiously after every stride. Sometimes for half a minute there was no sound, and then came the shuffle and creak which told of a fresh advance. My companion was trembling with excitement. His hand, which still held my sleeve, twitched like a branch in the wind.

"What is it?" I whispered.

"It's he!"

"Sir Thomas?"

"Yes."

"What does he want?"

"Hush! Do nothing until I tell you."

I was conscious now that someone was trying the door. There was the faintest little rattle from the handle, and then I dimly saw a thin slit of subdued light. There was a lamp burning somewhere far down the passage, and it just sufficed to make the outside visible from the darkness of our room. The greyish slit grew broader and broader, very gradually, very gently, and then outlined against it I saw the dark figure of a man. He was squat and crouching, with the silhouette of a bulky and misshapen dwarf. Slowly the door swung open with this ominous shape framed in the centre of it. And then, in an instant, the crouching figure shot up, there was a tiger spring across the room and thud, thud, thud, came three tremendous blows from some heavy object upon the bed.

I was so paralysed with amazement that I stood motionless and staring until I was aroused by a yell for help from my companion. The open door shed enough light for me to see the outline of things, and there was little Lord Linchmere with his arms round the neck of his brother-in-law, holding bravely on to him like a game bull-terrier with its teeth into a gaunt deerhound. The tall, bony man dashed himself about, writhing round and round to get a grip upon his assailant; but the other, clutching on from behind, still kept his hold, though his shrill, frightened cries showed how unequal he felt the contest to be. I sprang to the rescue, and the two of us managed to throw Sir Thomas to the ground, though he made his teeth meet in my shoulder. With all my youth and weight and strength, it was a desperate struggle before we could master his frenzied struggles; but at last we secured his arms with the waist-cord of the dressing-gown which he was wearing. I was holding his legs while Lord Linchmere was endeavouring to relight the lamp, when there came the pattering of many feet in the passage, and the butler and two footmen, who had been alarmed by the cries, rushed into the room. With their aid we had no further difficulty in securing our prisoner, who lay foaming and glaring upon the ground. One glance at his face was enough to prove that he was a dangerous maniac, while the short, heavy hammer which lay beside the bed showed how murderous had been his intentions.

"Do not use any violence!" said Lord Linchmere, as we raised the struggling man to his feet. "He will have a period of stupor after this excitement. I believe that it is coming on already." As he spoke the convulsions became less violent, and the madman's head fell forward upon his breast, as if he were overcome by sleep. We led him down the passage and stretched him upon his own bed, where he lay unconscious, breathing heavily.

"Two of you will watch him," said Lord Linchmere. "And now, Dr. Hamilton, if you will return with me to my room, I will give you the explanation which my horror of scandal has perhaps caused me to delay too long. Come what may, you will never have cause to regret your share in this night's work.

"The case may be made clear in a very few words," he continued, when we were alone. "My poor brother-in-law is one of the best fellows upon earth, a loving husband and an estimable father, but he comes from a stock which is deeply tainted with insanity. He has more than once had homicidal outbreaks, which are the more painful because his inclination is always to attack the very person to whom he is most attached. His son was sent away to school to avoid this danger, and then came an attempt upon my sister, his wife, from which she escaped with injuries that you may have observed when you met her in London. You understand that he knows nothing of the matter when he is in his sound senses, and would ridicule the suggestion that he could under any circumstances injure those whom he loves so dearly. It is often, as you know, a characteristic of such maladies that it is absolutely impossible to convince the man who suffers from them of their existence.

"Our great object was, of course, to get him under restraint before he could stain his hands with blood, but the matter was full of difficulty. He is a recluse in his habits, and would not see any medical man. Besides, it was necessary for our purpose that the medical man should convince himself of his insanity; and he is sane as you or I, save on these very rare occasions. But, fortunately, before he has these attacks he always shows certain premonitory symptoms, which are providential danger-signals, warning us to be upon our guard. The chief of these is that nervous contortion of the forehead which you must have observed. This is a phenomenon which always appears from three to four days before his attacks of frenzy. The moment it showed itself his wife came into town on some pretext, and took refuge in my house in Brook Street.

"It remained for me to convince a medical man of Sir Thomas's insanity, without which it was impossible to put him where he could do no harm. The first problem was how to get a medical man into his house. I bethought me of his interest in beetles, and his love for anyone who shared his tastes. I advertised, therefore, and was fortunate enough to find in you the very man I wanted. A stout companion was necessary, for I knew that the lunacy could only be proved by a murderous assault, and I had every reason to believe that that assault would be made upon myself, since he had the warmest regard for me in his moments of sanity. I think your intelligence will supply all the rest. I did not know that the attack would come by night, but I thought it very probable, for the crises of such cases usually do occur in the early hours of the morning. I am a very nervous man myself, but I saw no other way in which I could remove this terrible danger from my sister's life. I need not ask you whether you are willing to sign the lunacy papers."

"Undoubtedly. But *two* signatures are necessary."

"You forget that I am myself a holder of a medical degree. I have the papers on a side-table here, so if you will be good enough to sign them now, we can have the patient removed in the morning."

So that was my visit to Sir Thomas Rossiter, the famous bee-tle-hunter, and that was also my first step upon the ladder of success, for Lady Rossiter and Lord Linchmere have proved to be staunch friends, and they have never forgotten my association with them in the time of their need. Sir Thomas is out and said to be cured, but I still think that if I spent another night at Delamere Court, I should be inclined to lock my door upon the inside.

The Sealed Room

A solicitor of an active habit and athletic tastes who is compelled by his hopes of business to remain within the four walls of his office from ten till five must take what exercise he can in the evenings. Hence it was that I was in the habit of indulging in very long nocturnal excursions, in which I sought the heights of Hampstead and Highgate in order to cleanse my system from the impure air of Abchurch Lane. It was in the course of one of these aimless rambles that I first met Felix Stanniford, and so led up to what has been the most extraordinary adventure of my lifetime.

One evening—it was in April or early May of the year 1894—I made my way to the extreme northern fringe of London, and was walking down one of those fine avenues of high brick villas which the huge city is for ever pushing farther and farther out into the country. It was a fine, clear spring night, the moon was shining out of an unclouded sky, and I, having already left many miles behind me, was inclined to walk slowly and look about me. In this contemplative mood, my attention was arrested by one of the houses which I was passing.

It was a very large building, standing in its own grounds, a little back from the road. It was modern in appearance, and yet it was far less so than its neighbours, all of which were crudely and painfully new. Their symmetrical line was broken by the gap caused by the laurel-studded lawn, with the great, dark, gloomy house looming at the back of it. Evidently it had been the country retreat of some wealthy merchant, built perhaps when the nearest street was a mile off, and now gradually overtaken and surrounded by the red brick tentacles of the London octopus. The next stage, I reflected, would be its digestion and absorption, so that the cheap builder might rear a dozen eighty-pound-a-year villas upon the garden frontage. And then, as all this passed vaguely through my mind, an incident occurred which brought my thoughts into quite another channel.

A four-wheeled cab, that opprobrium of London, was coming jolting and creaking in one direction, while in the other there was a yellow glare from the lamp of a cyclist. They were the only moving objects in the whole long, moonlit road, and yet they crashed into each ether with that malignant accuracy which brings two ocean liners together in the broad waste of the Atlantic. It was the cyclist's fault. He tried to cross in front of the cab, miscalculated his distance, and was knocked sprawling by the horse's shoulder. He rose, snarling; the cabman swore back at him, and then, realizing that his number had not yet been taken, lashed his horse and lumbered off. The cyclist caught at the handles of his prostrate machine, and then suddenly sat down with a groan. "Oh, Lord!" he said.

I ran across the road to his side. "Any harm done?" I asked.

"It's my ankle," said he. "Only a twist, I think; but it's pretty painful. Just give me your hand, will you?"

He lay in the yellow circle of the cycle lamp, and I noted as I helped him to his feet that he was a gentlemanly young fellow, with a slight dark moustache and large, brown eyes, sensitive and nervous in appearance, with indications of weak health upon his sunken cheeks. Work or worry had left its traces upon his thin, yellow face. He stood up when I pulled his hand, but he held one foot in the air, and he groaned as he moved it.

"I can't put it to the ground," said he.

"Where do you live?"

"Here!" he nodded his head towards the big, dark house in the garden. "I was cutting across to the gate when that confounded cab ran into me. Could you help me so far?"

It was easily done. I put his cycle inside the gate, and then I supported him down the drive, and up the steps to the hall door.

There was not a light anywhere, and the place was as black and silent as if no one had ever lived in it.

"That will do. Thank you very much," said he, fumbling with his key in the lock.

"No, you must allow me to see you safe."

He made some feeble, petulant protest, and then realised that he could really do nothing without me. The door had opened into a pitch-dark hall. He lurched forward, with my hand still on his arm.

"This door to the right," said he, feeling about in the darkness.

I opened the door, and at the same moment he managed to strike a light. There was a lamp upon the table, and we lit it between us. "Now, I'm all right. You can leave me now! Good-bye!" said he, and with the words he sat down in the arm-chair and fainted dead away.

It was a queer position for me. The fellow looked so ghastly, that really I was not sure that he was not dead. Presently his lips quivered and his breast heaved, but his eyes were two white slits and his colour was horrible. The responsibility was more than I could stand. I pulled at the bell-rope, and heard the bell ringing furiously far away. But no one came in response. The bell tinkled away into silence, which no murmur or movement came to break. I waited, and rang again, with the same result. There must be someone about. This young gentleman could not live all alone in that huge house. His people ought to know of his condition. If they would not answer the bell, I must hunt them out myself. I seized the lamp and rushed from the room.

What I saw outside amazed me. The hall was empty. The stairs were bare, and yellow with dust. There were three doors opening into spacious rooms, and each was uncarpeted and un-draped, save for the grey webs which drooped from the cornice, and rosettes of lichen which had formed upon the walls. My feet reverberated in those empty and silent chambers. Then I wandered on down the passage, with the idea that the kitchens, at least, might be tenanted. Some caretaker might lurk in some secluded room. No, they were all equally desolate. Despairing of finding any help, I ran down another corridor, and came on something which surprised me more than ever.

The passage ended in a large, brown door, and the door had a seal of red wax the size of a five-shilling piece over the keyhole. This seal gave me the impression of having been there for a long time, for it was dusty and discoloured. I was still staring at it, and wondering what that door might conceal, when I heard a voice calling behind me, and, running back, found my young man sitting up in his chair and very much astonished at finding himself in darkness.

"Why on earth did you take the lamp away?" he asked.

"I was looking for assistance."

"You might look for some time," said he. "I am alone in the house."

"Awkward if you get an illness."

"It was foolish of me to faint. I inherit a weak heart from my mother, and pain or emotion has that effect upon me. It will carry me off some day, as it did her. You're not a doctor, are you?"

"No, a lawyer. Frank Alder is my name."

"Mine is Felix Stanniford. Funny that I should meet a lawyer, for my friend, Mr. Perceval, was saying that we should need one soon."

"Very happy, I am sure."

"Well, that will depend upon him, you know. Did you say that you had run with that lamp all over the ground floor?"

"Yes."

"All over it?" he asked, with emphasis, and he looked at me very hard.

"I think so. I kept on hoping that I should find someone."

"Did you enter all the rooms?" he asked, with the same intent gaze.

"Well, all that I could enter."

"Oh, then you did notice it!" said he, and he shrugged his shoulders with the air of a man who makes the best of a bad job.

"Notice what?"

"Why, the door with the seal on it."

"Yes, I did."

"Weren't you curious to know what was in it?"

"Well, it did strike me as unusual."

"Do you think you could go on living alone in this house, year after year, just longing all the time to know what is at the other side of that door, and yet not looking?"

"Do you mean to say," I cried, "that you don't know yourself?"

"No more than you do."

"Then why don't you look?"

"I mustn't," said he.

He spoke in a constrained way, and I saw that I had blundered on to some delicate ground. I don't know that I am more inquisitive than my neighbours, but there certainly was something in the situation which appealed very strongly to my curiosity. However, my last excuse for remaining in the house was gone now that my companion had recovered his senses. I rose to go.

"Are you in a hurry?" he asked.

"No; I have nothing to do."

"Well, I should be very glad if you would stay with me a little. The fact is that I live a very retired and secluded life here. I don't suppose there is a man in London who leads such a life as I do. It is quite unusual for me to have anyone to talk with."

I looked round at the little room, scantily furnished, with a sofa-bed at one side. Then I thought of the great, bare house, and the sinister door with the discoloured red seal upon it. There was something queer and grotesque in the situation, which made me long to know a little more. Perhaps I should, if I waited. I told him that I should be very happy.

"You will find the spirits and a siphon upon the side-table. You must forgive me if I cannot act as host, but I can't get across the room. Those are cigars in the tray there. I'll take one myself, I think. And so you are a solicitor, Mr. Alder?"

"Yes."

"And I am nothing. I am that most helpless of living creatures, the son of a millionaire. I was brought up with the expectation of great wealth; and here I am, a poor man, without any profession at all. And then, on the top of it all, I am left with this great mansion on my hands, which I cannot possibly keep up.

Isn't it an absurd situation? For me to use this as my dwelling is like a coster drawing his barrow with a thoroughbred. A donkey would be more useful to him, and a cottage to me."

"But why not sell the house?" I asked.

"I mustn't."

"Let it, then?"

"No, I mustn't do that either."

I looked puzzled, and my companion smiled.

"I'll tell you how it is, if it won't bore you," said he.

"On the contrary, I should be exceedingly interested."

"I think, after your kind attention to me, I cannot do less than relieve any curiosity that you may feel. You must know that my father was Stanislaus Stanniford, the banker."

Stanniford, the banker! I remembered the name at once. His flight from the country some seven years before had been one of the scandals and sensations of the time.

"I see that you remember," said my companion. "My poor father left the country to avoid numerous friends, whose savings he had invested in an unsuccessful speculation. He was a nervous, sensitive man, and the responsibility quite upset his reason. He had committed no legal offence. It was purely a matter of sentiment. He would not even face his own family, and he died among strangers without ever letting us know where he was."

"He died!" said I.

"We could not prove his death, but we know that it must be so, because the speculations came right again, and so there was no reason why he should not look any man in the face. He would have returned if he were alive. But he must have died in the last two years."

"Why in the last two years?"

"Because we heard from him two years ago."

"Did he not tell you then where he was living?"

"The letter came from Paris, but no address was given. It was when my poor mother died. He wrote to me then, with some instructions and some advice, and I have never heard from him since."

"Had you heard before?"

293

"Oh, yes, we had heard before, and that's where our mystery of the sealed door, upon which you stumbled to-night, has its origin. Pass me that desk, if you please. Here I have my father's letters, and you are the first man except Mr. Perceval who has seen them."

"Who is Mr. Perceval, may I ask?"

"He was my father's confidential clerk, and he has continued to be the friend and adviser of my mother and then of myself. I don't know what we should have done without Perceval. He saw the letters, but no one else. This is the first one, which came on the very day when my father fled, seven years ago. Read it to yourself."

This is the letter which I read:

"*My Ever Dearest Wife,*

"Since Sir William told me how weak your heart is, and how harmful any shock might be, I have never talked about my business affairs to you. The time has come when at all risks I can no longer refrain from telling you that things have been going badly with me. This will cause me to leave you for a little time, but it is with the absolute assurance that we shall see each other very soon. On this you can thoroughly rely. Our parting is only for a very short time, my own darling, so don't let it fret you, and above all don't let it impair your health, for that is what I want above all things to avoid.

"Now, I have a request to make, and I implore you by all that binds us together to fulfil it exactly as I tell you. There are some things which I do not wish to be seen by anyone in my dark room—the room which I use for photographic purposes at the end of the garden passage. To prevent any painful thoughts, I may assure you once for all, dear, that it is nothing of which I need be ashamed. But still I do not wish you or Felix to enter that room. It is locked, and I implore you when you receive this to at once place a seal over the lock, and leave it so. Do not sell or let the house, for in either case my secret will be discovered. As long as you or Felix are in the house, I know that you will comply with my wishes. When Felix is twenty-one he may enter the room—not before.

"And now, good-bye, my own best of wives. During our short separation you can consult Mr. Perceval on any matters which may arise. He has my complete confidence. I hate to leave Felix and you—even for a time—but there is really no choice.

"Ever and always your loving husband,

"*Stanislaus Stanniford.*

"June 4th, 1887."

"These are very private family matters for me to inflict upon you," said my companion apologetically. "You must look upon it as done in your professional capacity. I have wanted to speak about it for years."

"I am honoured by your confidence," I answered, "and exceedingly interested by the facts."

"My father was a man who was noted for his almost morbid love of truth. He was always pedantically accurate. When he said, therefore, that he hoped to see my mother very soon, and when he said that he had nothing to be ashamed of in that dark room, you may rely upon it that he meant it."

"Then what can it be?" I ejaculated.

"Neither my mother nor I could imagine. We carried out his wishes to the letter, and placed the seal upon the door; there it has been ever since. My mother lived for five years after my father's disappearance, although at the time all the doctors said that she could not survive long. Her heart was terribly diseased. During the first few months she had two letters from my father. Both had the Paris post-mark, but no address. They were short and to the same effect: that they would soon be reunited, and that she should not fret. Then there was a silence, which lasted until her death; and then came a letter to me of so private a nature that I cannot show it to you, begging me never to think evil of him, giving me much good advice, and saying that the sealing of the room was of less importance now than during the lifetime of my mother, but that the opening might still cause pain to others, and that, therefore, he thought it best that it should be postponed until my twenty-first year, for the lapse of time would make things easier. In the meantime, he committed the care of the room to me; so now you can understand how it is that, although I am a very poor man, I can neither let nor sell this great house."

"You could mortgage it."

"My father had already done so."

"It is a most singular state of affairs."

"My mother and I were gradually compelled to sell the furniture and to dismiss the servants, until now, as you see, I am living unattended in a single room. But I have only two more months."

"What do you mean?"

"Why, that in two months I come of age. The first thing that I do will be to open that door; the second, to get rid of the house."

"Why should your father have continued to stay away when these investments had recovered themselves?"

"He must be dead."

"You say that he had not committed any legal offence when he fled the country?"

"None."

"Why should he not take your mother with him?"

"I do not know."

"Why should he conceal his address?"

"I do not know."

"Why should he allow your mother to die and be buried without coming back?"

"I do not know."

"My dear sir," said I, "if I may speak with the frankness of a professional adviser, I should say that it is very clear that your father had the strongest reasons for keeping out of the country, and that, if nothing has been proved against him, he at least thought that something might be, and refused to put himself within the power of the law. Surely that must be obvious, for in what other possible way can the facts be explained?"

My companion did not take my suggestion in good part.

"You had not the advantage of knowing my father, Mr. Alder," he said coldly. "I was only a boy when he left us, but I shall always look upon him as my ideal man. His only fault was that he was too sensitive and too unselfish. That anyone should lose money through him would cut him to the heart. His sense of honour was most acute, any theory of his disappearance which conflicts with that is a mistaken one."

It pleased me to hear the lad speak out so roundly, and yet I knew that the facts were against him, and that he was incapable of taking an unprejudiced view of the situation.

"I only speak as an outsider," said I. "And now I must leave you, for I have a long walk before me. Your story has interested me so much that I should be glad if you could let me know the sequel."

"'Leave me your card," said he; and so, having bade him "good night," I left him.

I heard nothing more of the matter for some time, and had almost feared that it would prove to be one of those fleeting experiences which drift away from our direct observation and end only in a hope or a suspicion. One afternoon, however, a card bearing the name of Mr. J. H. Perceval was brought up to my office in Abchurch Lane, and its bearer, a small dry, bright-eyed fellow of fifty, was ushered in by the clerk.

"I believe, sir," said he, "that my name has been mentioned to you by my young friend, Mr. Felix Stanniford?"

"Of course," I answered, "I remember."

"He spoke to you, I understand, about the circumstances in connection with the disappearance of my former employer, Mr. Stanislaus Stanniford, and the existence of a sealed room in his former residence."

"He did."

"And you expressed an interest in the matter."

"It interested me extremely."

"You are aware that we hold Mr. Stanniford's permission to open the door on the twenty-first birthday of his son?"

"I remember."

"The twenty-first birthday is to-day."

"Have you opened it?" I asked eagerly.

"Not yet, sir," said he gravely. "I have reason to believe that it would be well to have witnesses present when that door is opened. You are a lawyer, and you are acquainted with the facts. Will you be present on the occasion?"

"Most certainly."

"You are employed during the day, and so am I. Shall we meet at nine o'clock at the house?"

"I will come with pleasure."

"Then you will find us waiting for you. Good-bye, for the present." He bowed solemnly, and took his leave.

I kept my appointment that evening, with a brain which was weary with fruitless attempts to think out some plausible explanation of the mystery which we were about to solve. Mr. Perceval and my young acquaintance were waiting for me in the little room. I was not surprised to see the young man looking pale and nervous, but I was rather astonished to find the dry little City man in a state of intense, though partially suppressed, excitement. His cheeks were flushed, his hands twitching, and he could not stand still for an instant.

Stanniford greeted me warmly, and thanked me many times for having come. "And now, Perceval," said he to his companion, "I suppose there is no obstacle to our putting the thing through without delay? I shall be glad to get it over."

The banker's clerk took up the lamp and led the way. But he paused in the passage outside the door, and his hand was shaking, so that the light flickered up and down the high, bare walls.

"Mr. Stanniford," said he, in a cracking voice, "I hope you will prepare yourself in case any shock should be awaiting you when that seal is removed and the door is opened."

"What could there be, Perceval? You are trying to frighten me."

"No, Mr. Stanniford; but I should wish you to be ready...to be braced up...not to allow yourself..." He had to lick his dry lips between every jerky sentence, and I suddenly realised, as clearly as if he had told me, that he knew what was behind that closed door, and that it was something terrible. "Here are the keys, Mr. Stanniford, but remember my warning!"

He had a bunch of assorted keys in his hand, and the young man snatched them from him. Then he thrust a knife under the discoloured seal and jerked it off. The lamp was rattling and shaking in Perceval's hands, so I took it from him and held it near the keyhole, while Stanniford tried key after key. At last one turned in the lock, the door flew open, he took one step into the room, and then, with a horrible cry, the young man fell senseless at our feet.

If I had not given heed to the clerk's warning, and braced myself for a shock, I should certainly have dropped the lamp. The room, windowless and bare, was fitted up as a photographic laboratory, with a tap and sink at the side of it. A shelf of bottles and measures stood at one side, and a peculiar, heavy smell, partly chemical, partly animal, filled the air. A single table and chair were in front of us, and at this, with his back turned towards us, a man was seated in the act of writing. His outline and attitude were as natural as life; but as the light fell upon him, it made my hair rise to see that the nape of his neck was black and wrinkled, and no thicker than my wrist. Dust lay upon him—thick, yellow dust—upon his hair, his shoulders, his shrivelled, lemon-coloured hands. His head had fallen forward upon his breast. His pen still rested upon a discoloured sheet of paper.

"My poor master! My poor, poor master!" cried the clerk, and the tears were running down his cheeks.

"What!" I cried, "Mr. Stanislaus Stanniford!"

"Here he has sat for seven years. Oh, why would he do it? I begged him, I implored him, I went on my knees to him, but he would have his way. You see the key on the table. He had locked the door upon the inside. And he has written something. We must take it."

"Yes, yes, take it, and for God's sake, let us get out of this," I cried; "the air is poisonous. Come, Stanniford, come!" taking an arm each, we half led and half carried the terrified man back to his own room.

"It was my father!" he cried, as he recovered his consciousness. "He is sitting there dead in his chair. You knew it, Perceval! this was what you meant when you warned me."

"Yes, I knew it, Mr. Stanniford. I have acted for the best all along, but my position has been a terribly difficult one. For seven years I have known that your father was dead in that room."

"You knew it, and never told us!"

"Don't be harsh with me, Mr. Stanniford, sir! Make allowance for a man who has had a hard part to play."

"My head is swimming, round. I cannot grasp it!" He staggered up, and helped himself from the brandy bottle. "These letters to my mother and to myself—were they forgeries?"

"No, sir; your father wrote them and addressed them, and left them in my keeping to be posted. I have followed his instructions to the very letter in all things. He was my master, and I have obeyed him."

The brandy had steadied the young man's shaken nerves. "Tell me about it. I can stand it now," said he.

"Well, Mr. Stanniford, you know that at one time there came a period of great trouble upon your father, and he thought that many poor people were about to lose their savings through his fault. He was a man who was so tender-hearted that he could not bear the thought. It worried him and tormented him, until he determined to end his life. Oh, Mr. Stanniford, if you knew how I have prayed him and wrestled with him over it, you would never blame me! And he in turn prayed me as no man has ever prayed me before. He had made up his mind, and he would do it in any case, he said; but it rested with me whether his death should be happy and easy or whether it should be most miserable. I read in his eyes that he meant what he said. And at last I yielded to his prayers, and I consented to do his will.

"What was troubling him was this. He had been told by the first doctor in London that his wife's heart would fail at the slightest shock. He had a horror of accelerating her end, and yet his own existence had become unendurable to him. How could he end himself without injuring her?

"You know now the course that he took. He wrote the letter which she received. There was nothing in it which was not literally true. When he spoke of seeing her again so soon, he was referring to her own approaching death, which he had been assured could not be delayed more than a very few months. So convinced was he of this, that he only left two letters to be forwarded at intervals after his death. She lived five year, and I had no letters to send.

"He left another letter with me to be sent to you, sir, upon the occasion of the death of your mother. I posted all these in Paris to sustain the idea of his being abroad. It was his wish that I should say nothing, and I have said nothing. I have been a faithful servant. Seven years after his death, he thought no doubt that the shock to the feelings of his surviving friends would be lessened. He was always considerate for others."

There was a silence for some time. It was broken by young Stanniford.

"I cannot blame you, Perceval. You have spared my mother a shock, which would certainly have broken her heart. What is that paper?"

"It is what your father was writing, sir. Shall I read it to you?"

"Do so."

"I have taken the poison, and I feel it working in my veins. It is strange, but not painful. When these words are read I shall, if my wishes have been faithfully carried out, have been dead many years. Surely no one who has lost money through me will still bear me animosity. And you, Felix, you will forgive me this family scandal. May God find rest for a sorely wearied spirit!"

"Amen!" we cried, all three.

Playing With Fire

I cannot pretend to say what occurred on the 14th of April last at No. 17, Badderly Gardens. Put down in black and white, my surmise might seem too crude, too grotesque, for serious consideration. And yet that something did occur, and that it was of a nature which will leave its mark upon every one of us for the rest of our lives, is as certain as the unanimous testimony of five witnesses can make it. I will not enter into any argument or speculation. I will only give a plain statement, which will be submitted to John Moir, Harvey Deacon, and Mrs. Delamere, and withheld from publication unless they are prepared to corroborate every detail. I cannot obtain the sanction of Paul Le Duc, for he appears to have left the country.

It was John Moir (the well-known senior partner of Moir, Moir, and Sanderson) who had originally turned our attention to occult subjects. He had, like many very hard and practical men of business, a mystic side to his nature, which had led him to the examination, and eventually to the acceptance, of those elusive phenomena which are grouped together with much that is foolish, and much that is fraudulent, under the common heading of spiritualism. His researches, which had begun with an open mind, ended unhappily in dogma, and he became as positive and fanatical as any other bigot. He represented in our little group the body of men who have turned these singular phenomena into a new religion.

Mrs. Delamere, our medium, was his sister, the wife of Delamere, the rising sculptor. Our experience had shown us that to work on these subjects without a medium was as futile as for an astronomer to make observations without a telescope. On the other hand, the introduction of a paid medium was hateful to all of us. Was it not obvious that he or she would feel bound to return some result for money received, and that the temptation to fraud would be an overpowering one? No phenomena could be relied upon which were produced at a guinea an hour. But, fortunately, Moir had discovered that his sister was mediumistic— in other words, that she was a battery of that animal magnetic force which is the only form of energy which is subtle enough to be acted upon from the spiritual plane as well as from our own material one. Of course, when I say this, I do not mean to beg the question; but I am simply indicating the theories upon which we were ourselves, rightly or wrongly, explaining what we saw. The lady came, not altogether with the approval of her husband, and though she never gave indications of any very great psychic force, we were able, at least, to obtain those usual phenomena of message-tilting which are at the same time so puerile and so inexplicable. Every Sunday evening we met in Harvey Deacon's studio at Badderly Gardens, the next house to the corner of Merton Park Road.

Harvey Deacon's imaginative work in art would prepare anyone to find that he was an ardent lover of everything which was outré and sensational. A certain picturesqueness in the study of the occult had been the quality which had originally attracted him to it, but his attention was speedily arrested by some of those phenomena to which I have referred, and he was coming rapidly to the conclusion that what he had looked upon as an amusing romance and an after-dinner entertainment was really a very formidable reality. He is a man with a remarkably clear and logical brain—a true descendant of his ancestor, the well-known Scotch professor—and he represented in our small circle the critical element, the man who has no prejudices, is prepared to follow facts as far as he can see them, and refuses to theorise in advance of his data. His caution annoyed Moir as much as the latter's robust faith amused Deacon, but each in his own way was equally keen upon the matter.

And I? What am I to say that I represented? I was not the devotee. I was not the scientific critic. Perhaps the best that I can claim for myself is that I was the dilettante man about town, anxious to be in the swim of every fresh movement, thankful for any new sensation which would take me out of myself and open up fresh possibilities of existence. I am not an enthusiast myself, but I like the company of those who are. Moir's talk, which made me feel as if we had a private pass-key through the door of death, filled me with a vague contentment. The soothing atmosphere of the séance with the darkened lights was delightful to me. In a word, the thing amused me, and so I was there.

It was, as I have said, upon the 14th of April last that the very singular event which I am about to put upon record took place. I was the first of the men to arrive at the studio, but Mrs. Delamere was already there, having had afternoon tea with Mrs. Harvey Deacon. The two ladies and Deacon himself were standing in front of an unfinished picture of his upon the easel. I am not an expert in art, and I have never professed to understand what Harvey Deacon meant by his pictures; but I could see in this instance that it was all very clever and imaginative, fairies and animals and allegorical figures of all sorts. The ladies were loud in their praises, and indeed the colour effect was a remarkable one.

"What do you think of it, Markham?" he asked.

"Well, it's above me," said I. "These beasts—what are they?"

"Mythical monsters, imaginary creatures, heraldic emblems—a sort of weird, bizarre procession of them."

"With a white horse in front!"

"It's not a horse," said he, rather testily—which was surprising, for he was a very good-humoured fellow as a rule, and hardly ever took himself seriously.

"What is it, then?"

"Can't you see the horn in front? It's a unicorn. I told you they were heraldic beasts. Can't you recognize one?"

"Very sorry, Deacon," said I, for he really seemed to be annoyed.

He laughed at his own irritation.

"Excuse me, Markham!" said he; "the fact is that I have had an awful job over the beast. All day I have been painting him in and painting him out, and trying to imagine what a real live, ramping unicorn would look like. At last I got him, as I hoped; so when you failed to recognise it, it took me on the raw."

"Why, of course it's a unicorn," said I, for he was evidently depressed at my obtuseness. "I can see the horn quite plainly, but I never saw a unicorn except beside the Royal Arms, and so I never thought of the creature. And these others are griffins and cockatrices, and dragons of sorts?"

"Yes, I had no difficulty with them. It was the unicorn which bothered me. However, there's an end of it until to-morrow." He turned the picture round upon the easel, and we all chatted about other subjects.

Moir was late that evening, and when he did arrive he brought with him, rather to our surprise, a small, stout Frenchman, whom he introduced as Monsieur Paul Le Duc. I say to our surprise, for we held a theory that any intrusion into our spiritual circle deranged the conditions, and introduced an element of suspicion. We knew that we could trust each other, but all our results were vitiated by the presence of an outsider. However, Moir soon reconciled us to the innovation. Monsieur Paul Le Duc was a famous student of occultism, a seer, a medium, and a mystic. He was travelling in England with a letter of introduction to Moir from the President of the Parisian brothers of the Holy Cross. What more natural than that he should bring him to our little séance, or that we should feel honoured by his presence?

He was, as I have said, a small, stout man, undistinguished in appearance, with a broad, smooth, clean-shaven face, remarkable only for a pair of large, brown, velvety eyes, staring vaguely out in front of him. He was well dressed, with the manners of the gentleman, and his curious little turns of English speech set the ladies smiling. Mrs. Deacon had a prejudice against our researches and left the room, upon which we lowered the lights, as was our custom, and drew up our chairs to the square mahogany table which stood in the centre of the studio. The light was subdued, but sufficient to allow us to see each other quite plainly. I remember that I could even observe the curious, podgy little square-topped hands which the Frenchman laid upon the table.

"What a fun!" said he. "It is many years since I have sat in this fashion, and it is to me amusing. *Madame* is medium. Does *madame* make the trance?"

"Well, hardly that," said Mrs. Delamere. "But I am always conscious of extreme sleepiness."

"It is the first stage. Then you encourage it, and there comes the trance. When the trance comes, then out jumps your little spirit and in jumps another little spirit, and so you have direct talking or writing. You leave your machine to be worked by another. Hein? But what have unicorns to do with it?"

Harvey Deacon started in his chair. The Frenchman was moving his head slowly round and staring into the shadows which draped the walls.

"What a fun!" said he. "Always unicorns. Who has been thinking so hard upon a subject so bizarre?"

"This is wonderful!" cried Deacon. "I have been trying to paint one all day. But how could you know it?"

"You have been thinking of them in this room."

"Certainly."

"But thoughts are things, my friend. When you imagine a thing you make a thing. You did not know it, *hein?* But I can see your unicorns because it is not only with my eye that I can see."

"Do you mean to say that I create a thing which has never existed by merely thinking of it?"

"But certainly. It is the fact which lies under all other facts. That is why an evil thought is also a danger."

"They are, I suppose, upon the astral plane?" said Moir.

"Ah, well, these are but words, my friends. They are there—somewhere—everywhere—I cannot tell myself. I see them. I could touch them."

"You could not make us see them."

"It is to materialise them. Hold! It is an experiment. But the power is wanting. Let us see what power we have, and then arrange what we shall do. May I place you as I wish?"

306

"You evidently know a great deal more about it than we do," said Harvey Deacon; "I wish that you would take complete control."

"It may be that the conditions are not good. But we will try what we can do. *Madame* will sit where she is, I next, and this gentleman beside me. Meester Moir will sit next to *madame*, because it is well to have blacks and blonds in turn. So! And now with your permission I will turn the lights all out."

"What is the advantage of the dark?" I asked.

"Because the force with which we deal is a vibration of ether and so also is light. We have the wires all for ourselves now— *hein?* You will not be frightened in the darkness, *madame?* What a fun is such a séance!"

At first the darkness appeared to be absolutely pitchy, but in a few minutes our eyes became so far accustomed to it that we could just make out each other's presence—very dimly and vaguely, it is true. I could see nothing else in the room—only the black loom of the motionless figures. We were all taking the matter much more seriously than we had ever done before.

"You will place your hands in front. It is hopeless that we touch, since we are so few round so large a table. You will compose yourself, *madame*, and if sleep should come to you you will not fight against it. And now we sit in silence and we expect—*hein?*"

So we sat in silence and expected, staring out into the blackness in front of us. A clock ticked in the passage. A dog barked intermittently far away. Once or twice a cab rattled past in the street, and the gleam of its lamps through the chink in the curtains was a cheerful break in that gloomy vigil. I felt those physical symptoms with which previous séances had made me familiar—the coldness of the feet, the tingling in the hands, the glow of the palms, the feeling of a cold wind upon the back. Strange little shooting pains came in my forearms, especially as it seemed to me in my left one, which was nearest to our visitor—due no doubt to disturbance of the vascular system, but worthy of some attention all the same. At the same time I was conscious of a strained feeling of expectancy which was almost painful. From the rigid, absolute silence of my companions I gathered that their nerves were as tense as my own.

And then suddenly a sound came out of the darkness—a low, sibilant sound, the quick, thin breathing of a woman. Quicker and thinner yet it came, as between clenched teeth, to end in a loud gasp with a dull rustle of cloth.

"What's that? Is all right?" someone asked in the darkness.

"Yes, all is right," said the Frenchman. "It is *madame*. She is in her trance. Now, gentlemen, if you will wait quiet you will see something, I think, which will interest you much."

Still the ticking in the hall. Still the breathing, deeper and fuller now, from the medium. Still the occasional flash, more welcome than ever, of the passing lights of the hansoms. What a gap we were bridging, the half-raised veil of the eternal on the one side and the cabs of London on the other. The table was throbbing with a mighty pulse. It swayed steadily, rhythmically, with an easy swooping, scooping motion under our fingers. Sharp little raps and cracks came from its substance, file-firing, volley-firing, the sounds of a fagot burning briskly on a frosty night.

"There is much power," said the Frenchman. "See it on the table!"

I had thought it was some delusion of my own, but all could see it now. There was a greenish-yellow phosphorescent light— or I should say a luminous vapour rather than a light—which lay over the surface of the table. It rolled and wreathed and undulated in dim glimmering folds, turning and swirling like clouds of smoke. I could see the white, square-ended hands of the French medium in this baleful light.

"What a fun!" he cried. "It is splendid!"

"Shall we call the alphabet?" asked Moir.

"But no—for we can do much better," said our visitor. "It is but a clumsy thing to tilt the table for every letter of the alphabet, and with such a medium as *madame* we should do better than that."

"Yes, you will do better," said a voice.

"Who was that? Who spoke? Was that you, Markham?"

"No, I did not speak."

308

"It was *madame* who spoke."

"But it was not her voice."

"Is that you, Mrs. Delamere?"

"It is not the medium, but it is the power which uses the organs of the medium," said the strange, deep voice.

"Where is Mrs. Delamere? It will not hurt her, I trust."

"The medium is happy in another plane of existence. She has taken my place, as I have taken hers."

"Who are you?"

"It cannot matter to you who I am. I am one who has lived as you are living, and who has died as you will die."

We heard the creak and grate of a cab pulling up next door. There was an argument about the fare, and the cabman grumbled hoarsely down the street. The green-yellow cloud still swirled faintly over the table, dull elsewhere, but glowing into a dim luminosity in the direction of the medium. It seemed to be piling itself up in front of her. A sense of fear and cold struck into my heart. It seemed to me that lightly and flippantly we had approached the most real and august of sacraments, that communion with the dead of which the fathers of the Church had spoken.

"Don't you think we are going too far? Should we not break up this séance?" I cried.

But the others were all earnest to see the end of it. They laughed at my scruples.

"All the powers are made for use," said Harvey Deacon. "If we can do this, we should do this. Every new departure of knowledge has been called unlawful in its inception. It is right and proper that we should inquire into the nature of death."

"It is right and proper," said the voice.

"There, what more could you ask?" cried Moir, who was much excited. "Let us have a test. Will you give us a test that you are really there?"

"What test do you demand?"

"Well, now—I have some coins in my pocket. Will you tell me how many?"

"We come back in the hope of teaching and of elevating, and not to guess childish riddles."

"Ha, ha, Meester Moir, you catch it that time," cried the Frenchman. "But surely this is very good sense what the Control is saying."

"It is a religion, not a game," said the cold, hard voice.

"Exactly—the very view I take of it," cried Moir. "I am sure I am very sorry if I have asked a foolish question. You will not tell me who you are?"

"What does it matter?"

"Have you been a spirit long?"

"Yes."

"How long?"

"We cannot reckon time as you do. Our conditions are different."

"Are you happy?"

"Yes."

"You would not wish to come back to life?"

"No—certainly not."

"Are you busy?"

"We could not be happy if we were not busy."

"What do you do?"

"I have said that the conditions are entirely different."

"Can you give us no idea of your work?"

"We labour for our own improvement and for the advancement of others."

"Do you like coming here to-night?"

"I am glad to come if I can do any good by coming."

"Then to do good is your object?"

"It is the object of all life on every plane."

"You see, Markham, that should answer your scruples."

It did, for my doubts had passed and only interest remained.

"Have you pain in your life?" I asked.

"No; pain is a thing of the body."

"Have you mental pain?"

"Yes; one may always be sad or anxious."

"Do you meet the friends whom you have known on earth?"

"Some of them."

"Why only some of them?"

"Only those who are sympathetic."

"Do husbands meet wives?"

"Those who have truly loved."

"And the others?"

"They are nothing to each other."

"There must be a spiritual connection?"

"Of course."

"Is what we are doing right?"

"If done in the right spirit."

"What is the wrong spirit?"

"Curiosity and levity."

"May harm come of that?"

"Very serious harm."

"What sort of harm?"

"You may call up forces over which you have no control."

"Evil forces?"

"Undeveloped forces."

"You say they are dangerous. Dangerous to body or mind?"

"Sometimes to both."

There was a pause, and the blackness seemed to grow blacker still, while the yellow-green fog swirled and smoked upon the table.

"Any questions you would like to ask, Moir?" said Harvey Deacon.

"Only this—do you pray in your world?"

"One should pray in every world."

"Why?"

"Because it is the acknowledgment of forces outside ourselves."

"What religion do you hold over there?"

"We differ exactly as you do."

"You have no certain knowledge?"

"We have only faith."

"These questions of religion," said the Frenchman, "they are of interest to you serious English people, but they are not so much fun. It seems to me that with this power here we might be able to have some great experience—*hein?* Something of which we could talk."

"But nothing could be more interesting than this," said Moir.

"Well, if you think so, that is very well," the Frenchman answered, peevishly. "For my part, it seems to me that I have heard all this before, and that to-night I should weesh to try some experiment with all this force which is given to us. But if you have other questions, then ask them, and when you are finish we can try something more."

But the spell was broken. We asked and asked, but the medium sat silent in her chair. Only her deep, regular breathing showed that she was there. The mist still swirled upon the table.

"You have disturbed the harmony. She will not answer."

"But we have learned already all that she can tell—*hein?* For my part I wish to see something that I have never seen before."

"What then?"

"You will let me try?"

"What would you do?"

"I have said to you that thoughts are things. Now I wish to prove it to you, and to show you that which is only a thought. Yes, yes, I can do it and you will see. Now I ask you only to sit still and say nothing, and keep ever your hands quiet upon the table."

The room was blacker and more silent than ever. The same feeling of apprehension which had lain heavily upon me at the beginning of the séance was back at my heart once more. The roots of my hair were tingling.

"It is working! It is working!" cried the Frenchman, and there was a crack in his voice as he spoke which told me that he also was strung to his tightest.

The luminous fog drifted slowly off the table, and wavered and flickered across the room. There in the farther and darkest corner it gathered and glowed, hardening down into a shining core—a strange, shifty, luminous, and yet non-illuminating patch of radiance, bright itself, but throwing no rays into the darkness. It had changed from a greenish-yellow to a dusky sullen red. Then round this centre there coiled a dark, smoky substance, thickening, hardening, growing denser and blacker. And then the light went out, smothered in that which had grown round it.

"It has gone."

"Hush—there's something the room."

We heard it in the corner where the light had been, something which breathed deeply and fidgeted in the darkness.

"What is it? Le Duc, what you have done?"

"It is all right. No harm will come." The Frenchman's voice was treble with agitation.

"Good heavens, Moir, there's a large animal in the room. Here it is, close by my chair! Go away! Go away!"

It was Harvey Deacon's voice, and then came the sound of a blow upon some hard object. And then . . . And then . . . how can I tell you what happened then?

Some huge thing hurtled against us in the darkness, rearing, stamping, smashing, springing, snorting. The table was splintered. We were scattered in every direction. It clattered and scrambled amongst us, rushing with horrible energy from one corner of the room to another. We were all screaming with fear, grovelling upon our hands and knees to get away from it. Something trod upon my left hand, and I felt the bones splinter under the weight.

"A light! A light!" someone yelled.

"Moir, you have matches, matches!"

"No, I have none. Deacon, where are the matches? For God's sake, the matches!"

"I can't find them. Here, you Frenchman, stop it!"

"It is beyond me. Oh, *mon Dieu*, I cannot stop it. The door! Where is the door?"

My hand, by good luck, lit upon the handle as I groped about in the darkness. The hard-breathing, snorting, rushing creature tore past me and butted with a fearful crash against the oaken partition. The instant that it had passed I turned the handle, and next moment we were all outside, and the door shut behind us. From within came a horrible crashing and rending and stamping.

"What is it? In Heaven's name, what is it?"

"A horse. I saw it when the door opened. But Mrs. Dela-mere——?"

"We must fetch her out. Come on, Markham; the longer we wait the less we shall like it."

He flung open the door and we rushed in. She was there on the ground amidst the splinters of her chair. We seized her and dragged her swiftly out, and as we gained the door I looked over my shoulder into the darkness. There were two strange eyes glowing at us, a rattle of hoofs, and I had just time to slam the door when there came a crash upon it which split it from top to bottom.

"It's coming through! It's coming!"

"Run, run for your lives!" cried the Frenchman.

Another crash, and something shot through the riven door. It was a long white spike, gleaming in the lamplight. For a moment it shone before us, and then with a snap it disappeared again.

"Quick! Quick! This way!" Harvey Deacon shouted. "Carry her in! Here! Quick!"

We had taken refuge in the dining-room, and shut the heavy oak door. We laid the senseless woman upon the sofa, and as we did so, Moir, the hard man of business, drooped and fainted across the hearthrug. Harvey Deacon was as white as a corpse, jerking and twitching like an epileptic. With a crash we heard the studio door fly to pieces, and the snorting and stamping were in the passage, up and down, up and down, shaking the house with their fury. The Frenchman had sunk his face on his hands, and sobbed like a frightened child.

"What shall we do?" I shook him roughly by the shoulder. "Is a gun any use?"

"No, no. The power will pass. Then it will end."

"You might have killed us all—you unspeakable fool—with your infernal experiments."

"I did not know. How could I tell that it would be frightened? It is mad with terror. It was his fault. He struck it."

Harvey Deacon sprang up. "Good heavens!" he cried.

A terrible scream sounded through the house.

"It's my wife! Here, I'm going out. If it's the Evil One himself I am going out!"

He had thrown open the door and rushed out into the passage. At the end of it, at the foot of the stairs, Mrs. Deacon was lying senseless, struck down by the sight which she had seen. But there was nothing else.

With eyes of horror we looked about us, but all was perfectly quiet and still. I approached the black square of the studio door, expecting with every slow step that some atrocious shape would hurl itself out of it. But nothing came, and all was silent inside the room. Peeping and peering, our hearts in our mouths, we came to the very threshold, and stared into the darkness. There was still no sound, but in one direction there was also no darkness. A luminous, glowing cloud, with an incandescent centre, hovered in the corner of the room. Slowly it dimmed and faded, growing thinner and fainter, until at last the same dense, velvety blackness filled the whole studio. And with the last flickering gleam of that baleful light the Frenchman broke into a shout of joy.

"What a fun!" he cried. "No one is hurt, and only the door broken, and the ladies frightened. But, my friends, we have done what has never been done before."

"And as far as I can help," said Harvey Deacon, "it will certainly never be done again."

And that was what befell on the 14th of April last at No. 17 Badderly Gardens. I began by saying that it would seem too grotesque to dogmatise as to what it was which actually did occur; but I give my impressions, our impressions (since they are corroborated by Harvey Deacon and John Moir), for what they are worth. You may, if it pleases you, imagine that we were the victims of an elaborate and extraordinary hoax. Or you may think with us that we underwent a very real and a very terrible experience. Or perhaps you may know more than we do of such occult matters, and can inform us of some similar occurrence. In this latter case a letter to William Markham, 146M, The Albany, would help to throw a light upon that which is very dark to us.

The Lord of Chateau Noir

It was in the days when the German armies had broken their way across France, and when the shattered forces of the young Republic had been swept away to the north of the Aisne and to the south of the Loire. Three broad streams of armed men had rolled slowly but irresistibly from the Rhine, now meandering to the north, now to the south, dividing, coalescing, but all uniting to form one great lake round Paris. And from this lake there welled out smaller streams—one to the north, one southward, to Orleans, and a third westward to Normandy. Many a German trooper saw the sea for the first time when he rode his horse girth-deep into the waves at Dieppe.

Black and bitter were the thoughts of Frenchmen when they saw this weal of dishonour slashed across the fair face of their country. They had fought and they had been overborne. That swarming cavalry, those countless footmen, the masterful guns—they had tried and tried to make head against them. In battalions their invaders were not to be beaten, but man to man, or ten to ten, they were their equals. A brave Frenchman might still make a single German rue the day that he had left his own bank of the Rhine. Thus, unchronicled amid the battles and the sieges, there broke out another war, a war of individuals, with foul murder upon the one side and brutal reprisal on the other.

Colonel von Gramm, of the 24th Posen Infantry, had suffered severely during this new development. He commanded in the little Norman town of Les Andelys, and his outposts stretched amid the hamlets and farmhouses of the district round.

316

No French force was within fifty miles of him, and yet morning after morning he had to listen to a black report of sentries found dead at their posts, or of foraging parties which had never returned. Then the colonel would go forth in his wrath, and farmsteadings would blaze and villages tremble; but next morning there was still that same dismal tale to be told. Do what he might, he could not shake off his invisible enemies. And yet it should not have been so hard, for, from certain signs in common, in the plan and in the deed, it was certain that all these outrages came from a single source.

Colonel von Gramm had tried violence, and it had failed. Gold might be more successful. He published it abroad over the countryside that 500frs. would be paid for information. There was no response. Then 800frs. The peasants were incorruptible. Then, goaded on by a murdered corporal, he rose to a thousand, and so bought the soul of Francois Rejane, farm labourer, whose Norman avarice was a stronger passion than his French hatred.

"You say that you know who did these crimes?" asked the Prussian colonel, eyeing with loathing the blue-bloused, rat-faced creature before him.

"Yes, colonel."

"And it was—?"

"Those thousand francs, colonel—"

"Not a *sou* until your story has been tested. Come! Who is it who has murdered my men?"

"It is Count Eustace of Chateau Noir."

"You lie!" cried the colonel, angrily. "A gentleman and a nobleman could not have done such crimes."

The peasant shrugged his shoulders. "It is evident to me that you do not know the count. It is this way, colonel. What I tell you is the truth, and I am not afraid that you should test it. The Count of Chateau Noir is a hard man, even at the best time he was a hard man. But of late he has been terrible. It was his son's death, you know. His son was under Douay, and he was taken, and then in escaping from Germany he met his death. It was the count's only child, and indeed we all think that it has driven him mad. With his peasants he follows the

German armies. I do not know how many he has killed, but it is he who cut the cross upon the foreheads, for it is the badge of his house."

It was true. The murdered sentries had each had a saltire cross slashed across their brows, as by a hunting-knife. The colonel bent his stiff back and ran his forefinger over the map which lay upon the table.

"The Chateau Noir is not more than four leagues," he said.

"Three and a kilometre, colonel."

"You know the place?"

"I used to work there."

Colonel von Gramm rang the bell.

"Give this man food and detain him," said he to the sergeant.

"Why detain me, colonel? I can tell you no more."

"We shall need you as guide."

"As guide? But the count? If I were to fall into his hands? Ah, colonel—"

The Prussian commander waved him away. "Send Captain Baumgarten to me at once," said he.

The officer who answered the summons was a man of middle-age, heavy-jawed, blue-eyed, with a curving yellow moustache, and a brick-red face which turned to an ivory white where his helmet had sheltered it. He was bald, with a shining, tightly stretched scalp, at the back of which, as in a mirror, it was a favourite mess-joke of the subalterns to trim their moustaches. As a soldier he was slow, but reliable and brave. The colonel could trust him where a more dashing officer might be in danger.

"You will proceed to Chateau Noir to-night, captain," said he. "A guide has been provided. You will arrest the count and bring him back. If there is an attempt at rescue, shoot him at once."

"How many men shall I take, colonel?"

"Well, we are surrounded by spies, and our only chance is to pounce upon him before he knows that we are on the way. A large force will attract attention. On the other hand, you must not risk being cut off."

"I might march north, colonel, as if to join General Goeben. Then I could turn down this road which I see upon your map, and get to Chateau Noir before they could hear of us. In that case, with twenty men—"

"Very good, captain. I hope to see you with your prisoner to-morrow morning."

It was a cold December night when Captain Baumgarten marched out of Les Andelys with his twenty Poseners, and took the main road to the north west. Two miles out he turned suddenly down a narrow, deeply rutted track, and made swiftly for his man. A thin, cold rain was falling, swishing among the tall poplar trees and rustling in the fields on either side. The captain walked first with Moser, a veteran sergeant, beside him. The sergeant's wrist was fastened to that of the French peasant, and it had been whispered in his ear that in case of an ambush the first bullet fired would be through his head. Behind them the twenty infantrymen plodded along through the darkness with their faces sunk to the rain, and their boots squeaking in the soft, wet clay. They knew where they were going, and why, and the thought upheld them, for they were bitter at the loss of their comrades. It was a cavalry job, they knew, but the cavalry were all on with the advance, and, besides, it was more fitting that the regiment should avenge its own dead men.

It was nearly eight when they left Les Andelys. At half-past eleven their guide stopped at a place where two high pillars, crowned with some heraldic stonework, flanked a huge iron gate. The wall in which it had been the opening had crumbled away, but the great gate still towered above the brambles and weeds which had overgrown its base. The Prussians made their way round it and advanced stealthily, under the shadow of a tunnel of oak branches, up the long avenue, which was still cumbered by the leaves of last autumn. At the top they halted and reconnoitred.

The black *chateau* lay in front of them. The moon had shone out between two rain-clouds, and threw the old house into silver and shadow. It was shaped like an L, with a low arched door in front, and lines of small windows like the open ports of a man-of-war. Above was a dark roof, breaking at the corners into little round overhanging turrets, the whole lying silent in the moonshine, with a drift of ragged clouds blackening the heavens behind it. A single light gleamed in one of the lower windows.

The captain whispered his orders to his men. Some were to creep to the front door, some to the back. Some were to watch the east, and some the west. He and the sergeant stole on tiptoe to the lighted window.

It was a small room into which they looked, very meanly furnished. An elderly man, in the dress of a menial, was reading a tattered paper by the light of a guttering candle. He leaned back in his wooden chair with his feet upon a box, while a bottle of white wine stood with a half-filled tumbler upon a stool beside him. The sergeant thrust his needle-gun through the glass, and the man sprang to his feet with a shriek.

"Silence, for your life! The house is surrounded, and you cannot escape. Come round and open the door, or we will show you no mercy when we come in."

"For God's sake, don't shoot! I will open it! I will open it!" He rushed from the room with his paper still crumpled up in his hand. An instant later, with a groaning of old locks and a rasping of bars, the low door swung open, and the Prussians poured into the stone-flagged passage.

"Where is Count Eustace de Chateau Noir?"

"My master! He is out, sir."

"Out at this time of night? Your life for a lie!"

"It is true, sir. He is out!"

"Where?"

"I do not know."

"Doing what?"

"I cannot tell. No, it is no use your cocking your pistol, sir. You may kill me, but you cannot make me tell you that which I do not know."

"Is he often out at this hour?"

"Frequently."

"And when does he come home?"

"Before daybreak."

Captain Baumgarten rasped out a German oath. He had had

his journey for nothing, then. The man's answers were only too likely to be true. It was what he might have expected. But at least he would search the house and make sure. Leaving a picket at the front door and another at the back, the sergeant and he drove the trembling butler in front of them—his shaking candle sending strange, flickering shadows over the old tapestries and the low, oak-raftered ceilings. They searched the whole house, from the huge stone-flagged kitchen below to the dining-hall on the second floor, with its gallery for musicians, and its panelling black with age, but nowhere was there a living creature. Up above, in an attic, they found Marie, the elderly wife of the butler; but the owner kept no other servants, and of his own presence there was no trace.

It was long, however, before Captain Baumgarten had satisfied himself upon the point. It was a difficult house to search. Thin stairs, which only one man could ascend at a time, connected lines of tortuous corridors. The walls were so thick that each room was cut off from its neighbour. Huge fireplaces yawned in each, while the windows were 6ft. deep in the wall. Captain Baumgarten stamped with his feet, tore down curtains, and struck with the pommel of his sword. If there were secret hiding-places, he was not fortunate enough to find them.

"I have an idea," said he, at last, speaking in German to the sergeant. "You will place a guard over this fellow, and make sure that he communicates with no one."

"Yes, captain."

"And you will place four men in ambush at the front and at the back. It is likely enough that about daybreak our bird may return to the nest."

"And the others, captain?"

"Let them have their suppers in the kitchen. The fellow will serve you with meat and wine. It is a wild night, and we shall be better here than on the country road."

"And yourself, captain?"

"I will take my supper up here in the dining-hall. The logs are laid and we can light the fire. You will call me if there is any alarm. What can you give me for supper—you?"

"Alas, monsieur, there was a time when I might have answered, 'What you wish!' but now it is all that we can do to find a bottle of new claret and a cold pullet."

"That will do very well. Let a guard go about with him, sergeant, and let him feel the end of a bayonet if he plays us any tricks."

Captain Baumgarten was an old campaigner. In the Eastern provinces, and before that in Bohemia, he had learned the art of quartering himself upon the enemy. While the butler brought his supper he occupied himself in making his preparations for a comfortable night. He lit the candelabrum of ten candles upon the centre table. The fire was already burning up, crackling merrily, and sending spurts of blue, pungent smoke into the room. The captain walked to the window and looked out. The moon had gone in again, and it was raining heavily. He could hear the deep sough of the wind, and see the dark loom of the trees, all swaying in the one direction. It was a sight which gave a zest to his comfortable quarters, and to the cold fowl and the bottle of wine which the butler had brought up for him. He was tired and hungry after his long tramp, so he threw his sword, his helmet, and his revolver-belt down upon a chair, and fell to eagerly upon his supper. Then, with his glass of wine before him and his cigar between his lips, he tilted his chair back and looked about him.

He sat within a small circle of brilliant light which gleamed upon his silver shoulder-straps, and threw out his terra-cotta face, his heavy eyebrows, and his yellow moustache. But outside that circle things were vague and shadowy in the old dining-hall. Two sides were oak-panelled and two were hung with faded tapestry, across which huntsmen and dogs and stags were still dimly streaming. Above the fireplace were rows of heraldic shields with the blazonings of the family and of its alliances, the fatal saltire cross breaking out on each of them.

Four paintings of old *seigneurs* of Chateau Noir faced the fireplace, all men with hawk noses and bold, high features, so like each other that only the dress could distinguish the Crusader from the Cavalier of the Fronde. Captain Baumgarten, heavy with his repast, lay back in his chair looking up at them through the clouds of his tobacco smoke, and pondering over the strange chance which had sent him, a man from the Baltic coast, to eat his supper in the ancestral hall of these proud Norman chieftains. But the fire was hot, and the captain's eyes were heavy. His chin sank slowly upon his chest, and the ten candles gleamed upon the broad, white scalp.

Suddenly a slight noise brought him to his feet. For an instant it seemed to his dazed senses that one of the pictures opposite had walked from its frame. There, beside the table, and almost within arm's length of him, was standing a huge man, silent, motionless, with no sign of life save his fierce-glinting eyes. He was black-haired, olive-skinned, with a pointed tuft of black beard, and a great, fierce nose, towards which all his features seemed to run. His cheeks were wrinkled like a last year's apple, but his sweep of shoulder, and bony, corded hands, told of a strength which was unsapped by age. His arms were folded across his arching chest, and his mouth was set in a fixed smile.

"Pray do not trouble yourself to look for your weapons," he said, as the Prussian cast a swift glance at the empty chair in which they had been laid. "You have been, if you will allow me to say so, a little indiscreet to make yourself so much at home in a house every wall of which is honeycombed with secret passages. You will be amused to hear that forty men were watching you at your supper. Ah! what then?"

Captain Baumgarten had taken a step forward with clenched fists. The Frenchman held up the revolver which he grasped in his right hand, while with the left he hurled the German back into his chair.

"Pray keep your seat," said he. "You have no cause to trouble about your men. They have already been provided for. It is astonishing with these stone floors how little one can hear what goes on beneath. You have been relieved of your command, and have now only to think of yourself. May I ask what your name is?"

"I am Captain Baumgarten of, the 24th Posen Regiment."

"Your French is excellent, though you incline, like most of

your countrymen, to turn the 'p' into a 'b.' I have been amused to hear them cry '*Avez bitie sur moi!*' You know, doubtless, who it is who addresses you."

"The Count of Chateau Noir."

"Precisely. It would have been a misfortune if you had visited my *chateau* and I had been unable to have a word with you. I have had to do with many German soldiers, but never with an officer before. I have much to talk to you about."

Captain Baumgarten sat still in his chair. Brave as he was, there was something in this man's manner which made his skin creep with apprehension. His eyes glanced to right and to left, but his weapons were gone, and in a struggle he saw that he was but a child to this gigantic adversary. The count had picked up the claret bottle and held it to the light.

"Tut! tut!" said he. "And was this the best that Pierre could do for you? I am ashamed to look you in the face, Captain Baumgarten. We must improve upon this."

He blew a call upon a whistle which hung from his shooting-jacket. The old manservant was in the room in an instant.

"Chambertin from bin 15!" he cried, and a minute later a grey bottle, streaked with cobwebs, was carried in as a nurse bears an infant. The count filled two glasses to the brim.

"Drink!" said he. "It is the very best in my cellars, and not to be matched between Rouen and Paris. Drink, sir, and be happy! There are cold joints below. There are two lobsters, fresh from Honfleur. Will you not venture upon a second and more savoury supper?"

The German officer shook his head. He drained the glass, however, and his host filled it once more, pressing him to give an order for this or that dainty.

"There is nothing in my house which is not at your disposal. You have but to say the word. Well, then, you will allow me to tell you a story while you drink your wine. I have so longed to tell it to some German officer. It is about my son, my only child, Eustace, who was taken and died in escaping. It is a curious little story, and I think that I can promise you that you will never forget it.

324

"You must know, then, that my boy was in the artillery—a fine young fellow, Captain Baumgarten, and the pride of his mother. She died within a week of the news of his death reaching us. It was brought by a brother officer who was at his side throughout, and who escaped while my lad died. I want to tell you all that he told me.

"Eustace was taken at Weissenburg on the 4th of August. The prisoners were broken up into parties, and sent back into Germany by different routes. Eustace was taken upon the 5th to a village called Lauterburg, where he met with kindness from the German officer in command. This good colonel had the hungry lad to supper, offered him the best he had, opened a bottle of good wine, as I have tried to do for you, and gave him a cigar from his own case. Might I entreat you to take one from mine?"

The German again shook his head. His horror of his companion had increased as he sat watching the lips that smiled and the eyes that glared.

"The colonel, as I say, was good to my boy. But, unluckily, the prisoners were moved next day across the Rhine into Ettlingen. They were not equally fortunate there. The officer who guarded them was a ruffian and a villain, Captain Baumgarten. He took a pleasure in humiliating and ill-treating the brave men who had fallen into his power. That night upon my son answering fiercely back to some taunt of his, he struck him in the eye, like this!"

The crash of the blow rang through the hall. The German's face fell forward, his hand up, and blood oozing through his fingers. The count settled down in his chair once more.

"My boy was disfigured by the blow, and this villain made his appearance the object of his jeers. By the way, you look a little comical yourself at the present moment, captain, and your colonel would certainly say that you had been getting into mischief. To continue, however, my boy's youth and his destitution—for his pockets were empty—moved the pity of a kind-hearted major, and he advanced him ten Napoleons from his own pocket without security of any kind. Into your hands, Captain Baumgarten, I return these ten gold pieces, since I

325

cannot learn the name of the lender. I am grateful from my heart for this kindness shown to my boy.

"The vile tyrant who commanded the escort accompanied the prisoners to Durlack, and from there to Carlsruhe. He heaped every outrage upon my lad, because the spirit of the Chateau Noirs would not stoop to turn away his wrath by a feigned submission. Ay, this cowardly villain, whose heart's blood shall yet clot upon this hand, dared to strike my son with his open hand, to kick him, to tear hairs from his moustache—to use him thus—and thus—and thus!"

The German writhed and struggled. He was helpless in the hands of this huge giant whose blows were raining upon him. When at last, blinded and half-senseless, he staggered to his feet, it was only to be hurled back again into the great oaken chair. He sobbed in his impotent anger and shame.

"My boy was frequently moved to tears by the humiliation of his position," continued the count. "You will understand me when I say that it is a bitter thing to be helpless in the hands of an insolent and remorseless enemy. On arriving at Carlsruhe, however, his face, which had been wounded by the brutality of his guard, was bound up by a young Bavarian subaltern who was touched by his appearance. I regret to see that your eye is bleeding so. Will you permit me to bind it with my silk handkerchief?"

He leaned forward, but the German dashed his hand aside.

"I am in your power, you monster!" he cried; "I can endure your brutalities, but not your hypocrisy."

The count shrugged his shoulders.

"I am taking things in their order, just as they occurred," said he. "I was under vow to tell it to the first German officer with whom I could talk *tete-a-tete*. Let me see, I had got as far as the young Bavarian at Carlsruhe. I regret extremely that you will not permit me to use such slight skill in surgery as I possess. At Carlsruhe, my lad was shut up in the old *caserne*, where he remained for a fortnight. The worst pang of his captivity was that some unmannerly curs in the garrison would taunt him with his position as he sat by his window in the evening. That reminds me, captain, that you are not quite situated upon a bed of roses yourself, are you now? You came to trap a wolf, my man, and now the beast has you down with his fangs in your throat. A family man, too, I should judge, by that well-filled tunic. Well, a widow the more will make little matter, and they do not usually remain widows long. Get back into the chair, you dog!

"Well, to continue my story—at the end of a fortnight my son and his friend escaped. I need not trouble you with the dangers which they ran, or with the privations which they endured. Suffice it that to disguise themselves they had to take the clothes of two peasants, whom they waylaid in a wood. Hiding by day and travelling by night, they had got as far into France as Remilly, and were within a mile—a single mile, captain—of crossing the German lines when a patrol of Uhlans came right upon them. Ah! it was hard, was it not, when they had come so far and were so near to safety?" The count blew a double call upon his whistle, and three hard-faced peasants entered the room.

"These must represent my Uhlans," said he. "Well, then, the captain in command, finding that these men were French soldiers in civilian dress within the German lines, proceeded to hang them without trial or ceremony. I think, Jean, that the centre beam is the strongest."

The unfortunate soldier was dragged from his chair to where a noosed rope had been flung over one of the huge oaken rafters which spanned the room. The cord was slipped over his head, and he felt its harsh grip round his throat. The three peasants seized the other end, and looked to the count for his orders. The officer, pale, but firm, folded his arms and stared defiantly at the man who tortured him.

"You are now face to face with death, and I perceive from your lips that you are praying. My son was also face to face with death, and he prayed, also. It happened that a general officer came up, and he heard the lad praying for his mother, and it moved him so—he being himself a father—that he ordered his Uhlans away, and he remained with his *aide-de-camp* only, beside the condemned men. And when he heard all the lad had to tell—that he was the only child of an old family, and that his mother was in failing health—he threw off the rope as I throw off this, and he kissed him on either cheek, as I kiss you, and he bade him go, as I bid you go, and may every kind wish of that noble general, though it could not stave off the fever which slew my son, descend now upon your head."

And so it was that Captain Baumgarten, disfigured, blinded, and bleeding, staggered out into the wind and the rain of that wild December dawn.

De Profundis

So long as the oceans are the ligaments which bind together the great broad-cast British Empire, so long will there be a dash of romance in our minds. For the soul is swayed by the waters, as the waters are by the moon, and when the great highways of an empire are along such roads as these, so full of strange sights and sounds, with danger ever running like a hedge on either side of the course, it is a dull mind indeed which does not bear away with it some trace of such a passage. And now, Britain lies far beyond herself, for the three-mile limit of every seaboard is her frontier, which has been won by hammer and loom and pick rather than by arts of war. For it is written in history that neither king nor army can bar the path to the man who having twopence in his strong box, and knowing well where he can turn it to threepence, sets his mind to that one end. And as the frontier has broadened, the mind of Britain has broadened too, spreading out until all men can see that the ways of the island are continental, even as those of the Continent are insular.

But for this a price must be paid, and the price is a grievous one. As the beast of old must have one young human life as a tribute every year, so to our Empire we throw from day to day the pick and flower of our youth. The engine is worldwide and strong, but the only fuel that will drive it is the lives of British men. Thus it is that in the grey old cathedrals, as we look round upon the brasses on the walls, we see strange names, such names as they who reared those walls had never heard, for it is in Peshawar, and Umballah, and Korti and Fort

Pearson that the youngsters die, leaving only a precedent and a brass behind them. But if every man had his obelisk, even where he lay, then no frontier line need be drawn, for a cordon of British graves would ever show how high the Anglo-Celtic tide had lapped.

This, then, as well as the waters which join us to the world, has done something to tinge us with romance. For when so many have their loved ones over the seas, walking amid hillmen's bullets, or swamp malaria, where death is sudden and distance great, then mind communes with mind, and strange stories arise of dream, presentiment or vision, where the mother sees her dying son, and is past the first bitterness of her grief ere the message comes which should have broken the news. The learned have of late looked into the matter and have even labelled it with a name; but what can we know more of it save that a poor stricken soul, when hard-pressed and driven, can shoot across the earth some ten-thousand-mile-distant picture of its trouble to the mind which is most akin to it. Far be it from me to say that there lies no such power within us, for of all things which the brain will grasp the last will be itself; but yet it is well to be very cautious over such matters, for once at least I have known that which was within the laws of nature seem to be far upon the further side of them.

John Vansittart was the younger partner of the firm of Hudson and Vansittart, coffee exporters of the Island of Ceylon, three-quarters Dutchman by descent, but wholly English in his sympathies. For years I had been his agent in London, and when in '72 he came over to England for a three months' holiday, he turned to me for the introductions which would enable him to see something of town and country life. Armed with seven letters he left my offices, and for many weeks scrappy notes from different parts of the country let me know that he had found favour in the eyes of my friends. Then came word of his engagement to Emily Lawson, of a cadet branch of the Hereford Lawsons, and at the very tail of the first flying rumour the news of his absolute marriage, for the wooing of a wanderer must be short, and the days were already crowding on towards the date when he must be upon his homeward journey. They were to return together to Colombo in one of the firm's own thousand-ton barque-rigged sailing ships, and this was to be their princely honeymoon, at once a necessity and a delight.

Those were the royal days of coffee-planting in Ceylon, before a single season and a rotten fungus drove a whole community through years of despair to one of the greatest commercial victories which pluck and ingenuity ever won. Not often is it that men have the heart when their one great industry is withered to rear up in a few years another as rich to take its place, and the tea-fields of Ceylon are as true a monument to courage as is the lion at Waterloo. But in '72 there was no cloud yet above the skyline, and the hopes of the planters were as high and as bright as the hillsides on which they reared their crops. Vansittart came down to London with his young and beautiful wife. I was introduced, dined with them, and it was finally arranged that I, since business called me also to Ceylon, should be a fellow-passenger with them on the *Eastern Star*, which was timed to sail on the following Monday.

It was on the Sunday evening that I saw him again. He was shown up into my rooms about nine o'clock at night, with the air of a man who is bothered and out of sorts. His hand, as I shook it, was hot and dry.

"I wish, Atkinson," said he, "that you could give me a little lime juice and water. I have a beastly thirst upon me, and the more I take the more I seem to want."

I rang and ordered a carafe and glasses. "You are flushed," said I. "You don't look the thing."

"No, I'm clean off colour. Got a touch of rheumatism in my back, and don't seem to taste my food. It is this vile London that is choking me. I'm not used to breathing air which has been used up by four million lungs all sucking away on every side of you." He flapped his crooked hands before his face, like a man who really struggles for his breath.

"A touch of the sea will soon set you right."

"Yes, I'm of one mind with you there. That's the thing for me. I want no other doctor. If I don't get to sea to-morrow I'll have an illness. There are no two ways about it." He drank off a tumbler of lime juice, and clapped his two hands with his knuckles doubled up into the small of his back.

"That seems to ease me," said he, looking at me with a filmy eye. "Now I want your help, Atkinson, for I am rather awkwardly placed."

"As how?"

"This way. My wife's mother got ill and wired for her. I couldn't go—you know best yourself how tied I have been—so she had to go alone. Now I've had another wire to say that she can't come to-morrow, but that she will pick up the ship at Falmouth on Wednesday. We put in there, you know, and in, though I count it hard, Atkinson, that a man should be asked to believe in a mystery, and cursed if he can't do it. Cursed, mind you, no less." He leaned forward and began to draw a catchy breath like a man who is poised on the very edge of a sob.

Then first it came to my mind that I had heard much of the hard-drinking life of the island, and that from brandy came those wild words and fevered hands. The flushed cheek and the glazing eye were those of one whose drink is strong upon him. Sad it was to see so noble a young man in the grip of that most bestial of all the devils.

"You should lie down," I said, with some severity.

He screwed up his eyes like a man who is striving to wake himself, and looked up with an air of surprise.

"So I shall presently," said he, quite rationally. "I felt quite swimmy just now, but I am my own man again now. Let me see, what was I talking about? Oh ah, of course, about the wife. She joins the ship at Falmouth. Now I want to go round by water. I believe my health depends upon it. I just want a little clean first-lung air to set me on my feet again. I ask you, like a good fellow, to go to Falmouth by rail, so that in case we should be late you may be there to look after the wife. Put up at the Royal Hotel, and I will wire her that you are there. Her sister will bring her down, so that it will be all plain sailing."

"I'll do it with pleasure," said I. "In fact, I would rather go by rail, for we shall have enough and to spare of the sea before we reach Colombo. I believe too that you badly need a change. Now, I should go and turn in, if I were you."

"Yes, I will. I sleep aboard tonight. You know," he continued, as the film settled down again over his eyes, "I've not slept well the last few nights. I've been troubled with *theolololog*—that is to say, *theolological*—hang it," with a desperate effort, "with the doubts of *theolologicians*. Wondering why the Almighty made us, you know, and why He made our heads swimmy, and fixed little pains into the small of our backs. Maybe I'll do better tonight." He rose and steadied himself with an effort against the corner of the chair back.

"Look here, Vansittart," said I, gravely, stepping up to him, and laying my hand upon his sleeve, "I can give you a shakedown here. You are not fit to go out. You are all over the place. You've been mixing your drinks."

"Drinks!" He stared at me stupidly.

"You used to carry your liquor better than this."

"I give you my word, Atkinson, that I have not had a drain for two days. It's not drink. I don't know what it is. I suppose you think this is drink." He took up my hand in his burning grasp, and passed it over his own forehead.

"Great Lord!" said I.

His skin felt like a thin sheet of velvet beneath which lies a close-packed layer of small shot. It was smooth to the touch at any one place, but to a finger passed along it, rough as a nutmeg grater.

"It's all right," said he, smiling at my startled face. "I've had the prickly heat nearly as bad."

"But this is never prickly heat."

"No, it's London. It's breathing bad air. But tomorrow it'll be all right. There's a surgeon aboard, so I shall be in safe hands. I must be off now."

"Not you," said I, pushing him back into a chair. "This is past a joke. You don't move from here until a doctor sees you. Just stay where you are."

I caught up my hat, and rushing round to the house of a neighbouring physician, I brought him back with me. The room was empty and Vansittart gone. I rang the bell. The servant said that the gentleman had ordered a cab the instant that I had left, and had gone off in it. He had told the cabman to drive to the docks.

"Did the gentleman seem ill?" I asked.

"Ill!" The man smiled. "No, sir, he was singin' his 'ardest all the time."

The information was not as reassuring as my servant seemed to think, but I reflected that he was going straight back to the *Eastern Star*, and that there was a doctor aboard of her, so that there was nothing which I could do in the matter. None the less, when I thought of his thirst, his burning hands, his heavy eye, his tripping speech, and lastly, of that leprous forehead, I carried with me to bed an unpleasant memory of my visitor and his visit.

At eleven o'clock next day I was at the docks, but the *Eastern Star* had already moved down the river, and was nearly at Gravesend. To Gravesend I went by train, but only to see her topmasts far off, with a plume of smoke from a tug in front of her. I would hear no more of my friend until I rejoined him at Falmouth. When I got back to my offices, a telegram was awaiting me from Mrs. Vansittart, asking me to meet her; and next evening found us both at the Royal Hotel, Falmouth, where we were to wait for the *Eastern Star*. Ten days passed, and there came no news of her.

They were ten days which I am not likely to forget. On the very day that the *Eastern Star* had cleared from the Thames, a furious easterly gale had sprung up, and blew on from day to day for the greater part of a week without the sign of a lull. Such a screaming, raving, long-drawn storm has never been known on the southern coast. From our hotel windows the sea view was all banked in haze, with a little rain-swept half-circle under our very eyes, churned and lashed into one tossing stretch of foam. So heavy was the wind upon the waves that little sea could rise, for the crest of each billow was torn shrieking from it, and lashed broadcast over the bay. Clouds, wind, sea, all were rushing to the west, and there, looking down at this mad jumble of elements, I waited on day after day, my sole companion a white, silent woman, with terror in her eyes, her forehead pressed ever against the window, her gaze from early morning to the fall of night fixed upon that wall of grey haze through which the loom of a vessel might come. She said nothing, but that face of hers was one long wail of fear.

On the fifth day I took counsel with an old seaman. I should have preferred to have done so alone, but she saw me speak with him, and was at our side in an instant, with parted lips and a prayer in her eyes.

"Seven days out from London," said he, "and five in the gale. Well, the Channel's swept clear by this wind. There's three things for it. She may have popped into port on the French side. That's like enough."

"No, no; he knew we were here. He would have telegraphed."

"Ah, yes, so he would. Well, then, he might have run for it, and if he did that he won't be very far from Madeira by now. That'll be it, marm, you may depend."

"Or else? You said there was a third chance."

"Did I, marm? No, only two, I think. I don't think I said anything of a third. Your ship's out there, depend upon it, away out in the Atlantic, and you'll hear of it time enough, for the weather is breaking. Now don't you fret, marm, and wait quiet, and you'll find a real blue Cornish sky tomorrow."

The old seaman was right in his surmise, for the next day broke calm and bright, with only a low dwindling cloud in the west to mark the last trailing wreaths of the storm-wrack. But still there came no word from the sea, and no sign of the ship. Three more weary days had passed, the weariest that I have ever spent, when there came a seafaring man to the hotel with a letter. I gave a shout of joy. It was from the captain of the *Eastern Star*. As I read the first lines of it I whisked my hand over it, but she laid her own upon it and drew it away. "I have seen it," said she, in a cold, quiet voice. "I may as well see the rest, too."

Dear Sir,
Mr. Vansittart is down with the small-pox, and we are blown so far on our course that we don't know what to do, he being off his head and unfit to tell us. By dead

reckoning we are but three hundred miles from Funchal, so I take it that it is best that we should push on there, get Mr. V. into hospital, and wait in the Bay until you come. There's a sailing-ship due from Falmouth to Funchal in a few days' time, as I understand. This goes by the brig *Marian* of Falmouth, and five pounds is due to the master, Yours respectfully,

Jno. Hines

She was a wonderful woman that, only a chit of a girl fresh from school, but as quiet and strong as a man. She said nothing—only pressed her lips together tight, and put on her bonnet.

"You are going out?" I asked.

"Yes."

"Can I be of use?"

"No; I am going to the doctor's."

"To the doctor's?"

"Yes. To learn how to nurse a small-pox case."

She was busy at that all the evening, and next morning we were off with a fine ten-knot breeze in the barque *Rose of Sharon* for Madeira. For five days we made good time, and were no great way from the island; but on the sixth there fell a calm, and we lay without motion on a sea of oil, heaving slowly, but making not a foot of way.

At ten o'clock that night Emily Vansittart and I stood leaning on the starboard railing of the poop, with a full moon shining at our backs, and casting a black shadow of the barque, and of our own two heads upon the shining water. From the shadow a broadening path of moonshine stretched away to the lonely sky-line, flickering and shimmering in the gentle heave of the swell. We were talking with bent heads, chatting of the calm, of the chances of wind, of the look of the sky, when there came a sudden plop, like a rising salmon, and there, in the clear light, John Vansittart sprang out of the water and looked up at us.

I never saw anything clearer in my life than I saw that man. The moon shone full upon him, and he was but three oars' lengths away. His face was more puffed than when I had seen him last, mottled here and there with dark scabs, his mouth and eyes open as one who is struck with some overpowering surprise. He had some white stuff streaming from his shoulders, and one hand was raised to his ear, the other crooked across his breast. I saw him leap from the water into the air, and in the dead calm the waves of his coming lapped up against the sides of the vessel. Then his figure sank back into the water again, and I heard a rending, crackling sound like a bundle of brushwood snapping in the fire on a frosty night. There were no signs of him when I looked again, but a swift swirl and eddy on the still sea still marked the spot where he had been. How long I stood there, tingling to my finger-tips, holding up an unconscious woman with one hand, clutching at the rail of the vessel with the other, was more than I could afterwards tell. I had been noted as a man of slow and unresponsive emotions, but this time at least I was shaken to the core. Once and twice I struck my foot upon the deck to be certain that I was indeed the master of my own senses, and that this was not some mad prank of an unruly brain. As I stood, still marvelling, the woman shivered, opened her eyes, gasped, and then standing erect with her hands upon the rail, looked out over the moonlit sea with a face which had aged ten years in a summer night.

"You saw his vision?" she murmured.

"I saw something."

"It was he! It was John! He is dead!"

I muttered some lame words of doubt.

"Doubtless he died at this hour," she whispered. "In hospital at Madeira. I have read of such things. His thoughts were with me. His vision came to me. Oh, my John, my dear, dear, lost John!"

She broke out suddenly into a storm of weeping, and I led her down into her cabin, where I left her with her sorrow. That night a brisk breeze blew up from the east, and in the evening of the next day we passed the two islets of Los Desertos, and dropped anchor at sundown in the Bay of Funchal. The *Eastern Star* lay no great distance from us, with the quarantine flag flying from her main, and her Jack half-way up her peak.

"You see," said Mrs. Vansittart, quickly. She was dry-eyed now, for she had known how it would be.

That night we received permission from the authorities to move on board the *Eastern Star*. The captain, Hines, was waiting upon deck with confusion and grief contending upon his bluff face as he sought for words with which to break this heavy tidings, but she took the story from his lips.

"I know that my husband is dead," she said. "He died yesterday night, about ten o'clock, in hospital at Madeira, did he not?"

The seaman stared aghast. "No, marm, he died eight days ago at sea, and we had to bury him out there, for we lay in a belt of calm, and could not say when we might make the land."

Well, those are the main facts about the death of John Vansittart, and his appearance to his wife somewhere about lat. 35 N. and long. 15 W. A clearer case of a wraith has seldom been made out, and since then it has been told as such, and put into print as such, and endorsed by a learned society as such, and so floated off with many others to support the recent theory of telepathy. For myself, I hold telepathy to be proved, but I would snatch this one case from amid the evidence, and say that I do not think that it was the wraith of John Vansittart, but John Vansittart himself whom we saw that night leaping into the moonlight out of the depths of the Atlantic. It has ever been my belief that some strange chance—one of those chances which seem so improbable and yet so constantly occur—had becalmed us over the very spot where the man had been buried a week before. For the rest, the surgeon tells me that the leaden weight was not too firmly fixed, and that seven days bring about changes which fetch a body to the surface. Coming from the depth to which the weight would have sunk it, he explains that it might well attain such a velocity as to carry it clear of the water. Such is my own explanation of the matter, and if you ask me what then became of the body, I must recall to you that snapping, crackling sound, with the swirl in the water. The shark is a surface feeder and is plentiful in those parts.

The American's Tale

"It air strange, it air," he was saying as I opened the door of the room where our social little semi-literary society met; "but I could tell you queerer things than that 'ere—almighty queer things. You can't learn everything out of books, sirs, nohow. You see it ain't the men as can string English together and as has had good eddications as finds themselves in the queer places I've been in. They're mostly rough men, sirs, as can scarce speak aright, far less tell with pen and ink the things they've seen; but if they could they'd make some of your European's har riz with astonishment. They would, sirs, you bet!"

His name was Jefferson Adams, I believe; I know his initials were J.A., for you may see them yet deeply whittled on the right-hand upper panel of our smoking-room door. He left us this legacy, and also some artistic patterns done in tobacco juice upon our Turkey carpet; but beyond these reminiscences our American storyteller has vanished from our ken. He gleamed across our ordinary quiet conviviality like some brilliant meteor, and then was lost in the outer darkness. That night, however, our Nevada friend was in full swing; and I quietly lit my pipe and dropped into the nearest chair, anxious not to interrupt his story.

"Mind you," he continued, "I hain't got no grudge against your men of science. I likes and respects a chap as can match every beast and plant, from a huckleberry to a grizzly with a jawbreakin' name; but if you wants real interestin' facts, something a bit juicy, you go to your whalers and your frontiersmen, and your scouts and Hudson Bay men, chaps who mostly can scarce sign their names."

There was a pause here, as Mr. Jefferson Adams produced a long cheroot and lit it. We preserved a strict silence in the room, for we had already learned that on the slightest interruption our Yankee drew himself into his shell again. He glanced round with a self-satisfied smile as he remarked our expectant looks, and continued through a halo of smoke,

"Now which of you gentlemen has even been in Arizona? None, I'll warrant. And of all English or Americans as can put pen to paper, how many has been in Arizona? Precious few, I calc'late. I've been there, sirs, lived there for years; and when I think of what I've seen there, why, I can scarce get myself to believe it now.

"Ah, there's a country! I was one of Walker's filibusters, as they chose to call us; and after we'd busted up, and the chief was shot, some on us made tracks and located down there. A reg'lar English and American colony, we was, with our wives and children, and all complete. I reckon there's some of the old folk there yet, and that they hain't forgotten what I'm agoing to tell you. No, I warrant they hain't, never on this side of the grave, sirs.

"I was talking about the country, though; and I guess I could astonish you considerable if I spoke of nothing else. To think of such a land being built for a few 'Greasers' and half-breeds! It's a misusing of the gifts of Providence, that's what I calls it. Grass as hung over a chap's head as he rode through it, and trees so thick that you couldn't catch a glimpse of blue sky for leagues and leagues, and orchids like umbrellas! Maybe some on you has seen a plant as they calls the 'fly-catcher,' in some parts of the States?"

"*Diancea muscipula*," murmured Dawson, our scientific man par excellence.

"Ah, 'Die near a municipal,' that's him! You'll see a fly stand on that 'ere plant, and then you'll see the two sides of a leaf snap up together and catch it between them, and grind it up and mash it to bits, for all the world like some great sea squid with its beak; and hours after, if you open the leaf, you'll see the body lying half-digested, and in bits. Well, I've seen those flytraps in Arizona with leaves eight and ten feet long, and thorns or teeth a foot or more; why, they could—But darn it, I'm going too fast!

340

"It's about the death of Joe Hawkins I was going to tell you; 'bout as queer a thing, I reckon, as ever you heard tell on. There wasn't nobody in Montana as didn't know of Joe Hawkins— 'Alabama' Joe, as he was called there. A reg'lar out and outer, he was, 'bout the darndest skunk as even man clapt eyes on. He was a good chap enough, mind ye, as long as you stroked him the right way; but rile him anyhow, and he were worse nor a wild-cat. I've seen him empty his six-shooter into a crowd as chanced to jostle him agoing into Simpson's bar when there was a dance on; and he bowied Tom Hooper 'cause he spilt his liquor over his weskit by mistake. No, he didn't stick at murder, Joe didn't; and he weren't a man to be trusted further nor you could see him.

"Now at the time I tell on, when Joe Hawkins was swag-gerin' about the town and layin' down the law with his shootin'-irons, there was an Englishman there of the name of Scott— Tom Scott, if I rec'lects aright. This chap Scott was a thorough Britisher (beggin' the present company's pardon), and yet he didn't freeze much to the British set there, or they didn't freeze much to him. He was a quiet simple man, Scott was—rather too quiet for a rough set like that; sneakin' they called him, but he weren't that. He kept hisself mostly apart, an' didn't interfere with nobody so long as he were left alone. Some said as how he'd been kinder ill-treated at home—been a Chartist, or some-thing of that sort, and had to up sticks and run; but he never spoke of it hisself, an' never complained. Bad luck or good, that chap kept a stiff lip on him.

"This chap Scott was a sort o' butt among the men about Montana, for he was so quiet an' simple-like. There was no party either to take up his grievances; for, as I've been saying, the Brit-ishers hardly counted him one of them, and many a rough joke they played on him. He never cut up rough, but was polite to all hisself. I think the boys got to think he hadn't much grit in him till he showed 'em their mistake.

"It was in Simpson's bar as the row got up, an' that led to the queer thing I was going to tell you of. Alabama Joe and one or two other rowdies were dead on the Britishers in those days, and they spoke their opinions pretty free, though I warned them as

341

there'd be an almighty muss. That partic'lar night Joe was nigh half drunk, an' he swaggered about the town with his six-shooter, lookin' out for a quarrel. Then he turned into the bar where he know'd he'd find some o' the English as ready for one as he was hisself. Sure enough, there was half a dozen lounging about, an' Tom Scott standin' alone before the stove. Joe sat down by the table, and put his revolver and bowie down in front of him. 'Them's my arguments, Jeff,' he says to me, 'if any white-livered Britisher dares give me the lie.' I tried to stop him, sirs; but he weren't a man as you could easily turn, an' he began to speak in a way as no chap could stand. Why, even a 'Greaser' would flare up if you said as much of Greaserland! There was a commotion at the bar, an' every man laid his hands on his wepins; but afore they could draw we heard a quiet voice from the stove: 'Say your prayers, Joe Hawkins; for, by Heaven, you're a dead man!' Joe turned round, and looked like grabbin' at his iron; but it weren't no manner of use. Tom Scott was standing up, covering him with his Derringer; a smile on his white face, but the very devil shining in his eye. 'It ain't that the old country has used me over-well,' he says, 'but no man shall speak agin it afore me, and live.' For a second or two I could see his finger tighten round the trigger, an' then he gave a laugh, an' threw the pistol on the floor. 'No,' he says, 'I can't shoot a half-drunk man. Take your dirty life, Joe, an' use it better nor you have done. You've been nearer the grave this night than you will be agin until your time comes. You'd best make tracks now, I guess. Nay, never look black at me, man; I'm not afeard at your shootin'-iron. A bully's nigh always a coward.' And he swung contemptuously round, and relit his half-smoked pipe from the stove; while Alabama slunk out o' the bar, with the laughs of the Britishers ringing in his ears. I saw his face as he passed me, and on it I saw murder, sirs—murder, as plain as ever I seed anything in my life.

"I stayed in the bar after the row, and watched Tom Scott as he shook hands with the men about. It seemed kinder queer to me to see him smilin' and cheerful-like; for I knew Joe's blood-thirsty mind, and that the Englishman had small chance of ever seeing the morning. He lived in an out-of-the-way sort of place, you see, clean off the trail, and had to pass through the Flytrap Gulch to get to it. This here gulch was a marshy gloomy place, lonely enough during the day even; for it were always a creepy sort o' thing to see the great eight-and ten-foot leaves snapping up if aught touched them; but at night there were never a soul near. Some parts of the marsh, too, were soft and deep, and a body thrown in would be gone by the morning. I could see Alabama Joe crouchin' under the leaves of the great Flytrap in the darkest part of the gulch, with a scowl on his face and a revolver in his hand; I could see it, sirs, as plain as with my two eyes.

"'Bout midnight Simpson shuts up his bar, so out we had to go. Tom Scott started off for his three-mile walk at a slashing pace. I just dropped him a hint as he passed me, for I kinder liked the chap. 'Keep your Derringer loose in your belt, sir,' I says, 'for you might chance to need it.' He looked round at me with his quiet smile, and then I lost sight of him in the gloom. I never thought to see him again. He'd hardly gone afore Simpson comes up to me and says, 'There'll be a nice job in the Flytrap Gulch to-night, Jeff; the boys say that Hawkins started half an hour ago to wait for Scott and shoot him on sight. I calc'late the coroner be wanted to-morrow.'

"What passed in the gulch that night? It were a question as were asked pretty free next morning. A half-breed was in Ferguson's store after daybreak, and he said as he'd chanced to be near the gulch 'bout one in the morning. It warn't easy to get at his story, he seemed so uncommon scared; but he told us, at last, as he'd heard the fearfulest screams in the stillness of the night. There weren't no shots, he said, but scream after scream, kinder muffled, like a man with a serape over his head, an' in mortal pain. Abner Brandon and me, and a few more, was in the store at the time; so we mounted and rode out to Scott's house, passing through the gulch on the way. There weren't nothing partic'lar to be seen there—no blood nor marks of a fight, nor nothing; and when we gets up to Scott's house, out he comes to meet us as fresh as a lark. 'Hullo, Jeff!' says he, 'no need for the pistols after all. Come in an' have a cocktail, boys.' 'Did you see or hear nothing as you came home last night?' says I. 'No,' says he; 'all was quiet enough. An owl kinder moaning in the Flytrap Gulch—that was all. Come, jump off and have a glass.' 'Thank ye,' says Abner. So off we gets, and Tom Scott rode into the settlement with us when we went back.

"An allfired commotion was on in Main-street as we rode into it. The 'Merican party seemed to have gone clean crazed. Alabama Joe was gone, not a darned particle of him left. Since he went out to the gulch nary eye had seen him. As we got off our horses there was a considerable crowd in front of Simpson's, and some ugly looks at Tom Scott, I can tell you. There was a clickin' of pistols, and I saw as Scott had his hand in his bosom too. There weren't a single English face about. 'Stand aside, Jeff Adams,' says Zebb Humphrey, as great a scoundrel as ever lived, 'you hain't got no hand in this game. Say, boys, are we, free Americans, to be murdered by any darned Britisher?' It was the quickest thing as ever I seed. There was a rush an' a crack; Zebb was down, with Scott's ball in his thigh, and Scott hisself was on the ground with a dozen men holding him. It weren't no use struggling, so he lay quiet. They seemed a bit uncertain what to do with him at first, but then one of Alabama's special chums put them up to it. Joe's gone,' he said; 'nothing ain't surer nor that, an' there lies the man as killed him. Some on you knows as Joe went on business to the gulch last night; he never came back. That 'ere Britisher passed through after he'd gone; they'd had a row, screams is heard 'mong the great flytraps. I say agin he has played poor Joe some o' his sneakin' tricks, an' thrown him into the swamp. It ain't no wonder as the body is gone. But air we to stan'by and see English murderin' our own chums? I guess not. Let Judge Lynch try him, that's what I say.' 'Lynch him!' shouted a hundred angry voices—for all the rag-tag an' bobtail o' the settlement was round us by this time. 'Here, boys, fetch a rope, and swing him up. Up with him over Simpson's door!' 'See here though,' says another, coming forrards; 'let's hang him by the great flytrap in the gulch. Let Joe see as he's revenged, if so be as he's buried 'bout theer.' There was a shout for this, an' away they went, with Scott tied on his mustang in the middle, and a mounted guard, with cocked revolvers, round him; for we knew as there was a score or so Britishers about, as didn't seem to recognise Judge Lynch, and was dead on a free fight.

"I went out with them, my heart bleedin' for Scott, though he didn't seem a cent put out, he didn't. He were game to the backbone. Seems kinder queer, sirs, hangin' a man to a flytrap; but our'n were a reg'lar tree, and the leaves like a brace of boats with a hinge between 'em and thorns at the bottom.

"We passed down the gulch to the place where the great one grows, and there we seed it with the leaves, some open, some shut. But we seed something worse nor that. Standin' round the tree was some thirty men, Britishers all, an' armed to the teeth. They was waitin' for us evidently, an' had a businesslike look about 'em, as if they'd come for something and meant to have it. There was the raw material there for about as warm a scrimmidge as ever I seed. As we rode up, a great red-bearded Scotchman—Cameron were his name—stood out afore the rest, his revolver cocked in his hand. 'See here, boys,' he says, 'you've got no call to hurt a hair of that man's head. You hain't proved as Joe is dead yet; and if you had, you hain't proved as Scott killed him. Anyhow, it were in self-defence; for you all know as he was lying in wait for Scott, to shoot him on sight; so I say agin, you hain't got no call to hurt that man; and what's more, I've got thirty six-barrelled arguments against your doin' it.' 'It's an inter-estin' pint, and worth arguin' out,' said the man as was Alabama Joe's special chum. There was a clickin' of pistols, and a loosenin' of knives, and the two parties began to draw up to one another, an' it looked like a rise in the mortality of Montana. Scott was standing behind with a pistol at his ear if he stirred, lookin' quiet and composed as having no money on the table, when sudden he gives a start an' a shout as rang in our ears like a trumpet. 'Joe!' he cried, Joe! Look at him! In the flytrap!' We all turned an' looked where he was pointin'. Jerusalem! I think we won't get that picter out of our minds agin. One of the great leaves of the flytrap, that had been shut and touchin' the ground as it lay, was slowly rolling back upon its hinges. There, lying like a child in its cradle, was Alabama Joe in the hollow of the leaf. The great thorns had been slowly driven through his heart as it shut upon him. We could see as he'd tried to cut his way out, for there was slit in the thick fleshy leaf, an' his bowie was in his hand; but it had smothered him first. He'd lain down on it likely to keep the damp off while he were awaitin' for Scott, and it had closed on him as you've seen your little hothouse ones do on a fly; an' there he were as we found him, torn and crushed into pulp by the great jagged teeth of the man-eatin' plant. There, sirs, I think you'll own as that's a curious story."

"And what became of Scott?" asked Jack Sinclair.

"Why, we carried him back on our shoulders, we did, to Simpson's bar, and he stood us liquors round. Made a speech too—a darned fine speech—from the counter. Somethin' about the British lion an' the 'Merican eagle walkin' arm in arm for ever an' a day. And now, sirs, that yarn was long, and my cheroot's out, so I reckon I'll make tracks afore it's later;" and with a "Good-night!" he left the room.

"A most extraordinary narrative!" said Dawson. "Who would have thought a *Diancea* had such power!"

"Deuced rum yarn!" said young Sinclair.

"Evidently a matter-of-fact truthful man," said the doctor.

"Or the most original liar that ever lived," said I.

I wonder which he was.

The Great Brown-Pericord Motor

It was a cold, foggy, dreary evening in May. Along the Strand blurred patches of light marked the position of the lamps. The flaring shop windows flickered vaguely with steamy brightness through the thick and heavy atmosphere.

The high lines of houses which lead down to the Embankment were all dark and deserted, or illuminated only by the glimmering lamp of the caretaker. At one point, however, there shone out from three windows upon the second floor a rich flood of light, which broke the sombre monotony of the terrace. Passers-by glanced up curiously, and drew each other's attention to the ruddy glare, for it marked the chambers of Francis Pericord, the inventor and electrical engineer. Long into the watches of the night the gleam of his lamps bore witness to the untiring energy and restless industry which was rapidly carrying him to the first rank in his profession.

Within the chamber sat two men. The one was Pericord himself—hawk-faced and angular, with the black hair and brisk bearing which spoke of his Celtic origin. The other—thick, sturdy, and blue-eyed—was Jeremy Brown, the well-known mechanician. They had been partners in many an invention, in which the creative genius of the one had been aided by the practical abilities of the other. It was a question among their friends as to which was the better man.

It was no chance visit which had brought Brown into Pericord's workshop at so late an hour. Business was to be done—business which was to decide the failure or success of months of work, and which might affect their whole careers. Between them lay a long brown table, stained and corroded by strong acids, and littered with giant carboys, Faure's accumulators, voltaic piles, coils of wire, and great blocks of non-conducting porcelain. In the midst of all this lumber there stood a singular whizzing, whirring machine, upon which the eyes of both partners were riveted.

A small square metal receptacle was connected by numerous wires to a broad steel girdle, furnished on either side with two powerful projecting joints. The girdle was motionless, but the joints with the short arms attached to them flashed round every few seconds, with a pause between each rhythmic turn. The power which moved them came evidently from the metal box. A subtle odour of ozone was in the air.

"How about the flanges, Brown?" asked the inventor.

"They were too large to bring. They are seven foot by three. There is power enough there to work them, however. I will answer for that."

"Aluminium with an alloy of copper?"

"Yes."

"See how beautifully it works." Pericord stretched out a thin, nervous hand, and pressed a button upon the machine. The joints revolved more slowly, and came presently to a dead stop. Again he touched a spring and the arms shivered and woke up again into their crisp metallic life. "The experimenter need not exert his muscular powers," he remarked. "He has only to be passive, and use his intelligence."

"Thanks to my motor," said Brown.

"*Our* motor," the other broke in sharply.

"Oh, of course," said his colleague impatiently.

"The motor which you thought of, and which I reduced to practice—call it what you like."

"I call it the Brown-Pericord Motor," cried the inventor with an angry flash of his dark eyes. "You worked out the details, but the abstract thought is mine, and mine alone."

"An abstract thought won't turn an engine," said Brown, doggedly.

"That was why I took you into partnership," the other retorted, drumming nervously with his fingers upon the table. "I invent, you build. It is a fair division of labour."

Brown pursed up his lips, as though by no means satisfied upon the point. Seeing, however, that further argument was useless, he turned his attention to the machine, which was shivering and rocking with each swing of its arms, as though a very little more would send it skimming from the table.

"Is it not splendid?" cried Pericord.

"It is satisfactory," said the more phlegmatic Anglo-Saxon.

"There's immortality in it!"

"There's money in it!"

"Our names will go down with Montgolfier's."

"With Rothschild's, I hope."

"No, no, Brown; you take too material a view," cried the inventor, raising his gleaming eyes from the machine to his companion. "Our fortunes are a mere detail. Money is a thing which every heavy-witted plutocrat in the country shares with us. My hopes rise to something higher than that. Our true reward will come in the gratitude and goodwill of the human race."

Brown shrugged his shoulders. "You may have my share of that," he said. "I am a practical man. We must test our invention."

"Where can we do it?"

"That is what I wanted to speak about. It must be absolutely secret. If we had private grounds of our own it would be an easy matter, but there is no privacy in London."

"We must take it into the country."

"I have a suggestion to offer," said Brown. "My brother has a place in Sussex on the high land near Beachy Head. There is, I remember, a large and lofty barn near the house. Will is in Scotland, but the key is always at my disposal. Why not take the machine down tomorrow and test it in the barn?"

"Nothing could be better."

"There is a train to Eastbourne at one."

"I shall be at the station."

"Bring the gear with you, and I will bring the flanges," said the mechanician, rising. "Tomorrow will prove whether we have been following a shadow, or whether fortune is at our feet. One o'clock at Victoria." He walked swiftly down the stair and was quickly reabsorbed into the flood of comfortless clammy humanity which ebbed and flowed along the Strand.

The morning was bright and spring-like. A pale blue sky arched over London, with a few gauzy white clouds drifting lazily across it. At eleven o'clock Brown might have been seen entering the Patent Office with a great roll of parchment, diagrams, and plans under his arm. At twelve he emerged again smiling, and, opening his pocket-book, he packed away very carefully a small slip of official blue paper. At five minutes to one his cab rolled into Victoria Station. Two giant canvas-covered parcels, like enormous kites, were handed down by the cabman from the top, and consigned to the care of a guard. On the platform Pericord was pacing up and down, with long eager step and swinging arms, a tinge of pink upon his sunken and sallow cheeks.

"All right?" he asked.

Brown pointed in answer to his baggage.

"I have the motor and the girdle already packed away in the guard's van. Be careful, guard, for it is delicate machinery of great value. So! Now we can start with an easy conscience."

At Eastbourne the precious motor was carried to a four-wheeler, and the great flanges hoisted on the top. A long drive took them to the house where the keys were kept, whence they set off across the barren Downs. The building which was their destination was a commonplace white-washed structure, with straggling stables and out-houses, standing in a grassy hollow which sloped down from the edge of the chalk cliffs. It was a cheerless house even when in use, but now with its smokeless chimneys and shuttered windows it looked doubly dreary. The owner had planted a grove of young larches and firs around it, but the sweeping spray had blighted them, and they hung their withered heads in melancholy groups. It was a gloomy and forbidding spot.

But the inventors were in no mood to be moved by such trifles. The lonelier the place, the more fitted for their purpose. With the help of the cabman they carried their packages down the footpath, and laid them in the darkened dining-room. The sun was setting as the distant murmur of wheels told them that they were finally alone.

Pericord had thrown open the shutters and the mellow evening light streamed in through the discoloured windows. Brown drew a knife from his pocket and cut the pack-thread with which the canvas was secured. As the brown covering fell away it disclosed two great yellow metal fans. These he leaned carefully against the wall. The girdle, the connecting-bands, and the motor were then in turn unpacked. It was dark before all was set out in order. A lamp was lit, and by its light the two men continued to tighten screws, clinch rivets, and make the last preparations for their experiment.

"That finishes it," said Brown at last, stepping back and surveying the machine.

Pericord said nothing, but his face glowed with pride and expectation.

"We must have something to eat," Brown remarked, laying out some provisions which he had brought with him.

"Afterwards."

"No, now," said the stolid mechanician. "I am half starved." He pulled up to the table and made a hearty meal, while his Celtic companion strode impatiently up and down, with twitching fingers and restless eyes.

"Now then," said Brown, facing round, and brushing the crumbs from his lap, "who is to put it on?"

"I shall," cried his companion eagerly. "What we do to-night is likely to be historic."

"But there is some danger," suggested Brown. "We cannot quite tell how it may act."

"That is nothing," said Pericord, with a wave of his hand.

"But there is no use our going out of our way to incur danger."

"What then? One of us must do it."

"Not at all. The motor would act equally well if attached to any inanimate object."

"That is true," said Pericord, thoughtfully.

"There are bricks by the barn. I have a sack here. Why should not a bagful of them take your place?"

"It is a good idea. I see no objection."

"Come on then," and the two sallied out, bearing with them the various sections of their machine. The moon was shining cold and clear though an occasional ragged cloud drifted across her face. All was still and silent upon the Downs. They stood and listened before they entered the barn, but not a sound came to their ears, save the dull murmur of the sea and the distant barking of a dog. Pericord journeyed backwards and forwards with all that they might need, while Brown filled a long narrow sack with bricks.

When all was ready, the door of the barn was closed, and the lamp balanced upon an empty packing-case. The bag of bricks was laid upon two trestles, and the broad steel girdle was buckled round it. Then the great flanges, the wires, and the metal box containing the motor were in turn attached to the girdle. Last of all a flat steel rudder, shaped like a fish's tail, was secured to the bottom of the sack.

"We must make it travel in a small circle," said Pericord, glancing round at the bare high walls.

"Tie the rudder down at one side," suggested Brown. "Now it is ready. Press the connection and off she goes!"

Pericord leaned forward, his long sallow face quivering with excitement. His white nervous hands darted here and there among the wires. Brown stood impassive with critical eyes. There was a sharp burr from the machine. The huge yellow wings gave a convulsive flap. Then another. Then a third, slower and stronger, with a fuller sweep. Then a fourth which filled the barn with a blast of driven air. At the fifth the bag of bricks began to dance upon the trestles. At the sixth it sprang into the air, and would have fallen to the ground, but the seventh came to save it, and fluttered it forward through the air. Slowly rising, it flapped heavily round in a circle, like some great clumsy bird, filling the barn with its buzzing and whirring. In the uncertain yellow light of the single lamp it was strange to see the loom of the ungainly thing, flapping off into the shadows, and then circling back into the narrow zone of light.

The two men stood for a while in silence. Then Pericord threw his long arms up into the air.

"It acts!" he cried. "The Brown-Pericord Motor acts!" He danced about like a madman in his delight. Brown's eyes twinkled, and he began to whistle.

"See how smoothly it goes, Brown!" cried the inventor. "And the rudder—how well it acts! We must register it tomorrow."

His comrade's face darkened and set. "It *is* registered," he said, with a forced laugh.

"Registered?" said Pericord. "Registered?" He repeated the word first in a whisper, and then in a kind of scream. "Who has dared to register my invention?"

"I did it this morning. There is nothing to be excited about. It is all right."

"You registered the motor! Under whose name?"

"Under my own," said Brown, sullenly. "I consider that I have the best right to it."

"And my name does not appear?"

"No, but—"

"You villain!" screamed Pericord. "You thief and villain! You would steal my work! You would filch my credit! I will have that patent back if I have to tear your throat out!" A sombre fire burned in his black eyes, and his hands writhed themselves together with passion. Brown was no coward, but he shrank back as the other advanced upon him.

"Keep your hands off!" he said, drawing a knife from his pocket. "I will defend myself if you attack me."

"You threaten me?" cried Pericord, whose face was livid with anger. "You are a bully as well as a cheat. Will you give up the patent?"

"No, I will not."

"Brown, I say, give it up!"

"I will not. I did the work."

Pericord sprang madly forward with blazing eyes and clutching fingers. His companion writhed out of his grasp, but was dashed against the packing-case, over which he fell. The lamp was extinguished, and the whole barn plunged into darkness. A single ray of moonlight shining through a narrow chink flickered over the great waving fans as they came and went.

"Will you give up the patent, Brown?"

There was no answer.

"Will you give it up?"

Again no answer. Not a sound save the humming and creaking overhead. A cold pang of fear and doubt struck through Pericord's heart. He felt aimlessly about in the dark and his fingers closed upon a hand. It was cold and unresponsive. With all his anger turned to icy horror he struck a match, set the lamp up, and lit it.

Brown lay huddled up on the other side of the packing-case. Pericord seized him in his arms, and with convulsive strength lifted him across. Then the mystery of his silence was explained. He had fallen with his right arms doubled up under him, and his own weight had driven the knife deeply into his body. He had died without a groan. The tragedy had been sudden, horrible, and complete.

Pericord sat silently on the edge of the case, staring blankly down, and shivering like one with the ague, while the great Brown-Pericord Motor boomed and hurtled above him. How long he sat there can never be known. It might have been minutes or it might have been hours. A thousand mad schemes flashed through his dazed brain. It was true that he had been only the indirect cause. But who would believe that? He glanced down at his blood-spattered clothing. Everything was against him. It would be better to fly than to give himself up, relying upon his innocence. No one in London knew where they were. If he could dispose of the body he might have a few days clear before any suspicion would be aroused.

Suddenly a loud crash recalled him to himself. The flying sack had gradually risen with each successive circle until it had struck against the rafters. The blow displaced the connecting-gear, and the machine fell heavily to the ground. Pericord undid the girdle. The motor was uninjured. A sudden strange thought flashed upon him as he looked at it. The machine had become hateful to him. He might dispose both of it and the body in a way that would baffle all human search.

He threw open the barn door, and carried his companion out into the moonlight. There was a hillock outside, and on the summit of this he laid him reverently down. Then he brought from the barn the motor, the girdle and the flanges. With trembling fingers he fastened the broad steel belt round the dead man's waist. Then he screwed the wings into the sockets. Beneath he slung the motor-box, fastened the wires, and switched on the connection. For a minute or two the huge yellow fans flapped and flickered. Then the body began to move in little jumps down the side of the hillock, gathering a gradual momentum, until at last it heaved up into the air and soared off in the moonlight. He had not used the rudder, but had turned the head for the south. Gradually the weird thing rose higher, and sped faster, until it had passed over the line of cliff, and was sweeping over the silent sea. Pericord watched it with a white drawn face, until it looked like a black bird with golden wings half shrouded in the mist which lay over the waters.

In the New York State Lunatic Asylum there is a wild-eyed man whose name and birth-place are alike unknown. His reason has been unseated by some sudden shock, the doctors say, though of what nature they are unable to determine. "It is the most delicate machine which is most readily put out of gear," they remark, and point, in proof of their axiom, to the complicated electric engines, and remarkable aeronautic machines which the patient is fond of devising in his more lucid moments.

The Last Galley

Mutato nomine, de te, Britannia, fabula narratur.

It was a spring morning, one hundred and forty-six years before the coming of Christ. The North African coast, with its broad hem of golden sand, its green belt of feathery palm trees, and its background of barren, red-scarped hills, shimmered like a dream country in the opal light. Save for a narrow edge of snow-white surf, the Mediterranean lay blue and serene as far as the eye could reach. In all its vast expanse there was no break but for a single galley, which was slowly making its way from the direction of Sicily and heading for the distant harbour of Carthage.

Seen from afar it was a stately and beautiful vessel, deep red in colour, double-banked with scarlet oars, its broad, flapping sail stained with Tyrian purple, its bulwarks gleaming with brass work. A brazen, three-pronged ram projected in front, and a high golden figure of Baal, the God of the Phoenicians, children of Canaan, shone upon the after-deck. From the single high mast above the huge sail streamed the tiger-striped flag of Carthage. So, like some stately scarlet bird, with golden beak and wings of purple, she swam upon the face of the waters—a thing of might and of beauty as seen from the distant shore.

But approach and look at her now! What are these dark streaks which foul her white decks and dapple her brazen shields? Why do the long red oars move out of time, irregular, convulsive? Why are some missing from the staring portholes, some snapped with jagged, yellow edges, some trailing inert against the side? Why are two prongs of the brazen ram twisted and broken? See, even the high image of Baal is battered and disfigured! By every sign this ship has passed through some grievous trial, some day of terror, which has left its heavy marks upon her.

And now stand upon the deck itself, and see more closely the men who man her! There are two decks forward and aft, while in the open waist are the double banks of seats, above and below, where the rowers, two to an oar, tug and bend at their endless task. Down the centre is a narrow platform, along which pace a line of warders, lash in hand, who cut cruelly at the slave who pauses, be it only for an instant, to sweep the sweat from his dripping brow. But these slaves—look at them! Some are captured Romans, some Sicilians, many black Libyans, but all are in the last exhaustion, their weary eyelids drooped over their eyes, their lips thick with black crusts, and pink with bloody froth, their arms and backs moving mechanically to the hoarse chant of the overseer. Their bodies of all tints from ivory to jet, are stripped to the waist, and every glistening back shows the angry stripes from the warders. But it is not from these that the blood comes which reddens the seats and tints the salt water washing beneath their manacled feet. Great gaping wounds, the marks of sword slash and spear stab, show crimson upon their naked chests and shoulders, while many lie huddled and sense-less athwart the benches, careless for ever of the whips which still hiss above them. Now we can understand those empty port-holes and those trailing oars.

Nor were the crew in better case than their slaves. The decks were littered with wounded and dying men. It was but a remnant who still remained upon their feet. The most lay ex-hausted upon the fore-deck, while a few of the more zealous were mending their shattered armour, restringing their bows, or cleaning the deck from the marks of combat. Upon a raised platform at the base of the mast stood the sailing-master who conned the ship, his eyes fixed upon the distant point of Megara which screened the eastern side of the Bay of Carthage. On the after-deck were gathered a number of officers, silent and brood-ing, glancing from time to time at two of their own class who stood apart deep in conversation. The one, tall, dark, and wiry, with pure, Semitic features, and the limbs of a giant, was Magro, the famous Carthaginian captain, whose name was still a terror on every shore, from Gaul to the Euxine. The other, a white-bearded, swarthy man, with indomitable courage and energy stamped upon every eager line of his keen, aquiline face, was Gisco the politician, a man of the highest Punic blood, a Suffete of the purple robe, and the leader of that party in the state which had watched and striven amid the selfishness and slothfulness of his fellow-countrymen to rouse the public spirit and waken the public conscience to the ever-increasing danger from Rome. As they talked, the two men glanced continually, with earnest anxious faces, towards the northern skyline.

"It is certain," said the older man, with gloom in his voice and bearing, "none have escaped save ourselves."

"I did not leave the press of the battle whilst I saw one ship which I could succour," Magro answered. "As it was, we came away, as you saw, like a wolf which has a hound hanging on to either haunch. The Roman dogs can show the wolf-bites which prove it. Had any other galley won clear, they would surely be with us by now, since they have no place of safety save Carthage."

The younger warrior glanced keenly ahead to the distant point which marked his native city. Already the low, leafy hill could be seen, dotted with the white villas of the wealthy Phoenician merchants. Above them, a gleaming dot against the pale blue morning sky, shone the brazen roof of the citadel of Byrsa, which capped the sloping town.

"Already they can see us from the watch-towers," he remarked. "Even from afar they may know the galley of Black Magro. But which of all of them will guess that we alone remain of all that goodly fleet which sailed out with blare of trumpet and roll of drum but one short month ago?"

The patrician smiled bitterly. "If it were not for our great ancestors and for our beloved country, the Queen of the Waters," said he, "I could find it in my heart to be glad at this destruction which has come upon this vain and feeble generation. You have spent your life upon the seas, Magro. You do not know how it has been with us on the land. But I have seen this canker grow upon us which now leads us to our death. I and others have gone down into the market-place to plead with the people, and been pelted with mud for our pains. Many a time I have pointed to Rome, and said, 'Behold these people, who bear arms themselves, each man for his own duty and pride. How can you who hide behind mercenaries hope to stand against them?'—a hundred times I have said it."

"And had they no answer?" asked the Rover.

"Rome was far off and they could not see it, so to them it was nothing," the old man answered. "Some thought of trade, and some of votes, and some of profits from the State, but none would see that the State itself, the mother of all things, was sinking to her end. So might the bees debate who should have wax or honey when the torch was blazing which would bring to ashes the hive and all therein. 'Are we not rulers of the sea?' 'Was not Hannibal a great man?' Such were their cries, living ever in the past and blind to the future. Before that sun sets there will be tearing of hair and rending of garments; but what will that now avail us?"

"It is some sad comfort," said Magro, "to know that what Rome holds she cannot keep."

"Why say you that? When we go down, she is supreme in all the world."

"For a time, and only for a time," Magro answered gravely. "Yet you will smile, perchance, when I tell you how it is that I know it. There was a wise woman who lived in that part of the Tin Islands which juts forth into the sea, and from her lips I have heard many things, but not one which has not come aright. Of the fall of our own country, and even of this battle, from which we now return, she told me clearly. There is much strange lore amongst these savage peoples in the west of the land of Tin."

"What said she of Rome?"

"That she also would fall, even as we, weakened by her riches and her factions."

Gisco rubbed his hands. "That at least makes our own fall less bitter," said he. "But since we have fallen, and Rome will fall, who in turn may hope to be Queen of the Waters?"

"That also I asked her," said Magro, "and gave her my Tyrian belt with the golden buckle as a guerdon for her answer. But, indeed, it was too high payment for the tale she told, which must be false if all else she said was true. She would have it that in coming days it was her own land, this fog-girt isle where painted savages can scarce row a wicker coracle from point to point, which shall at last take the trident which Carthage and Rome have dropped."

The smile which flickered upon the old Patrician's keen features died away suddenly, and his fingers closed upon his companion's wrist. The other had set rigid, his head advanced, his hawk eyes upon the northern skyline. Its straight, blue horizon was broken by two low black dots.

"Galleys!" whispered Gisco.

The whole crew had seen them. They clustered along the starboard bulwarks, pointing and chattering. For a moment the gloom of defeat was lifted, and a buzz of joy ran from group to group at the thought that they were not alone—that someone had escaped the great carnage as well as themselves.

"By the spirit of Baal," said Black Magro, "I could not have believed that any could have fought clear from such a welter. Could it be young Hamilcar in the Africa, or is it Beneva in the blue Syrian ship? We three with others may form a squadron and make head against them yet. If we hold our course, they will join us ere we round the harbour mole."

Slowly the injured galley toiled on her way, and more swiftly the two new-comers swept down from the north. Only a few miles off lay the green point and the white houses which flanked the great African city. Already, upon the headland, could be seen a dark group of waiting townsmen. Gisco and Magro were still watching with puckered gaze the approaching galleys, when the brown Libyan boatswain, with flashing teeth and gleaming eyes, rushed upon the poop, his long thin arm stabbing to the north.

"Romans!" he cried. "Romans!"

A hush had fallen over the great vessel. Only the wash of the water and the measured rattle and beat of the oars broke in upon the silence.

"By the horns of God's altar, I believe the fellow is right!" cried old Gisco. "See how they swoop upon us like falcons. They are full-manned and full-oared."

"Plain wood, unpainted," said Magro. "See how it gleams yellow where the sun strikes it."

"And yonder thing beneath the mast. Is it not the cursed bridge they use for boarding?"

"So they grudge us even one," said Magro with a bitter laugh. "Not even one galley shall return to the old sea-mother. Well, for my part, I would as soon have it so. I am of a mind to stop the oars and await them."

"It is a man's thought," answered old Gisco; "but the city will need us in the days to come. What shall it profit us to make the Roman victory complete? Nay, Magro, let the slaves row as they never rowed before, not for our own safety, but for the profit of the State."

So the great red ship laboured and lurched, onwards, like a weary panting stag which seeks shelter from his pursuers, while ever swifter and ever nearer sped the two lean fierce galleys from the north. Already the morning sun shone upon the lines of low Roman helmets above the bulwarks, and glistened on the silver wave where each sharp prow shot through the still blue water. Every moment the ships drew nearer, and the long thin scream of the Roman trumpets grew louder upon the ear.

Upon the high bluff of Megara there stood a great concourse of the people of Carthage who had hurried forth from the city upon the news that the galleys were in sight. They stood now, rich and poor, effete and plebeian, white Phoenician and dark Kabyle, gazing with breathless interest at the spectacle before them. Some hundreds of feet beneath them the Punic galley had drawn so close that with their naked eyes they could see those stains of battle which told their dismal tale. The Romans, too, were heading in such a way that it was before their very faces that their ship was about to be cut off; and yet of all this multitude not one could raise a hand in its defence. Some wept in impotent grief, some cursed with flashing eyes and knotted fists, some on their knees held up appealing hands to Baal; but neither prayer, tears, nor curses could undo the past nor mend the present. That broken, crawling galley meant that their fleet was gone. Those two fierce darting ships meant that the hands of Rome were already at their throat. Behind them would come others and others, the innumerable trained hosts of the great Republic, long mistress of the land, now dominant also upon the waters. In a month, two months, three at the most, their armies would be there, and what could all the untrained multitudes of Carthage do to stop them?

"Nay!" cried one, more hopeful than the rest, "at least we are brave men with arms in our hands."

"Fool!" said another, "is it not such talk which has brought us to our ruin? What is the brave man untrained to the brave man trained? When you stand before the sweep and rush of a Roman legion you may learn the difference."

"Then let us train!"

"Too late! A full year is needful to turn a man to a soldier. Where will you—where will your city be within one year? Nay, there is but one chance for us. If we give up our commerce and our colonies, if we strip ourselves of all that made us great, then perchance the Roman conqueror may hold his hand."

And already the last sea-fight of Carthage was coming swiftly to an end before them. Under their very eyes the two Roman galleys had shot in, one on either side of the vessel of Black Magro. They had grappled with him, and he, desperate in his despair, had cast the crooked flukes of his anchors over their gunwales, and bound them to him in an iron grip, whilst with hammer and crowbar he burst great holes in his own sheathing. The last Punic galley should never be rowed into Ostia, a sight for the holiday-makers of Rome. She would lie in her own waters. And the fierce, dark soul of her rover captain glowed as he thought that not alone should she sink into the depths of the mother sea.

Too late did the Romans understand the man with whom they had to deal. Their boarders who had flooded the Punic decks felt the planking sink and sway beneath them. They rushed to gain their own vessels; but they, too, were being drawn downwards, held in the dying grip of the great red galley. Over they went and ever over. Now the deck of Magro's ship is flush with the water, and the Romans', drawn towards it by the iron bonds which hold them, are tilted downwards, one bulwark upon the waves, one reared high in the air. Madly they strain to cast off the death-grip of the galley. She is under the surface now, and ever swifter, with the greater weight, the Roman ships heel after her. There is a rending crash. The wooden side is torn out of one, and mutilated, dismembered, she rights herself, and lies a helpless thing upon the water. But a last yellow gleam in the blue water shows where her consort has been dragged to her end in the iron death-grapple of her foeman. The tiger-striped flag of Carthage has sunk beneath the swirling surface, never more to be seen upon the face of the sea.

For in that year a great cloud hung for seventeen days over the African coast, a deep black cloud which was the dark shroud of the burning city. And when the seventeen days were over, Roman ploughs were driven from end to end of the charred ashes, and salt was scattered there as a sign that Carthage should be no more. And far off a huddle of naked, starving folk stood upon the distant mountains, and looked down upon the desolate plain which had once been the fairest and richest upon earth. And they understood too late that it is the law of heaven that the world is given to the hardy and to the self-denying, whilst he who would escape the duties of manhood will soon be stripped of the pride, the wealth, and the power, which are the prizes which manhood brings.

The Nightmare Room

The sitting-room of the Masons was a very singular apartment. At one end it was furnished with considerable luxury.
The deep sofas, the low, luxurious chairs, the voluptuous statu-
ettes, and the rich curtains hanging from deep and ornamental
screens of metal-work made a fitting frame for the lovely woman who was the mistress of the establishment. Mason, a young
but wealthy man of affairs, had clearly spared no pains and no
expense to meet every want and every whim of his beautiful
wife. It was natural that he should do so, for she had given up
much for his sake. The most famous dancer in France, the heroine of a dozen extraordinary romances, she had resigned her
life of glittering pleasure in order to share the fate of the young
American, whose austere ways differed so widely from her own.
In all that wealth could buy he tried to make amends for what
she had lost. Some might perhaps have thought it in better taste
had he not proclaimed this fact—had he not even allowed it to
be printed—but save for some personal peculiarities of the sort,
his conduct was that of a husband who has never for an instant
ceased to be a lover. Even the presence of spectators would not
prevent the public exhibition of his overpowering affection.

But the room was singular. At first it seemed familiar, and
yet a longer acquaintance made one realise its sinister peculiarities. It was silent—very silent. No footfall could be heard upon
those rich carpets and heavy rugs. A struggle—even the fall of a
body—would make no sound. It was strangely colourless also, in
a light which seemed always subdued. Nor was it all furnished

in equal taste. One would have said that when the young banker had lavished thousands upon this boudoir, this inner jewel-case for his precious possession, he had failed to count the cost and had suddenly been arrested by a threat to his own solvency. It was luxurious where it looked out upon the busy street below. At the farther side it was bare, Spartan, and reflected rather the taste of a most ascetic man than of a pleasure-loving woman. Perhaps that was why she only came there for a few hours, sometimes two, sometimes four, in the day, but while she was there she lived intensely, and within this nightmare room Lucille Mason was a very different and a more dangerous woman than elsewhere.

Dangerous—that was the word. Who could doubt it who saw her delicate figure stretched upon the great bearskin which draped the sofa. She was leaning upon her right elbow, her delicate but determined chin resting upon her hand, while her eyes, large and languishing, adorable but inexorable, stared out in front of her with a fixed intensity which had in it something vaguely terrible. It was a lovely face—a child's face, and yet Nature had placed there some subtle mark, some indefinable expression, which told that a devil lurked within. It had been noticed that dogs shrank from her, and that children screamed and ran from her caresses. There are instincts which are deeper than reason.

Upon this particular afternoon something had greatly moved her. A letter was in her hand, which she read and re-read with a tightening of those delicate little eyebrows and a grim setting of those delicious lips. Suddenly she started, and a shadow of fear softened the feline menace of her features. She raised herself upon her arm, and her eyes were fixed eagerly upon the door. She was listening intently—listening for something which she dreaded. For a moment a smile of relief played over her expressive face. Then with a look of horror she stuffed her letter into her dress. She had hardly done so before the door opened, and a young man came briskly into the room. It was Archie Mason, her husband—the man whom she had loved, the man for whom she had sacrificed her European fame, the man whom now she regarded as the one obstacle to a new and wonderful experience.

The American was a man about thirty, clean-shaven, athletic, dressed to perfection in a closely-cut suit, which outlined his perfect figure. He stood at the door with his arms folded, looking intently at his wife, with a face which might have been a handsome, sun-tinted mask save for those vivid eyes. She still leaned upon her elbow, but her eyes were fixed on his. There was something terrible in the silent exchange. Each interrogated the other, and each conveyed the thought that the answer to their question was vital. He might have been asking, "What have you done?" She in her turn seemed to be saying, "What do you know?" Finally, he walked forward, sat down upon the bearskin beside her, and taking her delicate ear gently between his fingers, turned her face towards his.

"Lucille," he said, "are you poisoning me?"

She sprang back from his touch with horror in her face and protests upon her lips. Too moved to speak, her surprise and her anger showed themselves rather in her darting hands and her convulsed features. She tried to rise, but his grasp tightened upon her wrist. Again he asked a question, but this time it had deepened in its terrible significance.

"Lucille, why are you poisoning me?"

"You are mad, Archie! Mad!" she gasped.

His answer froze her blood. With pale parted lips and blanched cheeks she could only stare at him in helpless silence, whilst he drew a small bottle from his pocket and held it before her eyes.

"It is from your jewel-case!" he cried.

Twice she tried to speak and failed. At last the words came slowly one by one from her contorted lips:—

"At least I never used it."

Again his hand sought his pocket. From it he drew a sheet of paper, which he unfolded and held before her.

"It is the certificate of Dr. Angus. It shows the presence of twelve grains of antimony. I have also the evidence of DuVal, the chemist who sold it."

Her face was terrible to look at. There was nothing to say. She could only lie with that fixed hopeless stare like some fierce creature in a fatal trap.

"Well?" he asked.

There was no answer save a movement of desperation and appeal.

"Why?" he said. "I want to know why." As he spoke his eye caught the edge of the letter which she had thrust into her bosom. In an instant he had snatched it. With a cry of despair she tried to regain it, but he held her off with one hand while his eyes raced over it.

"Campbell!" he gasped. "It was Campbell!"

She had found her courage again. There was nothing more to conceal. Her face set hard and firm. Her eyes were deadly as daggers.

"Yes," she said, "it is Campbell."

"My God! Campbell of all men!"

He rose and walked swiftly about the room. Campbell, the grandest man that he had ever known, a man whose whole life had been one long record of self-denial, of courage, of every quality which marks the chosen man. And yet, he, too, had fallen a victim to this siren, and had been dragged down to such a level that he had betrayed, in intention if not in actual deed, the man whose hand he shook in friendship. It was incredible—and yet here was the passionate, pleading letter imploring his wife to fly and share the fate of a penniless man. Every word of the letter showed that Campbell had at least no thought of Mason's death, which would have removed all difficulties. That devilish solution was the outcome of the deep and wicked brain which brooded within that perfect habitation.

Mason was a man in a million, a philosopher, a thinker, with a broad and tender sympathy for others. For an instant his soul had been submerged in his bitterness. He could for that brief period have slain both his wife and Campbell, and gone to his own death with the serene mind of a man who has done his plain duty. But already, as he paced the room, milder thoughts had begun to prevail. How could he blame Campbell? He knew the absolute witchery of this woman. It was not only her wonderful physical beauty. She had a unique power of seeming to take an interest in a man, in writhing into his inmost conscience, in penetrating those parts of his nature which were too sacred for the world, and in seeming to stimulate him towards ambition and even towards virtue. It was just there that the deadly cleverness of her net was shown. He remembered how it had been in his own case. She was free then—or so he thought—and he had been able to marry her. But suppose she had not been free. Suppose she had been married. And suppose she had taken possession of his soul in the same way. Would he have stopped there? Would he have been able to draw off with his unfulfilled longings? He was bound to admit that with all his New England strength he could not have done so. Why, then, should he feel so bitter with his unfortunate friend who was in the same position? It was pity and sympathy which filled his mind as he thought of Campbell.

And she? There she lay upon the sofa, a poor broken butterfly, her dreams dispersed, her plot detected, her future dark and perilous. Even for her, poisoner as she was, his heart relented. He knew something of her history. He knew her as a spoiled child from birth, untamed, unchecked, sweeping everything easily before her from her cleverness, her beauty, and her charm. She had never known an obstacle. And now one had risen across her path, and she had madly and wickedly tried to remove it. But if she had wished to remove it, was not that in itself a sign that he had been found wanting—that he was not the man who could bring her peace of mind and contentment of heart? He was too stern and self-contained for that sunny volatile nature. He was of the North, and she of the South, drawn strongly together for a time by the law of opposites, but impossible for permanent union. He should have seen to this—he should have understood it. It was on him, with his superior brain, that the responsibility for the situation lay. His heart softened towards her as it would to a little child which was in helpless trouble. For a time he had paced the room in silence, his lips compressed, his hands clenched till his nails had marked his palms. Now with a sudden movement he sat beside her and took her cold and inert hand in his. One thought beat in his brain. "Is it chivalry, or is it weakness?" The question sounded in his ears, it framed itself before his eyes, he could almost fancy that it materialised itself and that he saw it in letters which all the world could read.

It had been a hard struggle, but he had conquered.

"You shall choose between us, dear," he said. "If really you are sure—sure, you understand—that Campbell could make you happy as a husband, I will not be the obstacle."

"A divorce!" she gasped.

His hand closed upon the bottle of poison. "You can call it that," said he.

A new strange light shone in her eyes as she looked at him. This was a man who had been unknown to her. The hard, practical American had vanished. In his place she seemed to have a glimpse of a hero, and a saint, a man who could rise to an inhuman height of unselfish virtue. Both her hands were round that which held the fatal phial.

"Archie," she cried, "you could forgive me even that!"

He smiled at her. "You are only a little wayward kiddie after all."

Her arms were outstretched to him when there was a tap at the door, and the maid entered in the strange silent fashion in which all things moved in that nightmare room. There was a card on the tray. She glanced at it. "Captain Campbell! I will not see him."

Mason sprang to his feet.

"On the contrary, he is most welcome. Show him up this instant."

A few minutes later a tall, sun-burned young soldier had been ushered into the room. He came forward with a smile upon his pleasant features, but as the door closed behind him, and the faces before him resumed their natural expressions, he paused irresolutely and glanced from one to the other.

"Well?" he asked.

Mason stepped forward and laid his hand upon his shoulder.

"I bear no ill-will," he said.

"Ill-will?"

"Yes, I know all. But I might have done the same myself had the position been reversed."

Campbell stepped back and looked a question at the lady. She nodded and shrugged her graceful shoulders. Mason smiled.

"You need not fear that it is a trap for a confession. We have had a frank talk upon the matter. See, Jack, you were always a sportsman. Here's a bottle. Never mind how it came here. If one or other of us drink it, it would clear the situation." His manner was wild, almost delirious. "Lucille, which shall it be?"

There had been a strange force at work in the nightmare room. A third man was there, though not one of the three who had stood in the crisis of their life's drama had time or thought for him. How long he had been there—how much he' had heard—none could say. In the corner farthest from the little group he lay crouched against the wall, a sinister snake-like figure, silent and scarcely moving save for a nervous twitching of his clenched right hand. He was concealed from view by a square case and by a dark cloth drawn cunningly above it, so as to screen his features. Intent, watching eagerly every new phase of the drama, the moment had almost come for his intervention. But the three thought little of that. Absorbed in the interplay of their own emotions they had lost sight of a force stronger than themselves—a force which might at any moment dominate the scene.

"Are you game, Jack?" asked Mason. The soldier nodded.

"No!—for God's sake, no!" cried the woman.

Mason had uncorked the bottle, and turning to the side table he drew out a pack of cards. Cards and bottle stood together.

"We can't put the responsibility on her," he said. "Come, Jack, the best of three."

The soldier approached the table. He fingered the fatal cards. The woman, leaning upon her hand, bent her face forward and stared with fascinated eyes. Then and only then the bolt fell. The stranger had risen, pale and grave. All three were suddenly aware of his presence. They faced him with eager inquiry in their eyes. He looked at them coldly, sadly, with something of the master in his bearing.

"How is it?" they asked, all together.

"Rotten!" he answered. "Rotten! We'll take the whole reel once more tomorrow."

How it Happened

She was a writing medium. This is what she wrote:

I can remember some things upon that evening most distinctly, and others are like some vague, broken dreams. That is what makes it so difficult to tell a connected story. I have no idea now what it was that had taken me to London and brought me back so late. It just merges into all my other visits to London. But from the time that I got out at the little country station everything is extraordinarily clear. I can live it again—every instant of it.

I remember so well walking down the platform and looking at the illuminated clock at the end which told me that it was half-past eleven. I remember also my wondering whether I could get home before midnight. Then I remember the big motor, with its glaring head-lights and glitter of polished brass, waiting for me outside. It was my new thirty-horse-power Robur, which had only been delivered that day. I remember also asking Perkins, my chauffeur, how she had gone, and his saying that he thought she was excellent.

"I'll try her myself," said I, and I climbed into the driver's seat.

"The gears are not the same," said he. "Perhaps, sir, I had better drive."

"No; I should like to try her," said I.

And so we started on the five-mile drive for home.

My old car had the gears as they used always to be in notches on a bar. In this car you passed the gear-lever through a gate to get on the higher ones. It was not difficult to master, and soon I thought that I understood it. It was foolish, no doubt, to begin to learn a new system in the dark, but one often does foolish things, and one has not always to pay the full price for them. I got along very well until I came to Claystall Hill. It is one of the worst hills in England, a mile and a half long and one in six in places, with three fairly sharp curves. My park gates stand at the very foot of it upon the main London road.

We were just over the brow of this hill, where the grade is steepest, when the trouble began. I had been on the top speed, and wanted to get her on the free; but she stuck between gears, and I had to get her back on the top again. By this time she was going at a great rate, so I clapped on both brakes, and one after the other they gave way. I didn't mind so much when I felt my footbrake snap, but when I put all my weight on my side-brake, and the lever clanged to its full limit without a catch, it brought a cold sweat out of me. By this time we were fairly tearing down the slope. The lights were brilliant, and I brought her round the first curve all right. Then we did the second one, though it was a close shave for the ditch. There was a mile of straight then with the third curve beneath it, and after that the gate of the park. If I could shoot into that harbour all would be well, for the slope up to the house would bring her to a stand.

Perkins behaved splendidly. I should like that to be known. He was perfectly cool and alert. I had thought at the very beginning of taking the bank, and he read my intention.

"I wouldn't do it, sir," said he. "At this pace it must go over and we should have it on the top of us."

Of course he was right. He got to the electric switch and had it off, so we were in the free; but we were still running at a fearful pace. He laid his hands on the wheel.

"I'll keep her steady," said he, "if you care to jump and chance it. We can never get round that curve. Better jump, sir."

"No," said I; "I'll stick it out. You can jump if you like."

"I'll stick it with you, sir," said he.

If it had been the old car I should have jammed the gear-lever into the reverse, and seen what would happen. I expect she would have stripped her gears or smashed up somehow, but it would have been a chance. As it was, I was helpless. Perkins tried to climb across, but you couldn't do it going at that pace. The wheels were whirring like a high wind and the big body creaking and groaning with the strain. But the lights were brilliant, and one could steer to an inch. I remember thinking what an awful and yet majestic sight we should appear to any one who met us. It was a narrow road, and we were just a great, roaring, golden death to any one who came in our path.

We got round the corner with one wheel three feet high upon the bank. I thought we were surely over, but after staggering for a moment she righted and darted onwards. That was the third corner and the last one. There was only the park gate now. It was facing us, but, as luck would have it, not facing us directly. It was about twenty yards to the left up the main road into which we ran. Perhaps I could have done it, but I expect that the steering-gear had been jarred when we ran on the bank. The wheel did not turn easily. We shot out of the lane. I saw the open gate on the left. I whirled round my wheel with all the strength of my wrists. Perkins and I threw our bodies across, and then the next instant, going at fifty miles an hour, my right front wheel struck full on the right-hand pillar of my own gate. I heard the crash. I was conscious of flying through the air, and then—and then—!

****

When I became aware of my own existence once more I was among some brushwood in the shadow of the oaks upon the lodge side of the drive. A man was standing beside me. I imagined at first that it was Perkins, but when I looked again I saw that it was Stanley, a man whom I had known at college some years before, and for whom I had a really genuine affection. There was always something peculiarly sympathetic to me in Stanley's personality; and I was proud to think that I had some similar influence upon him. At the present moment I was surprised to see him, but I was like a man in a dream, giddy and shaken and quite prepared to take things as I found them without questioning them.

"What a smash!" I said. "Good Lord, what an awful smash!"

373

He nodded his head, and even in the gloom I could see that he was smiling the gentle, wistful smile which I connected with him.

I was quite unable to move. Indeed, I had not any desire to try to move. But my senses were exceedingly alert. I saw the wreck of the motor lit up by the moving lanterns. I saw the little group of people and heard the hushed voices. There were the lodge-keeper and his wife, and one or two more. They were taking no notice of me, but were very busy round the car. Then suddenly I heard a cry of pain.

"The weight is on him. Lift it easy," cried a voice.

"It's only my leg!" said another one, which I recognized as Perkins's. "Where's master?" he cried.

"Here I am," I answered, but they did not seem to hear me. They were all bending over something which lay in front of the car.

Stanley laid his hand upon my shoulder, and his touch was inexpressibly soothing. I felt light and happy, in spite of all.

"No pain, of course?" said he.

"None," said I.

"There never is," said he.

And then suddenly a wave of amazement passed over me. Stanley! Stanley! Why, Stanley had surely died of enteric at Bloemfontein in the Boer War!

"Stanley!" I cried, and the words seemed to choke my throat—"Stanley, you are dead."

He looked at me with the same old gentle, wistful smile.

"So are you," he answered.

A Pastoral Horror

Far above the level of the Lake of Constance, nestling in a little corner of the Tyrolese Alps, lies the quiet town of Feldkirch. It is remarkable for nothing save for the presence of a large and well-conducted Jesuit school and for the extreme beauty of its situation. There is no more lovely spot in the whole of the Vorarlberg. From the hills which rise behind the town, the great lake glimmers some fifteen miles off, like a broad sea of quicksilver. Down below in the plains the Rhine and the Danube prattle along, flowing swiftly and merrily, with none of the dignity which they assume as they grow from brooks into rivers. Five great countries or principalities,—Switzerland, Austria, Baden, Wurtemburg, and Bavaria—are visible from the plateau of Feldkirch. Feldkirch is the centre of a large tract of hilly and pastoral country. The main road runs through the centre of the town, and then on as far as Anspach, where it divides into two branches, one of which is larger than the other. This more important one runs through the valleys across Austrian Tyrol into Tyrol proper, going as far, I believe, as the capital of Innsbruck. The lesser road runs for eight or ten miles amid wild and rugged glens to the village of Laden, where it breaks up into a network of sheep-tracks. In this quiet spot, I, John Hudson, spent nearly two years of my life, from the June of '65 to the March of '67, and it was during that time that those events occurred which for some weeks brought the retired hamlet into an unholy prominence, and caused its name for the first, and probably for the last time, to be a familiar word to the European press. The short account of these incidents which appeared in the English papers was, however, inaccurate and misleading, besides which, the rapid advance of the Prussians, culminating in the battle of Sadowa, attracted public attention away from what might have moved it deeply in less troublous times. It seems to me that the facts may be detailed now, and be new to the great majority of readers, especially as I was myself intimately connected with the drama, and am in a position to give many particulars which have never before been made public.

And first a few words as to my own presence in this out of the way spot. When the great city firm of Sprynge, Wilkinson, and Spragge failed, and paid their creditors rather less than eighteenpence in the pound, a number of humble individuals were ruined, including myself. There was, however, some legal objection which held out a chance of my being made an exception to the other creditors, and being paid in full. While the case was being brought out I was left with a very small sum for my subsistence.

I determined, therefore, to take up my residence abroad in the interim, since I could live more economically there, and be spared the mortification of meeting those who had known me in my more prosperous days. A friend of mine had described Laden to me some years before as being the most isolated place which he had ever come across in all his experience, and as isolation and cheap living are usually synonymous, I bethought use of his words. Besides, I was in a cynical humour with my fellow-man, and desired to see as little of him as possible for some time to come. Obeying, then, the guidances of poverty and of misanthropy, I made my way to Laden, where my arrival created the utmost excitement among the simple inhabitants. The manners and customs of the red-bearded Englander, his long walks, his check suit, and the reasons which had led him to abandon his fatherland, were all fruitful sources of gossip to the topers who frequented the Gruner Mann and the Schwartzer Bar—the two alehouses of the village.

I found myself very happy at Laden. The surroundings were magnificent, and twenty years of Brixton had sharpened my admiration for nature as an olive improves the flavour of wine. In my youth I had been a fair German scholar, and I found myself able, before I had been many months abroad, to converse even on scientific and abstruse subjects with the new *curé* of the parish. This priest was a great godsend to me, for he was a most learned man and a brilliant conversationalist. Father Verhagen—for that was his name—though little more than forty years of age, had made his reputation as an author by a brilliant monograph upon the early Popes—a work which eminent critics have compared favourably with Von Ranke's. I shrewdly suspect that it was owing to some rather unorthodox views advanced in this book that Verhagen was relegated to the obscurity of Laden. His opinions upon every subject were ultra-Liberal, and in his fiery youth he had been ready to vindicate them, as was proved by a deep scar across his chin, received from a dragoon's sabre in the abortive insurrection at Berlin. Altogether the man was an interesting one, and though he was by nature somewhat cold and reserved, we soon established an acquaintanceship.

The atmosphere of morality in Laden was a very rarefied one. The position of *Intendant* Wurms and his satellites had for many years been a sinecure. Non-attendance at church upon a Sunday or feast-day was about the deepest and darkest crime which the most advanced of the villagers had attained to. Occasionally some hulking Fritz or Andreas would come lurching home at ten o'clock at night, slightly under the influence of Bavarian beer, and might even abuse the wife of his bosom if she ventured to remonstrate, but such cases were rare, and when they occurred the Ladeners looked at the culprit for some time in a half admiring, half horrified manner, as one who had committed a gaudy sin and so asserted his individuality.

It was in this peaceful village that a series of crimes suddenly broke out which astonished all Europe, and for atrocity and for the mystery which surrounded them surpassed anything of which I have ever heard or read. I shall endeavour to give a succinct account of these events in the order of their sequence, in which I am much helped by the fact that it has been my custom all my life to keep a journal—to the pages of which I now refer.

It was, then, I find upon the 19th of May in the spring of 1866, that my old landlady, Frau Zimmer, rushed wildly into the room as I was sipping my morning cup of chocolate and informed me that a murder had been committed in the village. At first I could hardly believe the news, but as she persisted in her statement, and was evidently terribly frightened, I put on my hat and went out to find the truth. When I came into the main street of the village I saw several men hurrying along in front of me, and following them I came upon an excited group in front of the little *stadthaus* or town hall—a barn-like edifice which was used for all manner of public gatherings. They were collected round the body of one Maul, who had formerly been a steward upon one of the steamers running between Lindau and Fredericshaven, on the Lake of Constance. He was a harmless, inoffensive little man, generally popular in the village, and, as far as was known, without an enemy in the world. Maul lay upon his face, with his fingers dug into the earth, no doubt in his last convulsive struggles, and his hair all matted together with blood, which had streamed down over the collar of his coat. The body had been discovered nearly two hours, but no one appeared to know what to do or whither to convey it. My arrival, however, together with that of the *curé*, who came almost simultaneously, infused some vigour into the crowd. Under our direction the corpse was carried up the steps, and laid on the floor of the town hall, where, having made sure that life was extinct, we proceeded to examine the injuries, in conjunction with Lieutenant Wurms, of the police. Maul's face was perfectly placid, showing that he had had no thought of danger until the fatal blow was struck. His watch and purse had not been taken. Upon washing the clotted blood from the back of his head a singular triangular wound was found, which had smashed the bone and penetrated deeply into the brain. It had evidently been inflicted by a heavy blow from a sharp-pointed pyramidal instrument. I believe that it was Father Verhagen, the *curé*, who suggested the probability of the weapon in question having been a short mattock or small pickaxe, such as are to be found in every Alpine cottage. The *Intendant*, with praiseworthy promptness, at once obtained one and striking a turnip, produced just such a curious gap as was to be seen in poor Maul's head. We felt that we had come upon the first link of a chain which might guide us to the assassin. It was not long before we seemed to grasp the whole clue.

A sort of inquest was held upon the body that same afternoon, at which Pfiffor, the *maire*, presided, the *curé*, the *Intendant*, Freckler, of the post office, and myself forming ourselves into a sort of committee of investigation. Any villager who could throw a light upon the case or give an account of the movements of the murdered man upon the previous evening was invited to attend. There was a fair muster of witnesses, and we soon gathered a connected series of facts. At half-past eight o'clock Maul had entered the Gruner Mann public-house, and had called for a flagon of beer. At that time there were sitting in the tap-room Waghorn, the butcher of the village, and an Italian pedlar named Cellini, who used to come three times a year to Laden with cheap jewellery and other wares. Immediately after his entrance the landlord had seated himself with his customers, and the four had spent the evening together, the common villagers not being admitted beyond the bar. It seemed from the evidence of the landlord and of Waghorn, both of whom were most respectable and trustworthy men, that shortly after nine o'clock a dispute arose between the deceased and the pedlar. Hot words had been exchanged, and the Italian had eventually left the room, saying that he would not stay any longer to hear his country decried. Maul remained for nearly an hour, and being somewhat elated at having caused his adversary's retreat, he drank rather more than was usual with him. One witness had met him walking towards his home, about ten o'clock, and deposed to his having been slightly I he worse for drink. Another had met him just a minute or so before he reached the spot in front of the *stadthaus* where the deed was done. This man's evidence was most important. He swore confidently that while passing the town hall, and before meeting Maul, he had seen a figure standing in the shadow of the building, adding that the person appeared to him, as far as he could make him out, to be not unlike the Italian.

Up to this point we had then established two facts—that the Italian had left the Gruner Mann before Maul, with words of anger on his lips; the second, that some unknown individual had been seen lying in wait on the road which the ex-steward would have to traverse. A third, and most important, was reached when the woman with whom the Italian lodged deposed that he had not returned the night before until half-past ten, an unusually late hour for Laden. How had he employed the time, then, from shortly after nine, when he left the public-house, until half-past ten, when he returned to his rooms? Things were beginning to look very black, indeed, against the pedlar.

It could not be denied, however, that there were points in the man's favour, and that the case against him consisted entirely of circumstantial evidence. In the first place, there was no sign of a mattock or any other instrument which could have been used for such a purpose among the Italian's goods; nor was it easy to understand how he could come by any such a weapon, since he did not go home between the time of the quarrel and his final return. Again, as the *curé* pointed out, since Cellini was a comparative stranger in the village, it was very unlikely that he would know which road Maul would take in order to reach his home. This objection was weakened, however, by the evidence of the dead man's servant, who deposed that the pedlar had been hawking his wares in front of their house the day before, and might very possibly have seen the owner at one of the windows. As to the prisoner himself, his attitude at first had been one of defiance, and even of amusement; but when he began to realise the weight of evidence against him, his manner became cringing, and he wrung his hands hideously, loudly proclaiming his innocence. His defence was that after leaving the inn, he had taken a long walk down the Anspach road in order to cool down his excitement, and that this was the cause of his late return. As to the murder of Maul, he knew no more about it than the babe unborn. I have dwelt at some length upon the circumstances of this case, because there are events in connection with it which makes it peculiarly interesting. I intend now to fall back upon my diary, which was very fully kept during this period, and indeed during my whole residence abroad. It will save me trouble to quote from it, and it will be a teacher for the accuracy of facts.

****

May 20th.—Nothing thought of and nothing talked of but the recent tragedy. A hunt has been made among the woods and along the brook in the hope of finding the weapon of the assassin. The more I think of it, the more convinced I am that Cellini is the man. The fact of the money being untouched proves that the crime was committed from motives of revenge, and who would bear more spite towards poor innocent Maul except the vindictive hot-blooded Italian whom he had just offended. I dined with Pfiffor in the evening, and he entirely agreed with me in my view of the case.

May 21st.—Still no word as far as I can hear which throws any light upon the murder. Poor Maul was buried at twelve o'clock in the neat little village churchyard. The *curé* led the service with great feeling, and his audience, consisting of the whole population of the village, were much moved, interrupting him frequently by sobs and ejaculations of grief. After the painful ceremony was over I had a short walk with our good priest. His naturally excitable nature has been considerably stirred by recent events. His hand trembles and his face is pale.

"My friend," said he, taking me by the hand as we walked together, "you know something of medicine." (I had been two years at Guy's). "I have been far from well of late."

"It is this sad affair which has upset you," I said.

"No," he answered, "I have felt it coming on for some time, but it has been worse of late. I have a pain which shoots from here to there," he put his hand to his temples. "If I were struck by lightning, the sudden shock it causes me could not be more great. At times when I close my eyes flashes of light dart before them, and my ears are for ever ringing. Often I know not what I do. My fear is lest I faint some time when performing the holy offices."

"You are overworking yourself," I said, "you must have rest and strengthening tonics. Are you writing just now? And how much do you do each day?"

"Eight hours," he answered. "Sometimes ten, sometimes even twelve, when the pains in my head do not interrupt me."

"You must reduce it to four," I said authoritatively. "You must also take regular exercise. I shall send you some quinine which I have in my trunk, and you can take as much as would cover a gulden in a glass of milk every morning and night."

He departed, vowing that he would follow my directions.

I hear from the *maire* that four policemen are to be sent from Anspach to remove Cellini to a safer gaol.

May 22nd.—To say that I was startled would give but a faint idea of my mental state. I am confounded, amazed, horrified beyond all expression. Another and a more dreadful crime has been committed during the night. Freckler has been found dead in his house—the very Freckler who had sat with me on the committee of investigation the day before. I write these notes after a long and anxious day's work, during which I have been endeavouring to assist the officers of the law. The villagers are so paralysed with fear at this fresh evidence of an assassin in their midst that there would be a general panic but for our exertions. It appears that Freckler, who was a man of peculiar habits, lived alone in an isolated dwelling. Some curiosity was aroused this morning by the fact that he had not gone to his work, and that there was no sign of movement about the house. A crowd assembled, and the doors were eventually forced open. The unfortunate Freckler was found in the bedroom upstairs, lying with his head in the fireplace. He had met his death by an exactly similar wound to that which had proved fatal to Maul, save that in this instance the injury was in front. His hands were clenched, and there was an indescribable look of horror, and, as it seemed to me, of surprise upon his features. There were marks of muddy footsteps upon the stairs, which must have been caused by the murderer in his ascent, as his victim had put on his slippers before retiring to his bed-room. These prints, however, were too much blurred to enable us to get a trustworthy outline of the foot. They were only to be found upon every third step, showing with what fiendish swiftness this human tiger had rushed upstairs in search of his victim. There was a considerable sum of money in the house, but not one farthing had been touched, nor had any of the drawers in the bedroom been opened.

As the dismal news became known the whole population of the village assembled in a great crowd in front of the house—rather, I think, from the gregariousness of terror than from mere curiosity. Every man looked with suspicion upon his neighbour. Most were silent, and when they spoke it was in whispers, as if they feared to raise their voices. None of these people were allowed to enter the house, and we, the more enlightened members of the community, made a strict examination of the premises. There was absolutely nothing, however, to give the slightest clue as to the assassin. Beyond the fact that he must be an active man, judging from the manner in which he ascended the stairs, we have gained nothing from this second tragedy. *Intendant* Wurms pointed out, indeed, that the dead man's rigid right arm was stretched out as if in greeting, and that, therefore, it was probable that this late visitor was someone with whom Freckler was well acquainted. This, however, was, to a large extent, conjecture. If anything could have added to the horror created by the dreadful occurrence, it was the fact that the crime must have been committed at the early hour of half-past eight in the evening—that being the time registered by a small cuckoo clock, which had been carried away by Freckler in his fall.

No one, apparently, heard any suspicious sounds or saw any one enter or leave the house. It was done rapidly, quietly, and completely, though many people must have been about at the time. Poor Pfiffor and our good *curé* are terribly cut up by the awful occurrence, and, indeed, I feel very much depressed myself now that all the excitement is over and the reaction set in. There are very few of the villagers about this evening, but from every side is heard the sound of hammering—the peasants fitting bolts and bars upon the doors and windows of their houses. Very many of them have been entirely unprovided with anything of the sort, nor were they ever required until now. Frau Zimmer has manufactured a huge fastening which would be ludicrous if we were in a humour for laughter.

I hear tonight that Cellini has been released, as, of course, there is no possible pretext for detaining him now; also that word has been sent to all the villages near for any police that can be spared.

My nerves have been so shaken that I remained awake the greater part of the night, reading Gordon's translation of Tacitus by candlelight. I have got out my navy revolver and cleaned it, so as to be ready for all eventualities.

May 23rd.—The police force has been recruited by three more men from Anspach and two from Thalstadt at the other side of the hills. *Intendant* Wurms has established an efficient system of patrols, so that we may consider ourselves reasonably safe. Today has cast no light upon the murders. The general opinion in the village seems to be that they have been done by some stranger who lies concealed among the woods. They argue that they have all known each other since childhood, and that there is no one of their number who would be capable of such actions. Some of the more daring of them have made a hunt among the pine forests today, but without success.

May 24th.—Events crowd on apace. We seem hardly to have recovered from one horror when something else occurs to excite the popular imagination. Fortunately, this time it is not a fresh tragedy, although the news is serious enough.

The murderer has been seen, and that upon the public road, which proves that his thirst for blood has not been quenched yet, and also that our reinforcements of police are not enough to guarantee security. I have just come back from hearing Andreas Murch narrate his experience, though he is still in such a state of trepidation that his story is somewhat incoherent. He was belated among the hills, it seems, owing to mist. It was nearly eleven o'clock before he struck the main road about a couple of miles from the village. He confesses that he felt by no means comfortable at finding himself out so late after the recent occurrences. However, as the fog had cleared away and the moon was shining brightly, he trudged sturdily along. Just about a quarter of a mile from the village the road takes a very sharp bend. Andreas had got as far as this when he suddenly heard in the still night the sound of footsteps approaching rapidly round this curve. Overcome with fear, he threw himself into the ditch which skirts the road, and lay there motionless in the shadow, peering over the side. The steps came nearer and nearer, and than a tall dark figure came round the corner at a swinging pace, and passing the spot where the moon glimmered upon the white face of the frightened peasant, halted in the road about twenty yards further on, and began probing about among the reeds on the roadside with an instrument which Andreas Murch recognised with horror as being a long mattock. After searching about in this way for a minute or so, as if he suspected that someone was concealed there, for he must have heard the sound of the footsteps, he stood still leaning upon his weapon. Murch describes him as a tall, thin man, dressed in clothes of a darkish colour. The lower part of his face was swathed in a wrapper of some sort, and the little which was visible appeared to be of a ghastly pallor. Murch could not see enough of his features to identify him, but thinks that it was no one whom he had ever seen in his life before. After standing for some little time, the man with the mattock had walked swiftly away into the darkness, in the direction in which he imagined the fugitive had gone. Andreas, as may be supposed, lost little time in getting safely into the village, where he alarmed the police. Three of them, armed with carbines, started down the road, but saw no signs of the miscreant. There is, of course, a possibility that Murch's story is exaggerated and that his imagination has been sharpened by fear. Still, the whole incident cannot be trumped up, and this awful demon who haunts us is evidently still active.

There is an ill-conditioned fellow named Hiedler, who lives in a hut on the side of the Spiegelberg, and supports himself by chamois hunting and by acting as guide to the few tourists who find their way here. Popular suspicion has fastened on this man, for no better reason than that he is tall, thin, and known to be rough and brutal. His chalet has been searched today, but nothing of importance found. He has, however, been arrested and confined in the same room which Cellini used to occupy.

****

At this point there is a gap of a week in my diary, during which time there was an entire cessation of the constant alarms which have harassed us lately. Some explained it by supposing that the terrible unknown had moved on to some fresh and less guarded scene of operations. Others imagine that we have secured the right man in the shape of the vagabond Hiedler. Be the cause what it may, peace and contentment reign once more in the village, and a short seven days have sufficed to clear away the cloud of care from men's brows, though the police are still on the alert. The season for rifle shooting is beginning, and as Laden has, like every other Tyrolese village, butts of its own, there is a continual pop, pop, all day. These peasants are dead shots up to about four hundred yards. No troops in the world could subdue them among their native mountains.

My friend Verhagen, the *curé*, and Pfiffor, the *maire*, used to go down in the afternoon to see the shooting with me. The former says that the quinine has done him much good and that his appetite is improved. We all agree that it is good policy to encourage the amusements of the people so that they may forget all about this wretched business. Vaghorn, the butcher, won the prize offered by the *maire*. He made five bulls, and what we should call a magpie out of six shots at 100 yards. This is English prize-medal form.

****

June 2nd.—Who could have imagined that a day which opened so fairly could have so dark an ending? The early carrier brought me a letter by which I learned that Spragge and Co. have agreed to pay my claim in full, although it may be some months before the money is forthcoming. This will make a difference of nearly £400 a year to me—a matter of moment when a man is in his seven-and-fortieth year.

And now for the grand events of the hour. My interview with the vampire who haunts us, and his attempt upon Frau Bischoff, the landlady of the Gruner Mann—to say nothing of the narrow escape of our good *curé*. There seems to be something almost supernatural in the malignity of this unknown fiend, and the impunity with which he continues his murderous course. The real reason of it lies in the badly lit state of the place—or rather the entire absence of light—and also in the fact that thick woods stretch right down to the houses on every side, so that escape is made easy. In spite of this, however, he had two very narrow escapes tonight—one from my pistol, and one from the officers of the law. I shall not sleep much, so I may spend half an hour in jotting down these strange doings in my dairy. I am no coward, but life in Laden is becoming too much for my nerves. I believe the matter will end in the emigration of the whole population.

To come to my story, then. I felt lonely and depressed this evening, in spite of the good news of the morning. About nine o'clock, just as night began to fall, I determined to stroll over and call upon the *curé*, thinking that a little intellectual chat might cheer me up. I slipped my revolver into my pocket, therefore—a precaution which I never neglected—and went out, very much against the advice of good Frau Zimmer. I think I mentioned some months ago in my diary that the *curé's* house is some little way out of the village upon the brow of a small hill. When I arrived there I found that he had gone out—which, indeed, I might have anticipated, for he had complained lately of restlessness at night, and I had recommended him to take a little exercise in the evening. His housekeeper made me very welcome, however, and having lit the lamp, left me in the study with some books to amuse me until her master's return.

I suppose I must have sat for nearly half an hour glancing over an odd volume of Klopstock's poems, when some sudden instinct caused me to raise my head and look up. I have been in some strange situations in my life, but never have I felt anything to be compared to the thrill which shot through me at that moment. The recollection of it now, hours after the event, makes me shudder. There, framed in one of the panes of the window, was a human face glaring in, from the darkness, into the lighted room—the face of a man so concealed by a cravat and slouch hat that the only impression I retain of it was a pair of wild-beast eyes and a nose which was whitened by being pressed against the glass. It did not need Andreas Murch's description to tell me that at last I was lace to face with the man with the mattock. There was murder in I hose wild eyes. For a second I was so unstrung as to be powerless; the next I cocked my revolver and fired straight at the sinister lace. I was a moment too late. As I pressed the trigger I saw it vanish, but the pane through which it had looked was shattered to pieces. I rushed to the window, and then out through the front door, but everything was silent. There was no trace of my visitor. His intention, no doubt, was to attack the *curé*, for there was nothing to prevent his coming through the folding window had he not found an armed man inside.

As I stood in the cool night air with the *curé's* frightened housekeeper beside me, I suddenly heard a great hubbub down in the village. By this time, alas! such sounds were so common in Laden that there was no doubting what it forboded. Some fresh misfortune had occurred there. Tonight seemed destined to be a night of horror. My presence might be of use in the village, so I set off there, taking with me the trembling woman, who positively refused to remain behind. There was a crowd round the Gruner Mann public-house, and a dozen excited voices were explaining the circumstances to the *curé*, who had arrived just before us. It was as I had thought, though happily without the result which I had feared. Frau Bischoff, the wife of the proprietor of the inn, had, it seems, gone some twenty minutes before a few yards from her door to draw some water, and had been at once attacked by a tall disguised man, who had cut at her with some weapon. Fortunately he had slipped, so that she was able to seize him by the wrist and prevent his repeating his attempt, while she screamed for help. There were several people about at the time, who came running towards them, on which the stranger wrested himself free, and dashed off into the woods, with two of our police after him. There is little hope of their overtaking or tracing him, however, in such a dark labyrinth. Frau Bischoff had made a bold attempt to hold the assassin, and declares that her nails made deep furrows in his right wrist. This, however, must be mere conjecture, as there was very little light at the time. She knows no more of the man's features than I do. Fortunately she is entirely unhurt. The *curé* was horrified when I informed him of the incident at his own house. He was returning from his walk, it appears, when hearing cries in the village, he had hurried down to it. I have not told anyone else of my own adventure, for the people are quite excited enough already.

As I said before, unless this mysterious and bloodthirsty villain is captured, the place will become deserted. Flesh and blood cannot stand such a strain. He is either some murderous misanthrope who has declared a vendetta against the whole human race, or else he is an escaped maniac. Clearly after the unsuccessful attempt upon Frau Bischoff he had made at once for the *curé*'s house, bent upon slaking his thirst for blood, and thinking that its lonely situation gave hope of success. I wish I had fired at him through the pocket of my coat. The moment he saw the glitter of the weapon he was off.

June 3rd.—Everybody in the village this morning has learned about the attempt upon the *curé* last night. There was quite a crowd at his house to congratulate him on his escape, and when I appeared they raised a cheer and hailed me as the *"tapferer Engländer."* It seems that his narrow shave must have given the ruffian a great start, for a thick woollen muffler was found lying on the pathway leading down to the village, and later in the day the fatal mattock was discovered close to the same place. The scoundrel evidently threw those things down and then took to his heels. It is possible that he may prove to have been frightened away from the neighbourhood altogether. Let us trust so!

June 4th.—A quiet day, which is as remarkable a thing in our annals as an exciting one elsewhere. Wurms has made strict inquiry, but cannot trace the muffler and mattock to any inhabitant. A description of them has been printed, and copies sent to Anspach and neighbouring villages for circulation among the peasants, who may be able to throw some light upon the matter. A thanksgiving service is to be held in the church on Sunday for the double escape of the pastor and of Martha Bischoff. Pfiffer tells me that Herr von Weissendorff, one of the most energetic detectives in Vienna, is on his way to Laden. I see, too, by the

English papers sent me, that people at home are interested in the tragedies here, although the accounts which have reached them are garbled and untrustworthy.

How well I can recall the Sunday morning following upon the events which I have described, such a morning as it is hard to find outside the Tyrol! The sky was blue and cloudless, the gentle breeze wafted the balsamic odour of the pine woods through the open windows, and away up on the hills the distant tinkling of the cow bells fell pleasantly upon the ear, until the musical rise and fall which summoned the villagers to prayer drowned their feebler melody. It was hard to believe, looking down that peaceful little street with its quaint top-heavy wooden houses and old-fashioned church, that a cloud of crime hung over it which had horrified Europe. I sat at my window watching the peasants passing with their picturesquely dressed wives and daughters on their way to church. With the kindly reverence of Catholic countries, I saw them cross themselves as they went by the house of Freckler and the spot where Maul had met his fate. When the bell had ceased to toll and the whole population had assembled in the church, I walked up there also, for it has always been my custom to join in the religious exercises of any people among whom I may find myself.

When I arrived at the church I found that the service had already begun. I took my place in the gallery which contained the village organ, from which I had a good view of the congregation. In the front seat of all was stationed Frau Bischoff, whose miraculous escape the service was intended to celebrate, and beside her on one side was her worthy spouse, while the *maire* occupied the other. There was a hush through the church as the *curé* turned from the altar and ascended the pulpit. I have seldom heard a more magnificent sermon. Father Verhagen was always an eloquent preacher, but on that occasion he surpassed himself. He chose for his text: *In the midst of life we are in death*, and impressed so vividly upon our minds the thin veil which divides us from eternity, and how unexpectedly it may be rent, that he held his audience spellbound and horrified. He spoke next with tender pathos of the friends who had been snatched so suddenly and so dreadfully from among us, until his words were almost drowned by the sobs of the women, and, suddenly turning he compared their peaceful existence in a happier land to the dark fate of the gloomy-minded criminal, steeped in blood and with nothing to hope for either in this world or the next—a man solitary among his fellows, with no woman to love him, no child to prattle at his knee, and an endless torture in his own thoughts. So skilfully and so powerfully did he speak that as he finished I am sure that pity for this merciless demon was the prevailing emotion in every heart.

The service was over, and the priest, with his two acolytes before him, was leaving the altar, when he turned, as was his custom, to give his blessing to the congregation. I shall never forget his appearance. The summer sunshine shining slantwise through the single small stained glass window which adorned the little church threw a yellow lustre upon his sharp intellectual features with their dark haggard lines, while a vivid crimson spot reflected from a ruby-coloured mantle in the window quivered over his uplifted right hand. There was a hush as the villagers bent their heads to receive their pastor's blessing—a hush broken by a wild exclamation of surprise from a woman who staggered to her feet in the front pew and gesticulated frantically as she pointed at Father Verhagen's uplifted arm. No need for Frau Bischoff to explain the cause of that sudden cry, for there—there in full sight of his parishioners, were lines of livid scars upon the *curé's* white wrist—scars which could be left by nothing on earth but a desperate woman's nails. And what woman save her who had clung so fiercely to the murderer two days before!

****

That in all this terrible business poor Verhagen was the man most to be pitied I have no manner of doubt. In a town in which there was good medical advice to be had, the approach of the homicidal mania, which had undoubtedly proceeded from over-work and brain worry, and which assumed such a terrible form, would have been detected in time and he would have been spared the awful compunction with which he must have been seized in the lucid intervals between his fits—if, indeed, he had any lucid intervals. How could I diagnose with my smattering of science the existence of such a terrible and insidious form of insanity, especially from the vague symptoms of which he informed me. It is easy now, looking back, to think of many little circumstances which might have put us on the right scent; but what a simple thing is retrospective wisdom! I should be sad indeed if I thought that I had anything with which to reproach myself.

We were never able to discover where he had obtained the weapon with which he had committed his crimes, nor how he managed to secrete it in the interval. My experience proved that it had been his custom to go and come through his study window without disturbing his housekeeper. On the occasion of the attempt on Frau Bischoff he had made a dash for home, and then, finding to his astonishment that his room was occupied, his only resource was to fling away his weapon and muffler, and to mix with the crowd in the village. Being both a strong and an active man, with a good knowledge of the footpaths through the woods, he had never found any difficulty in escaping all observation.

Immediately after his apprehension, Verhagen's disease took an acute form, and he was carried off to the lunatic asylum at Feldkirch. I have heard that some months afterwards he made a determined attempt upon the life of one of his keepers, and afterwards committed suicide. I cannot be positive of this, however, for I heard it quite accidentally during a conversation in a railway carriage.

As for myself, I left Laden within a few months, having received a pleasing intimation from my solicitors that my claim had been paid in full. In spite of my tragic experience there, I had many a pleasing recollection of the little Tyrolese village, and in two subsequent visits I renewed my acquaintance with the *maire*, the *Intendant*, and all my old friends, on which occasion, over long pipes and flagons of beer, we have taken a grim pleasure in talking with bated breath of that terrible month in the quiet Vorarlberg hamlet.

Spedegue's Dropper

The name of Walter Scougall needs no introduction to the cricketing public. In the nineties he played for his University. Early in the century he began that long career in the county team which carried him up to the War. That great tragedy broke his heart for games, but he still served on his county Club Committee and was reckoned one of the best judges of the game in the United Kingdom.

Scougall, after his abandonment of active sport, was wont to take his exercise by long walks through the New Forest, upon the borders of which he was living. Like all wise men, he walked very silently through that wonderful waste, and in that way he was often privileged to see sights which are lost to the average heavy-stepping wayfarer. Once, late in the evening, it was a badger blundering towards its hole under a hollow bank. Often a little group of deer would be glimpsed in the open rides. Occasionally a fox would steal across the path and then dart off at the sight of the noiseless wayfarer. Then one day he saw a human sight which was more strange than any in the animal world.

In a narrow glade there stood two great oaks. They were thirty or forty feet apart, and the glade was spanned by a cord which connected them up. This cord was at least fifty feet above the ground, and it must have entailed no small effort to get it there. At each side of the cord a cricket stump had been placed at the usual distance from each other. A tall, thin young man in spectacles was lobbing balls, of which he seemed to have a good supply, from one end, while at the other end a lad of sixteen, wearing wicket-keeper's gloves, was catching those which missed the wicket. 'Catching' is the right word, for no ball struck the ground. Each was projected high up into the air and passed over the cord, descending at a very sharp angle on to the stumps.

Scougall stood for some minutes behind a holly bush watching this curious performance. At first it seemed pure lunacy, and then gradually he began to perceive a method in it. It was no easy matter to hurl a ball up over that cord and bring it down near the wicket. It needed a very correct trajectory. And yet this singular young man, using what the observer's practised eye recognised as a leg-break action which would entail a swerve in the air, lobbed up ball after ball either right on to the bails or into the wicket-keeper's hands just beyond them. Great practice was surely needed before he had attained such a degree of accuracy as this.

Finally his curiosity became so great that Scougall moved out into the glade, to the obvious surprise and embarrassment of the two performers. Had they been caught in some guilty action they could not have looked more unhappy. However, Scougall was a man of the world with a pleasant manner, and he soon put them at their ease.

'Excuse my butting in,' said he. 'I happened to be passing and I could not help being interested. I am an old cricketer, you see, and it appealed to me. Might I ask what you were trying to do?'

'Oh, I am just tossing up a few balls,' said the elder, modestly. 'You see, there is no decent ground about here, so my brother and I come out into the Forest.'

'Are you a bowler, then?'

'Well, of sorts.'

'What club do you play for?'

'It is only Wednesday and Saturday cricket. Bishops Bramley is our village.'

'But do you always bowl like that?'

'Oh, no. This is a new idea that I have been trying out.'

'Well, you seem to get it pretty accurately.'

I am improving. I was all over the place at first. I didn't know what parish they would drop in. But now they are usually there or about it.'

'So I observe.'

'You said you were an old cricketer. May I ask your name?'

'Walter Scougall.'

The young man looked at him as a young pupil looks at the world-famous master.

'You remember the name, I see.'

'Walter Scougall. Oxford and Hampshire. Last played in 1913. Batting average for that season, twenty-seven point five. Bowling average, sixteen for seventy-two wickets.'

'Good Lord!'

The younger man, who had come across, burst out laughing.

'Tom is like that,' said he. 'He is Wisden and Lillywhite rolled into one. He could tell you anyone's record, and every county's record for this century.'

'Well, well! What a memory you must have!'

'Well, my heart is in the game,' said the young man, becoming amazingly confidential, as shy men will when they find a really sympathetic listener. 'But it's my heart that won't let me play it as I should wish to do. You see, I get asthma if I do too much—and palpitations. But they play me at Bishops Bramley for my slow bowling, and so long as I field slip I don't have too much running to do.'

'You say you have not tried these lobs, or whatever you may call them, in a match?'

'No, not yet. I want to get them perfect first. You see, it was my ambition to invent an entirely new ball. I am sure it can be done. Look at Bosanquet and the googlie. Just by using his brain he thought of and worked out the idea of concealed screw on the ball. I said to myself that Nature had handicapped me with a weak heart, but not with a weak brain, and that I might think out some new thing which was within the compass of my strength. Droppers, I call them. Spedegue's droppers—that's the name they may have some day.'

Scougall laughed. 'I don't want to discourage you, but I wouldn't bank on it too much,' said he. 'A quick-eyed batsman would simply treat them as he would any other full toss and every ball would be a boundary.'

Spedegue's face fell. The words of Scougall were to him as the verdict of the High Court judge. Never had he spoken before with a first-class cricketer, and he had hardly the nerve to defend his own theory. It was the younger one who spoke.

'Perhaps, Mr Scougall, you have hardly thought it all out yet,' said he. 'Tom has given it a lot of consideration. You see, if the ball is tossed high enough it has a great pace as it falls. It's really like having a fast bowler from above. That's his idea. Then, of course, there's the field.'

'Ah, how would you place your field?'

'All on the on side bar one or two at the most,' cried Tom Spedegue, taking up the argument. 'I've nine to dispose of. I should have mid-off well up. That's all. Then I should have eight men to leg, three on the boundary, one mid-on, two square, one fine, and one a rover, so that the batsman would never quite know where he was. That's the idea.'

Scougall began to be serious. It was clear that this young fellow really had plotted the thing out. He walked across to the wicket.

'Chuck up one or two,' said he. 'Let me see how they look.' He brandished his walking-stick and waited expectant. The ball soared in the air and came down with unexpected speed just over the stump. Scougall looked more serious still. He had seen many cricket balls, but never quite from that angle, and it gave him food for thought.

'Have you ever tried it in public?'

'Never.'

'Don't you think it is about time?'

'Yes, I think I might.'

'When?'

'Well, I'm not generally on as a first bowler, I am second change as a rule. But if the skipper will let me have a go—'

'I'll see to that,' said Scougall. 'Do you play at Bishops Bramley?'

'Yes; it is our match of the year—against Mudford, you know.'

'Well, I think on Saturday I'd like to be there and see how it works.'

Sure enough Scougall turned up at the village match, to the

great excitement of the two rural teams. He had a serious talk with the home captain, with the result that for the first time in his life Tom Spedegue was first bowler for his native village. What the other village thought of his remarkable droppers need not influence us much, since they would probably have been got out pretty cheaply by any sort of bowling. None the less, Scougall watched the procession to and from the cowshed which served as a pavilion with an appreciative eye, and his views as to the possibilities lying in the dropper became clearer than before. At the end of the innings he touched the bowler upon the shoulder.

'That seems all right,' he said.

'No, I couldn't quite get the length—and, of course, they did drop catches.'

'Yes, I agree that you could do better. Now look here! you are second master at a school, are you not?'

'That is right.'

'You could get a day's leave if I wangled with the chief?'

'It might be done.'

'Well, I want you next Tuesday. Sir George Sanderson's house-party team is playing the Free Foresters at Ringwood. You must bowl for Sir George.'

Tom Spedegue flushed with pleasure.

'Oh, I say!' was all he could stammer out.

'I'll work it somehow or other. I suppose you don't bat?'

'Average nine,' said Spedegue, proudly.

Scougall laughed. 'Well, I noticed that you were not a bad fielder near the wicket.'

'I usually hold them.'

'Well, I'll see your boss, and you will hear from me again.'

Scougall was really taking a great deal of trouble in this small affair, for he went down to Totton and saw the rather grim head-master. It chanced, however, that the old man had been a bit of a sport in his day, and he relaxed when Scougall explained the inner meaning of it all. He laughed incredulously, however, and shook his head when Scougall whispered some aspiration.

'Nonsense!' was his comment.

'Well, there is a chance.'

397

'Nonsense!' said the old man once again.

'It would be the making of your school.'

'It certainly would,' the head-master replied. 'But it is nonsense all the same.'

Scougall saw the head-master again on the morning after the Free Foresters match.

'You see, it works all right,' he said.

'Yes, against third-class men.'

'Oh, I don't know. Donaldson was playing, and Murphy. They were not so bad. I tell you they are the most amazed set of men in Hampshire. I have bound them all over to silence.'

'Why?'

'Surprise is the essence of the matter. Now I'll take it a stage farther. By Jove, what a joke it would be!' The old cricketer and the sporting schoolmaster roared with laughter as they thought of the chances of the future.

All England was absorbed in one question at that moment. Politics, business, even taxation had passed from people's minds. The one engrossing subject was the fifth Test Match. Twice England had won by a narrow margin, and twice Australia had barely struggled to victory. Now in a week Lord's was to be the scene of the final and crucial battle of giants. What were the chances, and how was the English team to be made up?

It was an anxious time for the Selection Committee, and three more harassed men than Sir James Gilpin, Mr Tarding and Dr Sloper were not to be found in London. They sat now in the committee-room of the great pavilion, and they moodily scanned the long list of possibles which lay before them, weighing the claims of this man or that, closely inspecting the latest returns from the county matches, and arguing how far a good all-rounder was a better bargain than a man who was supremely good in one department but weak in another—such men, for example, as Worsley of Lancashire, whose average was seventy-one, but who was a sluggard in the field, or Scott of Leicestershire, who was near the top of the bowling and quite at the foot of the batting averages. A week of such work had turned the committee into three jaded old men.

'There is the question of endurance,' said Sir James, the man of many years and much experience. 'A three days' match is bad enough, but this is to be played out and may last a week. Some of these top average men are getting on in years.'

'Exactly,' said Tarding, who had himself captained England again and again. I am all for young blood and new methods. The trouble is that we know their bowling pretty well, and as for them on a marled wicket they can play ours with their eyes shut. Each side is likely to make five hundred per innings, and a very little will make the difference between us and them.'

'It's just that very little that we have got to find,' said solemn old Dr Sloper, who had the reputation of being the greatest living authority upon the game. 'If we could give them something new! But, of course, they have played every county and sampled everything we have got.'

'What can we ever have that is new?' cried Tarding. 'It is all played out.'

'Well, I don't know,' said Sir James. 'Both the swerve and the googlie have come along in our time. But Bosanquets don't appear every day. We want brain as well as muscle behind the ball.'

'Funny we should talk like this,' said Dr Sloper, taking a letter from his pocket. 'This is from old Scougall, down in Hampshire. He says he is at the end of a wire and is ready to come up if we want him. His whole argument is on the very lines we have been discussing. New blood, and a complete surprise—that is his slogan.'

'Does he suggest where we are to find it?'

'Well, as a matter of fact he does. He has dug up some unknown fellow from the back of beyond who plays for the second eleven of the Mudtown Blackbeetles or the Hinton Chawbacons or some such team, and he wants to put him straight in to play for England. Poor old Scougie has been out in the sun.'

'At the same time there is no better captain than Scougall used to be. I don't think we should put his opinion aside too easily. What does he say?'

'Well, he is simply red-hot about it. "A revelation to me." That is one phrase. "Could not have believed it if I had not seen it." "May find it out afterwards, but it is bound to upset them the first time." That is his view.'

'And where is the wonder man?'

'He has sent him up so that we can see him if we wish. Telephone the Thackeray Hotel, Bloomsbury.'

'Well, what do you say?'

'Oh, it's pure waste of time,' said Tarding. 'Such things don't happen, you know. Even if we approved of him, what would the country think and what would the Press say?'

Sir James stuck out his grizzled jaw. 'Damn the country and the Press, too!' said he. 'We are here to follow our own judgment, and I jolly well mean to do so.'

'Exactly,' said Dr Sloper.

Tarding shrugged his broad shoulders. 'We have enough to do without turning down a side-street like that,' said he. 'However, if you both think so, I won't stand in the way. Have him up by all means and let us see what we make of him.'

Half an hour later a very embarrassed young man was standing in front of the famous trio and listening to a series of very searching questions, to which he was giving such replies as he was able. Much of the ground which Scougall had covered in the Forest was explored by them once more.

'It boils down to this, Mr Spedegue. You've once in your life played in good company. That is the only criterion. What exactly did you do?'

Spedegue pulled a slip of paper, which was already frayed from much use, out of his waistcoat pocket.

'This is *The Hampshire Telegraph* account, sir.'

Sir James ran his eye over it and read snatches aloud. '"Much amusement was caused by the bowling of Mr T. E. Spedegue." Hum! That's rather two-edged. Bowling should not be a comic turn. After all, cricket is a serious game. Seven wickets for thirty-four. Well, that's better. Donaldson is a good man. You got him, I see. And Murphy, too! Well, now, would you mind going into the pavilion and waiting? You will find some pictures there that will amuse you if you value the history of the game. We'll send for you presently.'

When the youth had gone the Selection Committee looked at each other in puzzled silence.

'You simply can't do it!' said Tarding at last. 'You can't face it. To play a bumpkin like that because he once got seven wickets for thirty-four in country-house cricket is sheer madness. I won't be a party to it.'

'Wait a bit, though! Wait a bit!' cried Sir James. 'Let us thresh it out a little before we decide.'

So they threshed it out, and in half an hour they sent for Tom Spedegue once more. Sir James sat with his elbows on the table and his finger-tips touching while he held forth in his best judicial manner. His conclusion was a remarkable one.

'So it comes to this, Mr Spedegue, that we all three want to be on surer ground before we take a step which would rightly expose us to the most tremendous public criticism. You will therefore remain in London, and at three-forty-five tomorrow morning, which is just after dawn, you will come down in your flannels to the side entrance of Lord's. We will, under pledge of secrecy, assemble twelve or thirteen groundsmen whom we can trust, including half-a-dozen first-class bats. We will have a wicket prepared on the practice ground, and we will try you out under proper conditions with your ten fielders and all. If you fail, there is an end. If you make good, we may consider your claim.'

'Good gracious, sir, I made no claim.'

'Well, your friend Scougall did for you. But anyhow, that's how we have fixed it. We shall be there, of course, and a few others whose opinion we can trust. If you care to wire Scougall he can come too. But the whole thing is secret, for we quite see the point that it must be a complete surprise or a wash-out. So you will keep your mouth shut and we shall do the same.'

Thus it came about that one of the most curious games in the history of cricket was played on the Lord's ground next morning. There is a high wall round that part, but early wayfarers as they passed were amazed to hear the voices of the players, and the occasional crack of the ball at such an hour. The superstitious might almost have imagined that the spirits of the great departed were once again at work, and that the adventurous explorer might get a peep at the bushy black beard of the old giant or Billie Murdoch leading his Cornstalks once more to victory. At six o'clock the impromptu match was over, and the Selection Committee had taken the bravest and most sensational decision that had ever been hazarded since first a team was chosen. Tom Spedegue should play next week for England.

'Mind you,' said Tarding, 'if the beggar lets us down I simply won't face the music. I warn you of that. I'll have a taxi waiting at the gate and a passport in my pocket. *Poste restante*, Paris. That's me for the rest of the summer.'

'Cheer up, old chap,' said Sir James. 'Our conscience is clear. We have acted for the best. Dash it all, we have ten good men, anyhow. If the worst came to the worst, it only means one passenger in the team.'

'But it won't come to the worst,' said Dr Sloper, stoutly. 'Hang it, we have seen with our own eyes. What more can we do? All the same, for the first time in my life I'll have a whisky-and-soda before breakfast.'

Next day the list was published and the buzz began. Ten of the men might have been expected. These were Challen and Jones, as fast bowlers, and Widley, the slow left-hander. Then Peters, Moir, Jackson, Wilson, and Grieve were at the head of the batting averages, none of them under fifty, which was pretty good near the close of a wet season. Hanwell and Gordon were two all-rounders who were always sure of their places, dangerous bats, good change bowlers, and as active as cats in the field. So far so good. But who the Evil One was Thomas E. Spedegue? Never was there such a ferment in Fleet Street and such blank ignorance upon the part of 'our well-informed correspondent.' Special Commissioners darted here and there, questioning well-known cricketers, only to find that they were as much in the dark as themselves. Nobody knew—or if anyone did know, he was bound by oath not to tell. The wildest tales flew abroad.

We are able to assure the public that Spedegue is a *nom de jeu* and conceals the identity of a world-famed cricketer who for family reasons is not permitted to reveal his true self.

Thomas E. Spedegue will surprise the crowd at Lord's by appearing as a coal-black gentleman from Jamaica. He came over with the last West Indian team, settled in Derbyshire, and is now eligible to play for England, though why he should be asked to do so is still a mystery.

Spedegue, as is now generally known, is a half-caste Malay who exhibited extraordinary cricket proficiency some years ago in Rangoon. It is said that he plays in a loincloth and can catch as well with his feet as with his hands. The question of whether he is qualified for England is a most debatable one.

Spedegue, Thomas E., is the headmaster of a famous northern school whose wonderful talents in the cricket field have been concealed by his devotion to his academic duties. Those who know him best are assured, etc. etc.

The Committee also began to get it in the neck. 'Why, with the wealth of talent available, these three elderly gentlemen, whose ideas of selection seem to be to pick names out of a bag, should choose one who, whatever his hidden virtues, is certainly unused to first-class cricket, far less to Test Matches, is one of those things which make one realize that the lunacy laws are not sufficiently comprehensive.' These were fair samples of the comments.

And then the inevitable came to pass. When Fleet Street is out for something it invariably gets it. No one quite knows how *The Daily Sportsman* succeeded in getting at Thomas Spedegue, but it was a great scoop and the incredible secret was revealed. There was a leader and there was an interview with the village patriarch which set London roaring with laughter. 'No, we ain't surprised nohow,' said Gaffer Hobbs. 'Maister Spedegue do be turble clever with them slow balls of his'n. He sure was too much for them chaps what came in the char-a-bancs from Mudford. Artful, I call 'im. You'll see.' The leader was scathing. 'The Committee certainly seem to have taken leave of their senses. Perhaps there is time even now to alter their absurd decision. It is almost an insult to our Australian visitors. It is obvious that the true place for Mr Thomas Spedegue, however artful he may be, is the village green and not Lord's, and that his competence to deal with the char-a-bancers of Mudford is a small guarantee that he can play first-class cricket. The whole thing is a deplorable mistake, and it is time that pressure was put upon the Selection Board to make them reconsider their decision.'

'We have examined the score-book of the Bishops Bramley village club,' wrote another critic. 'It is kept in the tap-room of The Spotted Cow, and makes amusing reading. Our Test Match aspirant is hard to trace, as he played usually for the second eleven, and in any case there was no one capable of keeping an analysis. However, we must take such comfort as we can from his batting averages. This year he has actually amassed a hundred runs in nine recorded innings. Best in an innings, fifteen. Average, eleven. Last year he was less fortunate and came out with an average of nine. The youth is second master at the Totton High School and is in indifferent health, suffering from occasional attacks of asthma. And he is chosen to play for England! Is it a joke or what? We think that the public will hardly see the humour of it, nor will the Selection Committee find it a laughing matter if they persist in their preposterous action.' So spoke the Press, but there were, it is only fair to say, other journals which took a more charitable view. 'After all,' said the sporting correspondent of *The Times,* 'Sir James and his two colleagues are old and experienced players with a unique knowledge of the game. Since we have placed our affairs in their hands we must be content to leave them there. They have their own knowledge and their own private information of which we are ignorant. We can but trust them and await the event.'

As to the three, they refused in any way to compromise or to bend to the storm. They gave no explanations, made no excuses, and simply dug in and lay quiet. So the world waited till the day came round.

We all remember what glorious weather it was. The heat and the perfect Bulli-earth wicket, so far as England could supply that commodity, reminded our visitors of their native conditions. It was England, however, who got the best of that ironed shirt-front wicket, for in their first knock even Cotsmore, the

Australian giant, who was said to be faster than Gregory and more wily than Spofforth, could seldom get the ball bail-high. He bowled with splendid vim and courage, but his analysis at the end of the day only showed three wickets for a hundred and forty-two. Storr, the googlie merchant, had a better showing with four for ninety-six. Cade's mediums accounted for two wickets, and Moir, the English captain, was run out. He had made seventy-three first, and Peters, Grieve, and Hanwell raked up sixty-four, fifty-seven, and fifty-one respectively, while nearly everyone was in double figures. The only exception was 'Thomas E. Spedegue, Esq.,' to quote the score card, which recorded a blank after his name. He was caught in the slips off the fast bowler, and, as he admitted afterwards that he had never for an instant seen the ball, and could hardly in his nervousness see the bowler, it is remarkable that his wicket was intact. The English total was four hundred and thirty-two, and the making of it consumed the whole of the first day. It was fast scoring in the time, and the crowd were fully satisfied with the result.

And now came the turn of Australia. An hour before play began forty thousand people had assembled, and by the time that the umpire came out the gates had to be closed, for there was not standing room within those classic precincts. Then came the English team, strolling out to the wickets and tossing the ball from hand to hand in time-honoured fashion. Finally appeared the two batsmen, Morland, the famous Victorian, the man of the quick feet and the supple wrists, whom many looked upon as the premier batsman of the world, and the stonewaller, Donahue, who had broken the hearts of so many bowlers with his obdurate defence. It was he who took the first over, which was delivered by Challen of Yorkshire, the raging, tearing fast bowler of the North. He sent down six beauties, but each of them came back to him down the pitch from that impenetrable half-cock shot which was characteristic of the famous Queenslander. It was a maiden over.

And now Moir tossed the ball to Spedegue and motioned him to begin at the pavilion end. The English captain had been present at the surreptitious trial and he had an idea of the general programme, but it took him some time and some consultation with the nervous, twitching bowler before he could set the field. When it was finally arranged the huge audience gasped with surprise and the batsmen gazed round them as if they could hardly believe their eyes. One poor little figure, alone upon a prairie, broke the solitude of the off-side. He stood as a deep point or as a silly mid-off. The on-side looked like a mass meeting. The fielders were in each other's way, and kept shuffling about to open up separate lines. It took some time to arrange, while Spedegue stood at the crease with a nervous smile, fingering the ball and waiting for orders. The Selection Board were grouped in the open window of the committee-room, and their faces were drawn and haggard.

'My God! This is awful!' muttered Tarding.

'Got that cab?' asked Dr Sloper, with a ghastly smile.

'Got it! It is my one stand-by.'

'Room for three in it?' said Sir James. 'Gracious, he has got five short-legs and no slip. Well, well, get to it! Anything is better than waiting.'

There was a deadly hush as Spedegue delivered his first ball. It was an ordinary slow full pitch straight on the wicket. At any other time Morland would have slammed it to the boundary, but he was puzzled and cautious after all this mysterious setting of the field. Some unknown trap seemed to have been set for him. Therefore he played the ball quietly back to the bowler and set himself for the next one, which was similar and treated in the same way.

Spedegue had lost his nerve. He simply could not, before this vast multitude of critics, send up the grotesque ball which he had invented. Therefore he compromised, which was the most fatal of all courses. He lobbed up balls which were high but not high enough. They were simply ordinary over-pitched, full-toss deliveries such as a batsman sees when he has happy dreams and smiles in his sleep. Such was the third ball, which was a little to the off. Morland sent it like a bullet past the head of the lonely mid-off and it crashed against the distant rails. The three men in the window looked at each other and the sweat was on their brows. The next ball was again a juicy full toss on the level of the batsman's ribs. He banged it through the crowd of fielders on the on with a deft turn of the wrist which insured that it should be upon the ground. Then, gaining confidence, he waited for the next of those wonderful dream balls, and steadying himself for a mighty fast-footed swipe he knocked it clean over the ring and on to the roof of the hotel to square-leg. There were roars of applause, for a British crowd loves a lofty hit, whoever may deliver it. The scoreboard marked fourteen made off five balls. Such an opening to a Test Match had never been seen.

'We thought he might break a record, and by Jove he has!' said Tarding, bitterly. Sir James chewed his ragged moustache and Sloper twisted his fingers together in agony. Moir, who was fielding at mid-on, stepped across to the unhappy bowler.

'Chuck 'em up, as you did on Tuesday morning. Buck up, man! Don't funk it! You'll do them yet.'

Spedegue grasped the ball convulsively and nerved himself to send it high into the air. For a moment he pictured the New Forest glade, the white line of cord, and his young brother waiting behind the stump. But his nerve was gone, and with it his accuracy. There were roars of laughter as the ball went fifty feet into the air, which were redoubled when the wicket-keeper had to sprint back in order to catch it and the umpire stretched his arms out to signal a wide.

For the last ball, as he realised, that he was likely to bowl in the match, Spedegue approached the crease. The field was swimming round him. That yell of laughter which had greeted his effort had been the last straw. His nerve was broken. But there is a point when pure despair and desperation come to a man's aid—when he says to himself, 'Nothing matters now. All is lost. It can't be worse than it is. Therefore I may as well let myself go.' Never in all his practice had he bowled a ball as high as the one which now, to the amused delight of the crowd, went soaring into the air. Up it went and up—the most absurd ball ever delivered in a cricket match. The umpire broke down and shrieked with laughter, while even the amazed fielders joined in the general yell. The ball, after its huge parabola, descended well over the wicket, but as it was still within reach Morland, with a broad grin on his sunburned face, turned round and tapped it past the wicket-keeper's ear to the boundary. Spedegue's face drooped towards the ground. The bitterness of death was on him. It was all over. He had let down the Committee, he had let down the side, he had let down England. He wished the ground would open and swallow him so that his only memorial should be a scar upon the pitch of Lord's.

And then suddenly the derisive laughter of the crowd was stilled, for it was seen that an incredible thing had happened. Morland was walking towards the pavilion. As he passed Spedegue he made a good-humoured flourish of his bat as if he would hit him over the head with it. At the same time the wicket-keeper stooped and picked something off the ground. It was a bail. Forgetful of his position and with all his thoughts upon this extraordinary ball which was soaring over his head, the great batsman had touched the wicket with his toe. Spedegue had a respite. The laughter was changing to applause. Moir came over and clapped him jovially upon the back. The scoring board showed total fifteen, last man fourteen, wickets one.

Challen sent down another over of fizzers to the impenetrable Donahue which resulted in a snick for two and a boundary off his legs. And then off the last ball a miracle occurred. Spedegue was fielding at fine slip, when he saw a red flash come towards him low on the right. He thrust out a clutching hand and there was the beautiful new ball right in the middle of his tingling palm. How it got there he had no idea, but what odds so long as the stonewaller would stonewall no more? Spedegue, from being the butt, was becoming the hero of the crowd. They cheered rapturously when he approached the crease for his second over. The board was twenty-one, six, two.

But now it was a very different Spedegue. His fears had fallen from him. His confidence had returned. If he did nothing more he had at least done his share. But he would do much more. It had all come back to him, his sense of distance, his delicacy of delivery, his appreciation of curves. He had found his length and he meant to keep it.

The splendid Australian batsmen, those active, clear-eyed men who could smile at our fast bowling and make the best of our slow bowlers seem simple, were absolutely at sea. Here was something of which they had never heard, for which they had never prepared, and which was unlike anything in the history of cricket. Spedegue had got his fifty-foot trajectory to a nicety, bowling over the wicket with a marked curve from the leg. Every ball fell on or near the top of the stumps. He was as accurate as a human howitzer pitching shells. Batten, who followed Morland, hit across one of them and was clean bowled. Staker tried to cut one off his wicket, and knocked down his own off-stump, broke his bat, and finally saw the ball descend amid the general *debris*. Here and there one was turned to leg and once a short one was hit out of the ground. The fast bowler sent the fifth batsman's leg-stump flying and the score was five for thirty-seven. Then in successive balls Spedegue got Bollard and Whitelaw, the one caught at the wicket and the other at short square-leg. There was a stand between Moon and Carter, who put on twenty runs between them with a succession of narrow escapes from the droppers. Then each of them became victims, one getting his body in front, and the other being splendidly caught by Hanwell on the ropes. The last man was run out and the innings closed for seventy-four.

The crowd had begun by cheering and laughing, but now they had got beyond it and sat in a sort of awed silence as people might who were contemplating a miracle. Half-way through the innings Tarding had leaned forward and had grasped the hand of each of his colleagues. Sir James leaned back in his deck-chair and lit a large cigar. Dr Sloper mopped his brow with his famous red handkerchief. 'It's all right, but, by George! I wouldn't go through it again,' he murmured. The effect upon the players themselves was curious. The English seemed apologetic, as though not sure themselves that such novel means could be justified. The Australians were dazed and a little resentful. 'What price quoits?' said Batten, the captain, as he passed into the pavilion. Spedegue's figures were seven wickets for thirty-one.

And now the question arose whether the miracle would be

repeated. Once more Donahue and Morland were at the wicket. As to the poor stonewaller, it was speedily apparent that he was helpless. How can you stonewall a ball which drops perpendicularly upon your bails? He held his bat flat before it as it fell in order to guard his wicket, and it simply popped up three feet into the air and was held by the wicket-keeper. One for nothing. Batten and Staker both hit lustily to leg and each was caught by the mass meeting who waited for them. Soon, however, it became apparent that the new attack was not invincible, and that a quick, adaptive batsman could find his own methods. Morland again and again brought off what is now called the back drive—a stroke unheard of before—when he turned and tapped the ball over the wicket-keeper's head to the boundary. Now that a crash helmet has been added to the stumper's equipment he is safer than he used to be, but Grieve has admitted that he was glad that he had a weekly paper with an insurance coupon in his cricket bag that day. A fielder was placed on the boundary in line with the stumps, and then the versatile Morland proceeded to elaborate those fine tips to slip and tips to fine leg which are admitted now to be the only proper treatment of the dropper. At the same time Whitelaw took a pace back so as to be level with his wicket and topped the droppers down to the off so that Spedegue had to bring two of his legs across and so disarrange his whole plan of campaign. The pair put on ninety for the fifth wicket, and when Whitelaw at last got out, bowled by Hanwell, the score stood at one hundred and thirty.

But from then onwards the case was hopeless. It is all very well for a quick-eyed, active genius like Morland to adapt himself in a moment to a new game, but it is too much to ask of the average first-class cricketer, who, of all men, is most accustomed to routine methods. The slogging bumpkin from the village green would have made a better job of Spedegue than did these great cricketers, to whom the orthodox method was the only way. Every rule learned, every experience endured, had in a moment become useless. How could you play with a straight bat at a ball that fell from the clouds? They did their best—as well, probably, as the English team would have done in their place—but their best made a poor show upon a scoring card. Morland remained a great master to the end and carried out his bat for a superb seventy-seven. The second innings came to a close at six o'clock on the second day of the match, the score being one hundred and seventy-four. Spedegue eight for sixty-one. England had won by an innings and one hundred and eighty-four runs.

Well, it was a wonderful day and it came to a wonderful close. It is a matter of history how the crowd broke the ropes, how they flooded the field, and how Spedegue, protesting loudly, was carried shoulder-high into the pavilion. Then came the cheering and the speeches. The hero of the day had to appear again and again. When they were weary of cheering him they cheered for Bishops Bramley. Then the English captain had to make a speech. 'Rather stand up to Cotsmore bowling on a ploughed field,' said he. Then it was the turn of Batten the Australian. 'You've beat us at something,' he said ruefully; 'don't quite know yet what it is. It's not what we call cricket down under.' Then the Selection Board were called for and they had the heartiest and best deserved cheer of them all. Tarding told them about the waiting cab. 'It's waiting yet,' he said, 'but I think I can now dismiss it.'

Spedegue played no more cricket. His heart would not stand it. His doctor declared that this one match had been one too many and that he must stand out in the future. But for good or for bad—for bad, as many think—he has left his mark upon the game for ever. The English were more amused than exultant over their surprise victory. The Australian papers were at first inclined to be resentful, but then the absurdity that a man from the second eleven of an unknown club should win a Test match began to soak into them, and finally Sydney and Melbourne had joined London in its appreciation of the greatest joke in the history of cricket.

LEONAUR

ALSO FROM LEONAUR
AVAILABLE IN SOFTCOVER OR HARDCOVER WITH DUST JACKET

THE EMPIRE OF THE AIR: 1 *by George Griffiths*—*The Angel of the Revolution*—a rich brew that calls to mind Verne's tales of futuristic wars while being original, visionary, exciting and technologically prescient.

THE EMPIRE OF THE AIR: 2 *by George Griffiths*—*Olga Romanoff or, The Syren of the Skies*—the sequel to *The Angel of the Revolution*—a future Earth in which nation states are given full self determination when the Aerians, the descendants of 'The Brotherhood of Freedom,' who have policed world peace for more than a century, decide they are mature enough to have outgrown war.

THE INTERPLANETARY ADVENTURES OF DR KINNEY *by Homer Eon Flint*—*The Lord of Death, The Queen of Life, The Devolutionist & The Emancipatrix.*

ARCOT, MOREY & WADE *by John W. Campbell, Jr.*—The Complete, Classic Space Opera Series—*The Black Star Passes, Islands of Space, Invaders from the Infinite.*

CHALLENGER & COMPANY *by Arthur Conan Doyle*—The Complete Adventures of Professor Challenger and His Intrepid Team-*The Lost World, The Poison Belt, The Land of Mists, The Disintegration Machine* and *When the World Screamed.*

GARRETT P. SERVISS' SCIENCE FICTION *by Garrett P. Serviss*—Three Interplanetary Adventures including the unauthorised sequel to H. G. Wells' *War of the Worlds-Edison's Conquest of Mars, A Columbus of Space, The Moon Metal.*

JUNK DAY *by Arthur Sellings*—". . . . his finest novel was his last, Junk Day, a post-holocaust tale set in the ruins of his native London and peopled with engrossing character types . . . . perhaps grimmer than his previous work but pointedly more energetic." *The Encyclopedia of Science Fiction*

KIPLING'S SCIENCE FICTION *by Rudyard Kipling*—Science Fiction & Fantasy stories by a Master Storyteller including 'As East As A,B,C' 'With The Night Mail'.

DARKNESS AND DAWN 1—THE VACANT WORLD *by George Allen England*—A Novel of a future New York.

DARKNESS AND DAWN 2—BEYOND THE GREAT OBLIVION *by George Allen England*—The last vestiges of humanity set out across America's devastated landscape in search of their dream.

DARKNESS AND DAWN 3—THE AFTER GLOW *by George Allen England*—Somewhere near the Great Lakes, 1000 years from now. Beneath our planet's surface tribes of near human albino warriors eke out an existence in a hostile environment.

LEONAUR

ALSO FROM LEONAUR
AVAILABLE IN SOFTCOVER OR HARDCOVER WITH DUST JACKET

THE COLLECTED SCIENCE FICTION AND FANTASY OF STANLEY G. WEINBAUM 1—INTERPLANETARY ODYSSEYS *by Stanley G. Weinbaum*—Classic Tales of Interplanetary Adventure Including: A Martian Odyssey, its Sequel Valley of Dreams, the Complete 'Ham' Hammond Stories and Others.

THE COLLECTED SCIENCE FICTION AND FANTASY OF STANLEY G. WEINBAUM 2—OTHER EARTHS *by Stanley G. Weinbaum*—Classic Futuristic Tales Including: *Dawn of Flame* & its Sequel The Black Flame, plus The Revolution of 1960 & Others.

THE COLLECTED SCIENCE FICTION AND FANTASY OF STANLEY G. WEINBAUM 3—STRANGE GENIUS *by Stanley G. Weinbaum*—Classic Tales of the Human Mind at Work Including the Complete Novel The New Adam, the 'van Manderpootz' Stories and Others.

THE COLLECTED SCIENCE FICTION AND FANTASY OF STANLEY G. WEINBAUM 4—THE BLACK HEART *by Stanley G. Weinbaum*—Classic Strange Tales Including: the Complete Novel The Dark Other, Plus Proteus Island and Others.

THE COLLECTED SCIENCE FICTION & FANTASY OF JACK LONDON 1—BEFORE ADAM & OTHER STORIES *by Jack London*—included in this Volume Before Adam The Scarlet Plague A Relic of the Pliocene When the World Was Young The Red One Planchette A Thousand Deaths Goliah A Curious Fragment The Rejuvenation of Major Rathbone.

THE COLLECTED SCIENCE FICTION & FANTASY OF JACK LONDON 2—THE IRON HEEL & OTHER STORIES *by Jack London*—included in this Volume The Iron Heel The Enemy of All the World The Shadow and the Flash The Strength of the Strong The Unparalleled Invasion The Dream of Debs.

THE COLLECTED SCIENCE FICTION & FANTASY OF JACK LONDON 3—THE STAR ROVER & OTHER STORIES *by Jack London*—included in this Volume The Star Rover The Minions of Midas The Eternity of Forms The Man With the Gash.

THE CRETAN TEAT *by Brian Aldiss*—The Cretan Teat is a wry and comic novel that interweaves its own fiction with an inner fiction about the discovery of a Byzantine painting of the Mother of the Blessed Virgin Mary suckling the infant Jesus and a fake ikon that becomes an instrument of Nemesis.

LEONAUR

ALSO FROM LEONAUR

AVAILABLE IN SOFTCOVER OR HARDCOVER WITH DUST JACKET

THE COMPLETE FOUR JUST MEN: VOLUME 2 *by Edgar Wallace*—*The Law of the Four Just Men & The Three Just Men*—disillusioned with a world where the wicked and the abusers of power perpetually go unpunished, the Just Men set about to rectify matters according to their own standards, and retribution is dispensed on swift and deadly wings.

THE COMPLETE RAFFLES: 1 *by E. W. Hornung*—*The Amateur Cracksman & The Black Mask*—By turns urbane gentleman about town and accomplished cricketer, life is just too ordinary for Raffles and that sets him on a series of adventures that have long been treasured as a real antidote to the 'white knights' who are the usual heroes of the crime fiction of this period.

THE COMPLETE RAFFLES: 2 *by E. W. Hornung*—*A Thief in the Night & Mr Justice Raffles*—By turns urbane gentleman about town and accomplished cricketer, life is just too ordinary for Raffles and that sets him on a series of adventures that have long been treasured as a real antidote to the 'white knights' who are the usual heroes of the crime fiction of this period.

THE COLLECTED SUPERNATURAL AND WEIRD FICTION OF WILKIE COLLINS: VOLUME 1 *by Wilkie Collins*—Contains one novel 'The Haunted Hotel', one novella 'Mad Monkton', three novelettes 'Mr Percy and the Prophet', 'The Biter Bit' and 'The Dead Alive' and eight short stories to chill the blood.

THE COLLECTED SUPERNATURAL AND WEIRD FICTION OF WILKIE COLLINS: VOLUME 2 *by Wilkie Collins*—Contains one novel 'The Two Destinies', three novellas 'The Frozen deep', 'Sister Rose' and 'The Yellow Mask' and two short stories to chill the blood.

THE COLLECTED SUPERNATURAL AND WEIRD FICTION OF WILKIE COLLINS: VOLUME 3 *by Wilkie Collins*—Contains one novel 'Dead Secret,' two novelettes 'Mrs Zant and the Ghost' and 'The Nun's Story of Gabriel's Marriage' and five short stories to chill the blood.

FUNNY BONES *selected by Dorothy Scarborough*—An Anthology of Humorous Ghost Stories.

MONTEZUMA'S CASTLE AND OTHER WEIRD TALES *by Charles B. Cory*—Cory has written a superb collection of eighteen ghostly and weird stories to chill and thrill the avid enthusiast of supernatural fiction.

SUPERNATURAL BUCHAN *by John Buchan*—Stories of Ancient Spirits, Uncanny Places & Strange Creatures.

Lightning Source UK Ltd.
Milton Keynes UK
UKOW051907071211

183362UK00001B/123/P